NASHVILLE BURNING

ALSO BY GERALD DUFF

FICTION

A Crop of Circles
Memphis Mojo
Dirty Rice: A Season in the Evangeline League
Decoration Day and Other Stories
Blue Sabine
Fire Ants and Other Stories
Coasters
Snake Song
Memphis Ribs
That's All Right, Mama: The Unauthorized Life of Elvis's Twin
Graveyard Working
Indian Giver
Playing Custer

POETRY

Calling Collect
A Ceremony of Light

NONFICTION

Fugitive Days: Trailing Warren, Ransom, Tate, and Lytle
Home Truths: A Deep East Texas Memory
Letters of William Cobbett
William Cobbett and the Politics of Earth

NASHVILLE BURNING

a novel

GERALD DUFF

TCU Press

FORT WORTH, TEXAS

Library of Congress Cataloging-in-Publication Data

Names: Duff, Gerald, author.
Title: Nashville burning : a novel / Gerald Duff.
Description: Fort Worth, Texas : TCU Press, [2017]
Identifiers: LCCN 2017017795 (print) | LCCN 2017018905 (ebook) | ISBN
   9780875656786 | ISBN 9780875656670?(alk. paper)
Subjects: LCSH: Nashville (Tenn.)--Fiction.
Classification: LCC PS3554.U3177 (ebook) | LCC PS3554.U3177 N37 2017
(print)
   | DDC 813/.54--dc23
LC record available at https://urldefense.proofpoint.com/v2/url?u=https-
3A__lccn.loc.gov_2017017795&d=DQIFAg&c=7Q-FWLBTAxn3T_E3HWr-
zGYJrC4RvUoWDrzTlitGRH_A&r=O2eiy819IcwTGuw-vrBGiVdmh-
QxMh2yxeggw9qlTUDE&m=OWEo9hLy7Smk-MTkItqCT353JO3SjPFLvF4O-
c7V-6vY&s=Fw06tMMbnCMfU9TcbwTge-98I8MEMf0DQDDIqc_N4Ow&e=

TCU Box 298300
Fort Worth, Texas 76129
817.257.7822
To order books: 1.800.826.8911

Text and cover design by Preston Thomas, Cadence Design Studio.

This is a work of fiction. Although the novel is centered around riots that actually took place in the
South in 1967 and 1968, other incidents, as well as characters, businesses, and places, are either
products of the author's imagination or are used in a fictitious manner. Any resemblance to actual
persons, living or dead, is purely coincidental.

For Patricia
Oh Heart! Oh Heart!

Fire is upon you, fire

That will not rest, invisible fire that feeds

On your quick brains, your beds, your homes,

your steeples,

Fire in your sons' veins and in your daughters',

Fire like a dream of Hell . . .

Rush out into the night, take nothing with you,

Only your naked selves, your naked hearts.

—"Fire on Belmont Street"
DONALD DAVIDSON

———————

I tried to sing the blues in Nashville

I couldn't find me no tune

I tried to eat me some Nashville barbecue

I got my taste all ruined

—"No Nashville Blues"
BLIND WILLIE BELL

CONTENTS

PART ONE
KINDLING

PART TWO
BLAZE

PART THREE
ASHES

PART ONE
KINDLING

1

THE ORIOLES, THE tomtits, the wrens, the cardinals, the finches purple and red, the robins, the mockers, the pileated woodpeckers and the downies, the larks, the doves, the wood pigeons, each and every songbird real and would-be in Nashville—all fowl large and small, regally colored or dun, admired, pestilent, or ignored, all able to sing, squawk, scream, shriek, or whistle—were tuning up at the first hint of light in the eastern sky across the Cumberland River. It was early spring, and all residents of the Athens of the South had to suffer being informed by birdsong of that stirring in the loins of each creature cursed with a pounding heart and pumping blood. Ever old, ever new.

The announcement by the birds of Nashville of the coming of the dawns of spring made the chancellor of Vanderbilt University stir a bit in his sleep, despite the thickness of the walls of the mansion on Cherry Mount Retreat in which he abided and despite its smoothly and quietly functioning climate control. It roused the residents of the stone homes farther west in Belle Meade, those with expanses of well-tended grounds set far back from the streets and boulevards and drives and courts and pikes and runs and ways and avenues and allées. The birds' songs spoke with strength and mindless purpose to those at rest in the homes built more closely together and nearer the streets of Hillsborough Village and Green Hills and West Meade and across the Cumberland in East Nashville. The song reached North Nashville, as well, where most of the Negroes or colored or blacks or whatever they currently called themselves in

3

1967 lived, and it bugled and rang in all parts of Metropolitan Nashville and beyond that throughout Davidson County, though no one worried much about what happened and what songs were sung outside the demarcated limits of the capital city of Tennessee.

The early spring caroling of the birds fell too upon the ears of an assistant professor in the English department of Vanderbilt University, Ronald Alden, PhD, who jerked awake in the house he rented on Graystone Lane at the first insult of bird squawk, as he had learned to do during his five years in Nashville, his acoustic memory operating to tell him that the crescendo of noise was not fully achieved yet, but would be in not more than two minutes. There had been a time when he'd clung to sleep as the birds tuned up each spring, trying to hold on to every moment of unconsciousness as long as possible, pulling his pillow over his head and burrowing deeply into whatever dream he was having that morning, even resorting once to wearing ear plugs all night in anticipation of the avian assault to come. That hadn't worked, and nothing he'd tried had insulated him from the morning song of the birds, and by his second year in Nashville, he'd become so enraged at the mindless honking at dawn he couldn't wait to wake up to curse the birds and what their aubade hinted about the natural drive of all things to procreate.

It was like having a bad tooth, one that had been aching for hours and now had stopped. If you left it alone, it might not crank up again immediately, but you knew the pain would resume at some point. Why not just suck at the sleeping bastard and make it roar? Steal a march on the enemy. Make it happen now, and get it over with. Make it know who's running this show.

"Goddamn the goddamn birds," Ronald said aloud, sitting up to slide out of the bedclothes, lurch around, and slam his feet to the floor.

"What?" Lily said in a blurred voice. "What'd you say?"

"The same thing. Six months out of the year I'm not allowed to sleep past five in the morning, no matter what I do. The damn birds won't let me."

"You shouldn't curse the birds," his wife said. "They're happy for the new day. That's all."

"That's because they're bird-brained. Dumb as rocks. Aubade-niks."

"Can't you do them this morning? I'm desperate for rest."

Ronald didn't answer her. He'd been doing them every morning of their lives, and he had nothing new to say about that chore. He could hear all three cranking up as he left the bedroom, each child greeting the dawn in his or her own way. Emily, the six-year-old, would be sitting quietly on the edge of her single bed, speaking to herself and to her imaginary companion, whose name and character changed with her moods. Sometimes her creation was Rum Tum, a male dwarf of enormous physical power and brooding anger, aching to destroy any and all who might oppose his mistress. "No, Rum Tum," Ronald would hear her saying to the empty air at moments when Emily felt the need to call upon her dwarf, her arm extended and her hand raised in a stop sign to hold back her minion, "you can't rip Daddy's guts out and make him shut up," or "Yes, Rum Tum, Mommy's sick and can't be bothered, and you're not allowed to hold the pillow over her face. No, sit down and play with your bashing machine. Don't spit on the floor."

Ronald knew that for Emily's mental well-being and psychic development he should prefer the other creature of his daughter's imaginings, Sarah, a sweet and invisible girl the exact size, shape, and eye coloring as Emily, a soft spoken waif who brought him gifts at the behest of her creator: scribbled pieces of paper, a crayon, a soggy bite of a Chips Ahoy! chocolate-chip cookie, a picture of a dog torn from a newspaper or magazine. But sweet Sarah was a bit too bland for Middle Tennessee, too much the goody-goody to fit comfortably into the state where she spent her invisible life. She was like the female students in his classes who did all their papers safely on time, knitted yarn they pulled from expensive and tasteful wicker baskets while he lectured about some ode by a Romantic poet, stopping the clash of their needles momentarily to write something short and pithy in their notebooks they figured he'd ask about on the exam, smiling prettily back at him when they detected him checking out how their hemlines rode up as they sat in the row of seats at the front of the room, legs neatly crossed at the ankle.

No, Rum Tum was a truer manifestation of the Zeitgeist, roughly defined, Ronald figured, not Sarah, and he found himself at specific times wishing the dwarf would suddenly appear, spring into action, and rip out a good chunk of the guts of certain colleagues, his eyes as cold and lifeless as dinner plates at a formal feed. Come to think of it, maybe it'd be even more fitting ironically if Sarah did that, Ronald considered as he worked at helping Emily pick out and put on her clothes of the day. Imagine those knitting needles in the hands of sweet Sarah.

"Why are you laughing, Daddy?" Emily said, turning her head to look back at Ronald as he worked to brush the tangles out of her mat of hair. "Is my hair funny?"

"No, your hair's not funny. It's serious as can be. I'm thinking about the Three Stooges."

"Hurry, but don't pull hard any more then," Emily said. "The stooges are about to come on, right?"

"Yes, they are. Just hold still, and I'll finish up."

From the room down the hall came the steady pounding of the slats of a crib being slammed against a wall, Julian at work, still in silence but for the dogged sound of steady impact, but that wouldn't last long. He'd be hungry, and pushing the end of his bed back and forth with a booming noise wouldn't hold him for long. Julian was much too old to be sleeping in a crib still, but there it was, paid for, and its ongoing destruction a source of amusement to him, so no need to add another debt just now. Julian was old enough to be perfectly capable of climbing up and out of his bed, but he preferred to be lifted by someone else as he hung like a sack of stones. He would wait for levitation.

"I'm coming, big boy," Ronald said, regretting instantly letting Julian knew he was being heard. The screaming started then, on a note high enough to shatter glass and then descending to a guttural growl as of a pit bull chewing at its muzzle. The tone ascended soon, though, and Ronald considered that a blessing. "See how long you can hold that note, Julian," he called out, releasing Emily to run out of the room into the hall and toward the kitchen.

"Come on, Rum Tum," she said. "Don't you want a chocolate Pop-Tart?"

Dylan, the year-old, would be dripping piss from every crevice of his diaper, Ronald knew, but he wasn't hollering yet. Let him stew in his own juice for a while longer while I warm up the Pop-Tarts and serve up the Three Stooges. It's show time. I got a class to teach.

A little over a mile away, in a brick home just at the end of one of the best streets in Highland Park, a structure of muted statement and faux columns marching whitely two by two across the façade facing the curb, Robard Flange lay on beige linens staring at the arm attached to the west side of his body. At retiring for sleep, he had left a wristwatch fastened just above the joint where the hand joined the forearm, knowing that device had at one time aided in getting him through the nights he spent alone with the arm, not counting Marie beside him. She slept like a stone always, mouth open, breath whistling in and out as regular as a blacksmith's bellows, head supported by solid rolls of fatty tissue at the throat and an oversized pillow beneath it, dead to the world and all that might be in it.

Daytime was easier, or had been, but now even the hours of good natural light were vexed by Robard's continual consciousness that the arm did not belong to him. It had at one point in that earlier life, the one that began in 1838 when he had been born in Mississippi as Rooney Beauchamp, the elder son of an old family in the Delta, its plantation well south of Memphis, populated by father and mother and sisters and younger brothers and a sufficient number of house servants to maintain the mansion and overseers to manage the work of over two hundred slaves cultivating the many acres of cotton contributing their share to the prosperity that marked the South before the war had come and destroyed an entire civilization.

Because the watch on the wrist of the arm was mechanical, a thing manufactured and sold by a merchant to a customer, it distanced the arm itself from Robard Flange's consciousness of its being there, attached to him, but not him, a parasite living on his blood, his breath, his nourishment. Or the timepiece had performed that function at one time. No longer was there comfort in that distancing, and no longer could Robard sleep in peace beside the thing not himself, yet attached to him. The watch proved no balm to him now, and Robard could date that loss of distancing precisely. He could point to the moment when he ceased to find relief in that trick he played on his mind by wearing the watch on the intruding thing lying beside him.

The student newspaper at the university, the *Vanderbilt Hustler,* had sounded the death knell for that mental contrivance Robard Flange had put to use to allow him to function day-to-day in his current life as professor of English at the birthplace of the Fugitive and Agrarian writers, the solid and true home of moral rectitude and honor and comprehension of the real and the good. The headline in the paper had caught his eye one noon in January, soon after the beginning of the spring semester, when he was passing through the student union on his way to the faculty dining hall, students jabbering at their tables, drinking their colas and smoking their cigarettes, ogling each other, sizing up possibilities, and pretending not to notice his progress among them. Robard could call up that instant of revelation in sharp and painful definition at any moment he allowed his mind to touch upon it. "Real World Comes to Vandy," the huge headline shouted on the first page of the *Hustler,* and that was enough to cause Robard to pause and pick up a copy of the rag the students were allowed to write, publish, and promulgate with no supervision of taste or decorum.

The story beneath was written by someone with a surname found most frequently on the East Coast, Robard Flange noted, its syllables filled with consonants and the most guttural of the vowels, and in the first paragraph, the owner of the outlandish name yelped and yodeled about the speakers confirmed to appear at the Vanderbilt IMPACT Symposium of 1967. "A coup for this student-run seminar," the young fool chortled. "Check this out, Vandy. VU will host Martin Luther King Jr., Allen Ginsberg, Stokely Carmichael, and—get ready for the dinosaur—Strom Thurmond on the same stage. It'll be a fireworks show you won't forget."

Robard had picked up the copy of the *Hustler* in his real hand, the right one, the one a part of his physical being in this current life, but as soon as he read the words announcing what was to come to Tennessee, to Nashville, to Vanderbilt, he shifted the rag to the hand not his own, the one belonging to death and loss and darkness, and the fingers of the thing had seized the announcement of apocalypse as though it were a Negro child being offered a lollipop.

Robard Flange groaned and shifted his body in his beautifully maintained home on Jefferson Street, twisting beneath the sheet covering him, the left arm dogging his every movement, and strained to put himself in psychic and spiritual position to revisit that early life, his time as Rooney Beauchamp, heir to Benevolence Plantation in Mississippi, two leagues south of Batesville, deep in the rich heart of the Delta. God, he said in a voice low enough not to arouse Marie at snore beside him, my Lord and Savior, please give me purchase on that moment. Allow your servant surcease from this hellish day.

Robard willed his eyes to close, repeating his words beseeching his Creator for translation and transcendence, and yet once again a tiny point of light stirred in the distance, gathering darkness to itself, dissipating the heavy grayness of fog that smothered the reality of what it covered, a spring morning early in the war west of Nashville centered at a great bend in the Tennessee River, close by a small chapel called Shiloh by the devout who gathered there to praise their Savior. Simple farmers, the yeomen of the Old South, tilling their acres unaided and alone, save for one or two slave families in due bondage to their masters. This bond was not a cold business culture of owner and vassal. It was a family farm arrangement, conceived in agreement and in a caring and fostering relationship for white and colored. That point silently made within, Robard Flange drew a full breath, his first inhalation of the day unfettered by doubt and tribulation, and the visitation began always as it did.

Early as it was in April 1862, in the valley of the Tennessee, the color of the leaves on every tree, every bush, every blossoming plant was a pale green, the hue sometimes seen in the gaze of a young woman of the South. Pure, pristine, unclouded, inviting and immediate, though chaste and maidenly and glowingly alive. Birds sang their chorus to the dawn, each different in tone and tenor, yet joined in single anthem to the appearance of the day. A new chapter in eternity, yet as old as the creation itself. Robard saw before him an abundance of grass, new sprung from the rich earth, and a shimmer of light as though of a bolt of lightning occurring far off and barely coloring the sky played briefly before his closed eyes in the bedroom in the current day in Nashville. He was wrenched by the moment, plunged into the paleness of green, lifted from the body which held him, that cage of middle-aged flesh in which he dwelled by force of time and circumstance. Yet again, he ascended from that self to the other. The essential, the true, the real. What he had been and would be again, if grace were granted.

Rooney Beauchamp, two days short of reaching the age of majority, sat his horse, a shining bay from Benevolence Plantation, steady and powerful, yet filled with a spirit which caused the animal to toss his head and shift his weight at the sounds coming from deep in the stand of timber and brush before him. Rooney leaned forward to calm Defiance with a pat on the neck, noting as he did the good order in which the men of the Fourth Mississippi stood in rank, seeing to their arms in anticipation of the charge they would shortly receive. It would come through the peach orchard before them, across the swale of water still standing from the spring rains, and it would likely be a blow launched by a regiment from Illinois, or perhaps from Michigan or Iowa, one of those blank midwestern states, and it would be made up of stolid farmers and mechanics, of German extraction most likely, well-supplied in material and sturdy in physical strength but lacking in one thing. That lack would be instrumental in the battle to come, and Rooney called out to the line of men near him to remind them of that virtue they possessed in full measure. "You fight today for home and hearth, Mississippians. Repel the invaders of your native land." Defiance whinnied, Major Rooney Beauchamp lifted his voice in bugle tone, and the men he led whooped, not yet in strong utterance of the rebel yell to come in the full heat and rictus of battle, but premonitory to that, nonetheless.

"What?" someone was muttering in Rooney's ear in a muffled tone, befogged and drowsy, a flattened female voice. "Did you say something, Robard?"

"Hush, Marie," Robard said, "go back to sleep." He reached out his live hand, Rooney Beauchamp's right one, to pat Defiance on that spot just behind his ear, hoping to hear the bay snort in appreciation of the attention from his rider, but the reassuring solidity of equine hair, bone, and muscle was not there to touch, and Rooney looked down to see what had happened to his mount. The steed was fading in color, the rich bay tint fading to gray, shimmering and breaking into pale fragments through which Rooney could see the darkness of earth tones rising and falling in small, then larger rhythmic waves. "No," Rooney Beauchamp said, his voice changing as he spoke, closer now to that of another man, a possessor of a tone weaker in timbre and force, not that of a leader of men in the Second War of Independence, but of a follower, a functionary, a clerk, that of Robard Flange, a mere teacher of the uncaring young.

"Stand to your arms," that voice cried, but the soldiers of the Fourth Mississippi gave no sign they heard, their holds on their weapons loosening as the vivid richness of light green leaves and gray uniforms slid into darkness. "Prepare to deliver a volley," the voice of Robard Flange begged, but now not a man stood to arms, and Defiance had vanished into mist, and Robard lay as himself, fastened to the dead arm on his left side, the limb of Rooney Beauchamp lost to cannon fire in defending the gray line against the charge of elements of the Fifteenth Illinois at Shiloh on the first day at the Peach Orchard on the margin of Megg's Creek.

"Honey, are you having a bad dream?" the female beside him asked, sitting up now, causing the mattress to buckle and sag, and leaning to peer into his face as Robard struggled to hold to what remained of the vision of valor and steadfastness and determination in the presence of certain defeat he had been granted yet again for a small and evanescent space. "Has your arm gone to sleep? Why are you rubbing on it so hard?"

"It is dead, Marie," Robard said. "It's not asleep."

"If it's tingling real bad, that's just the blood that's been cut off. It'll come back to normal in a minute."

"God, let it not return to normal," Robard said, rising in bed and swinging his legs to put his feet on the floor. "If this state be normal, normal be damned. Myself am Hell."

"It could be a pinched nerve. Please make an appointment with Dr. Lanier. That's been happening to your arm way too much this year. I'm worried, Sugar."

"I haven't got time for doctor's appointments. My ill will not yield to medical ministration."

"You don't know that until you try. They have medicine to treat everything at Vanderbilt Hospital. Wonder drugs that I hear about all the time. Let Dr. Lanier prescribe you a good strong drug."

"Medicos cannot treat what ails me, Marie," Robard said as he left the room. "Marvel sweetly at my condition though they may."

In the kitchen he wanted eggs and country ham and biscuit, the breakfast of a yeoman farmer of Tennessee, the fuel for a man, but he ate bran flakes and skim milk instead and thought about the meeting to come, his belly rumbling in protest at the insult of the pallid food given it. Robard seized the edge of the table with his living hand, the dead arm hanging heavy against his left side, and considered the matters to be addressed by the tenured members of the department not two hours in the future. Perhaps he could claim injury, bind up the superfluous arm in a sling, nod once toward it in explanation as he pursed his lips in pain, and not join in the discussion led by the Yankee chairman, an upstart crow in a tiger's hide, smirking and chuckling before the group as he ticked off item by item of his agenda.

But no, that would the coward's way, the habit of the shirker, the slinker from the field of battle, the one who flees in shame. Duty lies before each man, and response to that iron law is the measure of a gentleman and a warrior in the ongoing struggle. One may not flinch at the sound of impending combat, lest he be lost not only in body but in soul. The unseen minie ball may strike, but death from assault to flesh is singular and endurable. A life extended through retreat is naught but delay of the blowfly and the maggot. To blaze up in death is to live. To flinch in face of the foe is to drag a rotting corpse across a burned field, and that corpse be you.

Robard Flange shifted in his kitchen chair, stared into the patterned tablecloth beflecked with small red flowers before him, belched at the gorge of cereal rising in his throat, and rehearsed the words he would deliver in the conference room of Old Central two hours hence, come what may. He would take his stand.

2

"THESE GRITS IS KINDLY COLD," Tee Arnold said, poking at his plate with a fork and looking toward Minnie working at the sink with her back toward him. She said nothing, rattled a pan and ran water over it, using more motion than the cleaning job needed and grunting once as she put the pan on the drainboard with a bang.

"Said the grits is a mite cool," Tee Arnold said, his voice raised a little.

"I heard you the first time you complained about the grits," Minnie said. "You don't need to be repeating yourself. You lucky to be getting anything to eat at all this morning, much as I got to do before I get the chance to lay my head down tonight."

"Big doings ahead, huh, Sugar?"

"Don't be sugaring me, Tee Arnold. I got to put up with that woman from nine this morning to midnight tonight. I don't need no jollying and shucking from you."

"You got help, though, don't you, what all they got going on at the chancellor's house. That place going to be full of house niggers for you to boss around." Tee Arnold put a forkful of grits in his mouth, warm enough to eat but he wasn't going to remark on that. He could tell that woman was through talking about grits for the day, probably through talking about anything before she hit the door going out of the house on Manassas, just off North Eighth Street.

"Yeah, I got help, if you call trying to get that sorry bunch headed in one direction helpful. I be spending more time yelling at them than I will seeing anything get done at that damn dinner."

"He going to be there, though," Tee Arnold said. "You going to get to see him up close, maybe say hidy to the big man himself."

"He ain't going to have time to say hello to a nigger cook, her back in the kitchen, with all them bigshot honkies around to talk to, unless they got folks wanting to take pictures of him talking to a nigger."

"They do pop some flashbulbs, and you liable to be on the front page of the *Nashville Negro News* tomorrow morning, smiling and carrying on with Martin Luther King Jr. Get yourself famous on me here. Won't be able to even stand to talk to a maintenance man no more once you get on the front page."

"I can talk to that janitor, but he ain't going to listen, what I know about him," Minnie said. "I ain't studying meeting Dr. King. All I wants is just to be sure none of them sorry waiters don't spill no gravy on the man. That's what'll satisfy me."

"That other one's going to be there, too, I reckon."

"Which one you talking about? It's going to be twenty-one guests, not counting the two of them living in the house and thinking they run things every minute of the day."

"You running things, not them," Tee Arnold said, swallowing the last bite off his plate, a scrap of biscuit. "You know who I'm talking about being at that dinner. I don't mean them other rich white folks. I ain't talking about that old bastard senator neither nor them poem-writing fools. I mean that bad nigger from up north."

"His name be Stokely Carmichael, and I know they done asked him to be there. That's all I know."

"They hope he don't show up. I tell you that. They don't want no skinny-assed Yankee nigger hollering about black power in the chancellor's house. I seen on the TV set how he do."

"He knows how to act when, I imagine," Minnie said. "He knows who to cut up in front of and who not. He can talk just like a white man when he wants, like one of them on the TV set. Everything he says he's done figured out who's going to be listening to it. He ain't about to tear his britches."

"He tells them what they want to hear, all right. He please who he talking to."

"I love to see that old senator how he would look if that little nigger would holler black power at him, though," Minnie said, beginning to laugh a little. "His old mouth would turn upside down."

"He crap his pants," Tee Arnold said. "Look around for the police to protect him from that crazy Ubangi."

"Where you hear Ubangi?"

"I keep up with what's going on these days, Sugar," Tee Arnold said, standing up from the table to say good-bye to his wife on her way out the door. "I read the papers, watch the news. Listen, you going to be able to bring back something for me worth eating from that dinner at the chancellor's house?"

"They ain't be nothing served you'd like. I can't even spell what they got us cooking for them rich folks. They got a special little white sissy boy telling me what to cook and how to do it."

"I know what Dr. King like. Fried chicken and collard greens."

"Dr. King will eat what they give him. Stokely Carmichael now, he done put in a special request for vegetarian only," Minnie said. "No milk, nor not no butter, neither."

"You shitting me, woman. Don't be saying that."

"He a special kind of nigger," Minnie said, "in all kinds of ways. I'm gone. Keep this house locked if you wander off somewhere today."

"Tell that skinny little nigger I hear what he's saying," Tee Arnold hollered after Minnie as she let the door slam behind her. "Black power, oooweee."

Randall Eugene Puckett asked his mind to think hard now and be honest with the man it worked for. Realistic. Down to earth. Not going to lie to himself. Expect what might be likely to happen and not what he wanted to be true. Hope in one hand and shit in the other, and see which one filled up first.

Would Milton Drummond show up in his old Dodge after good dark, like he said he was going to, or would he find some reason not to make it? Some excuse like the Coronet wouldn't start, it had a flat and his spare wasn't no count, if he'd even had one in the trunk. One of his damn kids was sick, and Corinne had to get him to use the car to go to the clinic and fetch medicine or the young'un would start puking blood and go into a permanent fit. Maybe Milton would claim he was sick himself, not able to lift his head off the pillow, much less haul Randall Eugene to the Stop 'n' Shop to do the job.

"Goddamn it," Randall Eugene said out loud, staring at a water stain on the ceiling above his bed, one that looked like a duck riding a tricycle, except that one of the wheels looked wrong for the full picture. Putting up a hand to block his sight of part of the water stain, Randall Eugene was able to perfect the design to where it looked almost just like the duck was riding on a three-wheeled conveyance, sitting up straight and holding onto the handlebars like a man. A duck with his own vehicle, just as pretty as you please.

"Goddamn it," he said aloud again, keeping his voice down so Maureen wouldn't hear him talking to himself. Why can't I own a reliable car of my own, or find a man I can depend on to help me out, or a job that pays enough for me to get by without having to bust my ass wide open doing it, or live with a woman who would lie down beside me, look up at the water stain on the ceiling and see the same design I do, and not look at me like I was crazy for pointing out the resemblance? Is any of that too much to ask? Don't I deserve a little bit of reward for all I done and the time I put in doing it?

I went to high school, Ronald Eugene thought to himself, beginning to list the accomplishments which should have assured him success in Davidson County, Tennessee, if there'd been such a thing as justice or at least a connection between one thing done and another thing following that first one. I played a little football for the Raleigh High Bulldogs, as much time as that son of a bitch of a coach would let me get out on the field to do it. I worked after school at Booming Burger and cut grass in the summertime, I got up most mornings and went on to class and took a shot at doing what them ugly old women teachers kept on telling us to do. I turned in some assignments, wrote stuff down on the tests they would slap on us every time we turned around, sat quiet in the back row most of the periods, didn't talk back to them if they left me alone, did all a white man can do to get along and fit in like they kept wanting you to do. Hung around the damn building until I was in the eleventh grade and couldn't stand it no more. Walked out at lunch one day in April and never went up them steps again or spent a minute regretting what I'd done except when I'd drive back and forth by the schoolhouse with the cut-out wide open on the gutted muffler on my Ford until I got tired of doing that. Nobody ever come out of the building to watch me pass, anyway, no matter how that engine rumbled. And boy howdy, it did.

And what has all that effort got me? What has all that time put in trying to get along and get ahead done for me? What has keeping my head down and my eye on the ball and my back bowed up to work amounted to? Randall Eugene looked around the master bedroom of the mobile home he rented for him and Maureen in Cumberland Village Trailer Park, moving his gaze systematically from point to point of the space where he spent most of his time when he wasn't outside somewhere. He noted the chifforobe in one corner, the TV set in another, a stack of clothes folded up by Maureen and sitting on an ironing board, the door to the closet where the rest of his shirts and pants and her dresses and blouses hung on wire hangers, a couple of pairs of shoes—hers, not his—lined up like a bunch of little soldiers waiting for orders to advance, a tipped-over plastic bucket that had been in the same position for the last couple of months, and he waited with his mouth open a little to hear better for his brain to tell him the answer to his question. Nothing, a little voice said in the middle of his head, not a thing have you got to show for all that bearing down and trying hard, and Randall Eugene repeated out loud what the voice had whispered.

"Nothing," he said. "Nothing, unless a goddamn empty plastic bucket would count."

Maureen hollered from the kitchen to ask him what he was saying, and he said the word nothing again, thinking how you couldn't even think to yourself in a trailer home without somebody tuning in to what was in your head. Something about how thin the walls were, how tight together every damn thing in the house was, how shitty the insulation was, and how the doors to every room were no thicker than a page from the Nashville newspaper. No good insulation. Something thick between you and the rest of the world. That's what you didn't have in a manufactured home, and it was what you wanted and got to buy if you had the money—some building materials between you and other people thick enough to let you make a noise now and then that only you could hear.

"You going to want to eat breakfast before I take Herbert and Alice and Carolene next door? Because if you are, you are on your own. I ain't got time to fool around here another minute."

"Naw," Randall Eugene said. "Take them on. I've got stuff planned out to do today. I ain't going to eat nothing, and I sure ain't got time to mess with the kids."

"You better go outside and see what that fool Milton is wanting, then. He's been sitting out there in front of Miz Shipley's trailer in that old car of his for as long as I been up this morning."

"Shit, Maureen, why didn't you tell me Milton's out there? We got a thing we going to do today, and I expect he's waiting to talk to me about it."

"If it's something to do with Milton Drummond, I know one thing for sure," Maureen said, sticking her head in the bedroom door to look full into Randall Eugene's face.

"Yeah," he said, feeling the tingling start up in his belly, just below his rib cage, "what's that, Maureen?"

"It ain't going to involve work, and it won't make no money. That's for shit sure."

"That's what you think, huh?"

"Naw, that ain't what I think. That's what I know," she said, and started herding the kids out the door of the trailer. "I got that by heart."

"You going to get something up beside your head," Randall Eugene said. "You keep on talking to me like that."

"That kind of brag used to work for you, Gene, but not no more. You touch me one like that one more time, and you know what'll happen. I will waste your sorry ass."

"Goddamn you," Randall Eugene said, looking away from the burning gaze Maureen was putting on him. "Damn you to hell any way."

"That you've already done, Mister," the woman said, jerking her head around so that a big strand of dirty blonde hair flopped across her face. "And a damn good job you made of it. Come on, Herbert. Move your butt."

"Aw, Mama," Herbert said.

Milton Drummond had all the windows of his Dodge down, needing to get some air even as early as it was in the day and though he was parked in the shade of a big sweet gum tree. He was keeping a close watch on Maureen pushing Randall Eugene's kids across the weeds and sweet gum balls of the yard and through the door of the next trailer over from the Puckett's unit.

"Your wife going to work this morning?" Milton said as Randall Eugene walked up to the driver's side of the Dodge. Randall Eugene had put on shoes to save his feet from what might be lying just beneath the surface of the dirt streets of the Cumberland Village Trailer Park, broken glass or pieces of wire or bottle caps or a needle of some kind, but he hadn't bothered to put on a shirt yet. A tuft of yellowish body hair stuck straight out from the middle of Randall Eugene's chest like a rooster's topknot, his pants rode low on his hips, and the laces of his shoes flopped from side to side as he walked toward Milton's Dodge Coronet. "I see she's off loading y'all's kids on somebody."

"She better be going to work," Randall Eugene said, "if she wants any more money to spend. I'm about ready to wean her off my payroll."

Milton started to ask how much Maureen got paid on that Puckett payroll, but by the time he thought out a way to put that in words so it was funny it was too late to say it. Randall Eugene might think it wasn't a joke and take it wrong. He never laughed much when he wasn't drinking, wouldn't even crack a smile most of the time. Keep that thought to yourself, Milton Drummond said inside his head, about the payroll. Save yourself some trouble.

"You ready to get it on, Son?" Randall Eugene said. "Ready to hit a lick?"

"I wanted to talk to you about that, Gene. That's why I got here so early in the morning. Wanted to catch you at home."

"Chickening out, huh? Found yourself a way to stay broke and feel good about it. Be satisfied to eat some more pinto beans and drink some more Blatz."

"I ain't saying that," Milton said, leaning his head back and sucking at his teeth as though he was looking for room for some thinking to take place in his head, thoughts which needed a little space to develop. "No, it's something else. Two things, really."

"Two things? What two things? The only two things I can come up is two things you ain't got, Milton, and never have."

"What you mean?"

"Balls," Randall Eugene said. "Them two things that'll let a man do what he has to do, provided he's got them. And I ain't talking about knocking some woman up, neither. That takes balls, all right, but not the kind I'm talking about. I'm referring to the kind you ain't got."

"Listen to me first. Here's the two things I mean. One, how do we know it's going to be enough money at the Stop 'n' Shop for us to come out ahead on the deal if we was to go through with it?"

"That's one thing which I'll answer in a minute. What's the other one, Mr. Ball-less Wonder?"

"The other thing," Milton said, telling himself not to let that no-balls business get to him and fluster his mind, "is suppose we do it. You go in, and I sit in the car waiting with the motor running. What if that man behind the counter steps on an electric button he's got hid on the floor to call in the police with, or suppose he just drops down on the ground and won't open the cash register, or maybe comes up with a shotgun he's got hid? And all you are is just one man, and number one, you got to put the scare into him, number two, get the money in hand, number three, turn your back and get out the door while he's fixing to put a load of buckshot in your ass. See, that's the kind of things I'm thinking ahead about."

"I'm going to answer them questions of yours one at the time, see can I satisfy your chickenshit ass. Number one, the main girl that works in the Stop 'n' Shop has told her sister that the damn safe is full on Thursday nights, because they wait to then to take the whole week's money into the bank the next morning. And the sister goes to the New Bethel Baptist Church where Maureen hangs around with the kids every Sunday until they run them all off, and that sister let word about that business slip to Maureen who told me about it, and before you say what I know is working in your mind, let me tell you this. No, Maureen don't know a damn thing about what I'm planning to do. I never made a peep when she told me that little bit of news. See? So the money's going to be there just fine to make the deal worth doing. You understand that, Milton?"

"All right, if that's right, what you said, the money will be there. Okay. I'll give you that. But what about the rest?"

"I'm getting to that. Don't piss your pants until I do. Here it is. I know I can do all that. Put a scare into the man behind the counter, get the money, get out of the store, get in the car, and haul ass, and do all that in less than a minute."

"I ain't doubting you none, Gene, I'm just thinking about what might could go wrong. See, I'm looking for insurance on this deal."

"Insurance? What the fuck you talking about? That .38 I'll be carrying is all the insurance I'm going to need."

Milton looked down at the emblem on the steering wheel of the Dodge, got his words set right in his head, the ones he'd been saying over and over to himself on the way to Randall Eugene's place, and then he said them loud enough to be heard good but not beyond two or three yards of the car.

"This insurance deal I mean, it has to do with another man," he said. "I'm thinking we need to keep the scare up on the guy behind the counter at the Stop 'n' Shop while you get the money all scooped up. See, somebody else in there with you to take care of at least half the job you been thinking you'd have to do all on your own."

"You got to stay in the car with the motor running, Numbnuts, ready to get out of the parking lot as soon as I jump in the car. You can't come inside the store, too."

"I don't mean me," Milton said, staring down at the Dodge emblem on the steering wheel and speaking in its direction. "I know all that. I'm talking about another man, somebody else to go in there with you and put the scare on the man behind the counter. I ain't about to get out of the car myself."

"I lost my head for a minute. Why would I think you'd have the nerve to do anything but sit there revving the engine up and pissing your pants? I apologize, Milton. I really do. Shit, I owe you that."

Maureen had gotten the three kids delivered inside the door of the trailer next to hers and Randall Eugene's, and she was flouncing herself behind the wheel of her Chevrolet, throwing stuff into the passenger seat and not bothering to look over at her husband and Milton Drummond as she made ready to leave for work. Milton lifted his hand to wave at her, in case she was looking in the rear view mirror, but Maureen made no sign of seeing him do that. The Chevrolet cranked and Maureen gave it enough gas to make gravel fly up as she pulled away.

"Somebody else getting in this deal's going to mean that you and me get less money out of it, Milton," Randall Eugene said. "I bet you hadn't even thought about that."

"Yes, I have. I've studied it on out, and the man I'm talking about will do that scare job for a flat amount of fifty dollars. It wouldn't be no big deal to him, the money part. He got other things on his mind."

"Who would this dummy be, then? He don't sound smart enough to be able to pour piss out of a boot with the instructions wrote on the heel."

"That's what I'm trying to tell you. It's a guy I worked with at the Coca-Cola plant and I got to hear what all he's done before. And he ain't no amateur, neither."

"Yeah," said Randall Eugene in a way that sounded to Milton like he was holding his breath to keep from hollering. "Tell me about him. What's his name?"

"The name he goes by is Tooter, but his real name is Roosevelt Browning."

"Shit, he's a nigger, idn't he? I should've known that as soon as you said Coca-Cola."

"Well, yeah. That's what Tooter is, but I wouldn't call him that to his face. Him being a nigger, that's what makes him the right man for the job."

"You mean he'll work cheap."

"That, yeah, but the main reason is that's what makes him scary enough to do the job we talking about."

"Black as the ace of spades, I reckon. Dumb as a post," Randall Eugene said. "Goddamn, Milton. You just wear me out."

"Wait'll you see him. Soon as that man behind the Stop 'n' Shop counter hears y'all ask for the money, he won't do nothing but hand it over and lay down in the floor so Tooter won't do nothing to him. That fellow ain't going to be worrying about how to save that store's money from you. He just going to be thinking big scary goddamn nigger."

"Huh," Randall Eugene said, "maybe you on to something, Milton. Fifty dollars is all he wants, you saying. Why?"

"Yeah, Tooter ain't interested in the money side of things. He declares all he worries about is getting freedom and black power. He wants attention to the black man's predicament."

"He sounds like a nut. Is he a bad nigger, Milton?" Randall Eugene said. "Cause if he is, you can't trust him as far as you can throw the bastard. He's liable to go off like a unloaded gun at any minute."

"Tooter is cool. He keeps his head. All he wants to do is tear down the establishment. He reads books and makes speeches all the time on that very thing. He sounds like a preacher when he gets to going. Now's the time he says the blacks is got to start up doing direct action."

"He sounds crazy to me. He got a grudge. Like he hates white folks."

"Naw, not all white folks. Just the ones that runs things. Tooter despises that bunch. You ought to've seen what he did to that asshole straw boss at Coca-Cola when he give Tooter some shit one time. It put the fear of God into everybody that seen it."

Randall Eugene scratched at the tuft of yellow hair sticking out of the middle of his chest and looked up into the gum tree Milton's Dodge Coronet was sitting under. The sweet gum was filled with starlings, lined up on almost every branch, quarreling among themselves, dropping loads, and flapping their wings as they decided where to fly next.

"I want to meet this Tooter first," he said. "Before I let myself depend on a nigger with a lot on his mind to do this job."

"I figured you would. I told him we'd come over to that barbecue stand on Monroe about noon and see him there, if you'd go along with it. Want to do that?"

"Shit, why not? Let's see if the boy's got enough sense to give us a hand tonight. A big nigger will scare a man behind a counter. There ain't no doubt about that."

"Tooter looks like a regular Ubangi from Africa, Gene. Wait'll you see the way he looks out of his eyes."

3

IT HAD TAKEN ALMOST A YEAR to do it, given the windingly illogical layout of streets and roads in Nashville, undoubtedly not the result of a lack of planning traffic flow on the part of the city fathers, but the result of their building city streets along old cattle trails and Indian paths and farming byways from the nineteenth century. But Ronald Alden had finally figured out a route to the Vanderbilt campus that allowed him to avoid the rush and clot of cars on West End Avenue and Hillsborough Road in the early morning hours of the workweek. Following the road less traveled required him to send his elderly Chevrolet up narrow lanes, badly marked streets, and at least one that supposedly was dead-end but not really, all in service of getting to the faculty parking lot near the Student Union early enough to find a place to park.

He was a couple of minutes behind schedule because of having to re-dress Emily in an outfit suitable for some special day at the preschool, making the carpool driver have to wait in the process, Lily still unable to drag herself out of bed, so he didn't have time to dawdle once he'd hit the only major street he had to travel—Natchez Trace. He knew he'd have to gun it when he made the left turn, traffic allowing, and he was prepared to blast on down he road. He couldn't afford to be leisurely, and he certainly couldn't stop. But as soon as he saw her walking up Natchez Trace, her golden hair and her remarkable rear end unmistakable in the morning sun, Ronald Alden had no choice.

"Shit," he said out loud as all doubt of who she was vanished the nearer he got to her, and while it was still possible to pull over in front of her without being rear-ended by some redneck. "That's her on foot."

It was Josephine Carol Longineaux; she was carrying a small orange cloth bag in her left hand, walking like a refugee from a catastrophe with no set destination before her but certain ruin behind, and she was heart-breakingly desirable, just the way she was every Monday, Wednesday, and Friday morning at nine o'clock in Ronald Alden's sophomore survey of English lit. In the classroom, she sat in the second row, two in from the end, next to some smooth Sigma Chi from Birmingham with a great thatch of dark hair, a bored look on his doctor's son face, and an air of current, past, and future financial and social well-being in gated suburbs, tasteful downtown office buildings, and the best restaurants in any city he would ever visit.

His name was Gatewood Dunn, and he constantly made aside remarks to Josephine Carol Longineaux during the course of Ronald Alden's lectures on the *Canterbury Tales* and the seventeenth-century metaphysical poets and all the rest of that bunch of singing birds, but she never took her eyes off the teacher and she never acknowledged a one of Gatewood's sallies. Instead, she listened to all Ronald said, she recorded salient points in her notebook, she raised her hand when questions were posed, and she spoke clearly and well to each and every one of them, while projecting continually the bone-solid truth that she was the most wonderfully put-together young woman Ronald had ever been privileged to stare at for three hours a week. That was one of the side benefits of teaching, being able to study every detail of any woman before you with impunity, your motive for inspection above reproach.

A week ago, walking with George Gwaltney from the office in Old Central shared by three assistant professors toward the snack bar in Rand, they had seen Josephine Carol Longineaux proceeding toward them on the brick sidewalk. She was in the typical uniform of a Vanderbilt coed, nothing ostentatious nor revealing, only the garments that would look ordinary on an ordinary wearer, and she was carrying a load of books hugged up to her breast, her head bent a little forward. She was alone, it was late morning, and she was hurrying as though afraid she'd be late arriving to some class. She was all business.

Yet when she noticed the two young faculty members approaching, she began to smile in the obligatory manner of the Southern female college student and spoke to her teacher. "Hello, Dr. Alden," she said, and that was all.

"Hello, Miss Longineaux," Ronald said, and after she passed him and George Gwaltney, George threw an elbow into Ronald's side.

"There goes," he said, "what looks to be some of the finest pussy in the South."

"She's quite a good student, Josephine," Ronald said as though George had just asked about Josephine Longineaux's literary acumen, not her fuckworthiness. "She wrote a really nice paper on 'Batter My Heart, Three-Personed God' last week, the most complex of Donne's ecclesiastical sonnets, I think."

"I tell you what I'd like to have done. Batter her ass more likely," George Gwaltney had said, chortling like a moron. "All I know is I would eat her until her forehead caved in, if I ever got the chance."

"She focused on point of view in that poem," Ronald said. "Took a pretty original slant on it."

"Jump on her sweet little slant. That's what I want to do."

Ronald hadn't responded, hoping silence would convey a proper rebuke to his colleague for his remarks, but in his heart he agreed with what Gwaltney had said right down to the ground.

A car behind him honked as Ronald pulled the Chevrolet to the side of Natchez Trace just ahead of where Josephine Longineaux was walking, the driver shooting Ronald the finger as he passed and leaning on the horn again. Fuck you, Ronald lip-read from the face of the asshole blasting by.

As the next couple of vehicles slammed by on Natchez Trace, the wind of their passage raised dust from the roadway and caused Josephine's hair to lift as Ronald watched her in the rearview mirror. It looked burnished in the sun, moving like a sparkling stream between banks of ferns and water lilies. It shimmered in the light. Flow gently, sweet Afton, flow. Jesus, Ronald said aloud. Straighten up, fool. I've got to let her know who I am, he told himself, so she won't be alarmed that she's about to be confronted by some slavering old lecher. As soon as she realizes the driver of this worn-out old Chevy is trying to talk to her, she'll probably spin around and run.

"Miss Longineaux," he called in the direction of the open window on the passenger's side. "It's me, Dr. Alden," wishing he could use his first name to sound friendly but knowing that could be taken as beyond strange. Too meaningful, by far, too close, too familiar. "Do you need a ride to campus?"

She lifted her eyes then from where they'd been fixed on the bottle caps and scraps of paper and gravel of the roadbed trash and, it appeared to Ronald, recognized who was calling her name. The smile she directed toward the side mirror in return was not the usual conventionalized signal of greeting from a student to an authority figure—a teacher, a minister, a house mother of a dormitory, someone in a position of control—but an attempt to place an encounter into a safe category for polite communication. These women of her class would do that by instinct. And by will, if the need be. By the time Josephine Longineaux had reached the door on the passenger side, Ronald had hit the latch, and she was able to lean over and look directly into his face. She was wearing no makeup, Ronald noticed, and she looked exhausted.

"Need a ride?" he said. "I'm on my way to campus."

"If you don't mind, Dr. Alden. That would be nice. Thanks."

"Out early this morning," Ronald said, looking into the rearview mirror, letting two cars pass and then pulling into the flow up Natchez Trace, telling himself what a stupid thing he'd just said. It sounded like he was criticizing her for walking on the street and at the same time asking her to explain herself. What've you been up to? Where have you been? Were you with a man last night and now you're having to walk to school alone? Did you let him fuck you? Did you like it? Did you groan when he did? Did you come? How many times? What did you call out loud when you came? Just sounds or words?

"Yes sir," Josephine Longineaux said, "I am. It's really hot even this early, isn't it?"

"Very hot," Ronald said, trying to get the image out of his head of her sweating and moaning tangled in sheets beneath some son of the privileged South. She would be straining on the lip of orgasm and the boy would be holding back, trying not to lose it before she got to where she needed to be. Wait, wait, wait, she'd be saying. Not yet. Don't stop. I'm almost there. "It's Nashville in April, and it feels like summer already."

"Oh, that song," Josephine said, her voice breaking as she began to weep aloud in a sudden series of muted cries. "I can't bear to hear it."

The radio was playing at a fairly high volume, tuned to a contemporary music station, one of the few AM outlets in Nashville not devoted to country and western whines and squalls and foot stomps, but Ronald hadn't even been hearing it. Background thunder on the way to work. An auditory psyching up for the day's grief to come. "What's wrong, Miss Longineaux?" he said, leaning forward to turn the switch off. Jesus, had someone in her family died? Was the song about death?

"Oh, please leave it on," she said. "I've got to hear the last part. I can't stop a thing from hurting until I have it all happen to the very end."

The song was familiar to Ronald, though he couldn't have named it or the singer, and he focused immediately on the words as the plaintive tenor complained that he couldn't live if living was without the woman he was addressing and that she always smiled but in her eyes her sorrow showed. "Yes, it shows," the singer assured her, and then launched into a higher pitched and more agonized repetition of "I can't live if living is without you. . . . " He ended in a diminishing tone and volume of moans and whimpers, all masterfully consonant with the tune he'd set before. Woe ohh, woe ohh.

"You can turn it off now," Josephine Longineaux said, her eye bright with tears, two of which trickled thrillingly and slowly across and down her unrouged cheeks, the supporting bone structure beneath the flawless flesh insistent and perfect. That's it. That is always the true sign of ultimate female beauty, Ronald said to himself, the cheekbones, the goddamn wonderful cheekbones. These beautiful Southern women have a lock on that, no matter what their origin: girl children of millworkers, cosmeticians, waitresses, debutantes, Vanderbilt coeds, princesses or whores, daughters of privilege or poverty. His wife's face swam slowly into his mind unbidden, as though coming from deep under water, flat and unplaned as a board from eyesocket to jawbone. He pushed the image aside, all the way back to Mansfield, all the way back to central Ohio.

"Have you lost someone?" he heard himself say, and then spoke her given name directly instead of her surname, the first time he'd ever had occasion to call Miss Longineaux that personal label in a one-to-one encounter. He shivered once at the steering wheel at the thought and shook his head hard to clear it. "Did a relative pass away?"

"A relative?" she said. "You mean someone kin to me. No, I almost wish it was, Dr. Alden. I mean if it wasn't my parents or brothers, of course."

"Maybe a grandparent?" Ronald said, listening to himself offer up degrees of kinship for the dead, anything to keep her talking. "Or an elderly aunt or uncle?"

"No sir," she said. "Nobody's actually died. It's not that simple. It just feels that way."

Sir, she called him sir, Josephine Longineaux had just said that, and Ronald felt a pang both of relief and depression at what the term of her address demonstrated about the way she saw the relationship between the two of them as they proceeded up Natchez Trace at a slow rate behind a long string of cars headed for another day of servitude. He was her teacher, a safe old guy who'd offered her a ride to campus on a warm day in Nashville, and that's all he was. Remember that and get used to it. There's security and ease in the freedom of every man's chains.

"You've been disappointed somehow," he said, letting his gaze shift a little from the bumper of the car in front of him so that it could touch briefly on her face, composed and perfect despite the tears tracking over the sharp symmetrical angles of her cheekbones. "A shock of some sort."

"Not a shock. A shock is when you don't see something coming. I knew it would get here because it was on its way. And I dreaded it so much and now it's come, and I don't have to be afraid any more of when it will happen. It's here. It's over, and the worst has happened."

God, the way her mind works, Ronald thought. Such insight into relationships explains how she can read poetry so well and write such damn good analyses about how it works its magic. Josephine Longineaux was crying openly now in soft little whimpers, and Ronald watched his right hand leave the steering wheel and take her left hand. He marveled at the skill of his fingers as they enclosed the wonderfully shaped digits and palm of the young woman beside him. Her hand was cool, yet warm to the touch, and her fingers gracefully turned to allow his to intertwine with hers.

"Oh," she said. "My heart is broken, and I felt it happen at the exact moment he said what he did. It stopped being whole at exactly six o'clock in the morning by the clock radio. I can point to that time. The sunlight was coming through the blinds, Dr. Alden, and I memorized the pattern it made as it lay on the sheet. I can't stop seeing the way it changed when my heart broke. The light died in the world, and now light is just what lets you see things. Nothing but that. No more glow is left to make things mean beyond themselves. It's gone for good."

At that, Josephine Longineaux tightened her grip on Ronald's fingers, and he swung the car into a one-handed abrupt escape out of the traffic on Natchez Trace and onto a side street he'd never taken before. The sign at the corner identified it as Rowland Lane, and small houses lined both sides, all identical but for the color of the paint on the front doors. He pulled over to the side of the street before one with a greenish door trimmed in brown, a slab of wood mimicking a scene from nature. A glen in the forest, an opening in the wilderness wall, a pitiful attempt at the pastoral. Oh, the lies arising from the color green.

"Miss Longineaux," he said, lifting her hand entwined in his and allowing himself to look directly into her eyes, "there is no escaping sorrow. It must be borne alone." Why did I say those particular words, he asked himself. Borne? Sorrow? Miss Longineaux? Jesus! How soft-headed am I?

"I know," she said in a voice quavering on the lip of a full-throated sob. "I just have to get through it. But oh I don't know if I can. Not this time." With that Josephine Longineaux collapsed totally, allowing her upper body to fall toward Ronald, wedging her perfect face into his throat and weeping as though she would never be able to control her tears again. Ronald could feel them wetting his shirt collar, short-circuiting any possible thought process he might have attempted to launch, destroying any basis for logic, her hair pushing into his face and billowing abundantly against his lips and nose. The space she occupied smelled like flowers, some delicate perfume impossible to create in an industrial laboratory for commercial purposes, realer than that, honest and true and good. Then he was kissing that mouth he had studied for weeks as its owner sat before him in a classroom, a student of the masterpieces of English lyric verse and early Renaissance drama. She opened her lips to him, and Ronald sought his way inside, an explorer of the warmth and humid depth of her physical being. Sweet Jesus, she was both yielding and pushing back, hungry for contact and connection, yet afraid. Torn between animal need and cultural prohibition. The engine of the Chevrolet roared as Ronald's foot involuntarily pushed against the accelerator, all gears in neutral, all forward motion suspended in the moment. Warmth took him where it would. He knew there was no way he'd ever be able to turn off the ignition now.

West of Nashville near the end of the bitter highway between the capital of Tennessee and Memphis on the big river, a green sign announced that the first exit to downtown off I-40 lay eight miles ahead. As Tollman Briggs noted that announcement, he felt the engine of the VW van whine a bit louder as the top of a hill came into view, and he knew he would be able to see the tower of the Life and Casualty Building poking its way above the horizon in a short time, the first of the downtown structures to do that at such a distance. He felt a lift in his belly just below the rib cage and a bit above the navel, and he leaned forward to tap Cameron Semmes on the shoulder. If you stopped on the shoulder of I-40 at the right time, all you could see was the whited sepulchre of money the L&C building stood for. There was one vantage point and one only that filled the requirement and granted the focus on what Nashville truly meant.

"Pull over, Cameron," he told her as she lifted her shoulder at his touch as though she were trying to dislodge a fly that wanted to land on her bare back. "This is it."

"I can't pull over, Tollman. It's too late for that. We're on an interstate highway, and that's against the law. There's trucks everywhere."

"You can if I tell you to. It's an emergency. Pull way over on the shoulder once you get over the hill. It won't take but a minute."

He knew she'd want to argue and pretend she didn't know why he'd want to do such a thing. Then he'd have to explain again and listen to her expressions of disbelief and ridicule. She would say she was amazed, that the whole thing was amazing, that his not riding in all the way into Nashville in the van was weird and amazing, that word amazing being the one she was now using on every occasion to comment on all human action and thought and deed and insight. Last month her word had been fantastic, one she used so often even she got tired of it. Her theory, as she often explained, was that any word used frequently enough with variations in tone, duration, and strength would grow in talismanic power. Too many synonyms, that's what was ruining the world, particularly the United States and especially discourse among the learned and the hip classes. Strip away all modulation and nuance. Call all things the same thing over and over until the word became the thing again, until the split between thought and action, the world and comment on it, vanished.

Thus for a spell fantastic had been the word for Cameron Semmes, the talisman, the only signifier. Now the syllables making up amazing were taking on the task and would prove equal to the burden in all cases. Heal the linguistic breach, Cameron would say. Bend language to your use, not to its. You'd find the result amazing.

"You know why, Cameron," Tollman said. "Pull over or I'll just open the side hatch and bail out." That did the trick, since she knew he'd do what he said. That was his thing, and had been since he'd known her. A thing once said was a promise to Tollman Briggs, and he could and would deliver on every pledge of action. It only took a couple of events to convince Cameron that he meant what he said. One had been a dive he took from a moving car into a roadbed of gravel and bullnettles just outside Dyersburg, and the other had been a long step Tollman had taken out a second floor window just off Main Street in South Memphis. No bones were broken either time, but Tollman didn't count that as mere good luck. Fortune had nothing to do with the reward paid the truthful man. It·was the consequence the world sometimes offered a man of determination and commitment. Success, attainment of a goal. Not always, but often enough to justify sticking to the promise that language made. The word of the hour in Cameron's mind was amazing. To Tollman Briggs, the word was fate.

"Okay," Cameron Semmes said, "let me pull Van Johnson over. But I'm not coming back to look for you if you don't show up at Rainbow's pad on Belmont Street tonight. You're on your own, Hoss."

"What's this new label you're giving me?" Tollman said, picking up the duffle bag which he'd throw over one shoulder, leaving his hands free for the true work of the vagabond singer, the left to hold the guitar case and the right to support the universal signal of the rover, the lifted thumb. "Hoss? Have you gone Texan all of a sudden?"

"Amazing," Cameron said, bringing the VW which she was now calling Van Johnson to a stop on the shoulder. Her first name for it had been eVANgeline, but that word had lost its power through overuse. It had gone from clever to nondescript, missing somehow any transformational moment of talismanic significance. Words would do that, too. There is no guarantee in meaning. It can drain away like used dishwater. "Simply amazing."

"I'd call it complexly amazing, or it wouldn't be worthy of the name."

"See you in Nashville, I hope," Cameron said as Tollman unloaded himself and his gear onto the side of the interstate in the wash of air and dust from a trio of trucks blasting by. "But I'm not going to wait around until you show up."

"Just don't fuck the first guy you see," Tollman said. "That's bad karma and wrong juju."

"Amazing," Cameron said one last time before she pulled Van Johnson back into the flow of traffic headed for the Athens of the South.

The road before Tollman was clear now, and he settled into the hitcher's gait, his back to where he was going as he began the eternal drift, his duffle over one shoulder, guitar strapped across his chest. He was alone finally, working his way from the rural to the urban, from the green of the natural to the gray of cement, his part in the mythic necessity of bearer of the songs of the folk to the ears of those in need of hearing them now accepted, in progress, acted upon. "Beseige my heart," he said, "if you can, Old and Eternal Road, but know I will finally beat you. I will break on through to the other side."

Cars carrying lone salesmen and music executives and solitary middle-aged women, entire families, tourists from Ohio and Illinois and Missouri and Indiana, old black men broken by time and circumstance, the heedless redneck young, Mexican migrant workers in search of crops to harvest for a pittance, all the flotsam and float of America heading for Nashville, pounded their way by Tollman as he walked backwards into an unknown future, looking deeply into the history lying behind him. The way I walk is a statement, an icon of the wandering heart, he told himself, for where I go is unknowable until met and where I've been has meaning only as dead, lost, abandoned. The past cannot hold me, and the future waits for the shaping I will give it. I head East, the West rejected, and the long slender geographic configuration of the state of Tennessee apes my journey. For what I know I leave, and what I seek has yet to be realized. I give it life, my song gives it meaning, I move into myth.

It was fully a half hour before even one vehicle slowed down as it passed Tollman, broken now into a full and satisfying sweat and breathing deeply as he carried the load strapped to him. He had learned that feet grow more tired walking backward than turned in the conventional direction, and that dust blown up by speeding automobiles quickly turns to mud as it settles onto sweaty surfaces. He felt realer, knowing that, and he found himself unable to repress a broad grin as he thought about thinking what he was thinking. Layers of thought, not deep concentration on a single meditation, made for satisfaction. It was like filling his belly with a varied collection of dishes, not one huge chunk of meat. It rumbled, it mixed, and it drew strength from all parts of what his mind touched.

Behind his back Tollman heard the car pull off the road ahead, and for the first time, he shifted his attention from where he had been and toward where he had not yet arrived. He turned to trot toward the stopped vehicle ahead on the highway shoulder, the duffle moving on his shoulder as though it contained a living thing and the guitar case drumming against his chest as he jogged. Would this be his chariot to the heart of Music City, this beat-up gray Buick, its rear tilted to one side as though in favor of a old wound, a constant reminder of past mishap and present predicament? Yet the vehicle moves still, canted to one side though it may be, the unprotected heel and lean of the mechanical charger an emblem of wars fought, wars lost, wars survived, injuries overcome.

"Hello, young man," the driver called as Tollman Briggs wrestled the passenger door open. "Where are you headed?"

"Right now to Nashville," Tollman said, gesturing toward the rear door with his guitar case. "Ultimately, what man knows his final destination?"

"You got that right, I do believe," said the driver, a middle-aged sagging man wearing a white shirt and a loosened tie, and suit pants with no coat to match. "Put your stuff in the back seat, there with them boxes. I'm on my way to Church Street downtown, right close to the train station."

"That'd be a great advantage to me. I'm working my way to Belmont Street, somewhere close to Hillsborough Village."

"I can put you out pretty near that," the driver said. "Are you trying to break into the music business?"

"How did you know that?" Tollman said, thinking a little compliment about the astute insight of the Buick driver couldn't hurt, a payment to the old fellow, as obvious and tired though his comment was. He thought he was perceptive. Humor him.

"That guitar you got. That and the hair. That's the tipoff. You can see a hitchhiker carrying a guitar or a fiddle case on most any road leading into Nashville these days, every one of them hoping to make it big in Music City."

Gear loaded into the back seat half-filled with identical-sized cardboard boxes and the Buick back into the flow of I-40, Tollman looked closely about him at the details of the car carrying him where his journey might lead next. Worn upholstery, a steering wheel with a spinner knob added for extra purchase, scuffed and faded floor mats, a radio with an unlit dial, a driver with more miles on him than were indicated on the Buick's speedometer, a windshield with a long crack shaped like a river on a map from top to bottom on the passenger's side, vents pouring hot air at full volume, windows cracked for extra ventilation, all aspects necessary for proper conveyance of the man of the road into the next step of the journey.

"My Rosinante," Tollman Briggs said aloud. "Noble steed."

"What's that?" the driver said, taking a quick look at Tollman. "I didn't get what you just said."

"Nothing important. Just the name of a horse in a book I read a while back."

"You like horses, huh? I used to like them, too, back when I was a gambling man. I was a slave to the ponies. They owned me, though. Not me them."

"Not horses as horses, I don't like them that way, but for what they mean," Tollman said. "Ways to get to some place where you aren't now. That's what I like about them. Whether I'm actually riding one or not." Then, to offer a friendly response to the man at the wheel, selected by a fate he would never know or be capable of understanding, that of being Tollman's agent of transport into the next phase of the mythic journey, a question. "You say you used to be a gambler. No more? A bad run of luck?"

"I did. I was that. In another life before I began my real one, the one I'm living now and will live throughout all eternity. Name's Dean Slocomb, spelled with a b at the end of it, not just the m by itself."

"By that, you mean the b is silent, not sounded, but necessary anyway. It's got to be there doing its job, carrying the load but not worrying about getting credit for it. It serves the meaning of what you're called. Silence speaks volumes." At that, Dean Slocomb took a long look at his passenger and then allowed a smile to play across his face.

"I like what you're saying about my name. I'm gonna remember that. What label do you answer to, buddy?"

"I am Tollman," Tollman said. "In all senses of that word."

"That's your last name? Tollman?"

"It's my only name. I had a last name, and I still use it when the power structure demands full and official identification. But to myself and the world that matters, I am simply Tollman."

"You're not traveling under a consumed name, are you? I used to do that, back before I was born again. I did things I didn't want folks to know me in connection with, if you get what I mean. Not crimes now, though. Nothing indictable."

"A consumed name," Tollman said. "No, but I love the concept, and I'd like to use it someday in song, but no, Tollman is my real name, one of the ones I was given at birth. I'm trying to live up to it as best I can, each and every breath I draw."

"A new life asks you to get a new name," Dean Slocomb said, using only one hand to steer, the one holding the knob with the picture of a pretty girl adorning it, the nipples of her bare breasts pert and pink. With the other, he dug deeply at an ear and looked down to see what it might have fetched out for inspection. Satisfied, he put all fingers back on the wheel. "I learned that the hard way, and I want to tell you, Tollman, I praise the day I did that."

"Is it a long story? Do you have time to let me hear it?"

"I'll testify to any man who asks and who wants to listen, and let me tell you, I don't care if he stops listening along the way or just picks up part of what I'm saying. I figure anything that gets through is that much gain I made and that much of the message I've done got across. So I'll tell you my story, and I'll share my burden, but I want to ask you something first. Just a follow-up question, you understand."

"Ask me what you will, Mr. Slocomb, and I'll try to respond in a way that'll work for you."

"Call me Dean," the unindicted man said. "I don't believe in earthly titles, and I hope I done got beyond that, praise Jesus." He looked over at Tollman Briggs longer than a man driving an old Buick with shot brakes should advisably do, and then he went on. "You said something about how you was Tollman in every sense of the word. What'd you mean by that, Tollman?"

"I'm glad you asked, Dean, and I'm happy to try to answer it. A lot of people who're puzzled by something are afraid to admit their ignorance, and I believe that's the primary bar against enlightenment and understanding. Being humble enough to ask for explanation is the needful thing. Shows you're willing to be taught." Tollman paused to get his thoughts in order, to adjust what he had to say to the current audience, given its limitations in comprehension and cultural background, reminding himself to communicate his appreciation for the chance to explain the ramifications of the label put upon him at birth by happy chance by simple parents, and he leaned forward to tap three times with his knuckles on the sun-faded dashboard before him, a substitute for the guitar's not being in front of him to receive his muscle message. "Tollman the name suggests one who collects a fee from those privileged to travel the way he guards. Every step we take in this world is measured out and paid for one way or the other, and he who collects the fee and allows the advance of the traveler has the responsibility of measuring the worth of the supplicant and his suitability to continue the path he seeks to follow. Tollman is the keeper and the measurer, the defender of the path and the judge of the seeker before him. Tollman may communicate in simple words, in physical gesture, or visual signal. I choose as Tollman to convey my message in song."

"Oh, boy," Dean Slocomb said, letting off on the accelerator and slapping a hand on the steering wheel, "tell it, son. I'm liking where I think you're going. I've laid my money down at lots of tollbooths up yonder in the North, but I never thought about it that way when I was doing it. You telling me something."

"I'm glad to hear that, and I'm expecting we might be seeing things in the same way," Tollman said, feeling the tightness of a tear beginning to well up in his throat and chest. "Not much more to say about what the tollman does, but I think you'll understand his job is crucial and his task never-ending." Tollman had learned as a child he could bring tears to his eyes whenever he wanted, but no need now. It'd be overkill. All he had to do was think a young bird fallen out of its nest, alone and hungry and innocent about all dangers, and the tears would spring up until his eyes glistened.

"When you let yourself be directed, son," Dean Slocomb said, "you will be busy day and night. But that's where the joy is in this old world, taking directions, not in sitting around a crap table trying to predict the number of pips on a pair of dice."

And yet the naysayers will opine there's no knowledge in the folk,

Tollman said to himself, no comprehension of the true and the good in the common man. Look at this worn-out old salesman of goods un-needed and useless, driving a rusted-out old Buick, sweating like a work animal and steadily dying in his journey into the darkness, yet the bearer of gut and liver and lung and blood truths never to be recognized by the sophisticates.

"Can you sing without your guitar to help you along, Tollman? Because if you can, I'd be soul satisfied to offer a up a hymn of praise along with you while we work our way along this old I-40 into Nashville."

"I'm a great believer in a cappella duets," Tollman said. "What tune do you want to start with, Dean?"

"You know 'Trust and Obey'?"

"There's no other way to be happy in Jesus, but to trust and obey," Tollman said, beginning in flat recitation but ending the statement in song, Dean Slocomb joining in after the first few words were spoken. Tell me this is not a sign, Tollman told himself, that this is not the way to enter Nashville in the early spring, all leaves pale green and all buds poised to burst into bloom, the hitcher with his guitar riding with a man of the folk, giving voice to a simple sentiment set in rhyme and rhythm and aimed at those of low-level intellectual clout. As his voice blended with that of Dean Slocomb in the verse beginning with the words "As we do His good will," the Buick sailed by a road sign announcing that the next large clot of exits were to Nashville and the first one coming up was Charlotte Pike. Tollman was pleased but not surprised that his tenor floated in good counterpoint above the baritone of Dean Slocomb, not a bad combination for the hymn under treatment. Old Dean carries a pretty good tune for an ignorant redneck fundamentalist, Tollman admitted to himself, knowing the character of this entrance to Music City was doing him good mythically. "He abides with us still," he yodeled, his voice resting on the background growl of Dean Slocomb driving his Buick with its boxes full of pitiful sales samples riding along with Tollman's guitar in the vehicle's backseat. "We will trust His good will. He abides with us still and with all who will Trust and Obey."

I sweat an honest sweat, the heat from the wind of the highway pours over my face, ever eager-eyed, I arrive in Nashville singing a full song, harmonious brother to a man of the people. America, I will break your heart yet.

4

JONATHAN SETH MATTHEWS had worried about being able to recognize him in the crowd of people who'd be pouring off the TWA flight from New York, enough so that he'd brought along with him to the airport one of the placards announcing the student-run event. He had circled the name with a felt pen and underlined each letter in a contrasting color and drawn arrows from all points of the compass of the placard, each directed inward at the name. Jonathan knew that he himself could not but notice seeing his own name highlighted in bright shades and surrounded by arrows, and that had been reassuring for a while, right up to his sudden realization that the reason he'd notice his own name would be because he'd never seen it in letters larger than a twelve point typeface. What you weren't accustomed to seeing on a regular basis you would naturally be surprised by. Oh shit.

"What if he doesn't see us?" Jonathan said to Raymond Arceneau, loaded down with two cameras, a tripod, and a bag of equipment heavy enough to cause him to list badly to one side. "What if he just walks right by us, you know, as used as he is to seeing his name plastered everywhere? And we miss him and he wanders off and it takes us a long time to catch up with him and he'll be upset and out of sorts? And then when we get him back to campus, it'll be late and Dr. Haskell will chew our asses."

"He won't get by us, Jonathan," Raymond said, swinging the heavy bag from one shoulder to the other one, causing the tripod to clatter to the floor with a bang loud enough to cause an old lady standing nearby to jump and cry out. "We'll see him if he doesn't see us. That's what matters."

"What if we don't recognize him and he slips by?"

"How can you not recognize Allen Ginsberg, for Christ's sake? He'll be the only one with a beard and long hair and a crazed look in his eyes." Raymond paused and began to laugh at what he was going to say next, himself his own best audience. His only audience most of the time. "I take that back," he went on. "Part of it anyway. Ginsberg won't be the only one with a crazed look. About every third person in Nashville looks nuts. But Ginsberg will have his own kind of insanity. We'll know him, and so will everybody else that sees him. He'll stand out like a redneck at a sorority party."

"Maybe, maybe not," Jonathan Matthew said, adjusting the placard announcing the Vanderbilt Impact Symposium so that it could be better seen by anybody headed his direction. "Have you got your camera ready?"

"Yes, I do happen to have in mind getting some shots of Allen Ginsberg coming to Nashville, believe it or not. And I even remembered to bring a camera with film in it."

"Fuck you," Jonathan said in a distracted voice, his eyes on the passageway leading from where the TWA plane would land to the lobby area where the crew from the student newspaper, the *Vanderbilt Hustler,* waited.

"Fuck you very much right back," Raymond answered automatically. "I believe it's taxiing up to the gate. People are starting to swarm."

"Looking like they're glad to see whoever they're meeting. Putting on a welcome show," Jonathan said in a practiced jaded tone.

"Now, look, Raymond," he went on. "I'll go up to him as soon as we see him coming, and you be ready to take the first shot when I'm welcoming Ginsberg and shaking his hand and all that shit. I want that to be the lead picture on the front page of the *Hustler,* and if I'm lucky, on the *Nashville Tennessean* tomorrow morning."

"The *Tennessean* will not run a shot from us, Jonathan. They got their own photographers and reporter here, and they'll have them for everybody coming in."

"Martin Luther King Jr. is being driven in from St. Louis, they said. I don't know how Stokely Carmichael is getting to Nashville or where he's coming from. Have you heard?"

"No. But I know how Strom Thurmond is getting here."

"By jet from Washington, I guess."

"No, Jonathan. That old son of a bitch is flying in on a broom, dressed all in white with a pointy hat on."

"Very funny," Jonathan Matthews said. "And oh so original. They're coming down the passageway, the first bunch of them. Get ready."

"I was born ready, fool. Just don't get in my way."

Clots of passengers were heading down the corridor toward the bright lights of the waiting area, old ladies propping up old men in tentative toddle, freaks in tie-dye under clouds of hair and waves of body odor, incense, and weed smell, men in business suits looking around for pay phones hungry for quarters, children screaming from earache caused by the sudden change in atmospheric pressure, families looking for Maw Maws and Paw Paws and cousins and nieces, and finally near the end of the procession the man himself, the Beat poet Allen Ginsberg sporting thick eyeglasses, attired in a yellow robe and blue jeans and a heavy necklace supporting what looked to Jonathan to be a shrunken head complete with sewn-together eyes. Almost every finger of the author of *Howl* was adorned with at least one ring.

"Dig his eyes. He looks stoned," Raymond Arceneau said. "Blasted out of his fucking gourd."

"How else would you have him be?" Jonathan Matthews said. "That's why we invited him here, right?"

"Do you suppose he knows where he is? What if he believes we're narcs when we go up to him? He probably thinks he's in Rangoon."

"Get your camera ready," Jonathan said. "I'll shake his hand and welcome him and you get as many shots of me doing it as you can."

"Too late," Raymond said. "Look, the *Tennessean* reporter has already stuck a mike in his face. She's fixing to scoop us."

"Vanderbilt's paying for this, goddamn it. I'll break up this little party."

"Mr. Ginsberg," Jonathan cried out, moving at a lope toward the crew from the *Nashville Tennessean* and the minicam operator and team from WSM News. "I have seen the best minds of my generation destroyed by madness."

At that, Ginsberg looked away from the blonde woman pointing the mike at his teeth and instead toward the source of the mouther of his poetic feet. "Young man," he said. "What treasonous trash have you been reading? I bet you can't quote another line from it."

Jonathan did that instantly, shouting "starving, hysterical, naked," and praying Ginsberg wouldn't insist on more. "Come unto me," the poet yelled out loud enough to draw even more attention from those who'd been his fellow-travelers and the groundlings waiting for them, all shrinking away from where the disturbed-looking man was stopped in the middle of the passageway, forming as they did a ring of repugnance like the phenomenon discussed in Jonathan's botany class, involving something about a species of deadly mushrooms and root rot.

"Mr. Ginsberg," the blonde reporter was saying, adroitly and professionally blocking Jonathan from getting directly to the open arms of the poet, her arms spread wide to guard her catch from competitors. "Before you speak to anyone else, let me ask you the question all Middle Tennesseans have been eager to have you answer."

"Speak up, Child," Ginsberg said, trying to reach around the blonde journalist bimbo in Jonathan's path to take the hand offered him. "I'll be glad to try."

"Why have you come all the way to Nashville, why have you come to this year's Vanderbilt Impact Symposium?"

"Why, dear, that's an easy one. I've never fucked a Southern white boy before, and I think it's high time I did."

A great groan of shock and horror arose from those watching on the fringe surrounding the dangerous fungi, the ring of repugnance in the Nashville air terminal grew in diameter as though by magic, and the WSM lady reporter clicked off her microphone. "Let me tell you, Mr. Beatnik," she said off air and only loud enough for Ginsberg and Jonathan Matthews to hear her words, "I've tried them from everywhere, and there's not a dime's worth of difference between a Southern white boy and any other hard dick."

"Mr. Ginsberg," Jonathan broke in. "I'm from the Vanderbilt newspaper, the *Hustler,* and we're here to take you to campus and then to your hotel."

"Are you my angel?" the King of the Beats said, holding Jonathan's right hand in both of his, and squinting through his glasses. His eyes look as big as an owl's in those lenses, Jonathan heard a voice inside him say, small and meek and trembling in tone, and his hands are softer than any girl's I've ever touched. Oh, Jesus.

"My lyric from heaven? My gateway to the heart of the South?" the poet said. "Hustle me away from here. Put me in your chariot. Transport me where you will. Don't be gentle."

Alfred Buchanan sat at an angle on the leading edge of the desk in the vacated classroom in which the department of English was temporarily forced to meet, its traditional sanctum not available now because of renovation at the chairman's command in the face of supposedly unmoving opposition to any change of any sort. That refusal to move had not sped, Alfred mused smilingly, along with other obstacles overcome he could name. He was careful now in his physical posture not to push too strongly with his foot touching the floor, the left one. Probably the time-chewed piece of furniture on which he sat was heavy enough not to slide abruptly if he pushed too strongly with the anchored foot, but best to take precaution against slippage. It would look awkward, uncontrolled, and a shade embarrassing if he had to catch himself against the pull of gravity in front of the lot of them there assembling.

"Hello, Mr. Chairman," one of the older members of the department, Lawrence Hill Dunham offered, instinctively subservient to authority, his dentures a brilliant white against the mottled red of his face. "Not too pleasant in this classroom, is it?"

"No, Larry," Alfred Buchanan said, comfortably wondering what witty remark he'd utter next, and then it came to him, as it always did, synapses firing in perfect accord. "What I most dislike about our having to meet in this classroom while our real digs get refurbished is the odor."

"The odor?" Lawrence Hill Dunham said loudly enough that several others of those already gathered stopped their chats in progress and looked toward their chairman at casual lean and ease on the desk before them. What had made Dr. Dunham take notice and bark out a query?

"Yes, perhaps scent is a better and more precise term for it. When I walk into a room where freshman composition is ordinarily taught eight hours per day, I find that the smell of sentence fragments and imprecise word choice and butchered grammar can be positively overwhelming."

Dr. Dunham guffawed gratefully and several others joined in, one or two of those with substantial hearing loss asking others what Alfred had just said, and those yet able to parse initial consonants answering impatiently. Good to have said something surprising, complex enough not to have been immediately grasped, and above all apt, Alfred told himself as he watched the last three of the tenured members of the Vanderbilt English Department enter the room, talking among themselves so as to appear not to have realized where they had arrived or why they had set that place as their destination. All three looked up surprised when the first of them stumbled into a student desk, causing the other two to collide gently with him and each other, giving the impression of explorers happening on an unexpected clearing in a rain forest and peering about in search of the living quarters of a tribe newly discovered. Would their lodges be substantial? Would there be a special structure for ceremonial activities?

"This is the place, gypsy scholars," Alfred Buchanan said. "You have but to look about you to discover the heart of literary study at Vanderbilt, here gathered in Confederate Hall, room three eleven. Rest, rest, perturbed spirits." This jab earned more chuckles from a goodly and sufficient number, and Alfred was encouraged enough by that to smile broadly and then break off the expression of geniality at just the point when the last of the late-ish three wedged himself into a fifth row desk.

That would be Robard Flange, Alfred knew, fashionably laggard to any event for which he was expected and last to settle in place, and the other two were Gareth Lamb, chief among the adversaries of change and improvement, not only not agreeing with such developments but not believing in the very concept of their existence, and the third of the living dead, as Alfred referred to them in conversations with Phillipa those rare times he allowed topical events to be mentioned at the cocktail hour, was young Henry Hallam Horsham, a graduate of this university returned to serve his undergraduate mentors and masters after a stint at Yale, a lickspittle of the first water.

Dr. Robard Flange fiddled and fussed with what he was carrying and with locating his seat long enough to allow him to be the ultimate person in the room coming to attention, flinging his left arm haphazardly about more than was practically necessary, as was his wont, and then all there gathered focused on their leader at the front of the room in his casually graceful lean against the scarred oak desk. Alfred was pointedly not noticing the final settle of Robard Flange into his seat, timing the lift of his head to look at the assembled group until the more alert of the bunch realized it was he who was deciding to begin the meeting proper, not the laggard group of three. That moment and its effect accomplished, Alfred opened his mouth in greeting, showing his teeth in a wide and obviously calculated smile.

"Gentlemen," he said, "welcome to our monthly little get-together.

"I declare I've enjoyed being able to address the tenured members of the department by the single sobriquet of gentlemen," Alfred began, "but that won't be accurate much longer. I've received some most welcome news from the office of the chancellor, and I'm now prepared to share that with you. It is information of a most transformative nature."

That will get their attention, Alfred Buchanan said to himself as he noted a most perceptible stirring of feet and wobbling of heads follow what he'd just said. "What'd he announce?" Alfred heard Lawrence Hill Dunham ask the man next to him, Dr. Marvin Slope, medievalist and self-proclaimed linguist, though no credentialed evidence existed to substantiate that claim of competence. "What was that he said?"

"Let me answer, Marvin," Alfred said, "so that all may hear and applaud the news. My request has been approved by the chancellor that we launch a search for a senior scholar, specialty open, to be appointed full professor in the department as soon as a suitable individual may be identified and persuaded to join us."

"This is indeed news," Robard Flange said, his face darkening as he spoke without waiting for recognition by the chair to be allowed the floor. Alfred did what he had to do to control matters. Ignored the interruption and proceeded as though it had not occurred.

"I bring you this information a bit out of sequence with the announced agenda for our consideration today for a pair of reasons. First, to share the most agreeable news immediately and second, to describe to you the limitation imposed by the terms of the chancellor's agreement to my request."

"What are those, indeed, pray tell?" Gareth Lamb asked in a tone of energetic surprise, as though he'd just been told his wife had transferred all contents of his home on Blair Avenue into a Mayflower van while he was conducting a seminar on *The Rape of the Lock.*

"The limitation is that the scholar we hire shall be highly qualified, of course, and most crucially central to the permission given my request by the chancellor, the person shall be female."

"We had no notice that such a request had gone forward from the department for an additional senior position to be added to our number. You were not so instructed by us." The speaker was Robard Flange, his left arm aflap as though moved by a tempest wind and his right hand waving in the close air of Confederate Hall 311 as though to ward off an especially aggressive wasp intent on hanging its stinger in the middle of Robard's face. "What process was followed in connection with this matter?"

"The process was unusual," Alfred said, "I grant you that. And it was not of my choosing. The chancellor called me in, relayed to me the decision of the board of trustees of the university to establish a tenured senior position for a woman scholar in the College of Arts and Sciences, and added that if the department of English wished first innings in this cricket match, it was invited to do so. If not, the post would go to the social sciences, already slavering at the notion of a program in what they're calling women's studies."

"For God's sake, is that like home economics?" Samuel Vinson asked. "We had a course in that for girls in my high school in Macon. Cooking little pies and such. Small loaves of bread."

"Why were the pies little?" David McDavidson said.

"It's an outrage," Robard Flange said. "I still question your lack of consultation and seeking for direction, Mr. Chairman. We full professors needed as the heart of the department to be able to speak our will."

"The decision was made before it reached me, and the chancellor asked for a unilateral decision on my part. We have been directed. Should I have responded negatively, we should have seen the position go elsewhere and we should have seen a program in women's studies sans literary component at Vanderbilt as a result. Would you have that, gentlemen, or would you have an additional tenured position in English?"

"I propose," Buchanan said finally after a period of allowing outcries and groans to swell to a crescendo and then subside into a low mumble, "that we not debate a settled matter and that instead a small committee of the department come up with a bill of particulars about qualifications of candidates and procedures for search, present these to the department for its advice and consent, and then forward the result of that thinking to the chair for his use in decision making." Let's see if they buy that, Alfred said to himself, or if they perceive the ticking bomb there so beautifully and cunningly wrapped. As soon as Gareth Lamb offered to serve as chair of the committee, he knew he had them now, one of the Living Dead having fallen into the trap. Confederate Hall 311 a la Caesar. Or better yet, a la William Tecumseh Sherman at the gates of Atlanta.

"That settled by acclamation, let us proceed to the next matter of our agenda," he said instead of launching into a cavort, his tone now musing and thoughtful and composed, "if we may. That being the visit by a major American poet to Vanderbilt this week."

"If you are referring to that degenerate whose name I will not speak," Robard Flange said, "this so-called Beatnik mouther of obscenities and blasphemy, I question that characterization, sir."

"Robard, you speak well for me and for all of us," Alfred Buchanan said, "and I agree most wholeheartedly, yet the world at large considers him important and his appearance at Vanderbilt significant."

"This place, these grounds, I thank my Redeemer and praise Him, are not the world at large," Robard Flange went on, looking about him to garner nods of affirmation. These came in good number. "It is Vanderbilt University, birthplace of the only poetic movement of merit in the last century of American literary history."

"Truly spoken," Alfred agreed, "yet the world at large will judge us by our response to this upstart popinjay now come into our midst, the fact of which we must be cognizant. We must not allow him and those who notice him to use our response against us."

A short silence fell, heads swiveled in search of confirmation, and then Gareth Lamb spoke. "There is wisdom in what you say, Dr. Buchanan. We must be careful not to allow our literary heritage to be manipulated and turned against us. Ignoring him, this bearded pervert with the loud mouth, will serve us better than granting him notice and the hubbub about him which would result."

"Starve him of the publicity he craves," Samuel Vinson boomed, his voice a drum in the room. "Deny him the air he needs. Smother this pervert by our indifference."

"Well said, Samuel, and well argued, Dr. Buchanan," Robard said. "Shall we agree that the department shall make no formal statement about the momentary and meaningless presence of this poetaster at Vanderbilt?"

"I stand ready," Alfred Buchanan said, seizing the floor again, his floor, his department, his direction of events, "to receive such a motion."

Confederate Hall 311 trembled in the heat of discussion, the sweat and din of strongly held and poorly expressed opinions. "The most disgusting effect of this beatnik poetry that too many of our students are slipping off to read as they puff on their marijuana cigarettes," Gareth Lamb announced near the end of the hour, "is the atmosphere it creates in the classroom. I am increasingly forced to take notice of all the dirty bare feet I see on display as I try to teach the great works of the eighteenth century to these young louts. Encouraged by the mindless rant of today, they sit shoeless, picking at their toes monkeylike, grime all over them."

"We are in agreement, and we are adjourned," Alfred Buchanan said. A damn good meeting, he told himself, pushing off from his lean on the battered desk he'd ridden to a full and satisfying climax. Time to head to the barn and rub down the horses. The tenured members of the Vanderbilt department of English milled about, bumping into desks, stumbling into their fellows, seeking crushing rejoinders, and brushing up against walls and blackboards as they made their way toward the light of the hall, begging each other's pardon on the way.

5

"I DON'T BELIEVE I have to tell you what to do," Blanche Ann Weaver was saying to the young woman standing before her in a room on the second floor of what was in the 1920s a Davidson County Bank and Trust building on Second Street, now a mixed-use facility with a wig shop and a luncheon grill on the ground floor and rooms for transients and the Music City Magic Fingers Massage Salon occupying the floors above. The young woman was looking somewhere off to the left of Blanche Ann's face as though someone in another room had called her name and she couldn't place who it was without getting a good look at the speaker. She was wearing what reminded Blanche Ann of something she'd seen before, and when the girl lifted her hand to mess with a clump of hair dangling across her face, the connection came for Blanche Ann. The dishwater blonde was wearing clothes like her mother had made her on a pedal sewing machine back in Linden, a straight up and down dress from flour sack material of a mingled design. No brassiere on the girl, naturally, things being what they were these days, and a pair of breasts that would hang like flapjacks in a few years. Nice hips, though, and legs long enough to reach the ground without her looking like a frog squatting to jump. "I expect you already know what you do and how to do it, right?"

"Well, you know, I guess yeah," the girl said. "I'm nineteen and I was raised out towards Cookeville, so I guess I do know all that old stuff. It won't be nothing new to me."

"Like I said, I don't have to give you no detailed instructions about that part, but I do have to tell you what not to do. That's been my experience with girls just come to Nashville, anyway." Blanche Ann pulled a menthol cigarette from a package on the table before her and fired it up with a red plastic throw-away lighter. "What not to do, that's what you got to get straight in your mind. Want a cigarette, Lurleen?"

"I guess, but I don't like one lit by a lighter. It smells like kerosene to me."

"Light it off of mine, then. What you got against kerosene, Sugar?"

"I been smelling it all my life out there in the country, and I got my fill of the way it stinks a long time ago."

"Y'all cooked with it, huh?"

"For a while until the kitchen stove rusted out and broke down, and then they'd use kerosene to get the wood to burning. Daddy and the other ones would. My brother and Mama's boyfriends later on."

"Y'all had you a fireplace?"

"No, ma'am. Cook stove in the kitchen and a pot bellied one in the front room for heat. I hate and despise a wood fire."

"You won't run into many wood fires in Music City, if you stay out of North Nashville," Blanche Ann said, "and places out yonder in the country."

"I seen enough country to satisfy me. Is that where the colored folks live? North Nashville?"

"Yeah, but they spreading everywhere now. You'll see them popping up all over. Downtown, of course. In East Nashville some. Spreading into Hillsborough Village, all down in there. You name it, and they're coming into it."

"It ain't none comes in here, do they? Because I never been with one like that before. I don't know if I'd like it."

"That's one of the things I got to tell you not to do," Blanche Ann said.

"Not sell to coloreds?"

"No, I don't mean that. I mean not to think you have to like anything. The quicker you learn not to let one thing or the other matter to you, especially not whether you like what you're doing or not, the better it'll be for you. Liking don't mean nothing. But I guess that's a matter of personal choice and time going on by you. You get used to stuff you couldn't stand at first. I'm talking about me now, back when I was in the game, and girls I've seen get messed up along the way, you understand."

Lurleen didn't say anything to that, but she did nod her head and keep looking off to one side as though something behind Blanche Ann was drawing her attention. I'm not going to look around to see what it might be, Blanche Ann told herself. It ain't likely nothing, and if it is something I don't want to know about it.

"That's not the main thing, though," she went on. "Here that is. Don't offer to do nothing for nobody that comes in here. Not a soul, not even if he's a return customer and you think you know him good. Don't say a word about nothing but massage techniques and categories. Get me?"

"Not really. Do you mean I can't say do you want a massage to one of them?"

"Not even that. See, you got to act like you already know he wants a massage or he wouldn't have climbed up them three flights of stairs to get to Magic Fingers. Shit, who'd come all the way up here just to look around? He'll be carrying something he wants to get rid of, if he makes that climb."

Lurleen allowed her gaze to move for a quick look directly into Blanche Ann's face and then shifted back to whatever she was keeping an eye on off to the one side. She's either a little bit brain addled, Blanche Ann said to herself, or she's been knocked up beside the head so many times she's afraid to look somebody right in the eye and run the risk of pissing them off. Maybe she's learned by experience that lots of people don't like it when you stare at them straight on. Or maybe she's just dumb as a post.

"You get me on that?" Blanche Ann said, pitching her voice a little lower into what she figured would be a soothing range. No reason to get the girl from out near Clarksville all scared up. She may be a slow learner, but she'll maybe look good enough to the right kind of men to make me some money. "I'm not trying to make it look harder than it is, Sugar, but we always got to be careful what we say, and how we say it, and specially who we say it to."

"You talking about the police?" Lurleen said.

"Bingo," Blanche Ann said, taking a good long hit on her cigarette and stubbing it out in the ashtray. Maybe Daisy Mae from Dogpatch is got more sense than she looks like she does. "You got it. Anybody that comes in here and starts asking what kind of things will you do for him, and if it costs any extra, you got to figure him for maybe being a blue knocker. He starts saying shit like that, and you just act real surprised and say something like this. Do you mean will I use powder or oil or neither one in the massage I'm fixing to give you? That's your choice, Mister. See what I mean, what I'm saying about how to talk to them?"

"If he asks that before he takes his clothes off, is that the time when you mean? Or if he asks after he gets shucked down, is that different?"

"A good question, Sugar, but it ain't one with a perfect answer. You got to try to read each and every one of them, just one at the time every time. They all a little different, but not so much it's easy to tell them apart. You got to get your hands on them to tell for sure. And even then, maybe it's a cop. I've seen the bastards take a blowjob and then lie like hell and say they didn't. So I'm just telling you to keep your opinions to yourself, no matter what the shitasses ask you. Just act dumb and surprised, like you're a professionally licensed massage artist trying to practice your profession straight up. Then see how he takes it once you get to rubbing on him. Hell, it's easy enough to tell when one of them's faking it. Ain't you already learned that out there in Robertson County?"

"I never seen none of them fake nothing that I can think of, no," Lurleen said, looking down at the package of Salems on the table and pulling one out after Blanche Ann had nodded go ahead. "I guess I was the one doing the faking them times that happened."

"Sugar, I know what you're talking about, and I'm starting to believe you can learn this business right quick. Tell you what you do. Go get you a clean bucket and a washrag out of that closet over there, and the next one comes in here and starts wandering around that reception room, you go out and say howdy. Tell him welcome to the Music City Magic Fingers Massage Salon. Tell him he's come to the right place to get his kinks worked out, and ask him if his back's been getting real tied up in this hot old Nashville weather, spring time though it is."

"Yes, ma'am, I will," Lurleen said, pointing at Blanche Ann's burning cigarette to ask for a light. "But what kind of outfit do you want me to wear? Have y'all got something for me to change into?"

"Sugar, what you're wearing is fine. We don't do no kind of costuming here at Magic Fingers. There ain't no special uniform of no kind to wear, and my girls come to work in their regular clothes."

"Oh," Lurleen said. "I figured it was like I would have to wear some kind of a outfit that would, you know, show off my legs or something. 'Cause I ain't got that much on top to be an advantage to me. Legs, though, I do."

"Girl, you been being told about the old days in the game in Nashville," Blanche Ann said, with a sad little chuckle. "Them times are dead and gone. Used to be, though, not over ten or twelve years ago, back when I was in the middle of my time, why we'd bring a whole parade of girls into the front room where the hard dicks would be sitting. Some of the girls in swimming suits, or shorts, or nice-looking tight dresses. Some wearing like little shortie pajamas, some in full negligees, and I don't know what all. Yes, goddamn it, there was some class back then in whorehouses. Hell, this town is the capital of the fucking state, and people used to act like that made a difference."

"I've heard about things like that," Lurleen said. "Seen it in picture shows and all."

"Yeah, all that's gone now. Most men back then expected a night out on the town to look like everybody was having fun. Like they were going on a date. Hell, us girls used to call it dates. Lots of times we'd say to fellows coming in and they'd be wearing suits and ties, shiny shoes, and all spiffed up with their hair cut and combed. We'd say hello, sir. Would you like a date with me? Shit, they used to love that. Fuckers would blush when we asked them for a date, now and then. They'd appreciate us trying to make like things was real, and pretty, and sexy, you know."

"That's what I was maybe thinking," Lurleen said. "That I was going to be a lady of the night, like I heard an old fellow in Clarksville call it one time when he was with me. He was real nice. Worked in the drugstore."

"Nowadays," Blanche Ann, taking a savagely deep hit of smoke from her Salem, "they come in here wearing any kind of shit. They don't act happy to be here. They ain't looking for a nice time. They don't want to say a damn word to nobody. All most of them want is just a handjob, 'cause it's quick and cheaper, or they want you to lean over and stick your face down in a bad smelling wad of hair and give them a damn blowjob like a jackrabbit. They ain't hardly a man left in Davidson County coming in here who'll want a straight fuck, him on top looking you in the face and showing you how he likes it while he gets his rocks off. Shit."

"That's too bad, I reckon," Lurleen said. "You said the bucket and the washrag is in the closet?"

"Yeah, it's over yonder," Blanche Ann said, pointing toward a half-open door across the room. "Romance is gone now, Sugar. There ain't a soft heart left in Nashville in any of these fuckers."

"Well," Lurleen said. "I'll go get ready for my first one. I won't ask him nothing about what he wants."

"Just pray it's a handjob, Honey. If you touch him up pretty good during the massage, like it could be a accident but maybe not, he might get worked up a little and just settle for a jerkoff."

"I can do that real good," Lurleen said. "That's how I started out. It's been real nice talking to you, ma'am."

"Yeah, well. Welcome to Limp Dick City."

Felice Foldman stood in the foyer of Cherry Mount House, at its creation in 1850 the mansion of Belvoir Raphael Slade, timber and mining and land baron of historic note, and now the official residence of the Chancellor of Vanderbilt University, and she forced herself to stare deeply into the reception area which lay gleaming before her, a tasteful statement of substance, tradition, and meaningful wealth well managed, an invitation welcoming those who viewed it. Come, you may advance, all that was visible beckoned in measured tone. There is ease here, there is certainty, there is peace, prosperity, and above all assurance that what you see here will remain despite whatever mists may gather, whatever challenges may arise. You may come, sample, taste, and enjoy this moment. A polished and perfected bit of time here is yours for the taking and treasuring.

Sanford Temple stood speaking at the center of the circle of the household staff of Cherry Mount, his mane of blonde hair dancing, his gracefully long fingers pointing, gesturing, putting questions, making judgments and provisional decisions, working their way toward the creation of the beautifully realized event which lay before him and the staff responsible for carrying out what the fingers would shape. All was yet idea. All were poised to realize it.

"Where is Minerva?" Felice could hear Sanford asking the staff gathered around him, a touch of not annoyance precisely but intense interest evident in the answer he wished to hear. "I see everyone needful in their rightful places, ready to start the big, big push, but I don't detect Minerva's wonderful countenance. Where is she? Does anyone know?"

"Minnie said to tell you she right in the middle of one of her sauces. She frying it right now," one of the kitchen crew said, nodding and looking about him for agreement. Other heads nodded, and murmurs of assent arose.

"Oh, dear," Sanford Temple said, "I do hope she's not frying a sauce. Don't tell me that."

"That ain't just exactly what Minnie called it. Something else I can't say right."

"I surmised as much," Sanford said, "What a relief." He laughed in a high breathy tone, and Felice Foldman stopped listening to the exchange at that point, turning her attention instead to the location of a crystal vase on a side table near where she stood. Why was it there? Who had placed it? Was it part of a design? Had it been put there just so intentionally? By whose intention? Had Sanford seen it? Why did it look so centered on the table? Was that positioning conscious? Did it appear to be in its rightful spot? If Sanford took note of it, would he give that little look, the one with his wonderfully expressive lips pursed just a hair, the one that said without a word spoken "Oh dear, bad taste?" Admittedly, the morning sun touched it wonderfully, but the dinner was an evening event by definition. Had anyone considered how the vase would appear lit by artificial light?

Entertainment had been so much simpler before Malcomb had been appointed chancellor at Vanderbilt, coming as he had from his previous post as provost at Virginia, safely focused only on hosting a few annual receptions and dinners now and then for faculty mainly. That bunch seldom looked up from their plates of goodies and their glasses of various kinds of strong drink, except to argue minor points and make snide remarks to each other about their academic leader and his lady. No pressure there in tending to that task, other than remembering to keep smiling and read name tags as surreptitiously as possible.

Felice had even had her own work outside the house, a part-time appointment as a docent at the rather good museum at the university. She was able to slip invisibly out of the official home of the provost at UVA, have lunch with friends at leisure, even indulge in a small and emotionally meaningless affair of the glands, certainly not of the heart, with the architect husband of a colorless but very dear little woman in Charlottesville. That had gone on at a low level for several years, no one the wiser, with all players, consciously or not, benefitting from her little meetings here and there with her gentleman friend in quiet beds in the early afternoons in the Virginia highlands.

All had changed in Nashville, with the bright light of attention focused on the chancellor of Vanderbilt University and his family, and that was fitting and proper and well worth the trade-offs that had to be made. The loss of privacy, the need never to offend, the responsibility to be charming to people of power and significance, never being able to vanish or leave the stage or chance making a remark that might be used against her, Malcomb, the university, or the endowment, and the omnipresent pressure to maintain a positive and sunny mood in the face of whatever condition arose.

It had proved to be a shock and a burden at times, but well worth it, the elevation in rank and increase in monetary resources considered. To be able to keep up the pace, Felice had resorted to alcohol for a time, but that proved to be enervating and headache-making, and had led at points to some really rather harsh criticism from Malcomb, enough so that she had laid off the booze and sought other little helpers of a chemical nature. "It's all chemical," the wife of one of Nashville's financial heavy hitters had told her once. "Every damn thing in life is. Food, love, hate, fucking, peace, God, health. Find the right chemical compound, and you can understand and stand anything."

The conversation containing this advice had occurred, strangely enough, at a dinner in honor of one of the old Vanderbilt Fugitives, back to be lauded and sucked up to where once scorned, as Felice sat by Beth-Anne Lambert near the foot of the dinner table late after all had been eaten and drunk and the moment to retire to the withdrawing rooms had not quite arrived. Felice had ventured to say something she regretted as soon as the words left her mouth, a comment about how little she cared about poetry or novels or plays, whether by old famous writers or lively new up and comers. What she said had been in follow-up to a remark by BethAnne about the old Fugitive poet at home again, something to the effect that she had tried to read some of his poetry in preparation for meeting him at the chancellor's dinner and had yawned so widely she had dislocated her jaw for a full two minutes. "Jesus, Felice," she had said, a bit gone in her cups as was Felice, then still in her period of leaning on alcohol as self-medication, "I literally had to get Bobby to rub my jaw until it popped back in place, and he didn't know how to do it right. Surprise! As if he would, given his history of failure in satisfying the way a woman wants to feel. Tell yourself it's a hooker you're rubbing on, I told him. Bobby popped it back in then, by God."

Felice laughed so hard she snorted a bit of a quite good Margaux up into her nose, and then blurted out her confession as to how she made her way through reading a great work. "I have to get half soused to stand it, and then I get so sleepy after the first page, I fall into a doze." That's when BethAnne Lambert said what she said about the chemical basis of life.

"Give in to it, girl," she said. "Hunt until you find the right chemical compound, lay in a supply of that sucker, and don't stint on the dosage."

Remembering that, and watching the beautiful gesturing of Sanford Temple as he created in the perfectly measured inner climate of Cherry Mount House his vision of the evening event to come as it would be realized by the efforts of the staff, Felice thought of her stash in the secret little ivory chest in the closet of her special retreat upstairs. Tilting her head slightly to one side, she was able to make the sound of Sanford's wonderfully modulated voice become that of a stringed instrument, a zither, perhaps, in the practiced and skilled hands of a Renaissance troubadour, and she turned and headed for the stairs. Tonight she would be hostess to a United States senator, a Negro preacher known to all America, a Beatnik poet of New York Jewish background, and a radical young Negro who hated white people and chanted Black Power. That appointment would be later, though. Right now her chemical date was waiting upstairs, naked as an oiled savage.

"So this is the honeymoon suite of the Hermitage Hotel," the young black man said, looking around him at the wall paper in muted gold tones featuring representations of a classically influenced mansion with a carriage and horses just coming into view from the right side of the image. He was dressed in brand new pair of farmer's overalls, the creases of a long period of lying folded on a shelf clearly evident. The driver's whip in the sketch was poised to urge on the brace of steeds, repeated in each and every etching on all surfaces save the door facings each direction he looked but the whip not yet fallen in any location. "It makes you feel like something is about to happen, doesn't it? Something big, something that's going to last. All these pictures of Sambo in the driver's seat."

"That's right," Tilden said, looking up once briefly from what he was reading, and then immediately back down again to the place where his finger was pointed. He wore a dark suit, a white shirt with cufflinks, and a muted blue tie. "I can see why them honkies didn't want to let us stay here."

"Oh, we could stay without a whimper of objection if we were wearing the right kind of clothes. White jackets and black ties and all that shit. We could walk all the halls and enter every room if we knocked first and looked like we ought to. If we were carrying a rag to wipe stuff up with. I hate this fucking place."

"It's a lot better than where they wanted to put us there on the campus," Tilden said. "Some kind of a dormitory or something. Look like we was back at Howard."

"Yeah, a controlled environment for the bad niggers. Institutionalized racism. Keep your house servants close to you so you can keep a beady eye on what they doing and what they might be up to."

"That what you going to talk about, Stokely?" Tilden said. "Tomorrow when they get you up yonder on the stage with Martin and that old white bastard senator and that fag poet? That going to be the line you follow?"

"Maybe some of that to start with, but not mainly. I'm going to try to wing it a little, give Martin a chance to preach that old time religion at them for a while, and then see which direction I take with the motherfuckers. I know one thing, though, Tilden, I know what I'm going to end up talking about there at Vanderbilt."

"Where's that, Stokely? Like I don't know, huh?"

"Black power, brother, that's what I'm going to end up on. Black power. I'll be chanting that song and watching them squirm in their seats, looking like they about to piss their pants. That scares the honkies to death."

"That ain't hard to do these days. They on edge. These fuckers be as nervous now everywhere you look as a barefooted whore in a Baptist church."

"Without no hat on," Stokely said, laughing now and moving across the room toward the window to the west. "Feeling like she's underdressed, you know."

"Look here at all these hot chicken places they got listed in the phone book. Niggers in Nashville seem like they like a little heat in their vittles."

"Thank you for that nice rhetorical transition, Tilden, like old Dr. Blaylock used to say all the time back in English class. That lets me tell you gracefully what else I'm going to preach in Nashville here on a nice warm spring night. That's nature's time of renewal, you know. Spring-time in the South. In the season when all nature seems at peace."

"All right, what?" Tilden said, his big bald head lifted from the phone book, looking as though it had been polished to a high gloss by a soft rag. "Tell me what you talking about, son. Let's hear it. Preach it on out."

"I'm going to turn up the temperature here in the capital of Tennes-see. I'm going to see how hot these Nashville niggers like their grub to be. I'm going to tell them to burn this fucker down. See will they listen to me."

"Burn, baby, burn," Tilden said, rising from his chair and crossing the room to look out the window where Stokely stood, pointing into the distance.

"See that big old white stone building? Yonder on the hill?"

"I see it. I grew up seeing it. Hell, my eighth grade class at Carver Junior High toured it on a field trip. They give every one of us a sack with a baloney sandwich and a banana and some Oreo cookies to eat on the bus. My sack didn't have no cookies in it, though. Some asshole had done stole mine."

"We'll get you them cookies back in North Nashville, Tilden," Stokely Carmichael said. "You wait and see. You'll get to eat your fill."

"That ain't all that's on my menu for eating in North Nashville. Tell you one thing, though. Martin ain't going to like to hear you talk about burning shit down. He don't call that nonviolent. It will piss him off."

"Ain't that a shame?" Stokely said, "And us supposed to be on the same side and all."

"Burn the fucker down, that's what I say. Don't get me wrong," Til-den said. "But don't light that match until I get my full and fair share of chicken."

"Lord, Lord," Stokely Carmichael said, his eyes glistening as he looked from one golden mansion to the other pictured on the walls in the Hermitage Hotel, hundreds of them to choose from, each one crisp and clear in delineation. "Lord have mercy."

6

THE RAT HAD SET UP HIS TABLE again on the brick terrace of the student center, arranged to face the intersection of the two major sidewalks leading into Rand Hall where students drank coffee, made claims and excuses to themselves and others, studied flesh they couldn't touch, longed for witty rejoinders, and lusted for all they didn't have. Today a pile of several copies of the Rat's comic book *Cook's Night Out* were displayed on one end of the card table and a sheaf of flyers lay on the side opposite. That was new, Ronald Alden recognized as he passed by the Rat's signs leaning against the table— The Rat Loves You, Good News for Rats in Training, Kiss a Rat and Take Home a Fever, All Power to the Rat—and he stopped to pick one up to read. It carried the usual stylized drawing of a rat dressed in bell-bottoms and a T-shirt with a peace symbol held in a large disembodied hand with fingernails hooked into the shape of a claw. Across the top of the page were the words "Canine Sacrifice, Noon Today, at the Flagpole." Below that in smaller, though fatter, letters was the statement "Dog to Die for Your Sins, Vanderbilt. Don't miss the ceremony. Demand Your Rites."

"Hey, Greg," Ronald said. "Something new, huh?"

"Something old, something new, always a nod to history and a glimpse at what's to come," said a voice through the head-sized gray mask, complete with long whiskers, a drooping nose, and two prominent

60

yellow fangs, the whole effect looking tattered and bedraggled this deep into the academic year. The gray velour suit was badly pilled, and the big rubber representations of rodent feet were missing a couple of toes on the left one.

The white cloth gardening gloves looked brand new, though, and Ronald was strangely pleased to see the effort the rat was making to keep up appearances.

"The Rat brings the message," Greg said through the rat mask. "He does not create it. He is a blameless reporter of the world in which he skulks."

"A rat is without honor in his own country, right?"

"You beat me to it, Dr. Alden. The Rat couldn't have said it better himself."

"Who's going to sacrifice the dog, Greg?"

"The Blade Man. Who else?"

"It's almost eleven. When's the executioner going to get here? Is Dan doing him?"

Before the Rat could answer that, something else drew his attention, a pair of large young men, hulks dressed in khaki pants, white polo shirts, and sockless boat shoes, in full approach. They were not genetic twins, but their necks and heads appeared to have been forged in the same furnace and roughly shaped by the same coarse file. Each one held a copy of the flyer, obviously pulled from a dormitory bulletin board, judging by the torn corners, both leaned forward over the table toward the chair in which the Rat was seated, but only one spoke.

"Who says he's going to kill a dog by the flagpole, asshole?"

"No dog is going to be merely killed," the Rat said. "This will be a canine sacrifice on behalf of all Vanderbilt students. It is an act of love, bloody though it has to be. The canine sacrifice will made with all due ceremony."

"Bullshit," the other one of the two said. "We ain't going to let you hippie assholes kill a dog, especially by the flagpole. The football players ain't going to allow that kind of shit to happen. Not here at Vandy."

"Damn straight," said the first one, now holding a copy of *Cook's Night Out* picked up from the stack before him. "What is this funny book shit? Who do you think you are, you crazy little fucker?"

"I am the Rat. I speak for all ratkind. Fair play for rats. Equal rights for rodents."

Ronald knew he should say something to defuse what was going on between Greg and his guerrilla-theater act and the athletic defenders against canine sacrifice, but damn these two were big, and Greg was doing all he could to inflame and antagonize them. Irony was not the strong suit of the Vanderbilt undergraduate, particularly the ones recruited to get their brains beat out every weekend by bigger, stronger, meaner, and even less ironic young men from Alabama, Georgia, Tennessee, and the other well-functioning brutes of the Southeastern Conference.

"Boys," he said, instantly regretting that choice of address as he delivered it—what if they took the term as belittling and decided to give him a cuff or two?—"Greg is just fooling. There's not going to be any killing of a dog on campus, by the flagpole or anywhere else. This is all in fun."

"It ain't fun to talk about killing dogs," one of them said, the shorter of the two, though looking no less capable of great damage to someone off the football field, timid though he might be as a Commodore linebacker. "That's twisted shit, man."

"What about killing members of the NLF in Vietnam?" the Rat said. "Are you okay with that? The Rat's not."

"It's NFL, you little dummy, not NLF, and who gives a damn about killing communists?"

"National Liberation Front," the Rat said. "That's what NLF means. Dummy yourself, meathead."

With that, both defenders against canine sacrifice looked at Ronald Alden, at each other, and then simultaneously grabbed the edge of the rat's table, turning it over and scattering the flyers and the comic books to the bricks of the terrace. A cheer burst forth from the crowd of students who'd gathered to see what was going on, high pitched screams from the females and a variety of hoots and hollers from the males, all joyous at something happening at Rand Hall worth seeing for a change.

Ronald wanted to intervene, to show support for freedom of speech and toleration of irony and parody in an intellectual community, but his legs wouldn't move, his throat seized up, and he watched helplessly as the two louts moved in on the Rat, scuttling and crawling at a good rate of speed away from them, his rat feet getting good traction on the cement section of the terrace.

"Don't kick the Rat," someone in the crowd cried, and instantly a countervailing chant arose directing the attackers. "Do kick the Rat." Able now to speak, Ronald heard himself shout something about no rough-housing, and instantly was ashamed at the stupidity and inaneness of his outcry. Rough-housing? Jesus, how lame can I be? What am I going to say next? Play nicely?

"The dog will die for your sins," the Rat was saying in his scuttle away from the overturned table, his paws now slipping on the slick covers of the scattered copies of *Cook's Night Out*. "It is fated. It is complete."

"Shut up, Greg," Ronald yelled, and at that, the two louts looked at each other, as though checking off defensive signals, and moved away at a brisk pace, breaking into a full gallop at the sound of someone calling Ronald by his title. The tolling of chimes began to come from the bell tower to sound the hour, the crowd began to fray into parts and disperse, and by the time Ronald and a couple of female students had helped the Rat gather his comic books into a heap, all action was ended.

"Don't forget to return for the execution of the canine offering," Ronald could hear the Rat announcing as he headed toward his office in Old Central. "The dog will die for you before the cock crows thrice." Only one class taught today, he said to himself as he headed for his office, thinking of another one unprepared and looming like a case of terminal cancer, remembering the way Josephine Longineaux's lips had felt parting for his tongue to enter deeper into her mouth, and his weak paralysis on the Rand terrace as witness to Greg Donaldson's being physically attacked for his rat show. Enough this day already to regret, desire, dread, smoulder about, and moon over to last for a year, and Dr. Alden hasn't even checked his mail yet.

When he got there and leaned over to peer into the bottom row of open compartments, there was nothing in his mail slot outside the secretaries' office in Old Central of any consequence. The mail had come and been distributed, one of the major events of the departmental day, but pickings were slim in his box, though not in many others. Lodge Draper's box was overflowing with official looking stationery, damn his busy soul. Probably an acceptance of a submission to Notes and Queries about one line of a minor poem or to some other scholarly organ devoted to the miniscule products of small minds.

The chairman's box, that of Alfred Buchanan, was largest of all and placed highest to be most convenient, the amount of its contents beyond belief. In the box labeled Dr. Alden were a copy of the Rat's announcement about the canine sacrifice at noon, memos about due dates for department business, a catalogue from a book company about a wonderful new composition text for beginning writers, another reminder of an unpaid ticket for a parking violation on campus, a couple of unfamiliar items mailed at a junk rate, and that was it. No brown envelopes with his name and address in his own hand, so no news today of current rejections of his sent and re-sent articles to scholarly journals—with dazzling titles such as JEGP, MLN, PMLA, ELN, ELH, and others of the world of laboriously written and carefully submitted squibs to learning, fated never to be read by a living soul, yet treasured like moisture in a desert landscape.

Ronald tossed all but the Rat's announcement into the overflowing waste paper container next to the bank of English department mail boxes, and started upstairs toward the office he shared with Abe Lehman, the department's new and only Jew, ready to assume his role as Dr. Alden during the next hour in which he officially was open to visitations by students. It said that on the schedule pasted on the wall outside his office; therefore it was so. He'd returned a pile of graded papers to a freshman composition class two days earlier, and he expected a line of students to be waiting in the hall outside, outraged at grades and comments he'd scribbled in the margins and at the end of their productions, ready to demand reassessments and adjustments as any person of their socio-economic status would do at the incompetence of salespeople, clerks, and all other hirelings. Jesus, the help one must put up with these days.

Halfway up the first flight, he heard a sound of stumbling and unrhythmic footsteps coming from around the landing, and he moved to the side of the staircase to prepare to let whatever associate or full professor it was pass by him in safety, judging by the sound that it was much more likely to be a holder of the highest academic rank, perhaps even an occupier of an endowed chair, rather than someone in midcareer striving to climb the final slope to apotheosis. No one bounded up a set of stairs like an untenured assistant professor, nor did anyone else need to demonstrate that kind of energy and hunger for movement. Only the closely pursued, motivated by hope, despair, and brute fear, would move like an assistant professor, his ass on fire.

Ronald saw a shoe come into view, put forward as though to test strange waters for depth before making the final commitment of a full step, and he recognized its owner by its high state of shine and glow to be Dr. Robard Flange, always gleaming in his dress in every part that ought to reveal excrutiating attention to detail and preparation for public display. Taking a sudden indraw of breath, Ronald realized that he was climbing the stairs of Old Central on the left side, empty as it seemed to be as he'd started, and thus he was nearer the stair rail which Dr. Flange would cling to with his right hand as he descended, seeming never to favor his left, a fact well-known and well-observed by all and the subject of much argument as to reason. He would expect his way to be clear of all encumbrance as he descended the stairs, his left arm stiffly and strangely adangle. All knew that Dr. Robart Flange's way forward had to be kept clear of obstacles.

"He's like an Ay Rab," Ronald had heard a graduate student from Georgia explain once at a drunk gathering of the younger members of the worshippers of literature at Vanderbilt. "He uses only the one and the same hand to wipe his ass after every dump. It's his religion, see, and he's saving the clean hand for doing nice stuff."

That got a good laugh, naturally, though some kinder-hearted female student had remarked that her professor in eighteenth-century prose and poetry was by all indication simply limited physically because of injury or health condition, a notion quickly hooted down. "Bullshit, Martha," the graduate student from Georgia said. "He's been seen using his left paw to pick up things and open doors and all kinds of stuff. But, see, that's menial. He can do that without pissing off his God or committing a sin. I bet he jacks off left-handed without a damn bit of trouble."

Dr. Robard Flange turned the corner of the landing, depending heavily on his grip with the right hand on the stair post as he prepared to shift to the rail for support, and it was then that he saw Ronald coming up the stairs on the wrong side, blocking his way as the assistant professor bounded from one step to the next. When Ronald saw Flange see him and register he'd done so and had taken in the transgression against protocol which the untenured assistant professor of English was making on the stairway, several things happened at once.

First, Dr. Flange flinched and paled visibly, it appeared to Ronald, as though suddenly confronted by a locomotive of the L&N Line proceeding at full speed toward him. How had it gotten into Old Central, the hub of literary history and Southern cultural heritage at Vanderbilt and thus located at the center of civil society? Had some infernal Yankee inventor discovered a way to allow transport machinery to leave its duly appointed track to roam freely through the halls of antebellum mansions? Where was it headed in its mad career upward toward him?

Next, Ronald began to babble out an apology for having left the proper position for those ascending a staircase—to the right—attempting as he spoke to change in mid-placement where his foot would land on the next step up and in the process catching the toe of his unshined and dusty shoe on the riser. The mishap caused him to lurch to one side, his trailing foot sliding on the slick portion of wood uncovered by carpet, and finding himself in the early stages of falling forward headfirst. He put out a hand instinctly to catch himself, releasing the clutch of memos and junk mail he was still holding after the earlier discard. What he threw aside of that encumbrance carried well in the dead air of Old Central, including the Rat's flyer about the canine sacrifice due to come at noon, and Ronald watched that flutter, float, touch Robard Flange's extended leg and settle at his feet.

"Dr. Flange," Ronald said, levering himself up from the stair in a modified pushup and half crawling to the side of the set of risers where he should have been in the first place, "I'm so sorry. I should not have been in your way. I was in a rush. I'm a little late for office hours."

"Such haste is why I move with care and forethought," the holder of the Margaret Stone Wilson Peacock Chair in Literary Studies said, his words modulated and even for a man who'd just seen a locomotive of the L&N careening at him. "I consider consequence before I take a step. Always."

"Yes sir," Ronald said, leaning forward to retrieve the pitiful sheaf of the contents of his mailbox scattered in Robard Flange's way. "I should emulate that procedure."

That seemed to have been the right thing to say, Ronald considered as he observed an expression rise to the gray face of the full professor that on another man might have been read as a recognition by its bearer of his coming death but on Robard Flange was sign of bemused entertainment of a comment by an underling which surprisingly had struck him as being not completely worthless.

"I would not advise you, nor any man," Flange said. "Each of us must work out his own salvation, but I will commend such course as you just suggested as one which might redound to your future benefit."

"Thank you, Dr. Flange," Ronald said, beginning to work his way carefully past the endowed chair holder as he maintained his proper positioning on the right side of the staircase. "I'll just head for the office and my counseling sessions with students. May I relieve you of that flyer lying just in front of your shoe?"

"Yes," Flange said, "I have seen that communication, if you can call it that, and I'll be pleased to let you have your own copy to peruse at leisure." That's got to be a joke, Ronald told himself, and I probably should chuckle politely but make it short and quiet. He did that. It was wrong to have done so, he saw immediately, Flange's face darkening and his left hand twitching in its droop at an angle from his shoulder.

"Are you amused by this document?" he said. "I find it both alarming and beneath notice. Do you know that this young man, this fellow Gregory Donaldson, has declared a major in English?"

"I had not known that, no. But I have had him as a student in my nineteenth-century novel course."

"You may discover such information on departmental memos and notices. Up-to-date advisories and the lot. Well worth a daily notice. Are you his adviser?"

"No, Dr. Flange," Ronald said, not knowing if he was or not, but grateful that Greg Donaldson had never sought his advice about anything practical. Yet. Jesus, what if he's assigned to me, and he starts wandering up here to talk about schedule planning? He'll come as the Rat. I know he will, the little shit. Every time I see him these days, that's what he's wearing.

"He is insane, obviously," Robard Flange said. "Proposing to execute a dog as a sacrifice. Dangerous. Deluded. Blasphemous. Hell hath him in thrall."

"I think he's trying to be satiric," Ronald heard himself saying, instantly regretting his stupidity thus on display. "It's street theater, I think is how the term is used."

"Voicing such drivel maligns satire," Robard Flange said, his right hand now firmly in place on the stair rail as he prepared to take his carefully considered and projected next step. "And misrepresents the moral intent of the true satirist. Read Pope, I would advise this rat boy, should I choose to speak to him. Which I will not. Good day, Dr. Alden. Keep your feet beneath you."

"I will certainly attempt to, Dr. Flange," Ronald said, and then heard himself add as he watched the full professor of English make his accustomed way down the staircase. "Whatever is, is right." Jesus, I am insane. No, not insane. Delusional. I see what's not there, and say aloud whatever comes into my lame head. Don't I realize I'm in an English department? You can't use quotes from works of literature here as if they meant something.

When he reached the top of the stair and turned left toward the door of his and Abe Lehman's office, he could see two students waiting in the hall, both familiar and both dropping their gazes as they saw him, thus revealing they'd been sharing their opinion of their teacher—no doubt a low, vicious, and spiteful one—and both holding compositions in their hands. Ronald nodded to them, and they looked at each other to establish which got the first shot at confronting the man who'd wronged them, and the woman got the nod, following close on his heels as he headed for the chair behind his desk in the far corner of the room.

Putting the desk between him and Victoria Finucane, an expensively attired strawberry blonde from Birmingham, Ronald sat down with a show of energy and purpose, pointed toward the straight-backed chair facing him, and tried to smile agreeably as the plaintiff took the stand. Across the room, Dr. Abraham Lehman, expert on the prose of English clerical writers of the seventeenth century with a published book to prove it, stirred in his seat and showed deep interest in the pile of papers before him, letting all who might wonder know that he was oblivious to any but his own immediate concerns. Victoria Finucane accepted the gesture as a declaration that she and her instructor of freshman composition were alone and launched into a sidling attack on the evaluation that had been given her essay on the effect of the sonnet structure on a declaration of love by a minor poet of the Romantic era. "I'm just puzzled and a little concerned," she began, smiling enough to show a flash of teeth. "I'd like to hear an explanation, Dr. Alden."

She was well prepared to challenge, having learned in her upbringing in the Birmingham suburb of Hoover, Alabama, just how to explain to a servant what had gone wrong and how that lapse might now be profitably repaired to her satisfaction, ready to point out flaw and carelessness and not to lose control of the moment in the process. She was good, Ronald considered as he began the task of defending the justice of a grade of C for a paper shot full of comma faults and run-on sentences and paltry insights, not yet expert in achieving all she wanted as her mother assuredly had been for ages, but give her a few more years of seasoning and practice and no one would be able to stand against her. She'd whip her mate into shape with easy grace, whoever he might turn out to be and whatever position of authority and rank he would represent in the country club society of the Greater Metropolitan Area of Birmingham, and no member of the merchant class who faced her would be able to survive her velvet onslaught.

After a period of jousts, counterattacks, flanking movements, expressions of concern about the beauties of the sonnet form, and avowals of closer attention to the minor demands of effective writing in the future, Victoria Finucane left satisfied with a marked-through C on her composition, an addition of a B minus by her instructor in its place, and her gracious reminder that he change the grade in the official record as well as upon her original document now made whole.

After Ronald watched her gather her things, turn her back to him smartly and leave the room with a controlled twitch of her backside, he looked over at Abe Lehman who'd lifted his gaze from the surface of his desk to cast a cold eye in his direction. Ronald made a quick frowny face, turned his hands up in submission, and looked toward the male complainant now entering the office. Abe Lehman coughed once, deeply, turned away, and refocused on his task at hand.

That aggrievant was easier, Curtis Benoir Templeton, accustomed to taking doses of stronger medicine than a young woman of a social standing a bit above his, and he was easier to beat back into his cage, surly though it left him. He left the encounter with no change in grade, no yielding from his teacher, and no twitch of the hindquarters in farewell to the one he'd just dealt with. Abe Lehman watched him all the way out the door with much greater interest than he ever showed female visitors, but that was no news to Ronald Alden or to any other member of the English department.

"An interesting young man," Abe said, speaking for the first time now that the office was clear of squirmishers. "He shows signs of real intelligence, though not a grain of sophistication."

"I'll take your word for it, Abe," Ronald said. "I've never noticed him in the classroom. He just sits looking at the ceiling in a dull smoulder, most of the time."

"Not my experience in the course he had with me. But that aside, you had a young woman I've not seen before stick her head in the door just a few minutes ago. Asking for you in a pitiful little voice."

"Really? Who was she? What did she look like?"

"Oh, she looked like all of them, naturally. Out of a cookie cutter. Blonde, regular features, wearing the uniform. I didn't notice anything unusual except that she appeared a bit more forlorn than most."

"Probably another one suffering from a C," Ronald said, looking down at his desk and thinking it had to be Josephine Longineaux. Oh, shit. Oh, no. Here already? Thank God my office mate doesn't like the female sex. If it'd been a guy, Abe would have been able to tell me to a pound how much he weighed and whether he had a lot of hair on his forearms. She wouldn't be worth the time for Abe to scrutinize her. "An abused student looking for me to roll over and play dead, I expect."

"Probably. She didn't say whether she'd be back or not. Rather attractive if one likes Northern European types."

Abe left in a minute or so, headed for a class, and Ronald told himself to begin tending to one of the piles of ungraded papers on his desk and try to get what had happened that morning just off Natchez Trace out of his head. Let her not be offended or upset enough to say anything to anybody. Let her not think anything means anything. That'd be just what I need about now. Why did I use the word abused to Abe? Oh, fuck. Oh, Freud. Let me limber up my red pencil, look at the first paragraph on the first paper, and show how it doesn't make a damn bit of sense. Let me start drawing my red circles around all these stupid mistakes. Let me not think about her mouth.

7

THE POT OF GREASE WAS HOT, the bream were gutted and rolled in corn meal and sprinkled with salt, and it was time to start dropping them in and watching them roll up brown and crispy and ready to be dipped out to drain on the sheets of brown butcher paper on the picnic table in Tim Reynolds's backyard. The sun was just above the horizon, a sinking ball of fire in the western sky of Nashville, and almost all the graduate students that had declared intentions to come had been there long enough to have a good start on building a solid drunk or in some cases a good float toward a smooth high. Tim—calling himself Timbo to his fellow graduate students—had laid in a good stash of his own weed in addition to furnishing the fish and the cooking of it, so he had figured it was up to whoever showed to bring any extra medicine to suit a particular need.

That didn't mean all of them would do what they ought to, some of that bunch preferring to steal others' drink or dope, whether they could afford to rustle up their own or not, and of the faculty members invited, generally only the young ones would show, which meant a few bottles of cheap red wine would be set on the kitchen counters, carefully guarded by their owners against pilferage by anybody else. If one or two of the older tenured faculty showed, they wouldn't stay long and they'd take what remained in their bottles of gin and bourbon with them when they left. It was a dance, Timbo considered as he dropped a handful of bream into the seething pot of oil he was working on, and the right steps to take were familiar to everybody at the ball. They knew how to do, and they were doing their thing.

"Is that the way you cook them in Texas?" Lily Alden asked as the grease popped when the fish hit it going down, sounding as serious as though she were asking about the status of a terminal cancer case. "I didn't know you could get fish like that in your home state. That's where you're from, isn't it?"

"You can get anything you want in Texas," Timbo Reynolds said, falling into the act he performed whenever somebody in Nashville asked him about the place he came from. "And yes ma'am, Miz Alden, you can catch bream, at least in East Texas. All kinds of water where I'm from. Creeks and rivers and lakes and ponds. You name it, we got it."

"Don't call me that, please. I thought it was real dry everywhere in Texas."

"Don't call you what? Miz Alden or ma'am?"

"Either one. I'm Lily and I'm not old enough to be treated like an old lady yet."

"I never meant you're old," Timbo said. "I just thought you being Dr. Alden's wife and all that I ought to recognize that."

"Don't, please. I'm myself. He's himself. I am not just a part of him. And he sure isn't Dr. Alden to me."

"All right," Timbo said, "got you," thinking she is as crazy as they say she is. I wonder just how much to the bent side she might happen to be. "Watch out, now, Lily. I'm about to pull some of this fish out and throw some more in. Grease is going to be popping and spitting in every direction when I do it. It will burn you up if it hits you."

Timbo dropped the fish, and it sizzled when it hit the surface enough to make Lily give a little shriek and jump like she'd been stung.

Deeper and farther removed into Timbo and Marie's backyard on Evergreen Lane, a clot of folks had formed around one woman in particular, males mostly, all pointing inward at the same spot, like gypsy moths looking at a light. She was Therese Ellis Buchanan, daughter of Alfred and Phillipa Buchanan, and her hair and her carriage looked different from any other woman at Timbo's fish fry, whether female graduate student or a trailing wife of one of the men. As soon as Houston Stride had seen her earlier in the day entering Old Central looking for her father's office, he had known he had to approach her, tell her about the fish fry, and persuade her to come. He girded his loins and did it.

"Just something it may be fun to do," he'd said, after pointing out to her where in the old mansion the chairman of the English department had his digs. "I know you probably don't know anybody here much, and it'd give you a chance to meet some people your age, you understand. I bet your mother and father would like that to happen, wouldn't they?"

"If they don't have plans for me, I'll try to do that," she'd said. "Where will it be, this fish fry? I don't know Nashville that well. Just how to find my parents' place. I've been here so seldom."

Houston immediately offered transportation, but being wise to bull-shit and a woman who attended Barnard, she said she'd find her own way to the party and back, if she had the time open to do that. She had, and arrived in one of her father's cars, the red Triumph. Now she stood as a focus of a circle, her hair wound into an arrangement that must have originated in Paris, and her blouse, worn over well-tailored slacks, a kind of Hindu-looking item, as one of the female graduate students termed it.

"Houston thinks she's his date," Marlene Mercer said to two other women standing with her off to one side by a camellia bush coming into bloom, not yet full but close to a full burst of pink. Marlene took a healthy swig from the plastic cup in one hand and a strong puff from a cigarette in the other. "Look how he keeps moving in a little circle around her, with one arm stuck out to the side like he's protecting her from something."

"Houston thinks everybody is his date except for his wife, but I don't think this one needs protection," Betsy Ames said in a poisonous tone. "I expect she's been on the pill since she was nine years old."

"Either one of you talked to her yet?" Jennifer Smithing asked, knocking back a good slug of a red-colored drink.

"No, how could you, the way these fools have swarmed her," Betsy said, Marlene nodding agreement and throwing her cigarette butt at the camellia bush. "Have you?"

"Yeah, when I was getting out of the car, she'd just driven up and she asked me if this was where the Vanderbilt fish fry was. I knew who she was, as soon as I saw her. The car she was driving and the way she sounded and all."

"Vanderbilt fish fry, my ass," Marlene said. "I imagine she thinks she's come to Dogpatch, Tennessee. She thinks I'm Daisy Mae."

"I asked her what she was studying at Barnard, way up there in the big old city."

"What'd she say, Jennifer?" Betsy said.

"Fashion."

"Fashion?" Marlene said.

"Fashion," Jennifer repeated in a firm tone, nodding her head until her hair thrashed. "That's what Therese Buchanan told me."

"The fucking little bitch," Marlene Mercer said.

"She can kiss my ass, right up in the red part," Betsy said. Jennifer snorted agreement and kicked at the camellia bush beside her hard enough to jar some petals loose.

Across the way, Robert McLean of Memphis, graduate of Washington and Lee and a declared PhD dissertation specialist at Vanderbilt in late seventeenth-century metaphysical verse, was racking his brain to come up with a way to draw the attention of the woman Houston Stride was trying to establish claiming rights to for the night. Houston's wife hadn't been able to get a sitter for the party, and her husband was free to operate while she sat home and stared at the television screen and wondered whether to call her mother in Jackson to hear a little pep talk.

Probably not, she told herself, two miles away in a really sort of nice garage apartment her daddy had rented for her and Houston and the babies, both of them down for the night and an absence of human sounds reigning in all four graduate-schoolish rooms. Both she and her mother would just get emotional about relationships with spouses, Brenda Stride knew, and her mother would counsel her to grin and bear it. Live in the real world, she'd say. That romantic stuff stops as soon as the vows are said. Husbands will stop their wandering once they get a little age on them, she'd say, a story Brenda had been hearing ever since she got pregnant the first time and Houston began to come in late from what he claimed were study sessions with other graduate students preparing for exams. "He's not studying poems late at night, sweetheart. He's studying strange pussy," her mother had told her, shocking Brenda beyond any words she'd ever heard before from any woman, "and there's not a thing you can do about it if you want to stay with him. Make up your mind about that, and then learn to live with the consequences of your decision, whatever it happens to be. Hang in there and wait or seek divorce now, but realize what the result will be."

"Mother," Brenda had said, "I can't believe you're talking like this. It sounds so rude and obscene. It's so cold and unfeeling."

"Honey," her mother had said, "most of any marriage is just exactly that, and the alternative can be a lot worse. Do you want to go out on the market again with two dear little sweet children in tow? Do you think you'll be able to do any better than Houston Stride, if you do?"

"No, I don't want to do all that again. It's such hard work. And it's so uncertain."

"I know, Sweetness. Just keep your head down and don't think about what's going on. If you do, you'll drive yourself crazy, and if you confront him, all he'll do is lie and keep on doing it."

So Brenda stayed home when she had to, did her best not to think about Houston looking at other women that way he did when he wanted to get naked and fuck, and counted the days until his testicles began to fail him. Lie low, she told herself as she watched John Wayne doing something manly in a western on Movie of the Week, think on the sunny side, raise the kids, and plug in the vibrator when needed.

Now in Timbo's backyard fish fry, Houston had just managed to get Alfred Buchanan's prime piece-of-ass daughter Therese to reveal that she was into folk and blues, especially soul music, and Robert McLean walked up and stuck his head in the circle surrounding the foxy daughter of the English department chairman just as she was saying she had recently seen Otis Redding in concert somewhere in New Jersey. Sensing Robert McLean lean in beside him, Houston Stride wished McLean hadn't heard her say that.

He pounced immediately, like a falcon stooping to a sparrow foolishly showing itself to Death from Above. "Hey, Otis, you say," McLean said. "Amazing. I'm very familiar with Otis Redding. I'm from Memphis."

"No shit, Dick Tracy," somebody in the cluster muttered. "Who'd a thought that?"

A nice try to defuse what McLean had just said and one which drew a good laugh, but it wasn't witty enough to make Therese Buchanan not pursue what she'd just heard. "Have you seen Otis in Memphis?" she said, cocking her head to one side and lifting her eyes to look directly at the man from the Bluff City. She held out her plastic cup and somebody seized it and left for replenishment.

"Oh, hell, yeah," Robert McLean said in his best Delta drawl, the patented tone of good nature, wit, and a submerged capacity for violent action which drips from the weight male Memphis voices always aspire to carry. "When I'm in town, I go down to Stax Records and they let me in to listen to whatever's going on in the studio. One of the colored boys that works there is from a family that came off of my granddaddy's cotton plantation down close to Grenada, Mississippi. He's stayed close to our family. They'll do that for generations, you know, when they've been treated right."

"They still love the lash," Houston Stride thought to say, "his field hands."

"I'm sure it must go beyond that," Therese Buchanan said, still looking at Robert McLean but at least acknowledging she'd heard what Houston said. "Family ties and tradition, I expect. Tell me about Otis in the studio. Is he spontaneous or highly studied? How does he approach a song?"

"Otis starts slow," Robert McLean said, putting as much Old Memphis in his voice as he could manage as he looked into Therese Buchanan's fetching eyes, "but the heat builds as he works. You ought to hear him sliding his way into 'Try a Little Tenderness,' the way he does it in the studio. You can literally feel the temperature rising."

"Talking about heat rising and folks fixing to do it," Timbo Reynolds said, having just stuck his head into the charmed circle. "Time to eat this bream, y'all. It's hot, and that's when you got to eat it. Come get you some."

"That sounds tasty," the Barnard girl said, accepting her newly charged plastic cup from an anonymous hand thrust toward her. "Tennessee fish fry. I've never had that before. Downhome cuisine."

"These bream might've been caught in the Harpeth River in Tennessee, but they've been subjected to a Texas treatment," Timbo Reynolds said, falling into the studied affect of a Texan out of state. On the edge of innocent disinterest and guileless truth telling, but conscious of a burden of myth to bear and a responsibility to play an assigned role for all it was worth. "Y'all come on and get them." At that, the circle around Therese Buchanan scattered as the male students in English literature admitted to themselves that the fish to be eaten was a sure thing and the hope of pairing off with the strange new woman from the East was just a dream.

Houston Stride and Robert McLean weren't giving up the game yet, though, staying with Therese Buchanan as she wandered in the direction of the feeding trough, surrounded now by a crowd with plates in hand. Back in the house, someone had turned up the volume on the stereo feeding sound through the twin speakers positioned in the windows opening on the backyard of the rent house, and the wailing lead guitar of Cream burst out as accompaniment for the feeding in progress.

"I love Clapton's riffs in this one," Houston Stride said to Therese, "but then what's not to love once he gets cranked, right?"

"A little too derivative for my taste," Robert McLean said, "way yonder too white man, the way I see it. Give me that old Memphis blues sound, every time. Why settle for anything but the original?" Therese nodded yes to both of them, allowing her escorts to open the way for her to the fried fish, and it wasn't until she had a plateful and was seated on the ground that she had to say another word to either one of them.

"Who is that?" Lily Alden asked her husband as they stood together alone a few yards away near a crepe myrtle bush grown into a good-sized tree. It had needed cutting back years ago if any real blooming was to be expected of it, Lily had noted as soon as she and Ronald had arrived at the party, but nobody had tended to it. The series of tenants in the house just off Hillsborough Road where the graduate student couple now lived had been either too ignorant about ornamentals or too lazy to do anything about making the place where they lived look respectable. Trash, she thought, nothing but trash. If you act like where you live is not worth taking care of, everything around you will just go to hell, first bit by bit, little by little, and then all at once.

"That's Houston Stride," Ronald said. "You've seen him before, I believe. He's a grad student doing a dissertation with Abe Lehman. I believe it's on Milton's minor poems."

"I don't mean him or that other one, Bob McLean, either. I'm talking about the little cupcake they're slobbering over."

"Oh, her," Ronald said, taking a long look at the woman picking at a sliver of fish with a plastic fork. "I believe she must be Alfred Buchanan's daughter, if I'm not mistaken. I heard she was in town seeing her parents."

"If you're not mistaken, ha. Don't act like you haven't noticed her before, Ronald," she said. "You've been watching her ever since she drifted in here off the street afloat in that outfit."

"That you are wrong about. The first time I saw her was when you pointed her out."

"Yeah. Uh huh. Go get me something else to drink."

"You're not going to finish that one first?"

"Don't worry about what I'm going to do to this one. By the time you get back, I'll be ready for another one. This one'll be past history."

"Lily," Ronald said, looking toward her and away from the tableau of maiden and two ardent swains on display on the dark grass of spring, a little artificial light playing against the shadows.

"Don't Lily me. And get me enough in the next one for me to be able to taste it, too. Pep it up, Jack."

Jesus, Ronald told himself as he headed for the card table loaded with bottles of liquor and beer, I hope I don't have to end up carrying her out of here. Why in hell did I tell her about Timbo Reynolds inviting us to his fish fry? Why did I bring that bottle of vodka along? She is about to take off like a goddamn bird headed for the deep woods.

By the time he'd fought his way through the other revelers in line for drinks, been stopped by Jennifer Smithing to hear her quote what she thought was a line by Keats appropriate to the moment of the party—it was the one about what mad pursuit, naturally, about as clichéd an insight as could be imagined—found a new cup and put a tiny splash of vodka and two big glugs of grapefruit juice and ice in it, and fetched it back to the crepe myrtle where he'd left Lily, she wasn't there.

It wasn't hard to locate where his wife had gotten to, though, once he stopped looking for her beside the overgrown crepe myrtle and focused on one of the squares of light coming from a window holding a speaker. The singer was shouting about having heard it on the grapevine, and Lily was one of a clump of people moving to the beat the song was laying down. She had lost her empty cup, Ronald noted, and she was doing her best to match every move the man in front of her was making, starting her movements high and working down low enough to have to reverse directions to come back up or tumble to the stomped down grass of Timbo Reynolds's backyard. Lily wasn't quite keeping up with the beat, but she was doing her best to make up for the lapse by putting in as many extra moves as she could muster, snapping her fingers and throwing her head back as she sang along with the refrain. Honey, honey, yeah.

Her partner was David Mullins, a second- or third-year graduate student who hadn't quite settled in for the state of permanent residence at Vanderbilt many of his fellows seemed to have reached, and he had been enrolled in Ronald's novel course a year back, where he'd sat quietly, contributed nothing in class discussions, and written papers as unmemorable as yesterday's third glass of water. He looked lively now, though, arms lifted well above his head, pelvis thrust forward toward Lily's midparts, and his gaze fixed intently on her face as his head wobbled in time to the heavy beat of the bass drum and the shriek of the guitar overlay. Lily was humping right back at him, mouth ajar as though to announce the coming of a moment of imminent ecstasy if present conditions prevailed and all went right.

"Your wife really gets down, doesn't she, Dr. Alden?" Marlene Mercer was saying to Ronald. "It looks like she loves rock and roll."

"Don't let that fool you, Marlene," Ronald said. "Lily dances the same way to every song. She's like me. Caught in a time warp of Little Richard and Fats Domino from way back in our college years."

"That doesn't look like bop to me," Marlene said. "She must have taken some lessons after graduating. She looks like she's keeping up with the times." They both watched the song play out to the bitter end, silencing the beat and the need to move to it, but Lily and her partner didn't let the momentary quiet stop their movement. Ronald Alden's wife and the mother of his children did slow her hand movements and the major portion of her hip pumps, but she kept up a slow counter clockwise pelvic grind as she leaned forward to hear something David Mullins was saying to her.

"Maybe I ought to go rescue David," Ronald said to Marlene. "Can I fill your cup while I'm over there?"

"Later, maybe," Marlene said. "Look, the next song's started up. They haven't got done dancing yet. Why don't you and me try this one, Dr. Alden?"

"Oh, okay," Ronald said. "But I can't dance worth a damn, Marlene. And I sure can't keep up with you, I expect."

"All you got to do is nail your feet down so they don't move and let the rest of your body do what it wants to," Marlene said, crushing her paper cup and throwing it to the ground. "It'll come to you."

On another part of the field of battle, Therese Buchanan had finished eating all she could stand of the lumps of fried fish on her plate, and Robert McLean was the first to notice she needed to be relieved of the remains of the Harpeth River bream. "Let me take that for you," he said, "and refresh your drink." Therese said to make it a light one, and by the time Robert had headed for the liquor supply, Houston Stride saw his chance to take advantage of his absence.

"You wouldn't by chance want a little hit of something a little smoother than busthead gin?" he said. "Because if you do, I've got a little something good to share."

"I really don't want to smoke anything," she said, after pausing long enough to give the impression she was seriously considering what she'd just been offered. "I don't want to go to my parents' house in a messed-up state. I just got to Nashville, and I need to do the family-time thing with them."

"You didn't say home. You said your parents' house," Houston said, ready to demonstrate how closely he listened to what was said and how attentively he parsed it, knowing that a woman newly met was always gratified to detect signs of sensitive close attention in a man. "Don't you feel at home with Dr. Buchanan and your mother?"

"What a thing to say," Therese said. "That's a quaint thought. Home and parents. Sweet, though. Don't get me wrong. I suppose that's one of the identifiers of the Southern mind, what you just voiced."

"Quaint?" Houston said, thinking to himself that the condescending little Barnard bitch knows how to gig you. "You mean mentioning your parents?"

"No, I mean bringing up a concept of home. What does that mean, exactly, if you really consider it? Home? Is it possible for a sentient person to consider herself home anywhere? Is there a special place where you belong, where you can think here it is, I'm where I should be. This is me, and this place is where I belong. Here's the one and only fit for me."

"Now don't get me wrong, Therese," Houston said. "I'm as detached as the next guy, at large in the universe, wandering between two worlds, one dead and the other powerless to be born." Let's see how she handles that one, he congratulated himself. That ought to show her I don't believe a damn thing, either. She does not believe less than I do. I can match anybody in not believing shit.

"That's what I mean, exactly," Therese said with an East Coast tittering laugh. "That's another identifier of the Southern, I suppose. The resort to quoting poetry as an appeal to authority."

"Here's your vodka tonic," Robert McLean was back, speaking in his best Memphis voice, laden with that copyrighted sardonic Delta laziness, handing Therese a new cup. "I swear I had to fight my way through to get to the bottle. It's feeding time at the zoo up there around the firewater. What y'all talking about while I was fighting with the gorillas?"

"Oh, poetry," Therese said, trotting out that special laugh again. "Houston was quoting poetry. From the nineteenth century even."

"Houston knows some good lines to call on when he needs them," Robert McLean said. "He has got an instinct for that, I do believe."

"I believe that," Therese said. "I would not quarrel with that claim."

"Speaking of lines appropriate to the occasion," Houston Stride said, feeling heat rise in his head and his vocal cords beginning to tighten, "let me tell you about what a friend of mine from school was faced with and how he handled it. This girl he was really gone about and was getting dead serious about his relationship with her, what she did was go behind his back with one of his fraternity brothers."

"Did they do the nasty?" Robert McLean said. "Did she pull an Ole Miss on him?"

"Worse than that, Bob," Houston said. "If I know what you mean by an Ole Miss. What she would do after she and my friend had been out and been close, real real close, was after he'd let her off at the house where she lived, she'd leave after midnight to meet this other guy. You understand?"

"Did they read poems to each other?" Therese Buchanan said, pausing in the middle of taking a sip of her vodka tonic to pose the question in an innocent tone, both she and Robert McLean breaking into a laugh afterward.

"They fucked like dogs," Houston Stride said. "She and his brother Sigma Chi. That's what they did. But my friend found out about it, and the next time he and this girl he was planning to do the serious thing with went to bed together, here's what he did. He gave her a high grade Mexican coke suppository in the middle of things, see, because she'd fucked him over. She didn't even know he'd slipped it in her. And that was a lesson to her that she learned by heart. That was a signifier."

"Oh, my," Therese Buchanan said. "I'm glad it was high grade shit, that Mexican coke. If it was cheap stuff, she might have picked up a case of Montezuma's revenge. What line of poetry would fit that occasion, I wonder."

"Already with thee. Tender is the night?" Robert McLean offered up. "Therese, you hear who's coming out of that speaker, don't you? It's the man. Let's go dance to Otis. It's Memphis time in Nashville."

At that, Houston Stride left the pair of them and walked off at speed in the direction of a bunch of people near the gate in the wire fence part way around Timbo's backyard, trying not to hear the sounds of Memphis meeting Nashville and Barnard College and W and L laughing like hyenas at the intersection.

"Ronald Alden," a woman in a flowered silk outfit was yodeling as she worked her way through the gate into the backyard, followed by a man wearing a white Panama hat and a seersucker blazer with khaki pants, "I see you hiding over there in the bushes. Get your butt over here, Ronald, and bite me way up on the inside of my thigh." It was Lacy Bodean, wife to Chambers Bodean, a man from so old a Nashville family he didn't have to talk about it, though Lacy frequently made that fact clear to anybody she thought might need to hear it. He trailed behind her as she progressed across the Johnson grass and Bermuda of the yard, having let her get ahead of him as he paused to look with great interest at the way the gate in the wire fence fastened.

"I wish you would look at this hasp and latch arrangement, Lacy," Chambers Bodean called out to his wife. "I haven't seen a fastener like that on a gate since I was a little boy visiting Grandfather's place in Franklin. I don't mean the new place, now. I'm talking about the holdings down past the old battlefield."

Lacy wasn't listening to what Chambers was claiming, having learned years ago not to put much stock in what amazements her husband found in the natural world and in the methods used by Tennesseans to adapt to where they had to live in it. "Who do you reckon this gate latch belongs to, Sugar?" Chambers called after her. "You suppose he'd be open to selling it?"

By then Lacy had reached the corner of the yard where Ronald Alden was facing Marlene Mercer as she worked her way deeper into the bodily movements engendered in her by Otis Redding screaming and near to tears about somebody's raggedy old dress. Ronald was trying both to move in some rhythmic complement to what Marlene was doing and to keep watch on Lily several feet away as she jerked, trembled, shook, and vibrated before David Mullins, who now seemed to be showing a little slow-down in his own graceful hops and steps as he faced his professor's wife. He's realizing she's a little bit off, Ronald told himself, showing excitement just a hair or two in excess of what the situation reasonably requires. He'll either break and run as soon as he gets the chance or he'll try to drag Lily off to a dark place to do some pawing at her, depending on how much he's drunk or smoked or how loose in the cranium he happens to be.

"Didn't you hear me, Ronald Eugene Alden?" Lacy Bodean was yelling as she reached out a hand to grab his arm in the middle of the dance spasm he was supposedly caught up in as Marlene Mercer dipped and swayed six inches away from his belt buckle. "I swear I don't know whether to be insulted or to call a doctor for you, son."

"Hey, Lacy, my middle name's not Eugene," Ronald said, letting his attempts at moving to the music fade away, though Marlene kept the beat without his participation, rock steady and pelvis strong. "I was so busy trying to keep up with this young lady here I couldn't pull myself away."

"Well, that's reassuring, and your middle name ought to be Eugene. It fits you," Lacy said. "Generally when I offer a man a chance to bite my leg up above the knee, he falls all over himself to try to get at it."

"One of these days," Chambers Bodean said in a chirp, "I tell Lacy somebody's going to take her seriously and bite the fool out of her."

"Honey," Lacy said, "they already have, plenty of times, and all it's done is leave me with some nice blue hickeys." Marlene Mercer had slowed her gyration now and was looking at the new couple just arrived, an expression on her face which showed she'd welcome an introduction, so Ronald began performing that function.

"Lacy and Chambers Bodean, this young lady here is Marlene Mercer, one of our graduate students in English. Marlene, the Bodeans."

"I'm Lacy, Marlene, and the man looking at the ground and trying to figure out what kind of weeds are growing at our feet is my husband. He's the best I could do at the time. I hate to confess it, but I said yes to his plea. I believe I did, that is. I must have. I think I remember that."

"You said yes all right," Chambers said. "I don't know if I was asking you to marry me or let me see up underneath your dress, but you said yes to something. Next thing I knew, I was standing up in Saint Andrews Episcopal with the priest talking at me a mile a minute and everybody I knew in the world watching me. I couldn't find a way out of there."

"So I'm stuck with a Bodean," Lacy said, covering her eyes with a hand as though not to see Chambers, "the oldest son left in the line of that sorry collection, and I'm doomed to end up like the rest of the poor women who married into this bunch in Nashville. Deflowered, cast aside, and headed pell-mell for the last roundup."

"Are you the Bodean the building on the Vanderbilt campus is named for, Mr. Bodean?" Marlene said. "I teach a freshman English class in it on Tuesdays and Thursdays. That gray stone structure."

"Yeah, I guess I am," Chambers said. "Is that right, Lacy?"

"You are not. That's named for Daddy Will. He's dead now."

"That's right. I knew there was something wrong in what I was saying."

"Well," Lacy said, "They told me there'd be fried fish here, but I couldn't get Chambers pulled away from the Belle Meade bar in time to get here to eat some. I imagine it's all gone. Where is your wife, Ronald?"

"Uhh, she's dancing, I believe, the last time I saw her. Over yonder with some boy."

"Well, any time she can get out of the house away from all those rug-rats, I expect she deserves it. I'll go say hello to her and try to find that boy who invited us to this party and let him know we came. What is his name?"

"Timbo Reynolds," Marlene said. "There he is, and there's Mrs. Alden over there just beyond him, I believe."

"Is Robard Flange here?" Chambers asked. "I always like to talk to him about Shiloh. Especially that first day of the battle. He knows all about it. Everything you can think of. What they ate. How their horses looked. How hot it was underneath the shade trees."

"I don't think you'll find Dr. Robard Flange at a graduate student fish fry, Chambers," Ronald said. "A little too frivolous for him, I think."

"Wherever he is, he's reading in some book," Chambers said. "He will wear a book out. But you know what? He reads the same ones over and over, just like a kid chewing bubble gum to get all the taste out of it."

"Bubble gum?" Lacy said. "What do you know about bubble gum? Let's go do our duties, Chambers. We got two more parties to hit tonight, and I haven't got even the slightest buzz and haven't had a thing to eat."

Marlene and Ronald watched the Bodeans toddle toward the light coming through the back door of Timbo's rent house and falling onto the yard in tombstone-shaped patterns. "They're rich, huh?" Marlene said.

"Don't they act like rich folks in Nashville?"

"Well, they don't act like music people that're rich. You can look at music people and tell instantly they've got beaucoup bucks."

"The way you can tell Chambers Bodean is rich—old rich, I'm saying now—is that he will buy that gate latch from Timbo tonight. If he can't get it loose himself with a pair of pliers he borrows from Timbo and if Timbo can't do it, tomorrow he'll send out a three-man work crew in uniforms riding in two trucks to do it."

"Oh, well," Marlene said and waved as Ronald walked off looking to see where Lily had got to. He knew tonight, the way she was primed, he'd have to find means to gentle her into going home without her throwing a fit in front of all these graduate students. He hoped he was up to it.

8

ACROSS TOWN, out West End Avenue, south on Wisteria Lane and east on Hollyhock, up a broad drive between massive stone pillars, through the century-old oak doors opening into Cherry Mount House, deep into the recesses past the butler's pantry and positioned at the nerve center of all activities of preparation, cooking, and delivery of courses of cuisine to the long table of the formal dining room stood Minerva Monroe, a blackened wooden spoon in one hand and a checkered cloth in the other. She lifted the spoon to her mouth, tasted its clear contents, and frowned.

"Something wrong with that gravy?" the young woman standing next to her said. "I ain't put a thing in it that you didn't tell me to."

"I ain't worried about what's in it. What ain't there is what I'm tasting. Where's that pepper I told you to measure out and throw in there? How much did you put in?"

Laverne Magee pointed to a yellowed sheet of paper, stained with spots of grease and meat juices dried long ago and covered with extremely small handwriting. "There it say put in one quarter teaspoon. That's what I did. Ask Boleen. I showed it to her to be sure it was right."

"Fool," Minerva said. "Read all of it. It say one quarter teaspoon for every pint of liquid. How much liquid in there you see?"

"I don't know. I just work with what you give me to deal with. I ain't counted up them cups of broth."

"I don't know what they doing in the school houses these days. They sure ain't teaching you young'uns how to take instructions. I know that much. Least you ain't put too much pepper in there. I can take care of the messing you made of it so far. You a lucky girl."

Relieved, Laverne moved away from where she was standing next to the boss lady and headed for somewhere else in the work area of the kitchen, anywhere she could find something to pick up, wave around, and look busy doing it.

"And something else, girl," Minerva said as Laverne stepped away at a lively pace. "Listen to me."

"Yes, ma'am, Miss Minnie," Laverne said, keeping her head down as though she'd spotted just the thing she ought to be doing and was reaching out to seize it. "What's that you say?"

"Here's exactly what I mean for you to keep in your head. If anybody ask you what's the wet part in this dish here, don't you say the word gravy to them. The men folks won't give a damn what you call it and won't ask, but if some white lady hears you call it gravy, she ain't going to forget that. It is what now?"

"It's sauce," Laverne said in a strong tone, the way a child answers a teacher when she's figured out exactly what the teacher wants to hear. "That there is sauce."

"You got it. You got to always call gravy sauce around these kind of white ladies. It makes what they're eating taste better to them when you call it by the name they want to hear. These kind of folks, they don't want to hear no talk about gravy."

"I believe they ready to start that first course," Larry Gene Millard announced as he bustled into the heart of the kitchen, resplendent in a white coat, black bow tie matched perfectly to his trousers and to his shoes shined to a military gloss, his white hair in perfect complement to the shade of the serving jacket. "Toper, you and Perry get ready to start grabbing up them bowls of soup."

"Consomme, son," Minnie Monroe said. "Call it right. And you sure she's ready for you to start toting them bowls in there?"

"She just give me one of them hard looks," Larry Gene said, assertively nodding. "I do believe I know what that means when she put that eye on me. I done seen it enough times, Lord knows. Burn a hole in my head with it."

"All right, now, y'all remember where to start and when to do it. Toper, you and Percy watch Larry Gene to tell when it's time to put them bowls down. Do it nice and easy. Don't slop them. When you know you doing right is when they ain't making no sign of even seeing you. Keep that plan in your head I done wrote down and gone over with you all them times before. I don't want to hear her complaining to me about who got his soup first and wasn't supposed to. Remember who's sitting where. Don't you mess up and forget about what woman's sitting where and who's got the furtherance through the women and the men and on down the line."

"Futherance?" Percy said, looking at Minnie with his head slightly cocked to one side.

"Who gets his first and then next and so on. That's what I mean when I say furtherance."

"Miss Foldman, I ain't never hear her call it that."

"Don't you worry about what she call nothing outside of my kitchen. I call it right in here when I'm talking to you. Anything she say to you, you just smile and nod your nappy head. I'll tell you what to do when you out yonder, and I'll be standing right in this kitchen when I do it. Your job is to remember what I call a thing right here in this kitchen looking at you in the face. You understand me, son?"

Percy allowed as how he did, Toper nodding in agreement, and both looked toward Larry Gene Millard for walking orders. "Gentlemen," he said, "lift your first bowls of consomme. Keep them thumbs where they belong, and it ain't on the edge of the rim. Follow me into the dining room, and let's get this thing done."

Minnie looked about her as the three servants readied themselves for the serving of the first course during the dinner in the chancellor's home honoring the visiting speakers in the Vanderbilt University Impact Symposium of 1967, her gaze moving from the hands of one man to the other, to the ongoing flurry of the women around the cooking areas of her kitchen, to the black bow ties and the starched white front of the serving jackets, to the clock above a cabinet on a far wall, to the seethe and bubble of liquid and to the temperature gauges on the ranges around the room, and finally to the ceiling above holding it all in place. "All right," she said. "Go on out there, but remember not to go looking at Dr. Martin Luther King so hard you spill something on the tablecloth or on somebody. Don't you try to catch his eye. If you got to spill something, make it hit on that old bastard senator or that mean little skinny nigger sitting on the far side of the table or that big old sissy with the beard."

"See can you stir one of them up?" Toper said, breaking into a smile and looking at Larry Gene Millard for a show of support.

"Naw, fool," Minnie said. "That's just a joke. Don't you spill nothing on nobody. You do and you just start heading for the door and leave. Don't look back."

"And she do mean the back door, gentlemen," Larry Gene said. "Let's go feed Dr. King his supper."

The talk around the table had already cranked well up, as it always did after the cocktails beforehand, when the servers of the first course began their initial presentations, moving smoothly, quietly and with dispatch from one seated guest to the other, the pattern laid down by Minnie Monroe and burned into their heads doing its appointed work. The wives and widows of members of the Vanderbilt board and of assorted financiers of Nashville and beyond were chattering away comfortably to the persons on their right, prepared to shift their attention gracefully to those on the left, almost in unison at the appropriate time to be certain no one would suffer the chance of being ignored, overlooked, or allowed to eat from the plate before them in peace.

Dr. Martin Luther King Jr., seated to the right of Mrs. Chancellor Malcomb Foldman, had his head inclined toward her to listen to her commentary on the blooming habits of early flowering ornamentals at this horticultural moment in the warm days of early spring in Middle Tennessee, with its growing heat during daylight hours coupled with the delaying effects of cool nights and occasional showers. He was nodding in agreement and making an observation of his own about seasonal contrasts with similar blooms in Atlanta as Larry Gene Millard adroitly placed a bowl before Mrs. Chancellor Foldman, so handling the transaction as not to intrude on the space of either of the discussants of Southern spring floral events.

Dr. King's skin is a lot darker than mine, Larry Gene noted with approval. Look how pale my hand looks up against his. He wondered briefly how Dr. King got so far up in the world with that shade he had to work with. It generally pays to be yellow, Larry Gene knew, but he supposed that to be true more for a woman than a man.

Down the table, next to a gray-haired woman married to a last name famous in America for money and influence, sat the funny looking sissy man with the beard that Minnie had made the joke about spilling soup on. Placing the bowl before the woman, steady as a rock as it nestled onto the table, Toper McNab wondered how they had allowed a man dressed like he was and with such a beard to get to eat at the big table in the chancellor's house. They say he's a poet. How much money does a poet make? This one looks like he couldn't rub two dimes together. Shoot, Toper said to himself in that little voice inside his head that confided the things to him every day that let him keep on working for white folks, I know what this nasty looking old boy likes to do besides making up poetry. One thing is to eat, and the other thing is to eat, too.

Consomme bowls all laid with perfection and to the exact pattern set as it had been written in the Bible, Minnie's Bible of the Kitchen, which was a lot stronger than the one the preachers talked about and shook above their heads in the pulpits every Sunday, Toper and Percy readied themselves to transport every guest's fair share of the next dish when the time came. They'd know to do that when Larry Gene came back into the kitchen and gave them the sign to clear the bowls and get the next china plates of food ready to go.

"I wonder," Toper said to Minnie as she stood at the spot in the kitchen she liked to occupy when folks were eating her cooking out in the formal dining room of Cherry Mount House, a place which allowed her both to attend to the plating up of the next course and to maintain a close watch on any actual cooking still in progress, "I wonder, Miss Minnie, why me and Percy can't stand out there while them folks is eating what's in front of them right now, like Larry Gene be doing. It seem like it would save time for all of us to know when to start picking up and carrying off them plates soon as they done stop eating off of them."

"You can wonder all you want to, Toper McNab," Minnie said, directing the attention of one of the girls scurrying around before her to a flawed action now in progress. "Naw," she said to Boleen, "don't you flip that over yet. Ain't you learned nothing in all your time here?"

"Well, I was just wondering," Toper said. "Just curious about saving some steps."

"I'm going to tell you why," Minnie said, "just the one time. And don't never let your mind get curious again about how to do and when to do it. That ain't your business to question the way things is. You ain't out there standing up against the wall in that little alcove while them folks eats and talks and carries on, like Larry Gene is got to do to keep things running right, for one good reason. White folks don't want a gang of niggers looking over their shoulders and watching them eat and hearing what they saying to one another."

"But Larry Gene," Toper said. "He out there."

"Larry Gene is just the one light nigger and he knows how to stand back and blend into the wall like a stick of furniture. He ain't nothing more than a chifforobe to them white folks out there. They don't notice him and they don't think about him any more than they would about a place to hang up their clothes when they ain't interested in doing something like that right now. Get you and Percy out yonder, gawking and scratching, and the white folks be saying why are they looking at us guests. What they going to say I just said? What's all them niggers doing here?"

"I see what you saying," Toper said. "Now you explained it to me. But it's two niggers out yonder sitting there eating right along with them white folks."

"Son, them two ain't niggers no more. You only a nigger to the white folks when you somewhere you ain't supposed to be. Now let me ask you something," Minnie said, nodding in approval at a move well done by one of her assistants. "What was Dr. King talking about when you put that entrée in front of him?"

"He was talking about how good the weather in Nashville is up against Chicago. Everybody leaning in to listen to him, too."

"Hmm," Minnie said. "Did you hear that old senator talking?"

"Naw, Percy be waiting on him. I ain't had to go near him. I do be feeding that little real black nigger, though."

"He eating his vegetables only, like he ask for? He say anything to you none?"

"Nuh uh, he just poking at them peas and broccoli," Toper said. "He ain't interested in what's on his plate. He saying about how the times is changing for good. He be telling that Mrs. Rockefeller that. He ain't look at me a time. He say things is up in the air. He say something going on big. He smelling it, he say."

"He don't have to talk to you, sitting where he is. And he ain't going to. I knew he wasn't going to eat nothing."

"Old senator," Percy said, offering up his report on current events. "He telling people on both sides of him the same thing that little Carmichael nigger say. The senator say everything changing. Everything getting bad. We got to keep up a good eye on what be happening. Bad times getting worse all the time. It's coming like a freight train, he claim, lot worse than it ever was."

"The sissy man, that one with the old nasty suit on, look like it been through a washing machine and ain't been ironed, I heard him talking to that young lady in the blue dress," Toper said. "He be saying funny stuff to her."

"She laughing at him, at what he saying?" Minnie said, forgetting to keep an eye on some plating in process, enough so that Boleen was able to repair where she'd spilled some sauce by swabbing at the china with the end of her apron without the boss seeing her do it.

"Naw, that white girl ain't laughing. She be saying far out, saying some other stuff I don't remember. She say groovy, I recall that. She say revolutionary. Say she hates them Vietnam folks. She be asking the big sissy to sign her poem book."

"Looky yonder," Minnie said. "Y'all see Larry Gene just open and close that door. Start moving. Get them plates off that table and get the next ones out there."

As the servants bustled out the door to the formal dining room of Cherry Mount House at Minnie's command, Sanford Temple stepped into the kitchen from the opening cut into a side hallway parallel to the kitchen and running along the dining room. He was smiling, and his blonde mane was floating like a banner above his head.

"Minerva," he said. "All is going most well. Mrs. Rockefeller just told Teeny Sevier the shrimp dish is simply exquisite. Good show, Madam. I'm on pins and needles about what you've tried to do with the peaches in the dessert course, though. Do tell me you feel good about it, pretty please."

"Them peaches is from Georgia, way on down by Valdosta. They prime. Set your mind at ease, Mr. Temple, about that dessert."

"I know, I know, but I'm just like always, unbearably apprehensive. Ta for now, Minerva. I'll be back."

After Sanford Temple had slipped back into the hallway, easing the door closed behind him without making a sound, Laverne looked up from the plating she was arranging to put a question to the boss lady. "Miz Minnie," she said, "what's wrong with that man. He act curious to me."

"Ain't nothing wrong with that man, far as you concerned, girl. Get that sprig of mint looking right. Put every bit of your mind on that. We got to get these people fed and up from that table and out of my dining room before we can think about nothing else."

At least there's going to be plenty enough to carry home to Tee Arnold, Minnie considered as she looked at the clock above the cabinet, listened to the level of sizzle in the huge sauté pan Berthalene was shaking back and forth at the far range, and cocked her ear to pick up any sound of anything cooking too long or not long enough. Tee Arnold Monroe going to like the meat, anyway, just like Dr. King would out yonder in among all them people working their forks, if those fools would give him time to look down at his plate. He ain't like that skinny little Carmichael picking at them sour parsnips. He don't just focus on the vegetables.

9

"ROBARD, DARLING LOVE," Marie was saying to her husband as he sat with a glass of sour mash whisky on the table beside his reading chair in the study, a thin book in his hand and the look on his face of a man staring at a faint object moving in the distance he could not yet identify but was expecting to be a thing he dreaded. "I have heard something today from Arlene Youngblood that might interest you. It could be useful therapy for the muscle problem with your arm."

"I doubt that," Robard Flange said, turning his gaze from the object looming in the distance to the left arm lying dead in his lap, a placement for the missing limb of Rooney Beauchamp that Robard had discovered limited the feeling of dislocation and death in the limb to the area beginning two inches down from the shoulder joint. Should he allow the arm taken at Shiloh by enemy fire to be shifted in any manner from where he let it lay now, the feeling of loss, dismemberment, and death would climb inexorably upward into the left quadrant of the body itself. Lately it seemed headed that way. It seemed to be moving cell by cell, millimeter by millimeter, upward since the opening day of convocation at Vanderbilt in early September. Here in April in the midst of the spring term, it grew, it prospered, it rose, this desensitizing of the physical self. Would there be for him now no cessation, no surcease, no relief from creeping death? Robard shuddered and sipped deeply at his whisky.

"Don't take all your bourbon in one large gulp, dear," Marie said in solicitation. "It may interfere with digestion."

"It is not bourbon," Robard corrected. "It is Tennessee sour mash, my sole whisky of choice and of solace. Bourbon is made only in Kentucky."

"Of course. I speak generically, I suppose," Marie said, misusing the term. Robard did not choose to remark that lapse aloud. If he took that road at every opportunity, his sole conversation with his wife would consist of pointing out error, misstatement, and inaccuracy in word choice and grammatical arrangement.

"But what I was speaking of is what Arlene told me. And I hope you will consider it. She says that their elder son, Truman, you'll remember him, the young man who was such an athlete at Montgomery Bell Academy—can you call him to mind?—he has suffered since finishing school and college from an old injury to his arm, his left one, the same limb which troubles you."

"It's not the same limb," Robard could not help but respond. "It is my limb. His arm is his. This thing beside me is unfortunately mine and mine alone."

"Of course, I'm sorry. But Arlene said he tried all remedies prescribed by physicians and coaches and so on, and none availed. Then in desperation, he went to a massuesse, I believe she called it, at a place downtown, and began a series of treatments which improved his range of motion and his comfort just immensely. She gave me the address and the name of the place. It's a serious business, she said, though it has a quaint name. Would you like to hear it?"

"All right," Robard said to quiet her, sipping again at his sour mash and looking at the dead thing abandoned in his lap, the detritus of a battle begun well but fought to an inconclusive draw, which proved ominous in portent. "What's the name of the establishment?"

"I've got it here written on a scrap of paper," Marie said. "It's in one of the old bank buildings downtown, and it's called Music City Magic Fingers Massage Salon. It worked wonders for Truman Youngblood. Arlene gave me the number for it."

"Oh, I'll take a look at it," Robard said. "Perhaps. Could you bring me a refreshment of my drink, my love, in the meantime. I'm feeling a little twingy."

As Marie walked toward the sideboard where liquor and glasses were kept, swishing her way briskly since she'd made a suggestion not immediately rejected by her husband, Robard stared at the thing attached to his left side, the thing of flesh and bone which had once belonged to Major Rooney Beauchamp of the Fourth Mississippi and should have been buried for all eternity over a century ago after being blasted away by cannon fire from elements of the Fifteenth Illinois on the first day at Shiloh, and wondered how it would feel to a massage therapist to lay hands on a limb dead for so many years.

The spat had been silly, based on nothing substantial really and arising from its own sick energy. The stupidity and banality of its origin was precisely what made it consequential enough for Henry Hallam Horsham to find himself alone at two in the morning, driving down some outlandish pike in East Nashville, solitary and guilt stricken and victim to the kind of sick headache that plagued him each and every time he became emotional over a slight or insult or any manner of careless treatment he was forced to endure.

"I am not overly sensitive," Henry announced aloud in the enclosed and dead air of his sporty little deep maroon coupe, "and I'll have you know, my dear, that the presiding reason for my being upset is not anger, not pique, and certainly not my looking for an excuse to mope." There, Henry said silently to himself, the thought simultaneous with the words he was uttering aloud to the absent James Lane Allen, words he had not been allowed to speak in the midst of the really ugly moment that had occurred not thirty minutes ago. There, I've said clearly and well what James should have had the decency to hear from me with a willingness to hark and understand at the time of crisis. But would he? No, and here I ride along this deserted roadway, stricken with a pain hammering in my head and not an aspirin to be had anywhere in this automobile I can barely control in this state of agony. Physical pain coupled with emotional ache, and can those two sensations ever be truly separated?

"I will gladly suffer disagreement," Henry Hallam Horsham spoke aloud. "I will entertain argument and dissent. I am one educated and trained to relish the cut and thrust of intellectual debate, but let me say unequivocally this one thing." He paused and fumbled yet again with one hand in the glove compartment, hoping for the feel of a tin of aspirin with at least one tablet yet inside. Finding none for the seventh or eighth time, Henry returned to his solitary dialogue with James Lane Allen, one so dear and droll and delicate and yet so difficult, and spoke the words toward which his discourse had been building. "I welcome honest and open-hearted disagreement and the mental joy of attempting to show proof and, yes, running the chance of being disproved myself. Nothing ventured, nothing gained. No shame, no lasting hurt in such exchanges, no matter the result, whether in the classroom with my Vanderbilt students or in the sanctity of a private chamber with my sweet love, but one thing I will not abide." Henry paused, set himself, grasping the steering wheel firmly with both hands, and went on to speak the clinching conclusion. "I will never be willing to endure uncomplainingly and will never bear in silence deliberate cruelty."

Saying these words aloud, ones which he should have been allowed to express to James Lane and thus bring the stupid and meaningless spat to a satisfactory close and reconciliation, was freeing enough that tears instantly welled up in Henry's eyes, blurring briefly the flash and glow of neon lights from up ahead on a low roadside building but not enough to disguise the identity of the establishment. "Thank God," Henry said through his tears and flipped the turn button to signal his decision to leave the roadway, "it's a Stop 'n' Shop. They'll have aspirin aplenty, I do hope and pray."

The one automobile parked in front was a large, unwashed, and rather battered sedan, Henry Hallam noted, so he left a good bit of space between his coupe and the ancient hunk of rusting Detroit steel to his left as he brought his car to a halt. Too closely parked might mean the possibility of a dent or scrape on the finish of his coupe once the man behind the wheel decided to leave his vehicle and enter the Stop 'n' Shop for his beer or milk or the loaf of mushy white bread he'd be looking to purchase. He was sitting behind the wheel of the rusty heap with the motor loudly running, no doubt calculating how much of his purse he'd have to spend. If Henry moved quickly, he figured he could be first in the store, locate the aspirin and perhaps a diet cola to wash two or three tablets down, and be the first customer at the counter, thus avoiding the wait in line behind someone who undoubtedly would radiate an unpleasant odor.

Once through the door, Henry Hallam immediately spotted a shelf behind the counter where the clerk was standing at the cash register, on it a row of over-the-counter medications, cold tablets and cough syrups and Vicks salve and in the midst of it all the welcome colors of flat tins of aspirin. Two other men were already at the counter, though, so there was a line to deal with, after all. Oh, poo, Henry said to himself and looked around for where he might find a soft drink to ease the aspirin down his throat. As he did, he noticed a strange thing take place, and he threw up both hands in surprise.

One of the customers at the counter, a large Negro wearing a T-shirt with no sleeves, green workman pants, and rough shoes, was gesturing with something in his hand toward the clerk. At this, the clerk lifted his hands in the air, fell to his knees out of sight behind the counter, and the other customer, a white man with unkempt reddish hair, pale eyes, and tattoos all down both arms turned to look at Henry Hallam Horsham, said something to the Negro, and then hopped up on the counter and jumped down behind it.

"What you want, bubba?" the Negro said to Henry and then gestured with what he had in his hand, a silver gun like the ones in cowboy movies and in Bonnie and Clyde. "You don't look like a police to me. Is you?"

"No sir," Henry Hallam said. "I'm a college English teacher. This must be a stick-up, right?"

"Actually, it's an armed robbery. Lay down on the floor, English professor," the large Negro said, starting to frown and then as Henry Hallam felt his knees buckle and the floor fly up and hit him all down one side of his face and his upper body from the neckline to his waist, his legs for some reason not touching the floor at all as he fell, the Negro said something else, not a thing you'd expect to hear during an armed robbery of a convenience store. "Just be real still, and you're going to be able to witness some drama here in the next minute or two."

Try as he could, Henry Hallam Horsham could not get his legs to relax enough to allow his knees to bend, so as he lay facedown on the dirty tiles of the Stop 'n' Shop, his feet stuck up like the beginning of a set of parentheses. That would be called a paren, if only one were present, Henry remembered, and corrected his inner observation of how the angles of his lower body might appear to one accustomed to the written word. Oh, that damned James Allen, he was thinking as the large Negro leaned over and rapped the back of his head briskly with the barrel of his silver revolver, causing a bright light to bloom behind Henry's eyelids. Henry watched that grow and subside as he wondered whether his headache would become even more severe now. Oh, here it comes like a shooting star. Sleep.

"Here's that bag of money," Randall Eugene Puckett said in a yodel as he came bounding over the counter. "Just like that girl said it'd be."

"All right," Tooter Browning said. "I'm ready to go once I write something on the wall for these honkies to read."

"You didn't take that little fellow out, did you?" Randall Eugene said, pushing with the toe of his shoe at the man facedown on the floor with his feet sticking up. "I didn't figure you'd have to."

"Naw, hell," Tooter said, sticking his gun in his belt. "I just give him a love tap to help him doze off. Watch me now what I do with this can of spray paint."

"We got to get out of here quick," Randall Eugene said. "Hurry it up. I feel like I got to take a piss."

"Don't worry taking a leak," Tooter said, pointing with his spray can toward Randall Eugene's pants. "You already doing that."

"I'll be damned," Randall Eugene said. "When did that happen? I didn't even feel it. Shit."

"Don't be saying nothing about shit. You better be satisfied with pissing yourself, Randall. I ain't going to stand for you messing your diaper and thinking you going to get in that car with me."

"Sir," came a voice from behind the counter. "How long did you say you want me to wait before I get up? I ain't in no hurry now. Don't get me wrong. I just sure don't want to move before y'all tell me to. I'm just checking to see I got it right."

"Shut the fuck up," Randall said, walking toward the door with his legs spread apart as far as his dripping pants would let him. "This big nigger with me don't like you talking none."

"That gives this nigger an idea, Randall," Tooter said. "Take off them pants and throw them away before you get in the car. I got to write my message, and I'll be right with you."

A few minutes later when Henry Hallam Horsham's legs relaxed enough for his knees to flex and he woke up from his nap, the first thing he noticed was that his headache was gone completely, all passion spent. The second thing was a spray-painted statement in dark blue on the wall behind the counter where the clerk stood reading it. "What do you reckon it means?" he asked Henry Hallam as the first police car surged up to park beside the maroon coupe outside the Stop 'n' Shop on the Nolensville Road, the one with a single bullet hole through the windshield radiating cracks in all directions of the compass and a long and deep scratch in the paint of the panel on the driver's side.

"It's an appropriation from Ovid," Henry Hallam Horsham said, "but it's seriously altered to serve a contemporary purpose, it would appear."

"Uh huh. But what does it mean when it says None Dare Call Me Nigger. Black Power. That's what's bothering my ass."

"Indeed," Henry said, as the first policeman walked through the door, a notepad in his hand and his belt filled with weapons and restraining devices. The one behind him, younger and less hefty, was carrying a dark-colored shotgun at port arms. "My word," Henry added, "he was big and masterful, wasn't he, that Negro bandit? My God, what a noble head on the man."

10

THE SUN AROSE bright and burning on the day of the Vanderbilt Impact Symposium, and all the campus was madly astir and agog. The first news of the hour was that the Rat had announced that he would indeed lead a group in sacrificing a dog at the flagpole in front of Rand Hall, defying the threats by elements of the Fellowship of Christian Athletes, in particular the defensive line of the football team, to stomp a mudhole in the Rat's ass if he tried it. The Rat had issued a proclamation that the dog itself was in agreement with the plan, ready to die for the sins of the university, knowing only a public letting of canine blood would suffice. "Rover will go over," the Rat began chanting early in the morning before the mists were burned off the acacia and the red buds and the first hour of classes began. "To the other side." He sat on Rand terrace in a yoga position, and he called his chant the mantra of the mutt.

As soon as the first class hour was ended, though, attention shifted from the Rat and the planned sacrifice of the dog to a more enthralling topic. Word was that Allen Ginsberg had said things in Dr. Ronald Alden's modern poetry class, to which he'd been invited as visitor, that were seldom if ever heard in an officially sanctioned discussion of images, metaphors and metric feet at Vanderbilt. It all began with a student asking a question about the extreme length of lines in Mr. Ginsberg's poems, particularly in *Howl*. The student was Claire Troutt, a brunette Tri Delt from Bay St. Louis, an excellent interpreter of achieved meaning in poems and an astute describer of how lyric weight was carried by the structure of the individual work, and the possessor of a magnificent set of breasts and a pair of legs which went all the way up.

"Mr. Ginsberg," Claire Troutt had asked, smiling beautifully as she put her question to the famous Beat poet, "why are your lines so long?"

"The better to fuck you with, my dear," he had said, rolling his eyes and laughing like a jackal of the African veldt after he'd spoken. He went on to say stuff about Whitman and poetic feet and delayed finish and anticipatory expectation by the reader, but nobody in the class listened to all that business, knowing it was just filler until the visiting poet thought of something else shocking to say. They were prepared to wait for the good part. At the back of the classroom, the editor of the student newspaper, the *Vanderbilt Hustler,* Jonathan Seth Matthews, checked his tape recorder to be certain it was functioning right in capturing all that Allen Ginsberg was saying and was reassured by a blinking light and a view of rolling tape that it was. Technology is good, he told himself and looked back again at Claire Troutt, still smiling, still primo.

Across the campus from the Old Science building in which Dr. Ronald Alden's modern poetry class was meeting, another of the distinguished panelists scheduled for the symposium was addressing the introductory political science class of Dr. Moody Bossler, the oldest living Vanderbilt professor still upright and teaching, and the guest was finding himself facing a group of more senior, more serious, and more distinguished listeners, many of them full professors themselves.

Marvin Slope, medievalist scholar in the department of English, rose to stand at attention at his place, his hand raised politely to be recognized, and posed his query to Senator Strom Thurmond of South Carolina. "Senator," he began, "I must preface my question with an expression of gratitude for your magnificent leadership, wisdom, and statesman-like behavior during these difficult times for the nation we all love. Or may I amend that by saying the nation we all should love, whatever our rank and station in society."

Cries of "hear, hear" burst forth from many of the audience in the classroom, accompanied with thumps of approval on the student desks at which they sat. "Please," Dr. Marvin Slope said, raising one hand in gratitude at the expressions from his colleagues of support, yet modest in his desire to put his query, not himself, before the senator. "That said," he went on, "let me ask you, Senator Thurmond, what do you consider to be the reason for all the widespread upset among our colored citizens in America? I refer to the riots in northern cities, threats of revolution, instances of incivility, and declarations of dissatisfaction with our republic, marches in the streets, bottle throwing, intemperate language, and what have you."

"A wonderfully astute question, Doctor," Senator Strom Thurmond said, the nodding of his head slow, serious, and complimentary. "And one which plagues us all. What I can say in response is nothing that has not been said before more ably than many other wiser men than I. It is this. The Negro race in America resides in the most accepting, most progressive, and most rewarding nation that has ever existed on the face of the earth. Most of our colored friends recognize that fact, work away quietly at their jobs, keep their neighborhoods clean and neat, and raise their children properly. Those who do not, those who protest with no reason, those who wish to destroy the land in which they live, to set a blazing fire to our beautiful and good nation are misguided, misadvised, misled, incapable of rational thought, and doomed to misery, should they achieve their goals."

Applause, cries of hear, hear, and thundering poundings on the desks erupted at the statement by the senator, lasting for several seconds. As the sounds of approval diminished and Senator Thurmond licked his lips in preparation for his next utterance, a single voice spoke from the rear of the room, chanting over and over in a strong baritone bellow, "Bullshit, bullshit."

Later in the day, as Jonathan Seth Matthews worked on the special issue of the *Hustler* to be printed and distributed at the doors to the gymnasium where the symposium would be held that night, he looked deeply into the keys of his typewriter and penned what he hoped would win him his first taste of journalistic immortality. "Vandy Professors Riot in Confederate Hall. Black Power Student Advocate from Fisk University Chased by Gang of PhDs Across Quad. Medievalist Leads Pack of Blood-Thirsty Great Chain of Being Freaks."

"That is a busy headline," Raymond Arceneau, assistant editor and head photographer of the *Hustler* said, looking over Jonathan's shoulder at the headlines of the story slated for publication. "But if that doesn't get them all wound up, I don't know the Princeton of the South."

"I thought about focusing on Ginsberg saying fuck to Claire Troutt,"

Jonathan said. "But I figured that would get me kicked out of school too quick."

"Claire Troutt," Raymond said in a mournful voice, cupping his right hand into a cylinder and jerking it rapidly up and down close to Jonathan's right ear as the two journalists contemplated headline copy. "Ginsberg said fuck to Claire, and he doesn't even like pussy."

"Yeah," Jonathan said, refusing to acknowledge Raymond's fist-jacking motion. "That's the tragic part."

Chancellor Malcomb Foldman met weekly with his cabinet on Monday mornings at nine o'clock sharp, but in light of the sense of unease and perturbation on the day of the Vanderbilt Impact Symposium, he had thought it wise to call the group together for a little strategy session early Thursday. Take roll, he had told them, count noses, see who's smelled anything getting a little ripe, huddle up, see who's a little bilious, who's still happy, and who's feeling hot flashes. That's the agenda, gentlemen, that and checking for labor pains, false and otherwise.

They sat around the table in his conference room in Albert Sidney Johnson Hall, coffee at each place, sweet rolls on the side which none were eating, except for Lonsmith Meador, who never missed the chance to feed. Malcomb cleared his throat, all came to attention, utter quiet settled on the room but for the quiet chewing of Lonsmith, and the chancellor posed his first question.

"Who's handling this dog sacrifice business?"

"Security is on it, Mr. Chancellor," the VP for student affairs announced briskly. "There should be no real problem. All puffery and flapdoodle, I'm convinced."

"Yes, but the Fellowship of Christian Athletes has declared its intention to prevent any harm to animals, I notice," Malcomb said. "That group has a real potential for rough and tumble."

"They've been warned, Sir," the VP for student affairs said reassuringly. "Certainly they can be quite violent, particularly after a prayer meeting or a defeat on the field gets them all riled up, but I met with the leadership personally yesterday and laid down the law to them."

"At least we're in spring term," the Provost offered. "If it were football season, the Christian athletes would be much more bloody-minded. More losses to deal with."

"This young man who dresses up in the rat suit really doesn't intend to push it far, this dog sacrifice business," the VP for student affairs said. "He's just being theatrical. He hasn't even got a particular dog in mind."

"Did you talk to him, Terence, this rat lover?" the Chancellor said. "Gregory something, isn't it?"

"Yes, Gregory Donaldson. He's a senior honors major, unfortunately, and he craves attention."

"Studying English, no doubt," Chancellor Foldman said.

"What else?" the provost said.

"Those sons of bitches," the chancellor said and turned to the next item on the agenda of the special meeting.

Two buildings south of Albert Sidney Johnson Hall, another meeting was in progress, one called by special petition to the chairman from the senior members of the department of English, its agenda the coming agony in the garden of the Impact Symposium of the evening ahead. All tenured faculty were in attendance, even Henry Hallam Horsham, his head enclosed in a neatly arranged sterile bandage, the subject of marvel and sympathy from all. He was bravely pale, a trifle shaky in gait, but determined to participate in preparing for what upheavals of order might transpire, given the incendiary nature of at least two of the participants in the student-organized event rolling like a thunderclap toward the department and where it lived.

"First, I know we all want to extend our sympathy and best wishes to Professor Horsham this morning. He endured a most frightening experience last evening and has survived not unscathed but not much the worse for wear. I know you'll want to talk to him individually later. But this gathering is yours," Alfred Buchanan said to the group before him in classroom 311 of Confederate Hall. "In particular, I was asked to call us together by Professors Robard Flange and Gareth Lamb. Gentlemen, what topic would you have the senior members of the English department address in this extraordinary meeting?"

"With your permission, Gareth," Robard Flange announced, rising to his feet with the aid of his right hand on the chair back before him, the left arm conventionally adangle, even more so today, it seemed, "I will speak first." Gareth Lamb pursed his lips and nodded once in energetic agreement.

"At first blush and for initial reason, I wanted to ask the department's consideration of the topic of proper procedure in inviting visitors to Vanderbilt under our auspices, and that is a due and crucial topic for us to address. It cries out for solution. But an event occurred this morning in the classroom of an assistant professor of English that has changed, refocused, and made even more crucial the entire matter of allowing any visitors from outside the university to any area of its dominion. I think all of you may know what that event entailed."

"I must confess I do not," Alfred Buchanan said, his comment almost drowned out by the hubbub of agreement which Robard Flange's comment had caused. "I do know, of course, that the four participants in tonight's Great Ideas Symposium have been invited to meet with classes across the individually apposite sweep of academic disciplines here. I understand that Senator Thurmond and Dr. King and Mr. Carmichael have appeared or will be appearing for presentation and discussion in certain venues. There was a bit of a dust-up in the session with the senator, I've heard, involving a Fisk student. Do you refer to that, Robard?"

"I do not, Sir," Robard Flange shot back, his voice trembling a bit and his active arm lifted to eye level as though pointing toward some object of great interest behind Alfred's head. A spectre, perhaps? A lost bird flown where it ought not? "I've heard of the outside agitator who attempted to disrupt that event. But what I refer to occurred in the eight o'clock class devoted to so-called modern poetry taught by an assistant professor of English. You know him, and we all do. One Ronald Alden, a man who had the temerity to ask this Ginsberg creature to talk to our students about his putative poetry."

"What did Allen Ginsberg do?" Alfred Buchanan asked innocently. "Did our distinguished guest identify a metrical pattern wrongly? That I wouldn't be surprised at, given the too generous length of his usual line."

"I assume you are jesting, Chairman," Robard Flange said. "I prefer to believe that and give you the benefit of doubt. No, his lapse was not metrical. It was egregiously immoral, rude, and hellish."

"I have it on good authority," Dr. Gareth Lamb said, rising to stand by his chair, the posture of his body at the position called parade rest at the military prep school he'd attended as a youth, the Nathan Bedford

Forrest Academy in Port Gibson, Mississippi, at ease yet on guard, prepared for action should such be necessary, "that in response to a serious
and intelligent question put to him by a young woman of the class, this
beastly man not only did not take her query for what it was, a student's
earnest request for enlightenment, he seized the opportunity to use language never appropriate in a classroom at Vanderbilt. It is my heartfelt
hope that it will never become tolerated here."

"What did Ginsberg say?" Alfred Buchanan asked, "if I may inquire
as chairman of our meeting. Was it a quotation from one of his poetic
effusions? If so, we must admit that quoting from a work of literature
is in a sense protected discourse. I think of Robert Penn Warren's *All
the King's Men,* a repository of accurately reported rough words from
rough characters."

"Red Warren has never used obscene or profane language in a lyric,"
David McDavidson stated in the tone of an expert on all works Fugitive and Southern. "I challenge anyone to identify a single word in any
of Red's poems that one could not use in conversation with one's own
mother. I do not speak of his prose fiction."

"In prose fiction, the writer not only tells, but by the nature of the
genre, must also show," Samuel Vinson stated.

"True enough, more's the pity," Shoul Lambert mourned.

"A point well taken," Gareth Lamb said in a penetrating tone, feeling
the focus of discussion slipping away from him and his account of Allen
Ginsberg at loose among the young women of Vanderbilt, "but let me
respond to the chairman's question about the specific word choice of this
so-called poet, this bearded creature from beyond the pale. He used the
common and brutal Anglo-Saxon term for sexual intercourse in answering a question from a young woman many of us know, Claire Troutt, a
most admirable student and a lady of a distinguished family. He said it
loudly and laughed obscenely."

"Her people are Mississippians, I believe," David McDavidson said.
"From near Pass Christian, if I'm not mistaken. A very old and distinguished family."

"If he used the term I think you mean, this Ginsberg fellow," Marvin
Slope, medievalist and philologist, announced in the high-pitched voice
he used in conducting his history of the English language course, "it
comes from the Anglo-Saxon verb ficken, meaning to hit or to strike.

The alteration to a more guttural vowel sound came, of course, later with the Great Vowel Shift, thus resulting in the word used now by common speakers of the language. At its first appearance in the sixth century AD, the verb ficken did not carry the baggage it does today. Different times, different linguistic mores, I call it."

"The question I have," Robard Flange said, "is what did Dr. Ronald Alden do after Miss Troutt was assaulted verbally? Did he toss the fellow out on his filthy ear?"

Gareth Lamb said simply. "Dr. Alden did not remove the fellow from the classroom, he did not remonstrate, he did not reprimand, he said nothing. The class went on, and further discussion of this beatnik's poetry ensued for the remainder of the hour."

"That young woman, I do feel for her," Dr. Samuel Vinson said. "The shame and horror of the moment, the lack of any defense for her, her being of a fine old family from coastal Mississippi. It is all quite unspeakable."

All who spoke agreed that the matter was unspeakable, and detailed discussion of the unspeakability of that moment went on until the chimes of the great clock in Founder's Hall struck eleven.

11

TOLLMAN BRIGGS COULD TELL instantly that his guitar was out of tune, and he could point to when that had to have happened, at least to within an hour or two of the time when some fool had picked it up and begun strumming away in the middle of the night, trying to prove he could sing. What would any of this set of losers and dopers Cameron was hooked up with know about music, know about an instrument, know about life on the run? They knew how to light up a roach or a bong and how to suck down a lungful of smoke, and they knew how to stay up for three or four days without crashing, and that little blonde one with the popped eyes, Sunshine Mountain—how original she thinks the name is she dreamed up for herself, Tollman thought—she showed last night she knew how to give a dynamite blowjob. He'd give her credit for that. She'd paid attention to a teacher somewhere along the way, something that Cameron Semmes had never bothered to do.

Cameron didn't have to work to please, though, Tollman had to admit, as prime a woman as everybody recognized her to be on first sight. Everybody's always been ready to give her anything she wants, and she's never had to learn to give anything back. She's one of the takers and receivers, Tollman considered as he fumbled with trying to make the guitar sound right again, tightening and loosening and picking at first one and then another string and listening to the effects he was causing, and she doesn't have to worry about giving stuff up to get people to trade something back to her for it. No, all she's ever had to do is lie back, bend her knees, and listen to whoever's working on her moan about how beautiful and sexy and amazing she is. Easy taking, no need to give a thing away ever.

Uh oh, Tollman said to himself in the small quiet voice he tried always to use when he felt it starting up in his head or belly or sometimes as low as his balls, I'm about to get an idea for a song. If I don't scare it away by letting it know I'm eavesdropping, maybe I can get enough down to make it happen. Hell, no, I'm not just listening to it while it's caught off guard, he thought, feeling a surge and tickle working somewhere in the deep darkness of his inner organs. It's low down in my belly. It's coming to me. And it's not just one song that's snaking its head up over the edge of the bed this morning high enough for me to see it. It's at least two, twins on the way. I know what the first one's going to be called. It just told me its name. Idiot Savant. It said it as clear as spring water in East Tennessee flowing over a flat rock.

Jesus, Tollman Briggs spoke the name out loud, it's starting to happen, it's starting to work, Nashville is blooming in my brain. I came to this city right. I worked my way in here. I didn't drive into town in a car of my own, I hitched and caught a ride with a stranger who spoke in gnomic riddles, unconscious of what he was saying and what he was telling me, as unintentional as a blind seer in a thunder storm. I walked all the way from downtown Nashville south on Belmont and found the house Cameron Semmes said would be here, I moved in and got crystal-clear high, my head working like a fine watch without a speck of dust in the works, and now if I can get this guitar tuned, I can start laying some good shit down. Listen to it talking to me.

"Nashville," Tollman shouted out loud, "I will break your heart before you break mine. And when my ruin finally comes, I will embrace that, too, just like a lover."

A line of the first song came full-blown into Tollman's head, singing like an angel on coke. Where it would end up residing in the finished piece he could not yet tell, but it would fit somewhere, as tight and as loose at the same time as Sunshine Mountain's quick little mouth had been on his rig last night after Cameron had wandered off somewhere and given Tollman the chance to take and receive for a while. "Idiot savant," Tollman sang, not sure of the tune yet, but knowing it'd be a low growl for this part, "you don't know what you want. All you know is you want."

If only I could learn how to tune a guitar, Tollman thought, returning to savor the pure line from the folk he'd just been given, it'd save me a lot of grief. "All you know is you want. All I want is what you know."

The crowd was huge and nervous, overflowing Memorial Gymnasium, building in number and surliness since before five o'clock for an eight o'clock start, and spilling into the concourse leading to it, and it was more different in its makeup than any other event Major Bob Tomball had ever seen at Vanderbilt. That was because it had something for everybody, he figured, drawing people from more walks of Nashville life than he'd ever suspected even existed. You would find some mixing of different kinds of folks at a football game now and then, nothing like you'd see in Knoxville at a UT game, naturally, but if some real team was playing the Vanderbilt Commodores, say Georgia or particularly Alabama, people would turn out to see Vandy lose not only from Belle Meade and Green Hills and West Meade but from East Nashville and maybe a few from out in the country, come to town to get drunk, have a city experience, and watch Joe Namath pick apart a defense.

But Lord God, as one of Major Bob Tomball's officers in the Vanderbilt Security Force remarked, look at all these coloreds mixed in with the hippies in their damned old nasty dirty torn clothes, and the old boys with the big bellies and the overalls streaming in right next to ladies from Belle Meade being escorted by their lawyer and insurance executive and high-dollar-earning husbands, not even to mention the professor types, young and old, gray and bald and tottering and long haired and lively, and the damned students not only from Vanderbilt but the colored colleges, too. Fisk and Tennessee State and Meharry, and the other white schools in Nashville, Belmont and Trevecca and David Lipscomb and the Free Will Bible Baptist College and all the junior colleges and the fly-by-nighters downtown in the store fronts.

"A mess of them like this," Sergeant Bolt Compton said to Major Tomball, "all mixed up and not acting the same, how do you know how to handle such a bunch? Where are they coming from? What's going to set them off, if anything does? Not the same thing for all of them, right? You can't just look at them and say, oh, yeah, drunk fraternity boy, redneck UT fan, trailer trash, what have you, I know what makes you crazy. Your football crowd now, I can predict every time when I'm going to need to tell the boys to take notice. Hell, you can spot them by the damn clothes they're wearing. I can just look at the colors of their shirts and tell you exactly which one might need a knock upside the head in a minute or two. These ones here, I can't predict. It's like mixing a shot of bourbon with half a glass of kerosene and trying to drink it down. You might get around it all right and get it swallowed, and you might not. But even if you do, what's going to come of it? Will it come right back up or just lay there in your belly festering and making you nuts?"

"I appreciate what you're saying, Bolt," Major Tomball said, "but it might be even easier than policing a football game, this thing here. These folks at this symposium meeting aren't likely to be already drunked up when they get here, and the state of Alabama's not involved in a football contest, so we might get off real easy tonight. Hell, all these folks are going to do is listen to some people talk at them. That's all they're looking for. How much can that get them stirred up?"

"I hope you're right, Major, but I'm going to be as nervous as a one-legged man in a ass-kicking contest until this damn thing's over. Anytime you get a whole bunch of niggers and hippies and rednecks all mixed in together and them listening to this Stokely Carmichael and Martin Luther King jabbering at them, something's liable to blow any minute."

"Naw, naw," Major Tomball assured his officer, "don't be borrowing trouble now. Martin Luther King is a preacher, whatever else he is, and he's just likely to talk about Jesus and turning the other cheek and shit like that. That other little skinny bastard, he's an educated man, they say, and you know our darkies ain't going to understand a Yankee word he says to them, him being a nigger or not."

"Well, yeah," Sergeant Compton said, watching the flow of people sweeping through the doors of the basketball gymnasium in a steady stream, "but he's liable to talk about this black power bullshit, and Dr. Martin Luther King is bound to start ranting about peace. When a nigger starts talking about peace, you better be sure you got your gun loaded."

"Speaking of which," Major Tomball said, "you have gave the word to all officers not to leave a single round in any weapon, haven't you?"

"They know that, yeah."

"Just have their handguns strapped on so folks can see them, that's all we're going to need. The last thing we need is some fool popping a cap."

"It sure makes me nervous, though, Major, these boys being defenseless. There ain't nothing more dangerous than an unloaded gun."

"Sergeant, we got a secret weapon tonight you haven't even mentioned yet," Major Tomball said. "And that's going to have a real calming effect."

"What's that? Tear gas?"

"No, it's nothing like that. We got Senator Strom Thurmond up on that stage tonight. He'll talk some sense into the rednecks, and he'll scare the coloreds to death. He'll Dixiecrat the shit out of them."

"I tell you what scares me," Sergeant Compton said, allowing himself to laugh a little. "That big old hairy sissy that's going to be up there. He's liable to take off his clothes and show folks his pecker or something."

"They tell me he's a poet, Bolt. What I know about that breed of dipshit, he won't do a damn thing but jabber."

The teenage babysitter hadn't been ready to leave when Ronald Alden knocked on the door of her apartment just off Peabody, delayed by something happening or not happening at the Flaming Steer restaurant where she worked the afternoon shift. Having to wait the fifteen minutes it took for her to get ready had caused Ronald to get caught in the flow of traffic choking every street toward the Vanderbilt campus, and by the time he got home and got the sitter situated and Lily into the car, he knew they'd have a hard time parking, getting to and into Memorial Gymnasium, and finding a place to sit. The seats reserved for faculty would in all likelihood be filled by those unencumbered by children living at home, and any seats left over would be invaded by students, each with a settled sense of entitlement learned through a privileged upbringing in first and second homes that Ronald knew he'd never be able even to visit, much less own one of.

As he drove, he refused to look at Lily, and he managed to let her know he was purposely not looking at her even though he didn't have to say a word to accomplish that. She could tell how her husband was feeling by the deep and venomous curse he'd laid on the driver of a Lincoln Continental that had cut in front of him, causing him to hit the brakes hard enough to hear his Chevy tires squeal. Lily had been jolted forward in her seat, forced to put out a hand to keep from sliding into the dashboard, and made to add her own curse to the one Ronald had just vented. On the surface her expression of animus was directed toward a sudden physical dislocation and the damage that might have caused to the way her panty hose stretched over her kneecaps, but the real target was Ronald. He knew that, she knew the son-of-a-bitch ripped out of his throat was only occasioned by the Lincoln and had its true direction and home right between her eyes, and they relished in bitter silence together the fact that between a quarreling husband and wife the sweetest reproof is the one not verbalized.

Neither one said a word to the other all the way in the car to a parking place fully eight blocks from Memorial Stadium, during their walk together toward the site of the symposium, their entrance into the overheated building, and their final sitting places in temporary seats so far off to one side that anyone appearing on the speakers' platform could be seen only in a dim profile blocking the view of any other person up on stage.

"Do you see anybody you know?" Lily said. "I sure don't."

"A student or two, maybe. We're too far away over in this corner from where the real people sit to be able to see anybody."

"Your students aren't real? Is that what you're saying? That's not the way you act when one comes sucking up to you."

"You know what I mean. They aren't real in the aggregate, only one by one."

"That's true of everything in the whole fucking world, Ronald," Lily said, turning to look at her husband for the first time since they'd left their house. "Nothing exists in general."

"Listen to the deep thinker," Ronald said. "I bet you made an A in philosophy somewhere back in the distant past."

"Fuck you," Ronald's wife said in a voice a little too loud to be heard only by her husband, and just then someone began talking through the gymnasium loudspeakers in a booming volume overriding all other sound.

Almost a hundred feet away, immediately in front of the platform, squarely in the middle of the second row in a section roped off and reserved and fitted with padded chairs with arm rests, Felice Foldman was whispering in the ear of her husband, Malcomb Foldman, chancellor of Vanderbilt University. "Will you have to say anything tonight?"

He shook his head once, which Felice knew he would do, knowing already the event was student-initiated, student-run, and tuition-funded, obviating the need for the chancellor to take ownership and responsibility for the lineup of guests sitting on the stage before them and thereby giving him some cover in the event of embarrassment and/or total ruin.

She knew that, but by asking Malcomb if he had to speak she could gently remind him the event wasn't completely his baby. Relax a bit. It's all right to do that now. I'm glad to do that much for him, that bit of consolation, Felice considered as she focused her gaze tightly on the face of the student at the microphone. My part's done for this one, and it went off very well. Now it's his turn.

Anyone looking at the way Felice was gazing on the speaker before her would be convinced she was hanging on every word he uttered and would be able to summarize in great detail what was being said once he'd finished. That ability was a gift, Felice knew, her power to convince she was totally focused and of one mind, and it allowed her to think of anything she wished to consider or not to think at all whenever she wanted. That last part was hard, though, to keep nothing going on in your head, and when such moments of blankness came, that was a blessing. Right now, what I'll think of while this kid up on the stage jabbers introductions and directions and enjoys the attention he's getting is how well the dinner at Cherry Mount House went last night.

She had been afraid it could go completely off the rails in any direction, despite her faith in Sanford Temple's exquisite taste and his masterful handling of Negro servants and cooks. That overseeing-of-personnel part was taken care of and could be safely released into Sanford's capable hands always, but the people you had to invite to dinner parties and the dangerous mixes that sometimes occurred and couldn't have been anticipated—these were the landmines. At last night's dinner, to have at the same table two nationally known Negroes and a senator from South Carolina and a homosexual whose writings were beyond comment and, along with the outsiders, the necessary money people and the old Nashville family people and the token professor or two from the appropriate academic disciplines—all this could have trembled on the edge of explosion and gone off like a hydrogen bomb. It hadn't. It hadn't, Felice thought as she riveted her gaze on the young man bleating into the microphone. It hadn't, even though one of the token professors had been from the English department, DeWitt Vallandigham, a known incendiary on matters racial, social, civil, philosophical, sexual, and familial.

DeWitt had behaved himself, not saying much, and gazing about him like a Hottentot snatched up out of a jungle somewhere and put down at an Amish reunion. Perhaps it's best to overload them with strangeness, these token faculty members one had to invite to Cherry Mount House—fill their emotional circuits so full they become paralyzed and can't make spectacles of themselves. There was so much negritude and homosexuality present that DeWitt was overwhelmed. I'll have to ask dear Sanford about that notion of consciously overloading the social stimuli, Felice told herself, not Malcomb. My husband the chancellor would be so frightened by the idea he'd wet his panties.

At the microphone, Jonathan Seth Matthews looked down again at his written introduction of the symposium, its focus, and the descriptions of its eminent participants, all lined up behind him in their chairs. All but Allen Ginsberg, that is, his seat unoccupied though he had been seen behind the speaking area right before Jonathan mounted the platform to get things kicked off. He had even waved to Jonathan, a cheery little wiggle of his right hand that caused its target to blush, and he'd winked and nodded.

Jonathan had worked long and hard on the remarks he was to deliver, revising and practicing before a mirror, underlining certain words for emphasis, noting strategic points at which to pause, checking again and again the accuracy of biographical facts about the noted guests, and finally administering to himself the most important preparation of all, a fifteen minute deep and true toking of high grade hash brought back from Morroco by Boyd Ryman, a freshman-year roommate returned from abroad on a study trip to North Africa, full of new cultural awareness, an improved world view, and outlaw drugs.

The hash was working. Jonathan Seth Matthews was calm, he was ready, he was composed, he was speaking with utter confidence before the greatest number of people he had ever faced before, and he felt as though he could have witnessed a decapitation carried out before him without turning a hair. All I need to make it complete, Jonathan said to himself as he read aloud into a set of booming speakers the words he'd written about great issues of the time now under serious consideration at the Vanderbilt Impact Symposium of 1967, is for Allen Ginsberg to get up on this stage before I get to the part introducing him. And if he doesn't, Jonathan knew, kind hashish would say calmly in his ear the magic phrase who gives a fuck.

Nearing the end of a sentence which required a strategic pause and a lifting of his eyes to look out over the crowd before him, Jonathan

Seth Matthews glimpsed immediately before him in the second row a person who seemed familiar, met perhaps recently and acknowledged by an introduction maybe, someone whose name he'd heard and only half remembered now. He looked more closely, focusing on the face and the shape of the head and the sitting posture of the person so familiar to him. Jesus, he said to himself, I've got to look down at what's in front of me so I can keep reading and get it done, but what in hell am I doing sitting in the seat next to Chancellor Foldman wearing a woman's dress? I've got on earrings, and I've got tits and long hair, but my head is right out there in the middle of where I'm looking from up here. Have I lost my actual head? Has it floated off and left me?

Raising a hand to his brow, Jonathan was reassured when he touched a forehead and felt the sensation of his fingers on his skull, but he was afraid to move his hand further down. What if my nose and mouth are gone? How can I keep talking if I haven't got my mouth up here with me? Can I throw my voice and make my head on my woman's body say what I've got to say? Will the mike pick it up so everybody in the gym can hear me?

His mouth on the head next to the chancellor was moving, so Jonathan returned to his reading, looking down at the sheaf of papers to see what to say next, and then up at his head in the second row to see what it was doing. There was a delay between his mouthing a set of words and the head's saying it aloud, but the hesitation was brief and manageable, and most miraculous of all, the sound system was picking up what the head was saying and carrying it throughout the gym. Hell, my good old head, Jonathan Seth Matthews whispered beneath the prepared speech he was mouthing, we can do this thing together. Just hang on, and I'll do something for you, too, just as soon as I get the chance.

Besides, he thought to add, I got to admit seeing you there I look pretty damn good in that outfit that woman's body's wearing. The colors really match my eyes, complement my complexion, and it is so cool to have tits and be wearing rings on my fingers and panty hose on my legs. I bet my head thinks it feels sleek. I wonder if my head will get a chance to sneak a look at what that body's got underneath that dress in that bra? I don't see why it can't take a peek, but will I be there if my head goes home with the body and I'm up here introducing the symposium? Will I get to see my tits?

Before Jonathan Seth Matthews could untangle the problems of spatial location raised by that question, managing to keep on reading what was before him even as he attempted to adjust to the new circumstances he was having to face, a noise of chairs moving and people sounding surprised behind him and a rumble and beginning roar and gasp from the Symposium audience in front caused him to take a look to the rear to see what was going on. Had one of the old people on the platform toppled over with a heart attack or stroke? Had a dean kicked the bucket? Had Stokely Carmichael stood up and given a black power salute?

What Jonathan saw as he spun around was Allen Ginsberg, big as life, dressed not in the dark suit and tie he'd been wearing for the last two days but in a long striped robe and sandals, moving in a good trot from one side of the platform to the other, arms outreached and a huge smile of welcome and delight upon his face, toward the last man seated in the lineup of the Vanderbilt Impact Symposium of 1967, Senator Strom Thurmond of South Carolina. The senator was rising from his chair automatically, long accustomed to having admirers approach him hungry for handshakes, and he was extending his own good right hand toward the rough beast slouching toward him, ready to swap some skin.

Wanting closer contact than that, the King of the Beats embraced the senior senator from the Palmetto State, hugged him up tight to his dashiki and planted his mouth squarely in the middle of the dishpan-shaped gray face before him. The kiss was a full one, though it didn't land on the legislative lips, Strom Thurmond being able to turn his head gracefully to one side as though to receive the greeting of a friendly Frenchman, but Allen Ginsberg seemed satisfied and sated for the time being.

Would you look at that, Jonathan Seth Matthews said to himself where he stood and to his fugitive head on the female body in the second row of seats next to the chancellor, Ginsberg is as fickle as I feared he would be. Never, never again, will I trust my heart to know the truth or my ears to sort through lies spoken in passion. And now what this poet has done has got the crowd so worked up and crazy, I won't even be able to finish my introductory remarks. Listen to them screaming and laughing and whooping and hollering. I'll just stop, Jonathan said in a snit. I don't have to take this. I won't say another word, and I'll let them do whatever they want to in whatever order they choose, and I will not moderate or ask for questions from the audience, either. I'll sit down in the chair reserved for me, and my damn fool head is on its own out there. If it comes back to me from where it's so happy to be right now, it'll be because it chooses to, not because I beg and plead.

After Senator Thurmond had broken free from the smiling poet with the deeply foreign smell on his breath, he was able to sit back in his seat alongside his fellow participants, and when his turn to speak came, he dealt with the same topic addressed by the others. Power, variously defined. Dr. Martin Luther King spoke of the power of the powerless and the action of inaction, and the audience listened, some weeping, some applauding, but all used to hearing that story told. Stokely Carmichael called power by a new name, showing his teeth frequently in a smile that had no fun in it, and many older faculty and monied elders were roused from their stupor enough to quake a bit, look about them at the rabble applauding this advocate of violent action against the establishment, shake their heads in sorrow and dismay, and promise themselves to install sounder locks on all doors and windows no later than tomorrow.

When Senator Strom Thurmond arose to speak, these awakened faculty and many of the propertied Nashvillians present applauded loud and long, letting all with ears to hear know they were in accord with the senator's message of turn around, jump back, squat down, and hold on to what you got. As his last words thundered and boomed over the loudspeakers of Memorial Gymnasium—these being "as it was, as it is, as it shall be"—the answering bays and bellows from the crowd drowned out all electronically assisted sound.

The King of the Beats arose to speak, toddled toward the lectern, then lay on the floor to spin in a circle, arose again, launched into a deep hum, banged briskly on a portable set of chimes, and read at length from a work called "Wichita Vortex Sutra." "Here is the source of power, here is the healing of division, here is the past, present, and future," he howled. "Vortex, vortex, vortex." Many in the crowd took up the chant, particularly those hallucinogenically aided, and in due time and with much struggle and gales of breath, Ginsberg's presentation and the Impact Symposium of 1967 dissolved into separate clots of like-minded persons, fleeing in slow motion and in no sense part of a larger community, headed for the traffic jam of the outside air.

"I had hoped to hear Ginsberg read from *Howl*," Robert McLean was saying in a somber tone to Therese Buchanan as they left the gymnasium together, "or something at least from the early stuff. That's the real deal."

"Yeah, like the one about Whitman in the supermarket," Therese said. "He shows some real wit there. Eyeing the bag boys and fondling the melons."

"Everything is so boringly earnest now," Robert McLean said. "Even rock is getting too damned committed socially, don't you think?"

"Um," Therese said. "Poetry should be about dying, and rock should be about fucking. Things are getting turned upside down."

"I got some dynamite grass," Robert said. "Straight from Jamaica, as of yesterday. Want to get your head all torn up?"

"I'd love to, but not now. I promised my parents I'd go to a party at the house after this symposium thing and let them show me off a little. Maybe later. Is it Blue Mountain grass?"

By the time Ronald and Lily Alden had found where their car was parked almost a mile from the gymnasium, fighting their way across streets immobilized with traffic and down sidewalks crowded with students, townfolk, pickpockets, drug dealers, guitar pickers, and street whores—all high on something: snort, blow, suck, suppositories, Black Jack, gin, fear, hate, lust, loneliness, despair—they had been forced to talk to each other at least twice. Once when Lily walked out in front of a swerving pickup truck taking a shortcut across a lawn and Ronald felt he had no choice but to warn her, and the next time when Ronald heard his name called out loudly in a high-pitched voice with a deep bray beneath the tenor note. It was Lacy Bodean, and she was proceeding in a controlled totter alongside Chambers, tacking first to one side and then the other of their path as they drew near Dr. Alden and his wife and helpmate.

"Wait up," Lacy Bodean said, "I want to ask somebody that's supposed to know why it is they call what that hippie poet was hollering poetry. And that's not all I want to say. I been saving up questions for the last two hours."

Stepping off the sidewalk and taking advantage of the screening effect of a good-sized tree trunk, Ronald put out a hand to guide his wife in accompanying him and waited until Lacy and Chambers Bodean reached them, Chambers venturing cautiously off the cement of the sidewalk and tapping at the ground beneath the tree with the toe of one shoe. "I hope this is not a sweet gum tree," he said. "Those balls will roll under your feet and help turn you a flip if you step on these little suckers wrong."

"Chambers never needs any help to turn himself a flip," Lacy Bodean said. "I've seen him hit the floor so many times I can't count and there not be a single impediment to make him take a fall."

"My impediments come from within, my dear," Chambers said. "They are not real in a literal sense, like these damned old sweet gum balls. They're much more insidious than that."

"Tell it, Sugar," Lacy said, and then looking from Ronald to Lily and back again to the male of the pair, coming to a halt with the bole of the tree between her and the flow of refugees from the symposium down the sidewalk, she went on. "Have you ever in your life witnessed or imagined a thing like that before in Nashville, Tennessee?"

"You mean a symposium on current issues?" Ronald said, and then trying to sound less stuffily academic as he addressed the Bodeans of Middle Tennessee, "A bunch of folks talking about news of the day?"

"No, I mean the sight of a big crowd of white people in Nashville listening to two darkies just giving them what-for about the kind of life they've been living. And the white folks just shouting and clapping and saying pour it on, let us have it. Sock it to us, Negroes."

"It did seem strange to me," Chambers Bodean said, putting out a hand to brace himself against the tree trunk, "but I liked it. It was some real entertainment. Better than one of the old minstrel shows they used to have in the opera house downtown. Boy howdy, that was some fun. All those folks in blackface trading insults. It's tore down now, though, that building is, the old Frolic. Had naked dancers there, too. Real tastefully done, though."

"I would not have thought tonight's discussion was meant to be entertainment," Lily said, speaking in a way that Ronald was not used to hearing from her. Any expression of possible disagreement with the opinion of another person, except for any and all from Ronald, was not in Lily's social arsenal. "I think Dr. King and Mr. Carmichael were deadly serious."

"Of course they were, Honey," Lacy Bodean said. "That's what made it so funny. They were just carrying on, like a colored preacher in a hot church house in August, just raising Cain. And I kept waiting for the white folks in the audience to laugh and hoot and holler the more worked up the darkies got, and they never did."

"They hooted and hollered," Chambers said. "Now give the white folks credit where it's due."

"Chambers, hush. It's not just the hooting and hollering that matters. It's when they do it that counts."

"Oh," Chambers said. "You probably onto something. You know, this is a sweet gum tree. I can feel those little balls just working under my feet. They dying to turn me a flip."

"One other thing, now y'all," Lacy Bodean said. "Two things really, and here's the first one. Why do they call that old queer boy's shouting and carrying on a specimen of poetry? You are the expert, Dr. Alden. That's why they got you teaching English at Vanderbilt, right? So what is poetry, and how is Allen Ginsberg a poet? Answer that to my satisfaction, and I'll be able to go home, take off my girdle, drink half a bottle of something, and lie down and rest my eyes."

"Some say poetry is just the best words in the best order," Ronald said carefully, choosing a definition he thought might be simple enough to satisfy a monied matron from a fine old family in Davidson County. "That's one way to characterize it."

"That's a piss poor way then, I got to say," Lacy said. "Good lord, you could say that about anything anybody ever wrote down. I do that when I make out my grocery list for Lucille to take to the store and buy stuff. I do that when I write my mama a courtesy note."

"I tell you what," Chambers Bodean said. "I think you've hit on something that can furnish good fodder for discussion at one of our readings from the dramas of Shakespeare. What makes something be a poem? Let's ask these folks to come to our next reading, and then you can just rake Dr. Alden over the coals, Lacy Love. When is that next one, Honey?"

"It's going to be one of the special ones, you'll remember, Chambers. It's next Friday night at the house."

"That's right. I bet they wouldn't mind it being special. Would y'all?"

"I think it would be delightful," Lily said. "We'd love to come to one of your Shakespeare evenings."

"I'd love to see you at it, too," Chambers said, stepping away from the sweet gum tree and beginning to move back toward the sidewalk, a little less crowded by now. "I'd take a good long look at you while you're reading."

"Hush your mouth," Lacy said, chuckling as she put out a hand toward her husband. "I bet I'll do as much looking as you will."

"More, if the past is any indication. Maybe not looking at the same people as me, though," Chambers said. "Do y'all suspect the coloreds are going to be riled up by what that little skinny darky was saying to them tonight? Suppose some of them will want to go on the warpath? Do some of this black power boogie woogie?"

"The ones that get riled don't go to Vanderbilt to listen to people talk at them," Lacy said. "They don't hit the streets until after midnight anyway, the rowdy ones don't. I'll be in touch with you folks about next Friday. The reading's going to be from *Hamlet* if you want to brush up."

"That's the one about the crazy boy, isn't it? Wants to do it with his mama?" Chambers called after his wife, two or three steps ahead of him as they rejoined the retreat up the dark street away from Memorial Gymnasium.

"What do those two know about Shakespeare?" Ronald allowed himself to say to Lily, this deep into the end of the evening, as he watched the Bodeans move away, into the beam of a streetlamp and then out the other side. "Or Allen Ginsberg? Them and their literary friends. Jesus."

"They know how to be jolly and have a good time," Lily said. "And we're going to their place in Belle Meade next Friday for the reading from *Hamlet*. At least it'll give me a chance to get out of the house and away from the kids for a change."

"Lily, these people are old Nashville of the worst stripe. They're racists, born and bred. They are truly eaten up with prejudice."

"And you aren't?" she said. "Let's get to the car and go home. I'm freezing to death."

"It's not cold," Ronald said. "It's April, almost May. You can't feel like it's cold in this climate."

"I know how I feel," Lily said. "And you don't. You never do, no matter what you say."

Don't let her bait you into a prolonged argument over who feels what and to what degree and when, Ronald told himself, picking up the pace of his steps behind his wife as she moved briskly down the sidewalk with several more blocks to navigate before reaching the Chevrolet. She's looking for a reason to create an emotional display, and I won't even consider giving her the opportunity. Instead, I'll wonder what Josephine Longineaux is doing about now and who's there with her wherever she's doing whatever that might be. Did she go to the symposium tonight or is she still too distraught emotionally for such as that? I didn't see her there, though I looked hard enough. Did I do her any good by showing concern and care for her in that raw and early moment of despair she was feeling on Natchez Trace after being emotionally abused? Did she take what I did wrongly? Misinterpret my touching her? Did she think I was only interested in her physically? Does her quick little tongue feel as warm and new tonight as it did there in the car? Is someone kissing her right now? Which spoiled little fraternity bastard could be enjoying that?

12

ROBARD FLANGE HAD DREADED having to attend the Vanderbilt Impact Symposium this year. He feared having to endure the sight of rabble-rousers on a public stage supported by students, sponsored by the university, and allowed the free access to publicity this allowed. He foresaw the crowing and preening by the radical faculty in many parts of the university that would result, and he felt most deeply the insult to history and tradition such a congregation of Negroes and homosexuals and the sweepings of Nashville's lower classes would pose at the event.

He had informed Marie that she must not attend the spectacle for fear of what outbreaks of profanity and threats to civil and moral order might come as passions were inflamed and fed by such creatures as Dr. Martin Luther King and Stokely Carmichael and this great hairy Jewish pervert Allen Ginsberg. She had assured him she had no desire to be witness to whatever violations of decency might occur and that she would wait patiently at home, all windows and doors securely locked and all lamps lit, until his return.

"I must attend this abomination, my dear," Robard had told his wife, "to show the flag if nothing else. We cannot cede the field to these charlatans and filibusters, tempting though it is to boycott the gathering. Do that, and you allow what they say and threaten to go publically unchallenged. It is a duty I must discharge. I am compelled to take up the banner."

"I understand," Marie had said, standing straight upright, her makeup perfect, her posture that of the helpmate of a warrior, steadfast and un-afraid, steeled against tears. "Do you intend to speak out in public?"

"No, I shall not. All of us in the department of English—I refer to those right-minded few, of course, not to the hirelings brought in by this upstart crow Alfred Buchanan—have decided that we shall show our pres-ence by attendance in force, but that we shall demonstrate opposition not by lowering ourselves to verbal debate with this bunch. That they crave. But our posture, our presence, and our expression shall inform all with eyes to see what our assessment truly is and will continue to be. We shall condemn in silence. We shall not descend to their charnel-house level. "

"Splendid," Marie had said. "And will you gather at Marvin Slope's home afterward for discussion?"

"We shall," Robard Flange answered in a resigned and determined tone, suffering in silence.

"How does your arm feel, my dear?"

"I do not complain. I never whine. I shall endure. I shall bear it."

Enduring the actual period of the event in Memorial Gymnasium had not been nearly so disturbing as Robard had thought it would be. He had steeled himself to maintain his outward composure as he sat among his colleagues in the seats reserved for senior faculty in a section advanta-geous for viewing, and he had prepared mentally an exercise to which he would resort as need be when some particularly offensive or outrageous statement was made or insult committed by any of the three miscreants. Senator Strom Thurmond would be the sole voice of reason and truth on the platform during the event, and Robard intended to allow the asser-tions of the statesman from South Carolina to register in his conscious mind as they were offered. Those words of wisdom he would welcome.

When either of the other three spoke, Dr. Robard Flange of Vanderbilt University had decided that he would allow his current mind and soul to become quiescent and the selfhood of Rooney Beauchamp to make its presence known. The current moment in time would become not the year of 1967 in Nashville in an athletic auditorium filled mainly with rabble as audience and provocateurs as speakers, but instead an early morning on a day in the mists of early spring in 1862 near a small chapel on the Tennessee River called Shiloh. There Major Rooney Beauchamp would see to the readiness of the Fourth Mississippi regiment, as he bestrode his steed Defiance, his gaze alert, his will at full pitch and tone, his fate consigned to God and to the future of his state and nation, and his mood and temper in perfect ease and pure composure.

Whatever sound of discord and strife might come from a makeshift stage in the Nashville of 1967 or from opposing guns and cannon of Union forces in 1862, Rooney Beauchamp would drown such alarm by reciting to himself the names of all divisions, regiments, and squads of Confederate troops at the ready for the onslaught to come. He would name each man of his own command by initials and last name, all exactly precise and accurate, and all present in the mind of Rooney Beauchamp because Robard Flange had consigned them to memory over a century later. The names of the departed would be evident and available. The years might wither all flesh, blood, and bone, but the names of the valiant would be and were preserved for as long as God allowed Robard Flange a mortal presence in this fallen world.

So it had gone well for Robard, the onstage ranting and cavorting, the shouts and laughter and screams of approval from the audience, and the attempts to shock and appall notwithstanding, and he had arrived at the home of Dr. Marvin Slope not only encouraged by the success of his strategy but energized by having been able to recite interiorly over two hundred individual names and home locations of the troops of Rooney Beauchamp's command at Shiloh. He had gone through them alphabetically at a measured and respectful pace, twice completely, and by the time the Symposium event was over, he had gotten through over two-thirds of another recitation before having the opportunity to cease. In celebration of how well he had managed his showing of the flag, he completed that third recitation in true and good order, this time aloud as he drove his car to Marvin Slope's home in West Meade, each soldier remembered and duly honored, now dust in fact but alive in memory.

"Robard, old friend," Marvin Slope greeted him at the door, "I'd pour you a flagon of mead had I it to give. But alas, I do not. I do hope Jack Daniels Black Label will serve as suitable substitute."

"I don't see how it might could fail," Robard said, surprising himself by lapsing into the tenor lilt of an East Tennessee hill farmer and then, enjoying how he felt doing it, carried it a linguistic step further. "Let me have a sup of that good whisky you been hiding in the rafters, Marvin. See do it have the essence it ought to."

"I wish that little nigra up on stage that kept talking about black power could hear you say that just the way you did, Brother Robard," Marvin said. "It would scare the dickens out of the little runt. He wouldn't be thinking about black power. He'd be saying feet don't fail me now."

Buoyed by the hearty East Tennessee exchange, the medievalist and the enlightenment scholar joined their colleagues in the great room of Marvin Slope's well-appointed home, all now engaged in vigorous discussion not of the symposium event just ended but the next battle looming ahead for the Old Guard of the English department.

"He has proclaimed it," Gareth Lamb was saying with heat, "but it is not yet accomplished, this outrageous endeavor to appoint a woman to a named chairship. The department did not and does not seek it, and should not allow it to proceed."

"Nevertheless, it will be difficult if not impossible to derail the plan," David McDavidson said. "Our leader is a master manipulator. Buchanan has the ear of the chancellor."

"He has strong hold of more than just that one body part," Gareth Lamb said, looking about him to detect any signs of appreciation for the wit of his observation. Enough nods and chuckles came to encourage him to proceed. "The chancellor has instructed him to move forward with the search, and Buchanan has named a committee."

"I've not been approached about serving on such a task force," Robard said in his scholar's voice, setting the East Tennessee hill farmer dialect aside for the nonce. "Have any of you, as senior members of the department, been asked to take part?"

None said he had heard a word about the matter, all looking from one to the other for confirmation, with only Lawrence Hill Dunham not joining the chorus of denials. "Larry," Robard said. "I assume by your silence that you may have been asked by our Lord Alfred to join the witch's coven of this endeavor."

"Lord Alfred," Samuel Vinson said. "That's really good, Robard. What an apt label for our little leader from Harvard."

"He's a regular Adam with the naming process," Gareth Lamb announced in the midst of the chuckles, snorts, and belly laughs. A chorus of hear, hears burst forth.

After that died down, Lawrence Hill Dunham admitted he'd been asked by the chairman to represent the senior members of the department on the search committee for the female scholar slated to become the first of her gender to serve as a member of the Vanderbilt department of English. He then began to explain his reasons for accepting the appointment, an undertone of deep apology coloring his words, but Marvin Slope would hear none of it. "No need to feel you've let us down, Lawrence," he said.

"Dr. Dunham can burrow from within," Samuel Vinson said. "Be our man in disguise, our intelligence undercover." Applause ensued, Lawrence Hill Dunham beamed, Jack Daniels' finest whisky flowed more freely, and Robard Flange's dead arm, the one not his, the left one, the one belonging to Major Rooney Beauchamp, the limb shot away by elements of the Illinois regiment facing the Fourth Mississippi at Shiloh in the peach orchard on the first day, the constant reminder of loss and dislocation and displacement—that member—continued to buzz in a low dead tone to Robard Flange its message of impending doom, desolation, and defeat.

13

EARLY THE NEXT MORNING, Marie Summers Flange, after listening to her husband groan and toss in distress and despair in the bed beside her all night as he moved about the arm attached to him, attempting to sleep, dialed the telephone number given her by Arlene Youngblood, the number for the massage establishment which had benefited her son Truman with its professional services. Marie had misplaced the scrap of paper on which she'd written the number furnished by Arlene, so she spent some time searching through the medical section of the yellow pages of the telephone directory without being able to find any reference to the therapeutic service Arlene had recommended. She did finally locate the piece of paper with the number in one of her older purses she seldom used, so she didn't have to call Arlene to ask for the number again. That would have been only a small embarrassment of no real consequence, but not having to admit a lapse in organization to Arlene was a relief.

The telephone at the Music City Magic Fingers Massage Salon rang several times before someone finally picked up, and Marie admitted she was perhaps calling a bit early in the day, but it was after nine in the morning, for goodness sakes, ordinary business hours after all. "Hello," a woman said gruffly, not announcing the name of the establishment for which she was answering a ringing telephone, probably someone newly employed or if not that, certainly ill-trained in business etiquette.

"Is this the Music City Magic Fingers Massage Salon?" Marie said in a brightly serious tone. "If so, I'm calling about an appointment."

"She only talks to girls in person," the woman said. "If you want to let Blanche Ann take a look at you, just come down here in the afternoon. Not before one o'clock, though."

"Oh, it's not for me. It's for my husband I'm calling. He's been referred to your establishment by a friend to see if you can give him some relief. Well, actually, it's not the friend, but the mother of the young man who's suggested we contact you."

"The mother?"

"Yes, she may be in your patient files, but maybe not. Probably you'd have just the name of the patient. He's Truman Youngblood, if you need to look at that. He swears by the quality of the treatment y'all gave him."

"I don't look at no files," the woman said after a pause, "nor know nobody's name, neither. I don't know if we even got any such a thing as files."

Oh, dear, Marie thought. She really is a new hire or one who should've been replaced long ago. She sounds so rural and not really friendly at all, not pert and eager to communicate. She's hardly encouraging, but of course caregivers don't have to be these days. You are the supplicant, not they. "Let me just ask you this one thing, then," Marie said. "Does he need to make an appointment several days in advance? I do hope not, because he really needs attention now, and is just suffering and pining for relief."

"You say you're his wife? You married to this man you talking about?"

"Yes, and he doesn't know I'm calling, but if I'm able to get him in there today, I just know he'll appreciate it. He's still in bed after what all happened last night, and he still just can't turn any way or do anything that would provide relief or release this morning. He just carried on all night, poor thing, just desperate, and I couldn't do a thing for him. I never can, of course. Whenever I touch the affected member, he says he can't bear it. It just feels dead to him."

"I guess I know what you mean, but I never heard it said just like that before from a woman married to one of them. But if he wants to come on in here this afternoon, I imagine Blanche Ann will be able to find some one to take him on."

"A therapist? Licensed and all, just like the one that did such a service to Truman Youngblood?"

"Yep, that is exactly we call them, ever last one. A therapist."

"I'll get him down there, then. In the old bank building on Second, right? It is worth trying, I think. Don't you?"

"I ain't in that end of the business no more. I give it up a while back. Maybe it give me up, I don't know. You ain't saying you want to be there with him, are you? I don't think Blanche Ann will allow that kind of stuff. I know she won't, to tell you the truth."

"Why, no. I understand professional confidentiality. And Robard does too, of course. He is punctilious."

"You say he is, huh? Wait up a minute now. It's all just straight here, you understand. It ain't none of that stuff goes on. You looking for something different you ain't going to find it at Magic Fingers. Miz Blanche Ann Weaver she is old school and straight up, and that's all she's going to allow in her place of business."

"That is reassuring to hear, and I know my husband well enough to say that is what he's looking for. Some measure of relief in the most conventional and old fashioned sense."

"Well," the woman on the phone for Music City Magic Fingers Massage salon said after a pause, probably taken, Marie supposed, to allow her to pencil in a note about details of their conversation, "long as you understand the rules, just drop him off by himself, and I expect somebody'll be able to give him what he needs."

"That is most encouraging," Marie Flange said. "Thank you." Replacing the receiver in its cradle, she headed for the master bedroom where Robard lay suffering, emitting small peeps, hiccoughs, and moans of distress. Maybe some measure of release for him is not so far away, Marie told herself. Let me think of the most positively motivating way to put the matter to him. I will be so thrilled if I can help provide my husband a bit of surcease from sorrow.

She means well, Robard Flange told himself in midafternoon as his wife maneuvered the Buick Electra back and forth in a rather abbreviated parking space on Second Avenue, twisting the wheel first one way and then another in her attempts to get the machine close enough to the curb to be considered parked and ready to be left alone. She is limited educationally in comparison to me, but that is through no fault of her own. She is an Agnes Scott graduate, a fine arts major, and her training there has suited her well to be a helpmate and lady partner. I would have her even more narrowly focused, if I were forced to make a choice between a union with Marie or with an intellectual woman, perish that breed. Or a feminist with an agenda of rebellion and upheaval. Marie tends to my needs as husband and works to fulfill her role as wife, and what else could one reasonably wish?

"Dear," Marie said, giving up on her struggle to move the Buick nearer the curb and a successful parking, "are you sure you don't want me to accompany you into the waiting room of the massage salon? I can sit and read while you receive your treatment. It's no bother at all to me."

"I don't imagine I'll undergo any sort of treatment in a first visit, my dear," Robard explained. "That is typically a time of diagnosis and laying out a plan for attack on the problem at hand. It's much like a military campaign, I should imagine. Where is the enemy? What are his resources? What will be our strategy, given our strength and the lay of the land? What shall be our fallback position, if need arise? How shall we maintain morale and purpose? Where shall the blood letting begin?"

"I'm sure you're right, dear. But no talk of blood, my goodness. I'll be at Claudine's Dress Shop for a space and then perhaps at the little tea room in the Hermitage Hotel, and I'll be back here at the car in an hour. I do hope you won't have to wait for me."

"I have my keys, should I need them before you return. I shall not leave the car until you do, and if I'm not here when you return, simply wait for me. Lock the doors and keep a close watch for downtown types. Do you have those instructions straight in your mind now?"

"I do, dear, certainly. I so hope you'll have the same experience with massage therapy that Truman Youngblood did."

"I'm off then," Robard said, leaving the passenger seat of the Buick and heading for the massive old double doors of the former Bank and Trust of the Cumberland where withdrawals and deposits of great weight and value were once commonly conducted in the vanished days of business on the river. The dead arm dependent from the first day of Shiloh went with him but was not of him, and he had to struggle briefly with his one good hand to open the single slab of painted pine which had replaced the once magnificent brass and steel entry of the past.

An establishment selling wigs, hair pieces, cosmetics, phonograph records, and women's clothes of many colors now occupied the first floor of the old B and T of the Cumberland, and looking about him Robard discovered that a sign with the name of the massage therapy clinic pointed toward a staircase leading to the third floor of the stone building. The marble stairs were in good order still, he noted, and it was a comforting thought to consider that they had once been mounted by the financiers, entrepreneurs, and business giants of the Cumberland Valley over a century ago. O tempora, O mores, Robard said to himself in a small interior chant as he climbed the stairs, and then he found himself arriving at an anteroom containing a desk with a middle-aged woman in a blue smock-like dress behind it, several straight chairs lined up against the wall facing the desk, and nothing else of much consequence, save for a sign proclaiming that all employees were licensed therapeutic physical technicians with certifications available for inspection.

The woman behind the desk was taking a deep pull on a cigarette as Robard Flange entered the room, and she appeared to be using the smoke she'd just inhaled to mark the progress of the words she spoke to him, each syllable a well-shaped puff carrying a linguistic meaning. "How do? Looking for some massage therapy?" she said. "Feeling a little muscle tightness?"

"Not tightness, exactly," Robard said, noting the woman's badly arranged hairstyle, appearing to fall more to one side than intended. "Actually a sense of displacement and dislocation. Not even that, precisely. The arm on the left side of my body does not feel a part of me. It is foreign to my sense of self."

"You needing yourself a little adjustment, sounds like to me," the woman said. "This your first time at Magic Fingers? Reason why I ask is maybe if you been here before, you got a certain therapist in mind you want to see again."

"No, this is my first time. I was referred by a young man's mother. Truman Youngblood seems to have benefited from his treatment here, according to what she reports. Do you know him?"

"No, I don't know him exactly, but that's the second time I heard his name called today. A woman saying she's your wife called here this morning. Did she come here with you?"

"My wife's downtown shopping, but she's not with me here, no."

"That's good. I was afraid she might show up, even though I told her Blanche Ann won't allow that. I'm glad she listened to what I told her."

"My wife is most attentive," Robard said, a bit puzzled. "She understands and takes directions quite well, when they are clear and delivered simply."

"She sounds like a real different breed of cat to me, but I ain't got nothing against that, though. Don't get me wrong. That's between you and her, right? Different strokes for different folks."

Robard didn't respond, but the left arm seemed to hang a little heavier and announce its unwanted presence a bit more insistently. Time to move on with the exploratory visit at Magic Fingers. "Do you want to examine my insurance card or have me fill out a questionnaire about my past medical history?" he asked in a tone designed to let the woman know he saw no reason for further small talk.

"No," she said, pausing to light a new cigarette, "it's all cash on the barrelhead here for therapy. No checks, neither. Wait, I take that back. We will accept American Express Traveler's Checks. Miz Weaver says they're as good as gold."

"Well, I suppose insurance may not cover massage therapy. I understand that, and I am prepared to pay in cash for this exploratory session."

"Hokay," the woman in the blue smock said, "let me call in Lurleen for you to take a look at, see if you think she'll do the job for you. Wait'll you see her."

She got up from the desk, knocked some ashes off the front of her smock, and walked down a hall to the right. Robard could hear her talking to someone in a room at the end of the hall, though he couldn't make out the words, and the arm attached to his left shoulder seemed to sense something was going on, as well, twitching a bit on its own as Robard looked up at the ceiling to see if a pressed tin covering from the late century might still be in place from the previous life of the venerable B and T of the Cumberland. It was not; instead a dropped ceiling of painted plasterboard hung not five feet above his head. A pity, that, he was thinking as two sets of footsteps came toward him from the hall. All is finally taken. Nothing stays, naught abides, even lovely old pressed tin ceilings.

The receptionist came down the hall first, obscuring Robard Flange's immediate view of the therapist she had called by the name Lurleen, not the usual kind of identifier you'd expect on a health care specialist. The receptionist stepped aside, though, as soon as the two women emerged into the waiting area, and made a gesture of presentation with her right hand, the sort of thing a tuxedo-clad waiter in a restaurant called Justine's or Le Petite Chaise might do when placing the evening's entrée before a diner. "This here's Lurleen," the receptionist said. "Like I said."

The young woman Robard saw was dressed in a plain white outfit that looked somewhat like a uniform; she was wearing flat shoes of a dark color, and her hair reminded Robard of a moment he had experienced before but couldn't immediately identify. The way her hair suggested both abundant flow and a changing pattern of light caused a twitching sensation in the dead arm of Rooney Beauchamp hanging at Robard's side, surprising him enough to cause him to blink and stammer as he said hello to the therapist.

"I didn't hear you say what you wanted to be called, sir," the receptionist said, reaching for the cigarette pack in a pocket of her blue smock, "but I imagine you can tell Lurleen that back in the treatment room, if you need to be named something."

Robard's mind went blank for an instant. He soon cleared his throat, though, and made ready to give his full name, complete with title as he ordinarily did in the course of conducting any matter of business, having learned over the years that the announcement of the title of doctor gained instant attention and respect from tradesmen and functionaries of all stripes. After all, he was that, a doctor, and he was not required to specify that his terminal degree was not in medicine but in literature. His educational attainment was nothing to be shy or overly modest about. It should mean, and it should mean strongly.

When he began to let the therapist called Lurleen learn his name and title, however, Robard Flange was astounded not only to hear himself say, "I am Major Rooney Beauchamp," but to go on to add that he was of Benevolence Plantation in the Delta, currently serving as commanding officer of the Fourth Mississippi.

"Pleased to meet you," the therapist said, nodding and looking at a point a little above and to the right of Robard's head. "You want to come on back with me to the treatment room down the hall?" Then to the receptionist now behind the desk with a cigarette fully fired and smoking, "It's number three, ain't it?" The receptionist looked down at a sheet of paper, nodded, and Robard followed Lurleen down the hall to the second door on the right, his gaze riveted on the way her hair changed from shade to shade of color in the growing dimness of the hall.

"Is this your first time to come to Music City Magic Fingers Massage Salon?" Lurleen asked Robard as she ushered him into the treatment room, which held in the center of its space a bed elevated higher than one for sleeping would ordinarily be. The bed's legs were made of two by fours braced with several thinner pieces of lumber, a slab of plywood as its top surface, and a thin mattress covered by a pink sheet with a hospital tuck at all four corners. A waste basket, a small square table holding some plastic bottles of various sizes filled with different levels of liquid, a box of Kleenex tissues, and a large container of talcum powder made up the rest of the furnishings of treatment room three.

"Yes, it is," Robard said. "I've never had to seek the services of a massage therapist before, either here or elsewhere."

"Well, what are you looking for, Major?" Lurleen said, gesturing toward the treatment table.

"I have what the old folks might call a shortage in one of my arms," Robard said. "It's a matter not exactly of strange sensations in the limb, but of no sensation at all."

"In your arm? Just the one of them?"

She is from East Tennessee, Robard knew, judging from the way she said the words arm and just. She is of the hill folk, of Scotch-Irish yeoman stock, the backbone and core of the common people of our nation. Her ancestors fought for four years alongside each other and under the command of an aristocracy which knew and valued their character, their courage, their undying loyalty. The beauty and strength of their women shone like the glimmer of the sun on the flowing mountain streams of Tennessee and North Alabama and Georgia and the slow tidal rivers of the Deep South. Pure, lasting, glowing, and true.

The arm belonging to Rooney, the one lost at Shiloh on the first day at the peach orchard with the sun yet barely risen above the tree line, twitched with a small tremor. "Yes," Robard said. "Just the one. The one on this side."

"What you want me to do about it, then?" Lurleen said. "Do you want it massaged? Just the arm?"

"Do you think just doing the arm will suffice, Lurleen?"

"I don't know if it will or not," the therapist said, lifting her gaze from Robard's shoulder to look him straight in the face for the first time, her eyes a pale blue ringed by a darker shade about the iris. "You might ought to know more about what it'll take to satisfy you than I do. I could sure start with that and see."

"Please try that then. You know more than I do about massage therapy. I trust your superior insight and experience."

"Well, I tell you what, Major. Why don't you get ready, and I'll go get the stuff I need."

"How do I get ready?" Robard said. "Just get up on the table as in an examination in a physician's office?"

"Take off what you're wearing first. That's the way you start. But before you do that, we got to talk about the treatment fee."

"Oh, certainly. How much does a treatment require? I understand it must be paid in cash."

"That depends on what you want. If it's the full treatment, it'll be fifty dollars, and if it's just one thing or maybe two, it'll be less, depending. But you can always pay me what you think the massage is going to be worth to you. Not no less than fifty, though, for the full treatment. And I need to collect the money before I get down to business."

"I think it will require the full treatment, don't you, Lurleen?"

"That's up to you, Major," Lurleen said. "But I can sure give you that, and I think that'd have the best chance to fix you right up."

"Let's do that, then."

"All right, I'll be back after you take off all your garments. That's all of them, now, unless you want me to pull off your last 'un for you. That'd be extra. And one other thing, I got two ways of working during a full treatment. One is with all my uniform on, this 'un here I'm wearing now, and that's fifty dollars, like I said. The other way is I take off all my uniform, and that's some extra. See, they call that the Bald Uniform here at Music City Magic Fingers, but I think that's kind of an ugly name to give it. Don't you, Major?"

"Oh, yes," Robard said. "I do think it's an unfortunate label."

"It sure ain't bald is what I mean. I have got plenty of hair and I spend lots of time taking care of it. So when I've got my whole uniform off, I am certainly not bald. I mean just look at this big old head of hair I've got, Major, and you'll see why calling it the Bald Uniform bothers me. I may get naked as a jay bird, but I sure ain't getting bald."

"No, never," Robard said. "With that crown of glory. Never. And Lurleen, with the special do you take off your shoes, too?"

"Would you want me to, Major?"

"Oh, no, please leave them on. I don't know why I say that, though."

"Major, people say all kinds of things they don't know why they're saying them. Just lie back and relax and go with the flow, like Wanda Rene is always telling me. She's one of the therapists here, Wanda Rene is. A real little cute brunette girl. Woman I should say, the way she looks in a Bald Uniform. She's from over close to Memphis, Major. Ain't that right near to Mississippi where you come from?"

"You don't need to call me Major, Lurleen," Robard said, finding he was putting a good amount of firm determination in his voice. "I'm Rooney Beauchamp of Benevolence Plantation in Panola County, Mississippi. I'm a true son of the Magnolia State."

"All right, Rooney Beauchamp. Just get all your duds off, and I'll be right back to tend to what's bothering you. And you know what else?"

"No, what?"

"I am going to take off these old flat work shoes I'm wearing now, but I'll put on a pair of heels for you that I got back in my locker. They're just as red as fire, and I think they'll be a lot prettier for me to wear than these old flats when I'm giving you the full treatment with my Bald Uniform on."

"Oh, yes," Robard Flange said, beginning to loosen his tie and unbutton his shirt with his good hand. "Thank you, Lurleen, thank you. Bless you, Child."

The left arm twitched and buzzed, and from somewhere deep in the pale new green of April foliage facing the Fourth Mississippi at Shiloh came the rattle of musketry. See to your arms, Mississippians, Rooney Beauchamp said in a voice of bold brass and a clash of silver. Follow the flag, and cover your uniform with glory.

14

LILY ALDEN HAD ATTEMPTED to ask Lacy Bodean what would be the appropriate attire to wear to a participatory reading of scenes from Shakespeare's *Hamlet* as soon as the invitation had arrived in the mail. She had been looking for the written invitation ever since Lacy had informally made the offer to attend on the night of the Impact Symposium. That offer had been only oral and made outside under a sweet gum tree in the dark with a crowd swarming around, however, and Lily felt like she had to nail things down in detail as soon as the written document arrived. She had considered long and hard whether to inquire in writing to the address printed on the invitation Lacy Bodean had sent, 108 Fox Run, a location deep in Belle Meade, but to do that seemed awkward to Lily, enough so that she finally asked Ronald for his advice on the matter. He had no opinion, but made a smart remark anyway. She had tried to ignore it, but it joined the festering clump of other such sneers and jeers and put-downs Ronald used to dismiss her concerns, adding its weight and virulence to the seething pot.

Lily imagined the collection of remarks Ronald had made over the years to keep her in line, the curt dismissals, the raised eyebrows, the pursed lips, the little snorts and soft whistles of contempt—the whole evil mess simmering away—as being a large black cauldron on a low fire, maintained at just below the boil, the way you would slow-cook a pot of soup made up of root vegetables and greasy pork. No matter how well you tended to it, kept an eye on its progress and tried to add dill and pepper and salt and maybe a little basil to perk it up, it did nothing but grow nastier and less edible the longer it cooked. But there was no way you could get rid of that mess. It was all you had and all you could afford, and it had to be gotten down the best way you could manage it once it was slopped into cracked and dirty bowls and put on the table before you alongside the stained spoon you had to load and lift to your mouth.

What she had done finally to get some indication of how other women would dress for something as arcane and sophisticated as a reading aloud by guests at a party in Belle Meade from a Shakespeare play, all of them witty and sharp and educated and well dressed and getting drunker by the minute, unbothered by such matters as how to stretch an assistant professor's salary to feed three children and one mother and a father who spent most of his time preening and prissing and posing around rich little bitches at Vanderbilt, was to call Lacy Bodean on the telephone and ask her directly.

Lily had told Ronald she was going to pick up the phone and do just that, and he had advised against it instantly. Of course, if she had said instead she was going to write a polite note of inquiry to Lacy Bodean on good stationery, he would have called that stupid and wrong and ignorant. So she found herself calling just at eleven o'clock on a morning exactly six days before the date set in the written invitation from the Bodeans. Deciding on that timing had been exhausting. Any earlier than eleven in the morning might have seemed impertinent to Lacy. Maybe Lacy Bodean lay in bed until ten every day, sleeping off the festivities of the night before. Or perhaps she went to some spa for a physical tune-up every week on the very morning Lily was calling and would consider herself being rushed and bothered by having to answer the phone.

Could a later time in the afternoon be more appropriate, Lily asked herself as she sat in the kitchen with the telephone on the table before her, the Bodean number in the telephone directory underlined in red. Would Lacy Bodean be home at all in the afternoons? Wouldn't it be more likely you could find her at the Belle Meade Country Club having a late lunch, tipsy on white wine, putting a move on the club tennis pro? What would Lacy think if the phone rang and the little wife of an assistant professor of English was on the other end whining about which of her two outfits she ought to wear to an event where no one would notice her at all unless she vomited on the table?

"Fuck it," Lily had said, and dialed the number. Lacy Bodean answered on the third ring, sounding as she always did. Slightly surprised, maybe one sheet to the wind, pausing before responding to any comment made to her as she tried to come up with something witty or at least insulting, on that razor's edge between the Southern states of jolly and vindictive.

"Lacy," Lily said. "This is Lily Alden, and I'm calling to thank you again for the kind invitation to the *Hamlet* night at your place."

"To be or not to be, that is the question. I hope you're going to be, you and that handsome husband. Don't you be calling to tell me you have a prior engagement in Wittenburg and can't come to Denmark."

"Oh, we will be there. We wouldn't miss it. Did you get my note accepting your invitation? I sent it days ago. But the way the mail gets delivered, oh my."

"I bet I did, and made a little mark on a piece of paper as soon as I got it. That way I could forget it completely until I had to remember it again."

"Well, good. I just wanted to ask you about suitable attire for a reading from works by the Bard. I've never attended such an event before, and I want to be certain Ronald doesn't show up in blue jeans."

"Oh, Sugar," Lacy had said, laughing rather loudly to be on the telephone, Lily thought, "I'd say wear as little as possible. Maybe something frilly or filmy or low-cut. Men like that, don't they? But don't worry. With your cute little figure, nobody's going to care what you start off with."

Feeling still uninformed, Lily had talked a bit more about details of the evening to come—should she and Ronald bring their own copy of *Hamlet*? No, there'd be plenty of little old individual copies of a paperback edition which Chambers would pick out for everybody to have. He loves feeling like he's a scholar, poking around a bookstore and sucking on his pipe. Little does he know! Can I bring anything? Nothing but just as much of yourselves as you're willing to share—and she ended up staring at the receiver nestled back in its cradle while she listened to one of the kids piping up at some disaster in a tiny bedroom down a narrow hall. Lily had ended the fact-finding session the way she started it at 11 a.m. six days before the party was set to occur. "Fuck it," she said and gave the telephone the finger.

When she and Ronald arrived at the huge house on Fox Run on the night of the reading party, one they'd driven by many times on the Sunday afternoon jaunts they used to take after arriving in Nashville, thinking newly arrived that this first career step after graduate school would begin their journey to Eden—those drives ended when Julian was born and Ronald began spending Sunday afternoons grading freshman essays instead of looking for signs of promise in the physical environment— Chambers met them at the door, a brownish colored drink in his hand. He was wearing a tuxedo and an overly large top hat and gleaming spats, and Lily noted that he was actually heavily made up with blusher, lip-gloss, and eyeshadow.

"Oh," she said. "I didn't know dress was formal. Look at us."

"Shoot, it's not, honey," Chambers said. "Lacy just made me wear this monkey suit and she made me sit still while I let that cosmetics girl paint me all up. I don't know why Lacy did either thing. I just go along to get along. It's easier that way, I've discovered over the years. Y'all come on in and see who's here. Get you something to drink first before Lacy makes you do it, too."

"Do what?" Ronald said to his wife as they worked their way past Chambers Bodean, now focused on two other couples coming up the stone walkway behind them. "Make us do what?"

"It'll be something fun," Lily said. "And don't say anything snide when we see what it is."

"Calm down," Ronald said, lifting a hand to wave toward someone coming toward them as they moved slowly and more deeply into the reception area of the entry, a room paneled in dark wood with walls covered with portraits of grumpy looking men and of women with pro-nounced underbites and multitudes of pearl necklaces and brooches and lace. "Try to hold it in the road, Lily. We just got here."

"Looky, looky, looky," the woman coming toward them said before Lily had a chance to say something back to Ronald's nasty remark, "here's the intellectuals, the ones that's going to keep us honest about Hamlet and what all everything in that old play means." It was Lacy Bodean, and she carried a glass that matched her husband's in size and color of content. She was stepping high, landing hard, and moving steady as she came near them.

"Not me," Lily said. "I don't know a thing about Shakespeare. I just read a couple of his plays in college when they made me. And that one we had to do in high school about Caesar getting stabbed to death."

"Sugar, that's what we all did," Lacy Bodean said, "but that won't let you off. You can't plead ignorance around here. You do, and you'll be competing with champion dummies. There's not a soul at this party that claims to know a thing about anything. Just the opposite. Nobody but Chambers, that is. He believes for one thing he knows how to run a family business, but it sure ain't him that does it. It's Shirley Anne, his old accountant or secretary or former lover or current lover or something. She's the one that makes the money and puts the bread on the table here in this house."

Lacy paused, took a long look first at Lily, then Ronald, and shook her head. "Lord have mercy," she said. "Forsooth and lackaday, y'all are both just pale as ghosts. And you certainly know there's room for only one ghost in *Hamlet,* not three. Am I right or not, Mr. Scholarship?"

"He opens the play," Ronald said. "The apparition. Sets the stage for all that follows. Was he seen or not? Can you trust your eyes in the royal court of Denmark? Is what appears to be true really true? Can we tell a hawk from a handsaw?"

"When you talk like that," Lacy Bodean said, staggering back dramatically as she spoke, "I just can't stand it. It makes me get all wide-eyed and wet-thighed, I swear. Lily, I can tell exactly now how he gets you in the mood for bedroom sport and why all these little Vandy coeds want to sit at his feet and look up at him with their mouths watering."

"You're very kind and very wrong," Ronald said, not looking at Lily. "Where did you find that drink you're holding there, Lacy? Got any left over?"

"You can start loading up in a minute, but you got to listen to instructions first. You and your little wife here have got to go get in line in the library where Michele is set up with her magical potions and salves and pencils, and let her put some color into your cheeks and on those pale lips. She is the best makeup artist in Nashville, I can tell you. She does Johnny Cash every time he gets ready to go in front of an audience, and one time she even got to put a little color in Bob Dylan's dopey little face. It was like working on a living corpse, she told me."

"I don't think I want to do that," Ronald said. "I've got kind of a skin condition I have to watch."

"Oh, you got to if you're going to look right to read from *Hamlet* tonight. Everybody does. Besides, she uses an old Indian formula that wouldn't irritate the skin on a baby's butt. Get your drinks and go on back in there and let Michele make you up. We got a lot to do. We got to get drunk, eat a bunch of beef and boiled custard and faggots and

I don't know what all from the Shakespeare menu, get into something comfortable, and start reading the parts of *Hamlet* that Chambers has got picked out for us. Don't argue with your hostess, Dr. Alden. Just get with the program."

"Yes, of course we will, Lacy," Lily said, taking a good hold on the sleeve of Ronald's blue blazer, the one her mother had given him last Christmas. "He's just being shy. I want a gin and tonic, and I certainly could benefit from a nice facial."

By the time all potential readers of lines from the play about the melancholy Dane had had their faces painted, their eyebrows plucked, shaped and colored, their bellies filled, their livers assaulted, and the moods of some lightened by funny cigarettes, two hours had passed and the long table in the formal dining room had been cleared of empty glasses, bottles, and flasks, and the ruins of dinner. Lily stood talking to a young man who worked studio sessions on Eighteenth Avenue, did gigs, was now between all kinds of things in his life, as he put it, and was engaged for the night by Chambers Bodean to accompany the readings from *Hamlet* by strumming appropriate notes on his guitar and singing along as the moment and mood demanded.

"How long have you been working professionally in Nashville?" Lily asked him, reminding herself to back off from the drink for a round or two. Weren't you supposed to consume a glass of water for each one of alcohol you drank? A one-to-one ratio, right? If so, she better get started on a gallon jug of the hydration stuff if she was ever to catch up. Aren't his eyes strange, she thought, looking into the troubadour's face as she waited for him to answer her question and carry on his part of the obligatory small talk. They're very small, but intensely green, almost like they were dyed. Can you dye your eyes? How much chemical coloring would it take to get to that shade? Wouldn't it burn to pour that shit into your eye sockets?

"I don't call what I do work," he said after a pause while exchanging a long eyelock with Lily. "Work is what you do to keep the body functioning, isn't it? It's only instrumental, nothing in itself."

"I think anything you get paid to do is work," Lily said. "If you do something that they'll pay you for and that's the only reason you do it, then it's work."

"An economic definition, then. That's the way you see it. Work and life both, I bet."

Lily nodded, breaking her lock with the green eyeballs and looking toward the table for water. She didn't see any, so she took another slug of white wine. Where was Ronald, she wondered. Her husband was really kind of cute with lipstick and dark eyeshadow. Maybe a browner shade would suit his skin coloring more, though. Why did Michele choose the black family of color instead of the warmer browns for Ronald? Lily knew she wouldn't have made that choice. But who was she to quarrel with a woman who made up Johnny Cash and Kris Kristofferson before they went out on stage to sing about suffering and being dispossessed and in despair? Those two men always looked exactly the right shades in the face. The darkness of pain racked them, and their complexions showed it.

"I don't think of what I do," the troubadour was saying, a patch of his chest hair poking through the opening of his medieval-themed and be-stringed shirt, which looked to be better suited for a woman than a man. It works for him, though, Lily decided. "If I think, I'm splitting myself into separate parts," he added. "I want to be one thing always, and that's what my music lets me be."

"How does that work? How could you not think all the time?"

"It doesn't work all the time," the troubadour said. "But that's a goal, see, and without that goal, I'd be permanently shattered into pieces. Just split into parts and not whole."

"Aren't you thinking right now while you're talking? Doesn't that mean you're separated into parts, like you said you don't ever want to be?"

"True," the troubadour admitted. "But there is an upside to division. Right now, while I'm standing here, I'm thinking, and so I'm split into two minds, but one of them is saying what I'm saying now, here talking to you, and the other one's wondering what it'd feel like to stick my face and tongue between your breasts, close my eyes, and lose the world completely to that feeling."

"I need some water, I think," Lily said, lifting her hands to her neckline, which felt suddenly to be binding her throat, too small somehow for her blouse. "Real bad. I've got to find some water. What is your name, anyway?"

"I'm Tollman," the troubadour said. "I keep count. The days, the hours, the minutes, the measures of desire. Please forgive me for giving voice to what I was thinking."

"I guess you can't help what you think," Lily said. "Or what you don't think, either."

By the time Lily got back from finding a glass, filling it with water, drinking it, and trying to remember exactly what the troubadour had said about her breasts and his tongue, someone else was talking to Tollman Briggs, standing back from him at a distance as she looked up into his hatchet-shaped face framed by that tangle of dark hair matching in color the patch protruding from his open shirt. It was Brenda Gwaltney, the wife of George Gwaltney, an assistant professor of English with no more seniority or clout than Ronald. Nothing but an equal. Not only did Brenda not outrank Lily in that respect, she was a tiny dishwater blonde with no more going for her than an ability to look bewildered and dazzled by any man she talked to. Lots of men liked that, though, Lily knew, but she'd had enough wine to let her decide to send Brenda Gwaltney packing if she had to.

Look at her, peering up at this Tollman person with his shirt all unbuttoned and tie strings dangling, Brenda with her head thrown back and her mouth hanging open as though she'd just seen a solar event and was afraid the sun was about to explode. How can men be taken in by that little act? Maybe it was some instinctual ape-man response they all have when they see some gap on a woman's body opened up, whether it's her labia or her tonsils. All they see is a hole that they figure needs something stuck in it.

"Brenda," Lily said. "I swear I hadn't seen you until this minute. Have you and George been here along? How have I missed you? Where's your husband?" Lily made an exaggerated sweep of her head from side to side as though to seek out the puffy little figure of George Gwaltney, effectively shifting the attention of the troubadour from Brenda's popped mouth and glistening uvula to herself. "How much have I drunk already not to've even noticed you yet?"

"Oh, hi, Lily," Brenda said, returning her mouth to the usual firm little bow she presented when talking to another woman. "We got here late. Sitter problems."

"Isn't that always the case? I just wonder sometimes how it can be that mine and Ronald's entire connection with a social life and other people has got to depend on a bunch of teenage girls and little old ladies willing to watch our kids for a few hours every so often. I swear we are being held hostage on a daily basis by a bunch of high school dropouts, young and old."

The troubadour was backing away, Lily could see as she jabbered at Brenda Gwaltney, about to make his escape from two women communicating with each other, a scene most men enjoyed seeing about as much as they'd like watching a set of two-year-old twins for four hours. Gay men loved that, though, taking part in a conversation with two women, or even more women than that, getting just as girlish as the ones they were talking to. Why was that, Lily wondered as she watched the troubadour slide quietly away and begin to strum on the guitar he had slung about his neck, breaking into a little song as he turned tail and ran.

Why do gay men love to talk to women in groups? They're not women themselves exactly, she thought, promising herself she'd consider the topic more deeply at a later time when she wasn't feeling a bit woozy from wine. It seemed to be an interesting question at the moment, but maybe that was because she was on the edge of being almost, just about, a step or two away from, just teetering there, drunk. But nothing's very interesting when you're sober, after all, Lily knew, certainly not where she was now located in her life and in Nashville. But the troubadour had said, she reminded herself, he wondered how it would feel to have his face and tongue between her breasts.

Jesus, Lily said to herself, what a little tingle in my waterworks when I heard him say that. He just came flat out and told me. God!

"Hey, hey," Chambers Bodean was saying as he stood in the middle of the room and beat with a tiny hammer on a small ornate bronze gong, Chinese in origin and tuned to a melodious note, "all you literature lovers. All you fans of the Bard of Avon. We have got to get started with *Hamlet* if we're going to make any headway at all tonight. Now, my lovely wife, my beau ideal of the female species, informs me that as late as it is, we are going to have to forego the one by one removal of articles of clothing and go directly to full revelation."

"Oh, no," Margot Hardesty cried out, "I always like the gradual thing. The slow removal. One thing at the time. It's more titillating, I always think."

"You would," Harding Brockwood quipped. "Everybody knows you got what it takes to be titillating, Margot. Hell, you got two of what it takes."

"You hush, Harding," Margot said as all the veterans of Shakespeare Night at the Bodeans chortled and hooted, "You make it so easy to tell you're a UT graduate. And an old ATO."

"What are they talking about?" someone was saying in Lily's ear. Ronald, of course, who'd walked up as Chambers was beating his Chinese gong. "Is this actually going to be a strip show? Is that what he just said?"

"Just listen," Lily said. "Let's hear the rest of what Chambers has got to say."

"I've heard enough. You ready to go? I am. I'll let Lacy know we have schedule problems with the sitter. They can't take offense at that."

"I said to wait," Lily said in a muted but burning tone. "It could be fun."

"I don't want anyone but me to see you nude," Ronald said. "This is not our scene."

"Nice try, Ronald. But you don't want to see me nude," Lily said. "Not anymore you don't. That argument's not going to cut it, big boy."

"Big boy? How drunk are you?"

"Drunk enough to tell the truth. And I don't mind letting these people see my tits. They're still really nice ones."

"What? What're you saying?"

"Somebody's already told me tonight how he wanted to put his face between them, and I could tell he meant it in the nicest kind of way. If you don't want to take off your shirt and pants, why don't you just go home? You can relieve that baby sitter you're so worried about. I can find somebody around to give me a ride."

Chambers Bodean was pointing out directions for the ladies to take to find a private place to disrobe, knowing from past experience that anytime more than one woman is involved in removing clothing before a man, she will want to do it only as a member of a group in privacy as the process of discovery takes place. "Now you fellows, the ones of you not scared to let people see you with your girdle off, y'all go back in the study and get natural. It's all kinds of hangers and hooks in yonder to put your stuff on. Lacy will show the ladies where they can do their thing."

"Y'all got any shoe horns in this house, Chambers?" Townsend Northling asked. "I wore nice slippers tonight." That gave folks a chance for a big laugh, which everybody took, and people began to scatter for their designated staging areas.

Ronald Alden headed for the kitchen, thinking the best thing to do at this point is to fortify my drink and decide what to do. If I leave Lily here, there is no telling what the crazy bitch will end up doing, and depending on that, how the whole thing will play out between us now and later. Why is she so bound and determined to be insane? The new medication Dr. Strohmeyer prescribed was supposed to be a long step up from the one she's been on that's not really working, the new one a downer strong enough to stun a mule. She should be walking around daily in a fog, hardly able to do more than feed the kids and make up the beds in the morning. Instead she's babbling about her tits and what some drunk asshole with a Belle Meade address has said about what he wants to do to them.

Maybe, Ronald thought as he stood in a kitchen filled with silver pans and utensils and ranges and refrigerators and running water and black women working away at cleanup, and as he poured into his glass a good sized glug of expensive Scotch, a brand he'd never seen before and therefore undoubtedly worth drinking for the taste as well as the kick, maybe I should fuck her more often, but damn it's hard to do when she's so sour and crazy and zombified. When she shows some signs of normal human response, it's always in the form of bitchiness toward me. The only time she notices me is when she's lively enough to be pissed off and resentful. When we do fuck, she lies there like a stone. What have I done to deserve that kind of treatment?

What to do now? I can't physically drag her out of Lacy and Chambers Bodean's nude Shakespeare party, her with her tits on display while she screams bloody murder at me. I can't leave her while I go home and sulk. She'll end up in bed with some golf-playing, investment-overseeing, middle-aged fraternity boy in Belle Meade, and it'll be public knowledge, which means I'll have to do something about it and about her. And what would that be? Ronald drained the glass of Scotch, looked again at the name on the bottle he'd brought back into the kitchen with him, Famous Grouse, wondered briefly how a grouse could become renowned, and poured himself another shot, a lot bigger one this time.

Hell, he said as he took the first drink from that one. I'll just take off my shirt and join the rest of them at the big table. That way I can keep an eye on the crazy woman I'm married to, and nobody will notice I'm not really nude. It's only an excuse for the men to look at tits and ass and for women with a good endowment of those commodities to show them off to somebody other than their husbands without having to actually go to bed with them. That way it's not adultery with all the baggage that goes along with that. It's just Nashville.

Finishing his second glass of Famous Grouse, Ronald Alden began loosening his tie and unbuttoning his shirt, unfastening his belt to pull his shirt tail out, and unzipping his trousers part way down to make the job of de-shirting easier.

"Mister," someone said, one of the black women, the older of the two at work, "you can't get naked in here in the kitchen. This here's where we got to do our job. You got to go with the other white mens in the study if you fixing to take your clothes off."

"I'm sorry," Ronald said. "I'm not really taking all my clothes off, just my shirt, but I should've thought where I was. Is the study down the hall?"

"Yessir," the woman said, putting the silver ladle she was holding on the table, not looking up at Ronald. "That's where the mens always get naked. You can hear them in there having theyselves a good old time."

Ronald put down his glass, kept the bottle, and left the kitchen, fumbling with the buckle of his belt as he went down the hall toward the location of the hoots and hollers coming from a farther room. The younger black woman looked up from one of the sinks in the kitchen toward the woman who'd talked to the white man taking his shirt off and pulling the zipper down on his pants.

"You didn't want to see that man take his shirt off, huh, Miz Joleen? He sure is made up pretty in the face, idn't he? All that lipstick and rouge."

"I don't need to see that kind of foolishness, no," the older woman said.

"Did you use to?" the young woman said and chuckled. "Some time back?"

"I don't remember if I ever did, and if I did remember, I'd try to forget it. That old stuff ain't got no good in it."

"I don't like that kind of behaving yourself because I'm a Christian," the young woman said. "Get thee behind me, Satan."

"Christian or not ain't got nothing to do with a man taking his pants down," Joleen said. "That don't figure in it. I done learned that a long time ago. Look out now. That pan you fixing to put up ain't about to be clean. Wash that thing again, girl."

"All right, I'm just hurrying 'cause it's so hot in this old kitchen."

"That ain't no excuse. It's hot everywhere in Nashville, and it's getting hotter. All you can do about the heat in the Nashville is keep your head down and stick to your business."

Ronald drove exactly at the speed limit on the way home, observing all traffic regulations, even though the sitter had complained openly when he'd had to call her to say he and his wife would be getting back a little later from Shakespeare Night at the Bodeans than they'd thought. She had said she wouldn't be able to sit again for the Aldens, as late as she'd be getting home tonight. Her parents wouldn't let her, she just knew. Did he realize it was three in the morning? She had school to go to.

Careful, careful, Ronald told himself sternly. He knew if he was stopped by a police car on West End Avenue or Natchez Trace or any side street for any infraction, small or large, he'd never be able to convince an officer he wasn't guilty of driving under the influence. Influence, my ass, Ronald thought as he carefully shepherded the Chevrolet toward the hell waiting for him in the brick rent house on Graystone Lane. Why not call knee-walking drunk by its right label and be done with it? A rose by any other name and all that Shakespeare horseshit. It would stink as bad.

Lily sat beside him in the passenger seat, leaning back with her arms crossed as she hummed the tune to "Greensleeves" or "Hey Nonny, Nonny" or some other Renaissance tune the long-haired guitarist had sung as background accompaniment to the literary night at the home of Lacy and Chambers Bodean. She hadn't said a word to him after Ronald had finally got her in the car after the long process of pulling her away from the long table around which the naked and semi-naked guests had read lines from *Hamlet*, swigged away at tumblers of wine, liquor, and ale, and leered at the hundredweights of bare flesh there on display, tight and loose, firm and sagging, commodious and spare, wrinkled and smooth, behaired and shaven, lost and found.

Most of the women hadn't removed their panties, leaving something to the imaginations of their fellow lovers of the Bard, and not one man had bared his genitals for all to see, fearing his little soldier would have withdrawn so deeply into hiding that any bragging rights would have been forfeit, anyway. No straight man wants to show his dick in pub-lic for fear of not measuring up, Ronald knew. Ronald's wife, though, had joined with Lacy Bodean and one other woman in baring all, Lily retaining only her earrings and her necklace which lay brightly moving up and down with her breathing and just touching the edge of her nip-ples when she leaned forward to follow along in her copy of the Signet edition of *Hamlet* provided by the host as people took turns reading selected passages. She had reminded her husband of one of his students pretending to be interested in some dull text, eyes fixed on the distance and mind focused God knew where.

"Did you get your fill of showing your tits to one and all?" Ronald said, finally breaking the silence, holding his speed just at the limit and not under, that being a sure tipoff to police that the driver of a suspect vehicle was trying too hard to appear really sober. If you looked like you were conscious of not driving too fast and of the need to be responsible, that was a violation of protocol in itself, punishable by fine and forfeiture, like every damn thing else in life. Be careful, but not that careful.

Let's see how she responds to that question about the tit show, Ronald thought, riding along with her clothes back on as satisfied and happy as if she hadn't made a display of herself, hadn't made her husband a laughing stock, hadn't made it certain that he'd now be known as the Vanderbilt assistant professor of English married to the confirmed crazy woman. Does she even realize the damage she's done to me?

"Ronnie, baby," Lily said in a fake husky voice, "I haven't seen you look at my tits like that for years. I could've almost believed you were thinking I was sexy again." She turned her head and gave her husband a droop-eyed look, obviously fake, cackled a couple of times, and went on, "But then when I saw you looking at Brenda Gwaltney like you wanted to lick her poor little nipples, I knew you weren't seeing me at all. It was all just tits to you."

"I never even noticed that Brenda had her clothes off, if she did. There was nothing erotic about that whole scene. If I'd been a woman there, I would have felt demeaned by the whole pitiful display."

"Listen to the feminist, would you? I bet your little dick was hard as a rock under that table when you were thinking about getting in Brenda Gwaltney's panties."

"You're drunk," Ronald said, straining to see far enough ahead on West End to detect where the turn would come to head him home. Come on, damn it, get here, house, move. "You're talking nonsense."

"Oh, you're not bothered by nonsense," Lily said. "What scares you is the truth, and that's what all those bare tits and hairy triangles showed you tonight. Let me tell you something else. This was one of the best experiences I've had since we came to Nashville. I take that back. It was the single best experience I've had. I learned all kinds of things tonight.

And I learned it by taking off my dress and my bra and my panties and letting anybody that wanted to look at me do just that."

"They looked at you, all right. If that's what you were after. You are so fucking shallow, Lily. You just skim along the surface of reality. You have no idea why they were looking at you, women and men both. You don't understand implications."

"I understand all kinds of things, Sonny. When I heard what Ophelia said in the play when she was floating in that water before she drowned, I knew exactly what she meant. She was talking to me as I sat there naked, and I listened to what she was telling me, and I knew it was the truth. And I was able to hear it and understand what it meant to me because I wasn't wearing anything between me and the truth."

"That bit about Ophelia, the report of her death, that was read so poorly by George Gwaltney I wondered if he'd ever even dipped into *Hamlet* before. Jesus, his reading was awful. That drunk old woman, the one with her breasts hanging down to her waist, she read her part with so much more understanding than George did. Did you hear how he butchered the meter?"

"You are truly the crazy one, aren't you, Ronald?" Lily said. "You don't see anything but the forest and the trees."

"You can't even get your clichés right, Lily. It goes like this. You can't see the forest for the trees. See, what that means is . . . "

Lily didn't let Ronald finish the explanation. "Bullshit, bullshit, bullshit," she said. "Let's get home and get that sitter out of the house. I need a good fucking, and I need it right now. I'll even let you do it, asshole. Make like I'm Brenda, and maybe you can fool yourself enough to get your little prick up for me."

PART TWO
BLAZE

15

"HUSH, BIRDIES," Emily said out loud as she sat watching Miss Nancy on *Romper Room*. Miss Nancy was showing the children how to put on their romper stompers, and lots of them were doing it wrong, some because they were too little to follow directions and some because they weren't listening to what Miss Nancy was telling them. The rubber bands that were supposed to hold the plastic cups to their feet were not easy to put on and handle, Emily knew, since she'd asked Daddy last year when she was little to make her some romper stompers like the ones Miss Nancy showed on TV, and she'd found out it was hard to stretch the rubber bands enough to get them around her feet. They kept slipping off and sometimes even snapping against her fingers and making them sting enough she had to put her hand in her mouth to stop it from hurting.

"Birdies," Emily said again, looking away from the TV set and what Miss Nancy was having to do with one of the children, a little girl who'd just had the rubber band hurt her hand the same way the one on Emily's romper stomper had done when she was five. The little girl was making herself very troublesome, Emily knew. "Birdies," she said in a voice that was not trying to be funny, "I can't hear what Miss Nancy is saying to the little girl about being brave and big. You make too much noise, birdies. Stop all that racket."

The birds outside wouldn't stop singing to each other, though, and Emily didn't expect them to hush. They never would listen to her or to daddy. They did their singing every morning when it stopped being cold weather in Nashville and when the flowers started coming back to the yard and the leaves turned green. April showers bring May flowers. That's what a baby sitter had told Emily yesterday. Emily had to let the birds know when they were being too loud, though, just like Daddy had to do when Julian or Dylan started crying in the morning because they wanted something to eat or they wanted out of bed or they didn't like the way that their nasty old diapers felt when they'd messed in them. If you didn't tell the birds they ought to hush their racket while Mommy was trying to sleep, they'd probably be even louder than they were already. At least, quiet down a little, like Daddy would say to Dylan and Julian and even to Emily sometimes, though she was the big sister and knew how to act a lot better than her little brothers did.

"Birds," Emily said again, stopping to take a bite of her Pop-Tart which was now cool enough to put in her mouth after she'd made it get too hot in the toaster, "another thing you better listen to me about. Rum Tum can't hear what Miss Nancy is saying, either, and he just told me that. You don't want him to come out there and get you, do you?"

The Pop-Tart was blueberry, Emily could tell, not the kind she liked best, chocolate, but the picture on the package had showed the insides of the Pop-Tart to be brown like chocolate. "Old package," Emily said, slapping at the package on the sofa beside her, "you old story teller," her voice rising now, making Rum Tum look over at her from where he was sitting on the floor next to the TV set. He didn't look happy again, and he hadn't looked happy for a long time. Emily couldn't remember the last time when Rum Tum had wanted to play a fun game. Now he just got mad most of the time, and he told Emily why and what he was going to do about everything that wasn't nice and fun any more. It was getting a lot harder to make Rum Tum be quiet and not do what he said he wanted to. What a bastard worry and a nagging pain, Emily said to herself, just the way Mommy said it when she was talking to Daddy when he got home from Vanderbilt before time for supper everyday.

"Rum Tum," Emily said to the little man on the floor, dressed this morning in red pants and a black shirt and his really big boots, the black ones with the sharp silver points on their toes. They would cut anybody they touched and make the blood come out. He'd told Emily that before, lots of times. "I was just telling the Pop-Tart package it shouldn't lie to me about what tastes are inside of it. It showed chocolate, but when I bit it, look what it was." She held the Pop-Tart with one bite taken out of it up for Rum Tum to see. He nodded and made his mad growling sound and looked back at Miss Nancy and the romper room boys and girls. All of them had their romper stompers fastened to their shoes with the rubber bands now, and they were marching around the TV picture in a circle following Miss Nancy. She was singing the romper stomper song, and the boys and girls who were old enough to know how to sing it were trying to keep up with Miss Nancy. "Stomp your feet," she was singing. "Stomp your feet. It's real neat. Keep the beat. Clap your hands. All fall down. Roll on the ground. Make some sound."

When Miss Nancy said all fall down, all of the boys and girls but two fell down, and they began rolling on the ground like the song said to do, and they yelled and laughed and made some sounds like the song said to do. Emily jumped up, dropped her Pop-Tart, and fell down on the floor like the boys and girls on *Romper Room* and began yelling and laughing along with the ones on TV. Miss Nancy didn't fall down, since she was a big lady and big ladies don't lie down on the floor and roll around and yell, but Miss Nancy kept singing really loud, clapping her hands and opening her mouth so wide that the TV got close to her mouth to show how big her tongue and teeth were. It was black inside her head except where her teeth were white and sharp.

That's when Mommy started yelling from her room where she and Daddy slept in their bed. "For God's sake, shut up that racket, Emily. Please, please hush for Mommy. Where's your daddy?"

Emily stopped yelling for a while, but she kept rolling and she felt the Pop-Tart she'd dropped on the floor squishing under her back as she rolled over it. It felt soft and crumbly and funny, so she did it again, this time looking at Rum Tum to see if he saw what she was doing. He couldn't hear the TV set with Mommy yelling from the bedroom, so he was mad again. "Yell," he told Emily. "Clap your hands. Make some sound. Roll around." He showed her how big his teeth were, and he snapped them together hard like the alligators did on TV when they were eating baby ducks. Emily did what Rum Tum said, and he liked that and looked back at what Miss Nancy was doing on *Romper Room* on the TV set. Some boys and girls were looking sad, the ones who hadn't rolled around and yelled when the romper stomper song said to do that, and Emily didn't want to be sad. She didn't want Rum Tum to be mad, either, because he stayed that way so much now. She didn't want to be mad. She didn't want to be sad. She wanted the birdies to hush, and she wanted to do what Miss Nancy and the romper stomper song said to do. She rolled, she yelled, she made some sound.

Ronald Alden could see well before he got to Rand Terrace that the Rat was in business again. He actually had some action this morning, as early as it was, judging from the number of people gathered at his card table. It even looked like the rain might start up any minute now that the first of April had arrived, but something interesting enough was going on with the Rat to cause a few folks to pause before going into the student union to check mail, drink coffee, smoke cigarettes, and study each other for signs of weakness and possibility.

"Complete and total ratification," Greg Donaldson was saying as he stood behind his card table in costume, still complete this new spring but worn enough by hard use to be more pilled fiber than gray cloth. The head was still in the best shape of all, being made of durable rubber for the most part, but the feet had suffered more losses since the last time Ronald had seen them just before the Impact Symposium a year ago. Toes were gone from both sets of claws now, and when Greg happened to take a step the top of the feet moved immediately, but the soles flapped free and had to catch up.

"All will be ratified," the Rat said, his whiskers twitching as he talked, "get your copy of the new issue of *Cook's Night Out,* and learn the truth about the Vanderbilt underworld, the entire system of tunnels, avenues, connectors, and rat holes which cocoon the very ground on which we stand and scurry about."

"You talking about sewers, Rat?" a student in farmer overalls asked, a fraternity type Ronald recognized from his enrollment in the sopho-more survey class of a year ago when the young man had dressed in the standard uniform of a Deke. Now his overalls looked to have been sub-jected to judicious stylistic attack by bleach, beer can openers, scissors, and paint splatter. The boy's found Bob Dylan and gone counterculture, Ronald figured, and he's got the clothes to show it, just like he's done all his life, whatever dress is called for.

"In a metaphorical sense, my friend, the Rat's mind is always on and in sewers," the Rat said. "Get your exposé of Vandy Underground. Who's doing who and with what. Men and women, boys and girls, mammals and reptiles, who's on top and who's on bottom, and who likes where he's positioned and who wants to move. Instruments of flesh, tools of machine parts, shiny and new, used and rusty, able and disabled, the old in-out, in-out. Ever the same."

Ronald felt a chill settle in his bones, warm as it was on the first day of April in Nashville, and began to work his way toward the table covered with copies of *Cook's Night Out,* these beginning to go fast as the Rat rapped on about what this year's edition contained. What was the little shit doing this time, Ronald wondered. Has he turned from drawing Art Crumb-like pictures of naked women being slobbered over by a hot and bothered Colonel Sanders, hands filled with chicken legs and jewels as he begs the favor of overweight harem queens, to spreading libelous gossip about members of the Vanderbilt community? Who is Greg trying to nail this year? Surely only fraternity and sorority types, the usual targets of the excluded and marginal and twisted intellectual fringe dweller at any university. That's who he hates and envies and wants to be and never will be, the insiders, the ones who belong where they find themselves and never have to think about it. Maybe he's taking a shot or two at a generalized administration, but certainly not faculty. He wouldn't go after faculty. Not individual faculty. Not assistant professors of English. Not me.

Does this little bastard know I've been fucking Josephine Longineaux for months? If so, how did he find out? Who else knows? Who told him? Has he used my name in *Cook's Night Out?* Or some variant any fool can see through and figure out?

"Dr. Alden," Greg Donaldson said, holding out a copy of his magazine as he saw Ronald coming toward the table in fits and starts, "Here's you a copy of *Cook's Night Out,* hot and clammy from the hand of the Rat. Your assignment: read this squeal and write a two-page critique. The Rat craves commentary on his effusions."

At that, students and staff in the bunch still at the table, beginning to diminish in number as they picked up their copies of the Rat's magazine and moved off, tittered a bit at the Rat's thrust at the professor. "You going to grade Dr. Alden's paper, Rat?" one of them asked, a kid Ronald didn't recognize, knowing by that he'd probably had the student in class some time back and erased all memory of the relationship in the interest of maintaining room in his brain for the next crop coming through.

An unwatered plant of some ordinary variety, probably, resentful at not getting what it perceived to be its rightful share of attention and nourishment. "It won't be any better than a C plus, no matter how hard he worked on it," the former dandelion said.

"That's right," another voice piped up. "Nor which one of the fraternity files Dr. Alden copied it from. The Rat's onto that ploy."

"Have pity on an old worn-out professor," Ronald offered in a jovial tone, hoping to dull the edge of the verbal attack before somebody actually called him a name he wouldn't be able to ignore or laugh at. Play along, be the fool enough to a degree that you'll be able to walk into Rand without it appearing you're on the edge of a dead run. "I promise I'll make my paper better in revision, Mr. Rat. It was late when I wrote it, and I've been sick and under pressure in my real courses. And besides my grandmother just died, and we were real close, especially after my parents were killed in a plane crash in Peru."

It worked. Everybody in hearing range of what the professor had said guffawed, a couple even let out faint cheers, and in a minute or two, only Ronald and the Rat were left at the table, on which only a few copies of *Cook's Night Out* were left scattered. "What's the theme this year, Greg?" Ronald said, looking at the cover drawing, an involved map of a sewer system, filled with four-legged vermin with human heads popping up from all the manhole covers, four-color and detailed and caricatured.

"It's the old stand-bys, Dr. Alden," the Rat said. "Corruption in high and low places, expressing itself in the usual manner. Absolute power, absolute corruption. Bribes and special favors, sexual shenanigans, the old preying on the young, the young resorting to blackmail, the authorities shocked, shocked. A lot of head being given and a lot of heads rolling. What's nude in Gotham? That's the theme."

"Does the Rat name names?" Ronald said, thinking instantly why did I say that and then realizing an instant later that the comment was perfect for the occasion. The innocent man does not fear looking guilty. The guilty man fears looking, period.

"Never name names, the Rat says. Names will pop up on their own. All is known all the time. All will be revealed. Only the unknown is new, and that will not last. To judge is to forgive. The Rat reveals what is known but unforgiven."

"Have you been taking courses in Eastern religions again, Greg?" Ronald said, wanting to open to the first page of *Cook's Night Out,* but fearing it as though it were a letter to him from the *New Yorker* with his name typed as addressee. It looks to be individually tailored to him, it could be a letter accepting his essay on crucial trends in contemporary fiction for publication, but in his heart he knows it contains only a form rejection. As long as it's never opened, though, you'll never feel the finality of rejection. But until you do, you'll never live anywhere but in dread.

"Does the Rat sound Zen-like, Dr. Alden? Huh, huh? Is that what you're saying?"

"A little, maybe. Gnomic, certainly."

"Don't you worry, then, Dr. Alden. I didn't use your real name."

Laugh, damn you, Ronald said to himself in a directive as stern as a sudden massive blood loss, look amused, you piece of shit, stare the Rat in the eye. He did that, chuckling like a kindly academic adviser, rolling his copy of *Cook's Night Out* into a cylinder and heading for the door into the snack bar of Rand, not forgetting to raise a hand in casual farewell to his old student, the Rat, and steeling himself for what he knew he'd see once inside the building.

There she would be, as she was every Tuesday and Thursday after her modern European art history class was dismissed, sitting at a table with three or four of her Kappa Delta sorority sisters, smoking a cigarette, drinking hot chocolate, and surreptitiously watching the door for the entrance of her old teacher in a sophomore survey of English lit. They had agreed on arranging that sole semiweekly sight of each other, pledging no other encounters on campus except those happening by mere chance, careful never to reveal any hint of their attachment.

Ronald had come to live for those sightings, the fact that a woman of her age and beauty of flesh and status of social background and promise of an easeful future to come, not only would allow him access to her body but would present herself to him in public, hidden in plain view, to demonstrate to him what she felt during those other moments together in darkness and seclusion and delight. Those Tuesday and Thursday acknowledgments in privacy yet simultaneously in public were as thrilling to Ronald Alden as Fanny Brawne's mailed lock of hair must have been to John Keats. Meaningfulness at a distance, sweeter far than the actual contact of flesh itself.

All that relishment was richly true before he'd seen the Rat at work this morning in April, the first of the month, the sole day of the year designated for and dedicated to fools. To enter the snack bar of Rand with a copy of *Cook's Night Out*, ticking in his hand like a grenade with the pin pulled and lost and irreplaceable, felt to Ronald Alden this April Fools' Day like an entrance into the mouth of Hell itself. And not, Ronald said to himself as he stepped through the door, not the Hell of the Jewish faith, a kind of nothingness, or of the Roman Catholic one you could buy your way out of, or the existential one of Jean-Paul Sartre, that perdition of other people, but the real hell he'd been raised with, that of fundamentalist Protestantism. Fire, literal and burning forever, consuming for eternity, but never exhausting the sinner's capacity to sizzle, fry, and suffer.

"Dr. Alden," someone said in an obviously mocking and unctuous tone, and Ronald looked toward the table where he knew he'd see George Gwaltney sitting with coffee, a cigarette, and a stack of ungraded papers fastened together by a rubber band, a packet of pain as loomingly ominous as a tumor diagnosed malignant. "Please join me, learned sir, if you would so condescend." Looking at George Gwaltney meant Ronald could postpone scanning the territory to catch the first glimpse of Josephine, Josey, Joey, Jo Jo, JoBear, J Sweet, all the diminutives of endearment possible in her name. He knew them all, and invented new ones before each time they met. She let him tell her all the labels of lust and love he could come up with, amused as he gabbled his latest offerings into her ear. Jesus, get hold of yourself, he barked to himself. Straighten up.

"Got some papers you haven't gotten around to grading yet, I see," he said to Gwaltney. "Carrying them around like a leper with his bell. Unclean, unclean, clear the street for sorrow."

"These old things?" George said, hitching in his chair. "No, I've carried them around so long they're like a good luck charm to me. I don't know what I'd do without them, I swear."

"I know the feeling," Ronald said, making a production of looking at his watch, then around as though to find a wall clock to let him know how long he had to drink coffee and shoot the shit with George Gwaltney before leaving for his next appointment, two office hours in Old Central.

"Don't strain your neck so hard, Ron," George said. "You'll pop a vertebrae or something. She's right over there, three tables over, close to the window, with a whole gaggle of them surrounding her like an inferior setting for a gem of purest ray serene."

"Ain't you the literary man, though?" Ronald said. "And just who are you talking about?"

"Oh, Ronald, oh, Dr. Alden, how can you be so cruel and cold? There in the midst of a bunch of much lesser lights sits the finest looking little scoop of vanilla pussy to be seen at Vanderbilt. You know who I'm talking about."

"Oh, yeah, your flirtation with child molestation, I see where you're coming from. Miss Longineaux, I presume you mean."

"Don't look over there at her, Ronald," George Gwaltney said. "She's looking right at us, and that girl next to her just said something that made her laugh. No, take that back, smile. I don't think she knows how to laugh. She's so fucking good looking she's never had to learn to laugh at anything anybody's ever said to her since she hit puberty."

"Interesting theory. You're saying that physically attractive women don't have to laugh, huh? Laughter is simply an attempt by lesser persons to ingratiate themselves with those they perceive to be greater in some way." Not a bad comment to come up with on the fly, Ronald congratulated himself. That ought to change the subject and steer George away from what he knows makes me uncomfortable. He doesn't know why yet, the little bastard, but he senses what the Rat does. All is known, just not ripe for acknowledgment yet.

"Yeah, what you say is cute, but how do you account for Henry Fielding, then?" George said, and with that Ronald knew he could relax for now as far as George Gwaltney's supposings and wonderings and conjecturings about his interest in Josephine Longineaux were concerned. Safe waters, academic maundering taking place, nothing real to feel threatened about. And you know what else, Ronald thought, I could take what I just said, my insight about the source of laughter, and turn it into an article. Maybe focus on some contemporary novelist, say Roth or Heller. Maybe not, though. I don't know. It'd be a lot of work. I'd have to read what theorists say on the laugh impulse, and it's probably all in French. Shit.

Three tables over, at the one surrounded by four KDs between classes and before lunch and after two pre-dawn hours of careful and painstaking bathing and the applying of makeup and the arranging of hair and the choosing and donning of appropriate dress, Claire Hammond had just said something telling to Josephine Longineaux that Amy Newstead and

Stormy Meredith had appreciated enough to laugh out loud at. Stormy had to set her coffee cup down and check in a tiny mirror inside her bag to be sure she hadn't dripped something where it didn't belong when she'd burst out at what Claire'd said.

"There's your boyfriend," Claire had said, those words not the funny ones, but the next part of what Claire said was. "He looks kind of haggard."

"Well," Josephine said, after everybody had quieted down a little, "he has good reason to. Too much exercise late at night will completely tire an older man out."

That everybody really laughed at, all but Josephine, just smiling because she was the one that had said it, and she was way too cool to have to laugh at something witty she had come up with so that the ones listening would join in and help her out. Josephine Longineaux didn't need help from anybody, ever, and in no way, no matter how much she claimed to be like every other girl at Vandy. "I can't get dates when I want them, all the time," she'd once said famously. "With the right ones, somebody I want to be with, I mean. I just have to settle for the ones that want to be with me, like every other girl, and that is so boring. I just hate to be around somebody who's grateful, don't you? I want to be the grateful one, not the guy. Right?"

This morning in Rand, at the prime morning hour to see and be seen, all three of Josephine's KD sisters remembered that little plea she'd made to be seen as just like them and like most of the rest of the women at Vanderbilt, and they all remembered how it had made them feel when they'd heard it, whether first-hand by being there when Josephine had said it or hearing about it later when the news about it got around. Conflicted. That's the word that captures the response best. That's what Tanzie Blanchard had said to a bunch of girls one night late, all of them a little tipsy and some drunk as skunks, sitting around dateless in somebody's room together in the KD house.

"I really think two things at once," Tanzie had said, "when I think about what Josephine said about men problems. I say to myself she is so nice to feel that way for the rest of us so that she had to claim she's in the same fix. That is sweet and so thoughtful. And then that other little voice in my head that's always saying it's looking out for me first and nobody else, it pipes up and speaks. And you know what it says?"

"No," several girls all said together. "What?"

"That little voice says, 'That fucking bitch. I'd like to rip her tits off.'"

"Go, little voice. Tell it," Marilynn Morgan said and then everybody laughed until tears came and they drank everything alcoholic left in the room, even some wine that had turned weird and vinegary.

"So," Amy Newstead said, putting her cup down carefully on the table in Rand so that nothing would splash out of it and get on something, "Tell us, Josephine. In this little thing with Ronnie, who's the grateful one? You or him? Can you tell us?"

"Well," Josephine said, "that has changed over time, I guess is the best way to put it. When it all started up way last year right after spring break, after that terrible treatment I suffered from D. G., whose complete name I will never say again as long as I live, I got to confess I was the one filled with gratitude when the deal with Dr. Alden began. It was so exciting at first." Every girl at the table leaned in closer, as though to warm herself at a fire somewhere in a cabin in the Smoky Mountains late on a freezing night with the wind howling outside, a really studly guy beside her, shadows flickering on the wall, romance in the air. "But you know what, it's changed now, not just all of a sudden, but the way things will with a man, a little part crumbling off each time you're together and you hate it when you feel it, but you know it's happening, and there's not a thing you can do about it. It's the way of the world, like one of those old dramatists said somewhere, I guess it was during the Restoration."

Josephine paused and looked down at the little vase of plastic flowers at the center of the table in the Rand Hall snack bar, one just like all the others at every table in the room, except somebody had stuck a lit cigarette to one of the blooms in this arrangement and melted it a little. "Now Ronnie has gotten so grateful and so, I don't know, dependent somehow on me, that I'm really starting to feel a little freaked out. He wants to talk about how he feels all the time and stuff. Y'all know how that is." All three KD sisters nodded and said yes they did, and at least one of them halfway convinced herself she was probably telling the truth.

"When a man starts talking about the way he feels, it is so boring and such a downer," she said. "Why is that?"

"Who can tell?" Josephine Longineaux said. "When one of them wants to express himself like that, all whiny and stuff, it's all I can do to pretend to be listening and giving a shit. What I really want to say is something like 'Please shut up and keep your mind on fucking me right.'"

Everybody really laughed at that, loud enough to cause a cluster of girls two tables away to look in the direction of the KD table to see what was causing all that commotion on April Fools' Day. "Don't look back at that bunch," Stormy Meredith said. "Let the Tri Delts wonder whether or not we're laughing at them." That made them all laugh the harder, even Josephine Longineaux a little this time despite herself, but not enough to make her appear unserious.

16

"YOU REMEMBER that boy belongs to May Margaret?" Tee Arnold Monroe said to Minnie, seeing if he could get her to thinking about something other than getting ready to leave the house this morning. She was not exactly rushing around in a hurry like she was afraid of being late, but she wasn't acting like she even knew he was in the kitchen sitting at the table with his third cup of coffee. Not that he minded being out of the line of fire when Minnie had something on her mind to tend to, but when it looked like she wasn't even seeing he was there, Tee Arnold knew from experience it was not likely she had forgotten him completely. She had some things to say to him he probably didn't want to hear, but they hadn't reached the boiling point yet. When they did, she was liable to turn on him with her eyes blazing and deliver exactly what she'd been getting ready to unload. He couldn't think of a thing he'd done or not done lately which might set her off this particular morning, but that didn't mean much. Appearances could be deceiving with this woman. Hell, with any woman.

"I believe he got the last name of Brown or something like that," Tee Arnold went on and looked down at his coffee, spoon at ready if it looked like it would help him to be occupied with stirring his cup if Minnie decided to look at him.

"He ain't May Margaret's boy," Minnie said in a tone of correction, which Tee Arnold was pleased to hear. Nothing wrong with her setting him right about something that didn't have to do directly with him. That

168

might could satisfy her. "He's her grand, and his last name is Browning, first name Roosevelt. She raised him up over yonder on Washington Street. She call him Tooter when he was little. Always going around blowing on a whistle he carried everywhere he went."

"Say that who he is?" Tee Arnold said. "I had that wrong then. He must be her girl's boy, I reckon, with a last name of Browning like that."

"What about him?" Minnie said, looking not at her husband innocently stirring his coffee, but down at a piece of paper she'd pulled out of her purse. She studied the writing on it for a while and then stuck it back in the purse, snapping it closed and taking a long look around her kitchen, beginning with the stove, moving to the sink, and ending up with her eyes fixed on Tee Arnold, kind of at an angle, he noticed. Not head on and direct, but like she wasn't really thinking about what she was looking at. That relaxed him a little, and he took a sip of coffee.

"I been seeing him around, down in front of the barbershop and then at the fish house, just when I was walking by the place. I wasn't going in there now. I done lost my taste for gasper goo. It's done got too boney for me."

"Why you notice him?" Minnie said. "What's Roosevelt Browning worth you noticing him for?"

"He talking that Black Power business, that's what," Tee Arnold said. "He's just carrying on the other day, out there on Jefferson Street talking to a bunch of them sidewalk niggers like he was a preacher bringing the word of the Lord. Just a hollering."

"I expect May Margaret don't know about that. Last I heard, the police finally stuck him in the state pen for two to five for something he done. Took them a while to finally do it, though. He been messing up for a long old time."

"His eyes looked all red to me. He's dressed up in a suit, wearing a tie and all. He look like he fixing to foam at the mouth he's so mad at white folks."

"It's a lot of niggers mad at white folks," Minnie said. "That ain't nothing unusual in Nashville."

"I hear what you saying, but I was surprised a bad nigger like May Margaret's boy's done got himself interested in this Black Power business. That shit's for the college kids, ain't it? Them Fisk and Tennessee State bunch, that's who I'm talking about. They the ones got time for that kind of carrying on. Marching around and sitting in Woolworth's and saying what they fixing to do."

"If you got out of the house now and then and went somewhere else besides Jefferson Street, you hear a lot more of that business going on, Tee Arnold. I hear it on the bus from women going to work every morning. Stuff like that."

"What? Cleaning ladies be talking about Black Power? That's a surprise to me."

"Naw, not that. I mean them talking about getting even with white folks."

"Nuh-uh, no," Tee Arnold said, starting to laugh a little. "What they going to do? Pull them a strike for better pay? They going to unionize they own selves?"

"Some of these young ones is who I'm talking about, they saying crazy stuff you ain't never heard before. It's one of them the other morning I was riding behind, she's talking to somebody else sitting by her, and she say she heard a bunch of them going to organize and slip some poison into what they be cooking for the white folks. Going to do it all on the same day."

"That ain't right. That ain't going to happen."

"I ain't said it going to happen. They just talking, that's all," Minnie said and laughed some herself. "But they saying that, see, so some of the white folks can hear it said and get all scared up and nervous. That one I'm talking about, here's what she said she did to the woman she work for."

"What? Tell me."

"She said she went up to her after the old bitch had shorted her on how much she's supposed to be paying her. Tried to give her some old wore-out dresses instead of cash money or some crap like that, and here's what that girl said to her. She said, 'Ma'am, you ain't got to worry about your babies here. I love them like I love my own kids. And I sure ain't about to put no poison into what I cook for y'all to make them babies sick. I don't care what them women in North Nashville say they all going to do on what they calling the Great Getting Up Day. I ain't going to go along with it not one bit.'"

"What that white lady say to her when the girl tell her that?"

"I don't know what she said, but I know what the girl said the woman did. That white woman paid that girl the cash money she owed her and told her she could have them old dresses, too. Talked real sweet and bidable to her."

"Black Power," Tee Arnold said. "That's what Roosevelt Brown be talking about. Ooowee."

"Browning, not Brown. That's his name if he ain't changed it to Roosevelt X or something like that. I got to go. I got to get on that bus and ride out to Cherry Mount House and spend all day and night cooking and getting ready to feed some folks. They got a book-writing man they throwing a dinner for at the chancellor's tonight. He be what they say is a visiting writer at Vanderbilt, name of Kingsley or something like that."

"You don't mean Dr. King, do you? He done been here last year at Vanderbilt. He ain't back again, is he?"

"Naw, I didn't say King. I said Kingsley. He's a white man all the way from England, they said."

"Lord, Lord," Tee Arnold said, chuckling to show he was joking and that his wife shouldn't get mad at what he was about to say. "Don't you be poisoning them white folks while they eating tonight, now, Minnie, or telling them you going to."

"These rich folks ain't that easy to scare up," Minnie said. "They got more poison to use on niggers than niggers got to use on them. That's for sure. I'm gone. Don't eat no fish today. I'm going to bring you back some roast beef. Going to be a lot left over."

"Black Power, Sugar," Tee Arnold said as his wife left the house, but she didn't bother to answer back. "Power to the people. Heh, heh."

Marie had offered to drive him downtown, as she frequently did when Robard Flange visited his therapist for treatment of the dead arm attached to his left shoulder, claiming that by accompanying him to the address on Second Street she'd be relieving him of the responsibility of driving the Buick in all that traffic and him with but the one able hand on the wheel. She always said that concern was the true and full reason for the offer, but Robard knew the chance to poke her nose into one of the small dress shops in the Arcade and have tea in the Hermitage Hotel were the larger attractions drawing his wife downtown. He would not, however, allow himself to believe he did not appreciate, nor desire the company of his wife and helpmate on such an expedition from West Meade to the bustle of downtown Nashville. No, what led him to refuse her weekly offer to deliver him to the location of the Music City Magic Fingers Massage Salon was not a desire to escape Marie's presence but something essentially different.

He had explained it to Rooney Beauchamp one afternoon while he sat in the parked Buick after a session of treatment with his therapist, Lurleen Blankenship, she of the hair of gold and the dress she called the Bald Uniform with Red Pumps. The treatment had gone on at greater length than usual that day, and had been most fruitful, leaving its recipient for a full hour with no perceptible sense of detachment from the left arm dangling from his shoulder. It was not until turning off West End Avenue to wend his way home that he had to allow the arm to drop from the steering wheel where it had been assisting his other limb to direct the automobile. It had gone dead, completely and numbly, upon Robard's seeing the tower of the administration building at the center of the Vanderbilt campus rising above the great oaks that surrounded it. There death reclaimed the missing limb of Rooney Beauchamp, and the certainty of defeat at Shiloh settled once again into his blood, bones, and being.

Before that moment, however, he had sat in the Buick parked near but not directly in front of the old B and T of the Cumberland, feeling both buoyed and enervated from the after-effects of the therapy session with the young woman from the yeoman stock of the Old South, the great furnisher of the troops led so ably by the Cavalier class of that vanished civilization. "Major Beauchamp," Robard said aloud, leaning back against the headrest of his sedan, "I would not have you believe I choose to deliver myself for treatment at the Magic Fingers Salon unaccompanied by my dear wife for reasons other than those which preserve and protect her innocence."

"Dr. Flange," Rooney Beauchamp said in that voice long vanished from the earth in fact but now over a century later inhabiting the physical body of Robard, "I assure you I have no such doubts as to the nature of the motives which lead you to protect your lady wife from realities she is incapable of comprehending. I know you, Sir, and I trust your judgment and actions as I would those of General Albert Sidney Johnston himself."

"Major Beauchamp," Robard said in the voice he employed in the day-to-day reality of existence in the year of Our Lord 1968, "I thank you for that statement of confidence."

"Robard," Rooney Beauchamp said, "you need not call me by my military title when we are not engaged in martial action. We are friends and brothers under the flag, surely, and I am Rooney to you in all matters not directly associated with struggle on the field of battle."

"Thank you, Rooney," Robard said, shuddering a bit as he gathered himself to turn the key in the ignition and join the parade of automobiles swarming in the streets of Nashville. The return home would be difficult, as always, but immensely eased as a result of the therapeutic aid provided him by Lurleen Blankenship. God bless the child, her quick fingers, her easeful efforts, her glowing lips, and the warm darkness of her body, that eternal mystery of the female.

"I ride Defiance lightly now," Rooney Beauchamp said, "one with my steed. Onward to victory or to death."

"Yes, yes, onward," Robard answered. "No retreat, no turning back, and if a mortal wound comes in this next battle, I will lie me down a little to rest, and then rise again, unvanquished, to fight on."

"Look out for that old wreck of a Chevrolet," Rooney said. "It's being driven by a darky."

17

THE COCKTAIL HOUR would go on for a while, Chancellor Malcomb Foldman knew, since the guest of honor was a writer and an Englishman at that. That also meant that faculty members from the department of English had to be invited to Cherry Mount House, with all that entailed: the political divisions as long held as those between East and West, capitalism and communism, dogs and cats. The level of hatred and animus between literary types was fiercer even than that between sociologists and theologians, Malcomb considered, looking around him as he nursed his first glass of bourbon, so weak it looked like ginger ale, and observed the body language evident between the chairman of the English department, Alfred Buchanan, and the senior professor and occupier of a named chair, Robard Flange.

Buchanan was standing next to his wife, named Philip for some strange reason, smiling and leaning in toward Flange as though he was being restrained from tearing out his colleague's throat with his teeth only by an invisible wire attached to his back and holding him on leash. Robard Flange was baring his teeth as well, not so white and large as those of Buchanan's, of course, since Buchanan was chairman and in Malcomb Foldman's experience the choice of leadership for departments of English seemed always to depend on which man had the greater incisors. That was true with the great apes, too, wasn't it, Malcomb mused, as he leaned forward as though to hear more distinctly what Chambers Bodean, supposedly a possible major donor according to what Tony Kettleclap, VP and professional suck-up for money-getting, had told him. The alpha apes with the greater fangs always got first shot at the best fruit and sole access to the females in heat. Thus the need to smile a lot.

How could it be that the ones in Nashville with the most potential for giving were always so demented, Malcomb wondered, and why was Robard Flange there across the room swinging his strange dangling left arm about as he always did, seeming to want to shake it loose from him the way one did when a spider was discovered clinging to one's coat sleeve. "I understand that this Kingsley Amis fellow has written a book about teaching in a college," Chambers Bodean was saying. "My wife tells me it's all about burning up bed clothes and such, Chancellor. Made him a mess of money, I suppose, telling about that kind of goings-on."

"Oh, is that so?" Malcomb said. "I don't read much contemporary work, more's the pity. That does sound quite modern, doesn't it? A book about setting fire to where you're supposed to sleep."

"Lacy claims he's kind of famous. I guess that's why he's here, eh?"

"Everybody who comes to Cherry Mount House is famous in some way, I do believe," the chancellor said with a practiced chuckle. "Otherwise why would we waste good whisky on them? You're certainly in that category, Mr. Bodean. Famous in some most distinguished way."

"That's kind of you to say, Chancellor, but I swear I don't know what I could be famous for, except maybe that time my great granddaddy did all that messing up so bad down in Franklin, letting Slocomb slip by."

Oh, Jesus, Malcomb said to himself, another Middle Tennessee remembrance of the War Between the States. Where is that waiter with the real bourbon? Nod and laugh, nod and laugh, son, it's salary-earning time at Vandy.

Across the room near a small table covered with bric-a-brac probably worth more than all he would earn in ten years of teaching if he lasted that long, Ronald Alden was trying to catch the attention of a black man dressed in a white coat and carrying a tray of small brownish-colored clumps of something designed to look edible to anyone working to get drunk. Ronald knew the black man had seen him but was purposely ignoring his obvious desire to snag one of the fried-dough-looking things. He had let Ronald know he was not going to give him any num nums, as his daughter Emily would call them, and he had done that by looking directly at Ronald, pursing his lips as though to restrain a smile, and then turning his back to offer the tray to a woman who hadn't even noticed him and his tray of goodies.

"He knows what he's doing," Ronald said to Lily. "It amuses him, obviously. He's creating himself a little get-back at the man."

"What? Who? What are you talking about?" Lily said, not turning her attention away from her appraisal of the still-life scene before her of English novelist surrounded by admirers.

"Oh, nothing. The waiter who won't give me a fried goodie to eat, that's all. He's not going to vanish before you get a chance to talk to him, Lily."

"Who? What're you muttering about?"

"Kingsley Amis," Ronald said, "over there next to his long-legged blonde wife. She looks to be in agony, having to listen to Lacy Bodean yammer at her."

"I thought you were talking about a waiter," Lily said. "Now you're looking at a woman's legs. Make up your mind."

Lacy Bodean was leaning in toward the visiting novelist, even a bit on tiptoe as she worked to shoulder out another less physically powerful woman who had planted herself in front of the writer like a tick seized up for a blood picnic. Ronald had seen that wife before at various official faculty functions, but since she wasn't attached to any member of the English department, he had never thought it worth his while to learn who she was. Her hair was prematurely graying, allowed to hang as it would, wild and free and unadorned, and without seeing her face, Ronald knew from past encounters it would be devoid of makeup, she being the serious person she was, proud to be plain, to dress badly, and to speak out boldly against the war of American expansion in Southeast Asia.

Got to be married to somebody in the social sciences, Ronald thought as he sipped at his rapidly emptying glass, wandered off into darkest Tennessee and amazed it isn't Rhode Island. Maybe I should throw Kingsley Amis a lifeline, ask him what he thinks of Anthony Burgess or Philip Larkin. He'd appreciate some intelligent literary talk, I expect, might even invite me to join him for drinks some afternoon. Wouldn't that frost the asses of some of the old dogs in the department?

Amis was draining a glass and looking around as though he'd forgotten something essential to his well-being as Ronald walked up to the group surrounding him, three or four women and one male, a graduate student assigned by Alfred Buchanan to assist the writer-in-residence find his way around the university for the two months of his stay. Houston Stride the graduate student's name was, Ronald remembered, one of the hangers-on of the chairman and a man determined to rise, shine, and be visible in any way possible. The expression on Stride's face was a strange mixture, Ronald noted, of adoration and apprehension, as he looked back and forth from the woman in front of Amis to the focus of attention of all in the group, the writer in full speaking mode with his glass emptied of all but two cubes of ice.

"Hello, Alder," Amis said as soon as he saw Ronald approaching, breaking off in mid-word something he'd been saying to the social science wife. He knows me, Ronald thought, brightening as he realized those who'd heard the greeting by name would be impressed, even though Amis had gotten his label slightly wrong. Alder instead of Alden, but still pretty damn close to an indication that a literary man of note recognizes my specific existence. I wonder what about me has impressed him?

"Hello, Kingsley," Ronald said, changing in mid-pronouncement the greeting he'd intended to make, Mr. Amis or maybe just Sir. "How are you this evening?"

"Tip top," Amis said and extended his hand, shaking his glass and rattling its ice cubes. "Could you, dear friend?"

"Oh, yes," Ronald said, reaching past the swatch of prematurely gray, serious, and unmoving hair standing fixed in his way and taking the glass. "What are you drinking?"

"Just plain Famous Grouse, and do me a favor. Dump that infernal ice and make it a straight dose, would you?"

"I will, Kingsley," Ronald said, savoring the first name again, and then turning toward where he'd seen Amis's long-legged wife standing to ask if he might freshen her glass as well. She was not where she'd been, though, having turned her back and moved off to another clump of drinkers of a smaller number in need of some imposing figure to surround.

"And when you're back, Alder," Amis said, getting the name wrong again. Do I dare correct him, Ronald asked himself, deciding instantly he wouldn't. Who knows what witty injury Amis would deliver if someone made so bold as to point out an error he'd made? "I'd like you to help me explain to this charming lady why she's so mistaken about world affairs and the nature of power, its purpose and use."

Several listeners giggled at that, a couple guffawed, and the serious social-science wife showed no change of expression to indicate she'd heard what was said.

When Ronald got back, carrying the glass of single malt carefully since he'd insisted the person tending bar fill it to within a hair of the brim, Amis gestured to him to step aside from the group he'd been addressing. "Alder, could I speak to you for a moment about a matter of no interest to these good people? I don't want to bore them, but I promise," he said, breaking off and turning toward the group, "like your magnificent General MacArthur, I shall return."

More chuckles, and Houston Stride as handler of visiting writer began stepping in concert with Amis as he led Ronald toward a corner of the glittering cocktail space of Cherry Mount House. "Oh, Stride," Amis said, "you stay and entertain these people for half a tick. I need to speak in private to Alder here about a bit of business."

With the look of a survivor of the wreck of an ocean liner who'd just been informed he was not to be allowed to embark as the last passenger on the final lifeboat headed for salvation, Houston Stride nodded once and turned back toward the audience, stepping less lively now. "Look, Alder," Amis said, "I want to have a bit of fun with this sour little earnest bitch who's been raving on quite disloyally about the United States military venture in Vietnam. I'd like you to aid me in this, just for amusement's sake, and I didn't want to surprise you. Are you game?"

"Hell, Kingsley," Ronald said, feeling the whisky rising in him. "I was born dead game."

"Good, then. It'll be quite fun to tell Alfred about it. He so enjoys bearding professional liberals. That's what drew me to him when I met him at Harvard. Now you just look thoughtful and second my expressed opinions. Could be amusing, don't you think?"

Back with his audience, Kingsley Amis launched into an explanation of what he thought would be most advantageous for the sister leader nations of the West, the United States and the United Kingdom. By the time he'd braced himself, taken down a good half of his glass of Scotch, and gotten well started with his peroration, more and more smaller groups had disintegrated and become one with his. Ronald had been fed a generous portion of the brown fried things by the waiter who'd once shunned him, and he was in full cry of agreement with all that the visiting writer had to say.

"You understand," Amis announced to the social science wife, "the problems we have in the UK can be best solved by drastic but inevitable and finally most desirable measures, chief among these our becoming the fifty-first state of your nation. It's already been proved that a distance of an ocean between the mainland and another state poses no problem to annexation. I offer Hawaii as proof. I see it now. The United States of America welcomes mother home. Here, old girl, rest and be happy, mum. Play with the kiddies and tell old stories, while looking toward a glorious future."

"Hear, hear," Ronald said, and took a drink.

"Then the problem of Vietnam," Amis went on. "Need I say that the noble struggle in which America is now engaged, essentially alone, is for the continuation of civilization itself? Speak not to me of expansionism. Let us recognize instead the rightness of our fight for survival in a world increasingly overburdened with the colored nations."

"Hear, hear," Ronald said, joined this time by other voices, those of Robard Flange and Chambers Bodean.

It was after the third time that Ronald had seconded Amis's proposals for a newer whiter world order that he felt Lily tugging at his sleeve and digging her fingernails into the back of his hand, the one holding the empty glass. "Let's go," she was saying. "Now."

"But," Ronald said, "we're just getting started. It's just fun. It's all ironic. It's just satire. We still got to eat dinner at the chancellor's house."

"If you don't come with me, I'll start screaming. I'll have a fit. I know just how to do that, Ronald." She did, he knew, and he followed her out of the cocktail party right before dinner was slated to start. All the way out the door of Cherry Mount House and onto the walk Ronald could hear the notes from a musical gong being sounded behind him by a black waiter, calling the guests to feed. When he reached to open the door of his Chevrolet, he noticed he still had the empty whisky glass from which he'd been drinking, stamped with the Vanderbilt seal, in his hand.

Thinking back to the time before she'd met Ronald Alden in her junior year of college, Lily realized she'd not had a complete sexual experience until she was almost twenty years old. Oh, she'd played with herself a time or two and hadn't gotten anything out of it, unlike Onita Daniels who claimed she did to anybody who'd listen. You'd think Onita had discovered rubbing the clitoris. Lily had been pursued by boys in high school, fumbled with in parked cars, let two boys get their hands on her breasts for less than a minute total, combined, kissed on several occasions until her lips went numb, and had told girl friends about the close calls she'd had of going all the way, as it was called in Mansfield, Ohio, back in that simpler time. She'd even had boys, one in particular, Carl Swenger, force her hand onto an erection through their clothes, and finally on senior prom night, when everybody stayed out late and ate pancakes after midnight at the VFW hall in an event thought up by parents who hoped that would be a way to keep the seniors from getting drunk, driving cars off the road into trees, and fiddling with each other's private parts, she had allowed Carl to unzip his trousers, free his cock so she could get at it raw and she'd moved her hand up and down on it only a couple of times before stuff exploded all over the front of her dress, a really pretty one bought by her mother for her at Hart's on the square.

The stain Carl's eruption made on the material was impossible to remove, wet and sticky as it was, even after it had dried, and Lily had had to think long and hard about a lie that would convince her mother it was just maple syrup that had missed the pancakes and landed where it shouldn't. Worse even than that, after resting for a few minutes while he told Lily how much he loved her and wanted to spend the rest of his days bound to her in marriage, Carl had wanted her to do it again, this time with her mouth, and when she refused and flounced to the other side of the car seat, tempted to get out and walk home but it was really too far, particularly in heels, he had tried to stick his hand inside her panties and put his fingers inside her. She let him do that for a little while, found she didn't like it one bit, and made him drive her home without giving him even one more kiss.

When Carl Swenger let her out at the door, he repeated his offer of marriage, pledging his undying love, and Lily told him she'd think about that. She never went out with him again, naturally, and she told her best friend at the time, Linda Mayo, it was just because she didn't want to hook up with a boy who'd get a job in some business in Mansfield and never leave town until he died. That would be true of Carl Swenger, Lily knew, but the real reason she didn't want to marry him was not because she couldn't stand the thought of staying in Mansfield but that having his cock in her hand wasn't exciting, having to put it in her mouth later on after they got married would be gross and disgusting, and letting him put any part of his body inside her made her shudder to think about how it would feel.

So when she and Ronald Alden got together at Denison College, Lily did what she had to do. He proved not that disgusting to touch, and he never made her do anything with his cock she wasn't willing to try, and when they graduated, they were still going together. So they got married. The ceremony was nice, and her dress was beautiful, and all their Denison friends showed up and got drunk and partied and had a hell of a time, as the president of Ronald's fraternity said, so all that went all right. It was an okay time. Her parents liked her husband fine, even though he was an English major.

Then graduate school at Ohio State for Ronald, and the babies started coming, and finally her husband completed his goddamn dissertation and got offered a job at Vanderbilt, his first choice, and they were off to move to Nashville where he'd succeed as a scholar and Lily would raise the children and they'd have a happy life and then have grandkids and finally die in a quiet and painless manner.

Looking back over the course of her journey right up to now, as she lay nude on a mattress on the floor of an old rundown house on Belmont Street divided up into crappy apartments, and studied a poster of the Beatles someone had pinned on the wall with red thumbtacks—it was the one of the album cover of Sgt. Pepper with all those famous people on it, the one where you keep recognizing a new person popping up each time you look at it—Lily Schmidt Alden realized she hadn't had her first real orgasm until she had started letting Tollman Briggs fuck her.

It didn't seem fair somehow, she told herself, but maybe it was good she'd never matched up well sexually with anybody before, since it made the times now so newly sweet and special, the sessions she spent sweating and straining and feeling it happen once more under, over, next to, and with this folksinger who made up his own songs and wore his hair longer than she did. Every time it worked, Lily felt both like laughing and crying, laughing because it was so good and unexpected and weird, and crying because maybe this time would prove to be the last time it would happen. Maybe she'd forget how to come, since she'd gone so long without ever doing it before, or maybe she'd wear out in some way and her private parts would stop being able to do that any more, like an old refrigerator which had worked well and faithfully for years and then one day just quit. Used up and out of whatever made it freeze, freon or some other chemical, or maybe a part that had seized up and burnt away and would never function again.

But unlike an old refrigerator that stopped working, what she might lose in her body parts wouldn't be fixable. You can't replace a thing that makes you feel, that lets you forget your name and the fact you're married and have three children to love and raise, unloveable though they might be and broke as you are. You can't buy a new part for your body or mind or soul that will work right again and let you get outside and above and away from where you're settled and fixed and trapped in your life, never to escape being the thing and the person you are.

Tollman had laughed until his eyes watered the first time he'd heard Lily call that part of her body he did such incredible things to her private parts. "Your private parts?" he said. "Why don't you call it your vagina, if you want to be clinical about it? Or if you want to be real, call it your pussy or your cunt. Private parts? Where are you from, girl?"

"It has nothing to do with where I'm from, geographically," she'd said, instantly going midwestern on this man from somewhere down here in this part of the world. "I've heard every curse word and obscenity you hear all the time in Nashville, and I've heard them said in Mansfield and Granville and Columbus, Ohio. The South hasn't got a patent on shocking word choice. We can and do say fuck and shit and damn and all the rest of the litany of filth, including that word you just used."

"What?" Tollman said. "Vagina? Pussy?"

"No. The other one."

"Say it, Lily," he told her, and she'd refused, not complying until a few minutes later in the midst of things when he'd told her to say it then, and she did, over and over, shrieking it aloud until somebody in the next room beat on the wall to make her stop.

But Lily knew what she feared most was not her body failing her, or her mind, or her soul or whatever part of herself it was that operated at the moment of translation that was the truth of her orgasm. It wasn't really that she was a mammal and an animal and a woman and a human, all that which was not something inanimate like a refrigerator—fixable, replaceable, immortal because it really wasn't alive—it was something else she knew was never in her control and could never be.

It was not she herself who controlled those moments that wiped out all that was Lily in her everyday life in Nashville. It was another person. It was not her husband, but it was a man. And he was by definition untrustworthy, and this particular one was a fool to boot. He thinks he's an artist, Lily told herself as she looked at the Sgt. Pepper poster, searching for the bearded face of Walt Whitman, the mustache and haunted eyes of Edgar Allan Poe; he thinks he's different, even unique, and that he has something to say that's never been said before. He can't even play a guitar worth a damn, and here he is in Nashville.

He hath me in thrall, Lily said to herself, remembering that line from some poem, telling herself she wasn't even able to recall it correctly, much less name the poet who'd thought it first and then written it. This Tollman has me, and I'll pay for what I've bought, and it will cost me more than I can afford. But the payment's not due just now, and I won't think about being unable to meet the bill until it comes. I'll put it off until the bill collector comes for good.

"Come in here," Lily called out in a voice loud enough that Tollman could hear her in the next room where he was plunking away at his guitar, hitting close to the same note again and again, but just missing it. "Come in here now, Tollman," she called again. "Give that guitar a rest. I need another good fuck."

18

THEY HAD GOTTEN a little over eight thousand dollars from the Stop 'n' Shop that April night last year out on Nolensville Road, Randall was thinking as he lay in bed listening to one of the kids hollering at another one, claiming a toy or a bottle cap or something was his and not the other one's. Why in hell wasn't Maureen knocking the hell out of one or the other or both of them little bastards? She was still in the house, wasn't she? He'd heard her feeding the bunch of them a little while ago, or maybe he'd just half dreamed it. She was bound to have woke him up before she left the house for work. She couldn't stand to see him resting and at his ease, and she would roust him out before she left, whether it benefited anybody to do it or not. She had to still be around somewhere then or Randall would've known for sure she was out and gone.

Eight thousand, one hundred and twenty seven dollars and eighty four cents, that had been the total amount Randall and Milton Drummond had counted out on the kitchen table, though it had taken three or four times by each of them working separately before they found a number they could agree to settle on. So they ought to have had over four thousand dollars apiece as each man's fair share, since Tooter had said all he wanted was fifty dollars to help make the deal go down easy and quick. All he was going to be there in the Stop 'n' Shop for was to put the scare on, to be a great big nigger, black as the ace of spades, and paralyze the clerk behind the counter. That's all the money he wanted, except he wanted to write that shit on the wall with the blue-colored spray can. Something about don't you call me nigger, but it was said better than that, so as to get attention, as Randall remembered.

That part had been put in the *Tennessean* newspaper the next morning and again in the *Nashville Banner* that afternoon. They played that up bigger than the hold-up at the Stop 'n' Shop itself, like it was the main thing that happened. The damn papers had called it an alarming trend, saying it was political or some shit like that, when all it really was was a bad nigger who didn't like white folks getting the chance to have his say and get it noticed. And then, when it came right down to the nut-cutting, and Randall Eugene had held out two twenties and two fives to the big scary-looking bastard, what he'd done was just look at it like it was a horse turd Randall was offering him.

"What's that?" he said, sitting at the kitchen table in Milton's house, not looking up at first and then when he did, fixing his eyes directly on Randall's face. They was all red looking and bloodshot, Tooter Browning's eyes was, like a nigger's will get when he's getting mad and maybe about to go nuts on you. "What's that shit?" he said, not taking the money out of Randall's hand, just sitting there long enough that Randall started feeling funny holding the twenties and fives out toward Tooter and finally laid the bills on the table, careful not to make it look like he was throwing the money down but laying it there nice and easy. The way he was doing it wasn't saying a thing, that's what Randall Eugene was indicating to the scary looking black fucker. I'm just gently putting it down on the table. I don't mean a thing by it, the way I'm laying it down.

"Why, that's the fifty dollars Milton said you wanted to help us out back yonder," Randall said, then turning his head toward where Milton was sitting behind his pile of bills and change, "ain't that what you told me, Hoss?"

"I don't remember what I said exactly," Milton said. "I believe it was something like Tooter said he wouldn't want a lot to help us out."

"You told me, right out yonder in front of my trailer, that he wanted fifty dollars, and he'd call it even, numbnuts," Randall said, letting how he was feeling about the whole deal be shown in the way he spoke to Milton. "That's what the fuck you said, out in front of my house, sitting in your car under that damn sweet gum tree, them balls just a-popping on the roof."

"I don't remember it just that way," Milton said. "I do remember saying Tooter wanted to let the Man know what this whole thing meant. That's why he wrote on the wall with his spray can. Right, Tooter?"

"Writing on the wall was my own thing," Tooter Browning said. "That ain't none of your business, neither one of you. I ain't charging you for that. What I want to get paid for is making that motherfucker lay behind the counter and stay scared enough not to move none for ten minutes after we left the 7-Eleven."

"It was a Stop 'n' Shop," Randall said. "Not no 7-Eleven."

"I don't give a shit what the damn store's called," Tooter said. "I want more money than fifty dollars."

"How much do you believe would be fair, then?" Randall said. "A couple of hundred? You got to remember I set the deal up. I was the one that knowed about the money going to be there."

"I give you that," Tooter had said. "You did that, and I got my message in the newspapers all right, so I'll settle for a thousand dollars and y'all do what you want with the rest of it. Buy you a new used car and a mess of grits. I don't give a fuck."

That's the way it ended up, with Tooter's thousand gone and the rest of the take from the hold-up split between Randall Eugene and Milton. Tooter left Milton's house as soon as they counted out his thousand, spinning the tires of his Pontiac as he pulled away, making gravel fly up and hit against the grill of Randall's car. As soon as the sound of Tooter's busted muffler faded, Randall considered whether or not to whip Milton's ass, but decided against it. Shit, what if Milton told Tooter about it and the crazy bastard would decide to go African on Randall? It ain't worth taking the chance, but Lord it would be sweet to bust this weak-ass lying little fucker upside the head. Don't remember it being said that way, my ass.

The thing of it was that the half of what was left after Tooter took his thousand dollars, though it was over three thousand bucks and change, just didn't last no time. Maureen was suspicious about where the part of it she found came from—Randall Eugene had hid it down in the mouth of a big old boot back in the closet and God knows how she ran up on that—but not knowing where the money came from didn't stop Maureen from spending the shit out of it. She'd blown most of it on bills and a new dinette set, and by the time a month had gone by, there wasn't enough money from what Randall Eugene had busted his ass to get to buy a sick Mexican his supper.

It ain't no work worth doing in Nashville for a man with any self-respect, Randall Eugene said to himself as he got up to go in the kitchen and keep the kids from killing each other, and I'll be damned if I'm going to lower myself to work on a minimum wage deal. My daddy didn't raise me to think that way about myself and take that kind of treatment. I am worth a whole lot more than a pissant little job like that.

By the time he got into the kitchen, the kid that had wanted what the other had been playing with was satisfied for some reason, and the other one was squalling a little but not making much noise with it. Sometimes you leave things alone and they'll work out on their own, Randall thought philosophically, and then he noticed through the window over the sink of the mobile home that Maureen was outside talking to Milton Drummond who'd got out of his car and was standing beside it with the door still open. If Maureen takes a mind to slap him, Milton wants to be able to jump in fast for a quick get-away, Randall said to himself, laughed a little at what he'd come up with, and walked outside.

"You trying to pick up my old lady, Milton?" he said. "Toll her off to a dance somewhere? Do a little honky tonking?"

"Naw, naw," Milton said, shaking his head back and forth so hard he got ahead of his ballcap a little, making it slide around on his head some.

"I wish somebody would," Maureen said, "get me out of that kitchen for a while." She sounded good natured for a change, and Randall congratulated himself of thinking of a thing to say that would make her feel good about herself. You got to jolly a woman along, now and then. Throw her a compliment and let her think you might be jealous of another man looking at her. She don't need to hear the truth all the time.

"I got work to do," Maureen said to Milton. "You got to ask me some other time to go dancing. I'll take a rain check on this thing."

"I wasn't really going to ask you that, Maureen," Milton said, looking not at Randall's wife but at him. "Seriously now."

"Well, just don't you try it," Randall said. "That's all I got to say. Don't be getting no ideas about my baby." At that, Maureen laughed, the first time Randall had heard that since he couldn't remember when, and she went up the steps into the trailer, slamming the door hard behind her so it would catch.

"She's still a pretty good-looking woman now and then," Randall said to Milton, watching the shadow of his wife through the plastic pane in the door. "Hard to keep noticing that when she rides me so hard about getting tied down to a steady job, though. Women will stop trying to please a man, and I don't know why."

"I know what you're saying," Milton said. "Back before me and Donnell split the sheets, she would never let up on me. Not enough money, not enough money, not enough money, that was the song she sang from morning to night."

"They want it to spend as fast as you can tote it to them. It stays on their mind."

"That's kind of why I'm over here. I got something that might do us some good."

"What would that be? Janitoring at the schoolhouse? Picking up garbage for the city of Nashville? Anything like that, and I ain't interested, Milton. I got to keep my options open for something that'll pay a living wage and not break my goddamn back for me while I'm doing it."

"It's a thing like that deal last year, Randall," Milton said in a low voice, looking around as though to spot potential eavesdroppers, though the closest living thing in sight, that belonging to the neighbor in the next trailer, was only Wanda Sue Matlock's half-grown cat, knocking a sweet gum ball back and forth in the skinned-off yard. "But a whole lot better. Let's get in the car so we can talk."

"I'll listen to you, Milton," Randall Eugene said, walking around the car and sliding into the front seat, "but you got to realize every time you see a convenience store, you ain't necessarily looking at over eight thousand dollars just waiting to be picked up. That was a special deal and a one-time thing, and all that came from me doing some investigating and planning. You walk into your ordinary Stop 'n' Shop and nine times out of ten, all you going to find in the till is about fifty bucks. They throw every bill that comes in over a twenty in a safe cemented in the floor just as soon as they get it. That is the policy, and it fucks everything up."

"No, I ain't talking about a little old store like that," Milton Drummond said, rolling up his car window in case Wanda Sue Matlock's cat was listening, Randall Eugene told himself, laughing a little at what he'd just come up with in his head about the cat. "I mean a whole different deal with a lot more money," Milton went on.

"I ain't about to try to rob a fucking bank, Milton," Randall Eugene said. "The police catch nearly every fool who tries that, and they stick his ass in the pen for a long stretch. I don't know about you, but I need me fresh air outside every day that rolls. In these banks, they got dye packs that blow up on your ass. You can't even spend the money if you get away with it. It's all red colored."

"It ain't nothing like that. See who we'd be taking the money from, they ain't on the up and up themselves. It ain't no legitimate business where the Man will give a shit about it getting knocked over. It ain't the Man's money. That's what I'm saying."

"The man? Who you been talking to, Milton?"

"Tooter," Milton Drummond said simply. "Tooter Browning. It's his deal, and they's enough money to be had in it to where that three thousand dollars apiece we got last year'll look like nothing."

"Tooter Browning? Why would he want to do something with us again, Milton? He hates white folks. Last time I saw that nigger he was so mad at us his eyes was red as fire and drawed up like B B's. I was afraid he was going to pull some kind of a Ubangi stunt on us. Go for a machete or something, I don't know. Some kind of a big old blade. Tooter Browning is as prejudiced as a motherfucker."

"Tooter says the ones holding the money would for sure know him or any other brother he could get to help him. He's got to find somebody else. Us, they wouldn't know. We all look just alike to them, Tooter says, white folks do."

"See what I'm telling you about nigger prejudice? So we'd be holding up some kind of nigger establishment? That's what you saying, Milton? Shit, man, them drug pushers use machine guns and German shepherd dogs to guard their money. They'd waste our asses in a New York minute, as soon as we said stick 'em up."

"It's women holding the money, Randall Eugene," Milton said. "And it won't even be but one of them there, and Tooter knows when the money's going to be give to her to hold for about a half a day at the longest. So when we'd go in, it would be just the one woman by herself, not even knowing what all is in that big old bag they give her to keep until the next bunch comes in to make the transfer."

"One woman, huh? Where's the money come from? How much is it?"

"It's over eighty thousand dollars, Randall. Hell, we could retire on our part of that. It comes from a week's worth of dope money in Nashville all collected together to be took off to Memphis by somebody Tooter knows. That's all he told me about it."

"How much do we get?" Randall Eugene said, counting and dividing numbers in his head, trying to remember what it meant to carry a number. He needed a piece of paper and a pencil and about fifteen minutes, damn it.

"Tooter will take a third of it, and let us have the rest, he says. That's the deal he's ready to make with us."

"That black son of a bitch will misremember and change a deal on you," Randall Eugene said. "As I recollect. But still, that's a chunk of money, even with his part gone. Where is this woman going to be located, this nigger lady with the eighty grand she's fixing to lose?"

"Down on Second Street. She runs a wig shop."

"Wig shop?"

"Yeah, for colored women to put on their heads to change their looks and stuff, I guess. It's named Wilma's Wild Wigs, and it's in a old building used to be a bank."

"Let's go get us a twelve pack and talk about this thing, Milton. I can be persuaded, but you got to talk sweet and play with me a little bit first. I ain't easy."

"The beer's already in the back floorboard," Milton said, cranking the engine. "I knowed you'd want me to come prepared."

The department meeting had gone quite well, up to this point, Alfred Buchanan considered as he focused on appearing to listen closely to the discussion of possible alterations to the format of the comprehensive examination for candidates for the doctoral degree in English at Vanderbilt University. The issue divided always along the same lines, though these were not acknowledged publicly or ever discussed in plain view. Here it was then. Was it easier and less tiring for the faculty examiners to subject each candidate to a two-hour oral ordeal, or should the examinations be written? Should the candidates be tortured and humiliated in a public display of oral questions and answers, sneering laughs, and witty asides by questioners, or should they be made to write long responses over a period of days to queries dreamed up by the inquisitors?

It was vexed and vexing question. Making the ordeal all oral was simpler, easier, and more humbling to the candidates, in some cases utterly destroying self-confidence and causing reconfiguration of entire life plans, and that was strong argument for retention of the current system. Yet there were those faculty, typically the newer ones, who argued strongly for the revelation of mind and knowledge which written responses to questions forced candidates to display. The uncertain glibness of speech against the agonized refusal to commit to a point and express an opinion in written prose. This issue was the yearly torment for those professing literature at Vanderbilt.

The whole matter was a pointless and irresolvable one, Alfred Buchanan knew in his role as leader of the pack, but that fact was what made the subject so endlessly fascinating for the department of English. It could never be finally decided, so discussion of the topic could last until each participant in the debate was dead, buried, and turned to dust. Each nuance of argument on each point of contention was sweet relishment to the soul.

"Cogent and telling points on each side of this question have been made," Alfred announced. "Now let me inform you of a directive from the office of the chancellor which we have been bound to follow."

"Yet another?" Shoul Lambert asked in near full voice. "Is there no end to the niggling harassment and command from that quarter?"

"Ours not to reason why," Alfred Buchanan answered. "Ours but to do or die. And the charge this time will be not into the roar of literal cannon, but into the thicket of the literary one."

Members of the department looked from one face to the other of those of the group with whom each still communicated, some in surprise, others with expressions in keeping with those of men condemned to death in the moment of being informed that their last-minute pleas for a stay of execution had been denied, a few with the puzzled open mouths and popped eyes of the committed deaf. What did the chairman just say? Huh?

"Let me detail the message from on high which I have to deliver," Alfred Buchanan said, "and it is this. The powers that be have decided that a course in the literature of the Negro in America is to be taught in the Vanderbilt Department of English. We are to select an instructor, and he is to design the course for teaching in the next semester and deliver it then. We must expand the literary canon, and the university cannot afford to appear to be reluctant to recognize the need to accommodate the changes in higher education being wrought nationally."

"Preposterous," Shoul Lambert thundered. "Is there no academic freedom left at this university?"

"Must we obey this dictate from the chancellor?" Robard Flange asked, annoyed that Shoul had begun with the strongest argument that could be launched, that of the maintenance of academic freedom, thereby leaving no final shot in the locker for the ultimate moment. A tactician must never show his all to the enemy before the attack is well launched. Rooney Beauchamp always held a surprise or two in reserve. "Can't we appear to cooperate, but delay the process? Can we not state that no one of us senior professors is conversant with whatever it is that constitutes Negro literature?"

"You could learn it in an afternoon, I'd hazard," Gareth Lamb said to a spatter of muted laughter. "What is it Negro literary aspirants do? Do they have poems? Novels? Drama? Is aught even written down by these people? What do they scribble on? Do they use crayons?"

"It's field hollers and simple pleadings to Jesus," Samuel Vinson said. "Swing low, sweet chariot and so on. Lift that load, tote that bale, et cetera."

"I would not attempt to go down that path," Alfred Buchanan said.

"Listen to our chairman," Lawrence Hill Dunham said. "He is informed about this matter."

"Thank you, Larry," Alfred said, giving his lapdog a verbal pat in public. "Here it is then. If we do not pick up the gauntlet, the chancellor will appoint a visiting professor from Fisk University to teach the course in question."

"Would he be a Negro?" Henry Hallam Horsham asked. "There are white faculty at Fisk, I understand. Would the course be taught on the Fisk campus?"

"He would be a Negro, I have it on good authority," Alfred said. "A distinguished scholar of the field of literature under discussion. And the course would be taught on this campus as an ordinary Vanderbilt course for credit in the study of English."

"Distinguished? What does that mean?" David McDavidson said. "He owns a suit and tie?"

"Let that day not come," Robard Flange said. "We must walk this path on our own, and we must not allow such appointment of a Negro to be made to this faculty, even temporarily. Once taken, that step is irreversible and must lead to others."

"Now," Alfred said, "what I hear is this, and please check me on it. We all agree that none of the senior faculty has expertise in this branch of literature—no, hold yourselves in check. We must call it literature, like it or not. No grumbling about definitions at this point—and we will inform the chancellor that, eager as we are to expand our academic offerings in such manner, none of us has the time to move away from our own fields of expertise to learn the literature of the Negro in America. Though we could do so and would, of course, any number of us, particularly those in American literature. So we will assign the task to a junior member of the department. Give him a reduced load to learn it, and we'll move forward cheerfully and publicly without the need to seek outside aid."

"One question," David McDavidson said. "To whom shall you assign this task? Which of the junior faculty can we trust to carry out this responsibility?"

"I propose to let someone teach it who wants to do so," Alfred said. "We want no reluctance to be evident for the administration to seize upon. I propose a young man who is ever at the cutting edge of so-called popular culture. The name that comes to mind is Ronald Alden."

"Does he know this assignment might well tarnish his reputation?" Gareth Lamb said. "After all, to use an old East Tennessee axiom, if you lie down with dogs, you get up with fleas."

"I think Dr. Alden will relish it," Alfred said, "and give it his all."

Not too shabby, Alfred told himself, we'll get a course taught in Negro lit, then I'll lobby for a black man to teach it on a permanent basis, and Malcomb Foldman won't be able to say no and get away with it. If my achieving that appointment of a Black scholar to the English faculty at Vanderbilt University doesn't get me good attention from somewhere on the Coasts, I don't know Princeton or UCLA.

19

"WHY ARE WE in this shitty little place?" Betsy Ames asked, wiping the lip of the bottle of Stroh's beer carefully with a tissue from her purse, not wanting to use one from the paper napkin container, though it was probably cleaner than any other surface in the bar on Blair Avenue. That probably depends on the way the napkins were inserted in the metal holder, though, she thought, and who had done it. Oh, well. She was going to have to pay for the beer, so she took a sip.

"Because of who goes here, of course, Betsy," Marlene Mercer said. "That's why people go anywhere, not because of the place they're going but because of who else they're going to see there in the same place with them."

"I've been in worse," Betsy admitted. "And what you just said makes some sense. That applies not just to bars like Brown's Diner, either, if you think about it."

"Of course. Why'd you come to Vanderbilt for graduate work? You could have gone to Georgia just as well, probably got scholarship money."

"Point taken," Betsy said. "But you know what?"

"What?" Jennifer Smithing said. "But I bet I know what you're going to say."

"Probably. I thought I'd meet a better run of men here than I would at Georgia. You know, somebody with some background and some money and who'd gone to a better college than I did. Somebody who might be going somewhere."

"And you did," Marlene said. "You truly made the right decision."

"Don't fuck with me, Marlene," Betsy said. "Yeah, I met exactly the kind of man I was hoping I would. He's been places, got a daddy with money, went to a college in Virginia, for God's sake. Likes poetry, doesn't drive a pickup and go dove hunting and chew Redman, all that shit."

"Tell us the rest, girl," Jennifer said. "Don't hold back now."

"You know the rest, and you just want to watch me suffer."

"Hell, yes," Marlene said. "We're all voyeurs. Why do you think we read fiction and write papers about it and teach rich little freshmen how to put commas in a series? Tell us. We want some sublimation, too."

"I met the son of a bitch, all right," Betsy Ames said. "But he's married, and each time he fucks me, he gets up from wherever we are on some floor or up against the wall or in a bed somewhere, if I'm lucky that night, and he puts his clothes back on. And then you know what he has the gall to do?"

"What?" Marlene and Jennifer said almost at the same time. "What?"

"He asks me to look and see if his shirt and trousers are hanging right, so when he goes home to Brenda she won't be able to tell what he's been doing."

"Who he's been doing, more likely," Marlene said, but Betsy didn't bother to come back at her about that. Scar tissue does get to the point where it doesn't hurt so much any more, no matter how much you scratch it. Sort of.

"And you know what he asked me to do the other night when we'd done it on the floor in the seminar room in the Divinity School building?"

"You did it there?" Jennifer said.

"Yes," Betsy said in a snarl, which made both the other women laugh. "We did it there. That's where we happened to be, wasn't it? Where else was I going to let him do it? Was I going to say 'Hold that thought while we go somewhere else first'?"

"Tell us what he asked you to do after you'd sinned in the very house of God," Jennifer said, looking at Marlene for a sign of appreciation and getting it.

"The asshole asked me to smell his breath to see it was all right for him to pass muster when he got home."

"What had he been doing that he was worried about how his breath smelled, Betsy?" Jennifer said. "Do tell."

"None of your bees wax, Sweet Child," Betsy said. "And now here I am in Brown's Diner where everybody but us is an old confirmed drunken bum drinking at two in the afternoon, and I'm here because it's where the English department graduate students get together to drink before they play softball."

"He does play with that bunch sometimes," Jennifer said. "I've seen him in here more than once. I told you that."

"Don't I know it. Here I sit drinking out of a bottle which has probably been handled by somebody with syphilis, just on the off-chance that Houston Stride will come in here and see me and maybe say to himself, 'Oh, look. There's Betsy Ames. Don't I fuck her off and on and now and then? Maybe I'll do it now, if Jennifer Smithing's not around.'"

"Wait a minute, bitch," Jennifer said. "Watch what you're saying."

"Watch who you're spreading your legs for, whore," Betsy said.

"Girls, girls," Marlene said. "Let's just get drunk and not fight. Houston's not cheating on y'all. He's cheating on the woman he's married to. Get your facts straight before you start pulling each other's hair out."

Cameron Semmes was finding herself a little short of funds, here at the end of a fading day in April, and she looked up from the cookbook she was reading to recheck who else in addition to her was in the house on Belmont Street. Maybe somebody had wandered in, but in the meantime, she'd look at the cookbook she'd found in a pile of other books in one of the closets. When people moved out of a house in a hurry, they always left the books, if they had any.

Cookbooks were good to consider sometimes, telling you just what to do step by step and how to measure exactly what amount of each ingredient to use to make a thing come out right, showing a pretty picture of the final product, as it shined and glistened in the light, ready to ingest. Actually going into a kitchen, though, firing up a stove, getting stuff together, mixing it up, putting it in pans and skillets and pots and letting the fire get to it—all that wasn't worth the time and effort, but imagining what it would be like to follow a plan with a beginning, a middle, and an end product, that could help keep stuff in your head beat back and at bay for a while. How nice to be persuaded you could think like that and believe in what cookbooks celebrated: starting somewhere, having faith in being able to figure out what to do next, then doing it, and being satisfied by what you end up with. Amazing.

But just now, Cameron wanted to see who was around of the ones staying in the big house on Belmont. Not that anyone of that bunch would have a dime or would let her borrow it if they happened to have it at hand, broke as she was this late in the day. Could be, though, that Morning Glory might still be holding a stash somewhere, and if approached right would let her have a little to tide her over until the check from Daddy Semmes got there. It was a day late, and that was worrisome to Cameron, since her father was always punctual to a fault, even with things he disapproved of doing. Once he took on a job, though, he'd carry it out, like a professional plumber dedicated to finding where the leak in a line was, hunting it down, and then plugging it up for good.

That's what Daddy does, Cameron mused, and that's what he's done all his life and will be still doing when he's dead if God'll give him the chance to keep looking for leaks. That's my old man, practicing the craft of the plumber, the current heir and placeholder in line of the largest plugging-up and toilet-installing family firm in Little Rock, Arkansas, a man like Grand Pop and all the other Grand Pops before him. It was ending now, though, the dominance of the dynasty of the plumbing Semmes family in Arkansas's capital city, since there wasn't a single male heir left to give a damn about finding why drains were plugged and pipes were leaking and commodes wouldn't flush.

"I am a great disappointment," Cameron said out loud to Wrong Hand, the only other person she'd seen in the house when she'd come in from a day hanging around Blue Moon Studio just off Eighteenth Avenue, on the prowl for something. Wrong Hand looked up from the bass guitar he was picking with his left hand, that the reason for what he was called and answered to, and nodded politely. He hadn't understood a word Cameron had said, she could tell, and that was promising. He'd eaten or sucked or smoked or snorted or shot up something strong, or maybe all that, in the last little while. His eyes seemed to be working independently of each other, one pointed up and the other down, one blinking and the other intermittently closed, one focused and the other wandering off to the side as though seeking the direction of a sudden clap of thunder.

"I broke my daddy's heart," Cameron said, "when after I turned the age of twelve I refused to pick up a wrench again. Hell, I wouldn't even touch a plumber's friend any more. I didn't give a shit if every pipe in every house in Little Rock sprung a leak. If a commode didn't want to flush, my attitude was let it do its own thing. Who was I to define another thing's bliss?"

"Cool," Wrong Hand said, looking back down at his left hand as though it belonged to someone else and he'd been instructed to watch what it was doing and maybe learn a thing or two from studying its skillful movements. "I can dig that."

"But you know what, Wrong Hand?" Cameron Semmes said. "My daddy forgave me for that, and you know why? I'll tell you why. He figured anybody with Semmes blood, girl or not, would finally give in to the impulse to plumb. They'd finally pick up that wrench, listen real hard to where the leak was coming from, no matter how faint or far off, hunt that sucker down, and fix it. That's why he never gave up on me and never will, and that's why he still sends a check made out to me every month from Semmes Plumbing, Inc., still believing I'll eventually come to my senses and reach for that monkey wrench and put on some overalls."

"You say you got a check?" Wrong Hand said. "Can you loan me a little until I get paid for this gig I got coming?"

"I don't have any money now, and you haven't a gig coming, and you know what else, Wrong Hand?"

"Decca wants me to do some studio work. They sure do. A cat done told me that this morning," Wrong Hand said. "Or maybe it was yesterday morning. The sun was shining real bright when he told me, I remember that."

"I'm going to tell you what else, whether you want to hear it or not," Cameron said. "As long as pipes leak in Little Rock, I got a future I can count on."

"It's dark outside now, though. I don't see the sun shining nowhere."

"It ought to be dark, Wrong Hand. It's nighttime, and I know you're holding something. What is it? And give me a little hit of it."

The front door to the big house on Belmont was closed, but it hadn't been lockable for as long as Cameron had been staying there and maybe for years before that, so when Tollman Briggs pushed it open, neither Cameron nor Wrong Hand saw him enter the front alcove and come down it into the room where they sat.

"How long have you been standing there, Tollman?" Wrong Hand said, looking up from the bass guitar. "I guess I thought you was a chifforobe or something. I only just now saw you."

"I was a chifforobe," Tollman said, "and now I changed back to me after listening to what y'all were saying."

"Huh," Wrong Hand said. "I figured it was something like that you was, some kind of furniture. Did you know I got me a gig over at Decca, Tollman?"

"That's good to hear. And a great big old white whale just surfaced in the Cumberland River today and started prophesying, Wrong Hand. Everybody in downtown Nashville's gone on down to the edge of the river to listen to him."

"He did? What's he saying?"

"He said as soon as Wrong Hand Stubbins freely shares his stash with those that love him, the whale will heave up out of that water, walk out of the river, and deliver blessings to every man in Tennessee."

"What about blessings for every woman, Tollman?" Cameron said. "Is the whale a male chauvinist pig?"

"He's a white whale, Cameron," Wrong Hand said. "Not no pig. Didn't you hear what Tollman just said?"

"When are you going to start sharing your dope, then?" Cameron said, "so the whale can come out of the water and get all this good shit started?"

Wrong Hand hit a lick on the bass guitar, closed both eyes for almost half a minute, and when he opened them again, both seemed in relatively good synch. "Okay, eyes," Wrong Hand said, "let's go in the kitchen and see what's cooking. Guide me in yonder."

It wasn't until a good two hours later that Cameron decided it was time to take Tollman into one of the rooms off the long hall at the top of the stairs and see if a little workout would relax her enough to be able to sleep a few hours, if not all the rest of the night, but at least until the birds of Nashville cranked up their songs for the new day to come, the hour when nobody in the city could stay asleep. She hadn't been with Tollman for several days, as far as she could remember, and from past experience she knew he'd be so grateful for the favor she was about to confer upon him that he'd stay on the job maybe long enough to listen to where the leak was coming from, hunt it down, and plug it up for a while.

"Tollman," she said, taking a last hard toke from the final roach of Mexican weed Wrong Hand had come up with. "I hear the sound of water coming from somewhere. It's dripping like a bad faucet. You want to go help me track it down?"

"Oh, hell, yeah, Cameron," Tollman said. "Is it a bad leak, you think?"

"What I'm hearing tells me it's bad enough to need a good stoppage," she said and ate the last of the roach.

Later that night a little after two in the morning, Lily Schmidt Alden sat behind the wheel of the Chevrolet, parked in front of the house on Graystone Lane where she hardly ever parked, chiefly because she was usually having to unload three children and a load of groceries and bags and boxes, and she wanted that disgorging to take place as close to the back door of the house as possible. If she parked on the street, not only did she have to carry all the stuff in on her own, but she had to hold Dylan and make sure Emily or Julian wouldn't run out into the street and get hit by some idiot driving by at Nashville speed, too fast always for current conditions. Both of the kids who could walk knew better than to venture out of the yard onto the pavement, but they did that whenever they got the chance anyway. They did that for at least two reasons: because they didn't think ahead to what might happen, and they did it to spite their mother because she had told them not to do it.

One reason, then, she hadn't pulled up into the driveway this late at night was on the off-chance that Ronald was asleep and maybe wouldn't wake up when she came into the house, and the other was that she was crying so much she could barely see where to turn the car into the driveway through the stream flowing from her eyes as though something in her tear ducts had broken that ordinarily controlled the amount possible for discharge. She wasn't sobbing as much as she had at first, and the moaning sounds she'd been making all the way home as she drove through the streets of Nashville with all its streetlights befogged and haloed by her drowning eyes had died down some.

On the way home, Lily had hoped she could get control of herself enough to be able to hide her condition from her husband if he was awake or woke up when he heard her moaning, but by the time she pulled the Chevrolet over and parked in front of the rent house in which her family lived, she'd decided she didn't give a shit. Let the bastard see what shape she was in if he happened to rouse up and see her. Who fucking cares, a voice inside her said, and then she said that out loud, as she sat in front of the house, with the car's engine still running and its lights still on. The worse thing had already happened. After that, what could Ronald's judgment of her mean or matter?

When she'd walked up to the door of the house on Belmont where Tollman stayed—he refused to say he lived there, he'd told her more than once, or that he lived anywhere in fact; he just stayed places, a wanderer of and among the folk always—the door was standing half open and new tender leaves were being blown in by a pretty strong spring breeze, pushing at her from behind as though to say she should just walk in and not bother to knock and wait for somebody to come to the door and invite her to step inside. No one had made social calls at this old wreck of a house in the last thirty years anyway, Lily thought as she pushed the door open enough to allow her to enter. The kind of people that she'd seen wandering in and out of this place during the times she'd been there with Tollman acted like a bunch of cave dwellers as they came and went, hardly ever noticing anybody but themselves, and when they did see another being, not displaying a bit of interest, not even to mention a shred of courtesy. All they'd do if they deigned to take notice of her was to ask if she was holding anything or if she had any spare change. Jesus! What a bunch of losers most of them were, though one or two were interesting in odd ways, the kind of people you might see in documentaries about protests and hootenannies and folk concerts and sit-ins, pale and hairy and sullen and thin to the point of emaciation.

So when she'd walked into the old house sometime after midnight— it had taken that long for Ronald to grade all his damned papers and drink enough bourbon to make him go to bed and fall asleep like a stone, thus giving Lily the opportunity to leave their house, get in the car and drive to Belmont Street, something she'd never had the nerve to do before, but tonight she just had to touch Tollman—the only person she saw was skinny, longhaired, barefoot, and dressed in dirty jeans and a T shirt, picking at a guitar with his eyes closed. "Pardon me," Lily said, "is Tollman in his room asleep?'

"Oh, you got here," the man said, not opening his eyes at first and then when he did, blinking and looking behind Lily as though someone had followed her into the room. She looked back over her shoulder, putting a smile on her face to show she was prepared to be civil to the person who'd perhaps walked in behind her with no announcement, but no one was there.

"I am here, yes," Lily said, this time nodding and smiling in the direction of the guitar plucker. "Is Tollman Briggs here tonight?"

"Yes, ma'am. He's still upstairs, I guess. Did he send you over here?"

"Tollman? No, I haven't spoken to him in a couple of days, and I just wanted to see him. About an event I'm planning, something he might want to sing at."

"No, I meant the whale. Did he send you to deliver a message? I didn't think he'd send a lady."

"A whale? Some person you call whale? I don't know him. No, no one by that name sent me. In fact, as I said, no one did."

"I guess he'll come himself, then," the man sitting on the floor with the oversized guitar said. "He's a mammal, you know. He breathes air, just like us. He comes up to the surface to do that, because he has to, if he wants to keep on living. They say he can walk."

"I see," Lily had said, thinking here's another one, a lost soul and a destroyed mind. But maybe he's just drunk or drugged up and can get better with care. Then she stepped carefully around the guitar player, giving him enough room not to have to shift his position to let her by, and went upstairs to the room where Tollman stayed and where he made her delirious those heated and transforming times on that magic mattress. The door was closed, probably to allow Tollman to block the sound of the guitar and the comings and goings of the others who wandered in and out of the house on Belmont Street, a girl called Rainbow and another one who said she was Morning Glory and some hairy young men with names she'd either never heard or never wanted to remember: Snake Music and Slick and Hole Jumper among them.

She knocked gently at the door, heard someone shift on the mattress on the floor as though half consciously aware of a sound filtering through to him in his sleep, and it came to Lily to surprise Tollman by softly entering his room while he lay nude on his bed, as he always slept as he'd told her, covered by a sheet at times, but beneath that always wearing no more in the world of dream than he did when he came forth from his mother's womb. When I sleep, he liked to whisper in Lily's ear after they'd come together in the act that began as fucking but ended in love, I would always have my body remember its bare beginning and its eternal self.

There was light in the room, Lily discovered as she cracked the door, a soft and flickering glow from candles, inconstant but sufficient to reveal clearly what lay before her. Tollman's face was buried between the woman's legs, his head tilted up and his eyes half closed as he moved slowly and rhythmically with upward strokes of his tongue, lit redly by candles placed just outside the widely spread legs of the woman who lay back with her head supported on what looked like a throw pillow from a sofa. Tollman's hands moved in a slow caress from a spot just above the knees of the woman up along the outside of her legs. As Tollman's hands reached the woman's rib cage, she turned her face toward Lily and smiled, making a beckoning gesture with her left hand. "Hi, there," she said. "Want to join us, Lily? Always room for one more."

As she stumbled down the stairs, feeling her throat beginning to constrict and the sobs gathering deep inside her chest before the racking delivery of moans, cries, and tears she knew would come, Lily could think of only one thing. Not what she'd seen Tollman and the woman doing on the bare mattress beneath, not the way his eyes looked half-closed like those of a child biting into a sweet often forbidden but now miraculously available, not the way the candle light flickered on his hands moving up her sides in total caress and adoration, none of those things of the physical world held in suspension in that room, but one overwhelming question instead. How did the bitch know her name?

I won't let myself answer that now, Lily repeated again and again as she drove the Chevrolet home, not knowing when she'd gotten into the car or when she'd started the engine or how she'd found her way to Graystone Lane where her husband and children were sleeping, I'll wait until I think I can stand it before I let myself know that.

Ronald was asleep when she went into the bedroom. At least his eyes were closed, and he was breathing the way an unconscious or dying man will do as he waits for the last inhalation and the final expulsion of breath to arrive. He didn't move when Lily slipped into bed beside him, no alteration in his position or breathing, not even when she put her hand on his to see if he would pull away at the touch. She hated him then, knowing she'd never forgive her husband for that, for not being awake, for not having to fake sleep, and she pulled away to her side of the bed, lying near enough to the edge of it to feel she might fall if she moved one hair closer. I'll never be able to fall asleep again, Lily said to herself, not tonight, not ever.

But she did, and she did not dream, and she remained unconscious until the mixed and raucous song of all the birds of Nashville woke her at dawn.

20

ROBARD FLANGE HAD LAGGED in his timing this spring and had failed to deliver what had come to be expected of him. It was the first occasion anyone at Vanderbilt could remember his April Fools' Day poem not appearing in the special satiric edition of the student newspaper, and he was sitting in his study at home staring blankly at a yellow pad of paper on the desk before him. Why even continue with the effort, he had asked himself when the editor of the rag had called him to inquire when the April Fool poem from Dr. Flange would arrive for placement in the special edition.

"It's become one of the Vandy traditions," the editor had said. "Every time a new editor is named for the *Hustler* one of the first things he hears from the guy who's outgoing is to be sure to remind Dr. Flange about the deadline for his April Fools' Day poem. The students all look forward to it, Sir, and it's printed right in the middle of the second page, like always. Everybody always wants to see it there. It's a fixture."

"I appreciate the sentiment," Robard had said, his left arm twitching at the untruth he was offering this Jonathan Seth Matthews, an editor whose tenure should have concluded at the end of last year's second semester, a young man who'd praised this Allen Ginsberg creature upon his barbarous actions as one of the participants in the infamous Impact Symposium of 1967, an event which celebrated sodomy, encouraged Negro unrest at Vanderbilt and in Nashville at large, and which featured the two national leaders of such behavior in the entire nation, this Stokely

204

Carmichael incendiary and Martin Luther King Jr., a so-called minister of the gospel but in true fact a Communist and provocateur manqué. *Time* Magazine's "Man of the Year," indeed.

"I've enjoyed bringing a bit of levity to the campus over the years," Robard Flange said, "particularly at the time for good-natured satiric fun and the poking of pins into inflated egos which is the purpose of such a time as April Fools' Day. Being a scholar of the literary products of the great English satirists, I've ventured so boldly as to offer each year my humble contribution to the tradition of the Manichean impulse, which as you may know, is a satire which aims not only to criticize and bring down vanity, but in that process to improve public behavior and the morality of the powerful. It attacks, but shows the truly moral way to virtue."

"Yessir," Jonathan Seth Matthews said in response, taking advantage of the fact that Dr. Flange couldn't see him over the telephone by moving his cupped right hand rapidly up and down in a jacking motion for the benefit of Raymond Arceneau, the *Hustler* reporter listening in on another receiver. Raymond had bent over at that as though to offer his rectum for penetration, and Jonathan had risen from his chair and air-humped at him for a couple of strokes. "I don't know that much about satire, Dr. Flange, but I do know everybody that reads the April Fools' edition of the *Hustler* never misses your poem each and every year."

"Isn't your major field of study English?" Robard Flange had asked in an innocent tone, putting the incompetent young editor on notice that his comments on satire were not only less than acceptable but revelatory of one not serious about literature, particularly that of the eighteenth-century Enlightenment, and in crucial need of amendment.

"Yessir, Dr. Flange, but I never took your satire course. I really wanted to, but every semester I had some conflict with it I couldn't avoid."

"Oh, well," Robard had said, "I'll see what I can do, if the demand for my bit of funning is what you say it is. A bit of informed laughter, not mindless hooting, can be a great support to the intellect and a relief to the emotions of students."

Despite the request from the degenerate editor of the *Hustler*, Robard Flange had not written a poem for the 1968 April Fools' edition of the paper. He had sworn an effort to comply only to the extent of saying he would make fair trial, and did not pledge a poetic product. There was therefore no violation of honor or of commitment to a task due for completion. His promise to attempt to do so was driven entirely out of his head by a more pressing matter, his weekly treatments for the misfortune of the dead arm belonging to Rooney Beauchamp, that limb lost in 1862 at Shiloh and now attached through work of the Prince of Darkness to Robard's shoulder and self, existing now in the desolate and blasted heath of twentieth-century Nashville.

The treatments by Miss Lurleen, as Robard had come to call her, the pet name, he knew, pleasing her greatly, though modesty forbade her saying so, had been going most well. Each trip from his home in West Nashville to the once-thriving downtown area of the city left Robard not only energized, but sated; not only relieved of pain, but emotionally restless; not only for a spell unconscious of the dead weight of the Rooney limb dependent, but intensely aware of the personality of the young officer which dwelt each week more strongly in the mind and soul of Robard himself. Through the expert and loving—yes, call it that, use that word: loving. Lord God, the services this child of the mountains supplied—ministrations of Lurleen Blankenship of Music City Magic Fingers Massage Salon and of the country yeomanry and womanhood of East Tennessee, Robard had been feeling a steady healing develop, not simply physical, but a mending and joining, a true melding of the selfhood of the gallant Rooney Beauchamp of Benevolence Plantation, commanding officer of the Fourth Mississippi, with that of Dr. Robard Flange, professor of English at Vanderbilt University. It was a gift, it was a miracle, it was a blessing, being made whole.

Now Robard drew from a desk drawer a copy of last year's special April Fools' edition of the student newspaper and began to read from the poem he had penned for the *Hustler* and published there. He read with a growing sense of disappointment the bit of satiric fluff before him that he had seen fit to publish a short year before, realizing now that the new state he had achieved revealed how vapid, how surface, how silly and jejune, the product of his imagination showed him to have been only months earlier. First of all the title, one he'd thought clever and catchy enough to attract the admiration of students, now struck him as simplistic, juvenile, thin, and finally, the worst sin of all for a satirist, not funny.

It was called "Rhonda, the Red Lipped Coed," an obvious take-off on Rudolph, the Red Nosed Reindeer, that ditty in itself out of season. Worse, though, was the fact that even a superficial reading of the poem itself showed its author to be enamored of spoiled, upper-class, vapid sorority girls with no sense of obligation to tradition, to the need for struggle in the face of adversity, young women who if asked to minister to the arm of a man dead for over a century and now attached to a full professor of English would have screamed something like "gross" and have fled instantly to the comfortable cocoons of their sheltered lives. Would they bend to the tasks which Lurleen, a simple maiden from Cookeville, performed with such dignity, dispatch, and diligence? No need to ask that question.

As Robard turned from the poem he had written and published for all to see, now realizing that the genuine fool on April the First of 1967 had been not Rhonda, the Red Lipped Coed, but none other than himself, he lifted his hands to shield his eyes from the condemnation before him, the dead arm quivering with the strain and falling back before reaching halfway to his face, and he distinctly heard a voice speak. Calm, deep, insistent, and loud enough to have been heard outside his study, were there an auditor to witness, the words came.

"Do not grieve overmuch. That poem was not written for a living woman, but for a phantasm. There can be no lasting shame in that for one grown finally into the fullness of his manhood and character."

"What can I do to atone?" Robard asked. "To whom am I speaking now? Is it the immortal Alexander Pope?"

"Pope is among the shades, where he remains isolate and completed in paradise, his work done. Do you not know me?"

"Major Beauchamp?" Robard said. "Of Benevolence Plantation, in Panola County?"

"You know me as no man has," the voice said, this time with a touch of humor. "You know me as Rooney. You are Robard to me, my friend."

"What can I do? I cannot disavow my deed. I cannot retrieve what has been published."

"No, you cannot change the past. But that's of no consequence. Turn your face and your pen to the present and to what will come. Write a true poem, truly directed and truly addressed to she who merits it."

"Lurleen Blankenship," Robard breathed the name. "She must be the maiden of whom you speak."

"Lurleen of the yeoman stock of Old Tennessee. Speak to and of her in verse. That must be your goal."

"I will bend my efforts to do so, Major Beauchamp," Robard said, looking toward the source of the voice, somewhere deep in the shadows of the darkly timbered room of books and framed photographs of Confederate officers and private soldiers, but in vain.

"Please, Robard," the voice spoke once again with a cordial tone of amusement, trailing in volume as though it were moving away down a forest track, becoming muted by distance, "why would you not call your friend by his Christian name?"

"Rooney," Robard said, through a catch in his throat, "I promise no merit in the product of my wit, but I pledge complete allegiance to my effort."

Listen though he did for a full minute, his breath held and his good ear cocked toward the door from which Rooney Beauchamp had spoken, Robard could hear no hint of another sound. Turning his attention toward the yellow pad of blank paper before him, he lifted his pen and began to write the words which he began to hear dictated to him in the quiet of his study, audible to none but himself. It was a complete iambic pentameter heroic couplet, the choice of the masters of satiric verse of the golden age of literature in England, the eighteenth century, and it glowed before him on the page as though indicted in living light.

"The bird's wing sweeps at end of Southern day
As on dead arm your living tongue doth play."

Robard Flange saw his work, knew it was good, granted and begun by grace, and he bent to the task before him, the creation of "An Ode to Old Tennessee's Daughter." He paused, poised to hear a telling rhyme for lick, heard it granted, and fell into poetic fit.

Across the western verge of Nashville, on Belmont Street, in a crumbling mansion built in the 1870s by Solomon Sprinkle, founder of a tobacco snuff company which boomed in that period of commercial growth after the unpleasantness between the States of the Union had finally resolved, Tollman Briggs plucked at the strings of a guitar in a garrett room just under the rafters, his eyes closed in a spasm of imaginative concentration. Near him, Cameron Semmes sat scribbling with a number two pencil on a torn-open and flattened envelope the words which Tollman spoke as each note was teased from the strings he caressed.

"You ask if my love's of the body or of the soul," he was saying, speaking slowly to allow Cameron to keep up with what his muse was telling him, "you say if my love's of another, it can't be of you. Yet if you let your body talk, the answer's waiting somewhere in blue."

"In blues?" Cameron said. "Like in Memphis stuff? Memphis Slim and Memphis Minnie and that bunch?"

"No," Tollman said, opening his eyes to let Cameron see she was bugging him, interrupting the creative flow, and should just write down what she heard and let him see what he'd said later. Jesus, you can't comment on what you're doing while you're doing it. It'd be like wondering if you were keeping your rig up while you were in the middle of putting it where it had to be put. Dick, hey, dick, are you being a dick? Thinking about what you're doing while you're doing it is like your belly trying to figure out how to digest what it's digesting while it's doing it.

"No, not like the blues, like blue, you know," Tollman said. "Like something is blue colored."

"That doesn't make sense," Cameron said, erasing the letter s from the last word she'd written.

"Exactly," Tollman said. "Thanks for that. Now write this down. I just thought it up after you asked me about the blues. Here it is. Get it down now, before I lose it. 'My belly knows its job, my body stays true, what I eat is bound to feed me, what you ask me is nothing but blue.' "

"Far out," Cameron said in full scribble. "Amazing."

"Yep, and you ain't heard nothing yet. Get this part. 'Lay on back on my bed, don't question me and what I do. All you need to know about me is blue.' "

"You're smoking, Dude."

"Tell me about it. Here comes another line. 'Close your eyes, open your mouth, and taste the blue.' "

"Wow," Cameron said. "Amazing. This is about Lily, that married chick you've been boning, right? Is it about her catching you going down on me?"

"No, it's not about that. It's about nothing. It's like all my stuff. It's elemental, girl. It's not about Lily Alden. It's about blue. Hell, what I hope it's about is getting me produced on Eighteenth Avenue."

21

RANDALL EUGENE PUCKETT knew they'd get there late, even just for the first drive-by when all they were going to do is look things over, check out just where the wig place was, see where it'd be easiest for Milton to park while him and Tooter did the job, all that getting ready stuff. Then they'd go back home to wait until time to come do it. It wasn't his fault they didn't get to Second Avenue at the time they'd planned for the scouting-things-out cruise, that was for damn sure, and he knew in his bones without having to be told that Tooter Browning wasn't one to keep anybody waiting. That big black bastard was born ready to be on time, from the looks of him. I ain't talking about being on time for doing a job of work now, Randall Eugene said to himself as Milton worked his old Pontiac through the early morning traffic in downtown Nashville. I expect Tooter Browning's just like every other nigger when it comes to doing real work for wages. A day late, a dollar short, and looking for a way to get out of doing what he's hired to do.

Randall Eugene's old daddy had always told him the way to act when you're a working man is give the boss a good day's work for what he's paying you for every day when the job starts. Do that, don't talk back, and don't shirk. That's what John Calvin Puckett told all his kids, the sorry old bastard. He was damned good to give advice while he was laid up at the house saying his back was out and claiming there wasn't a single lick of work in the county for a man to get hired to do. He could forevermore talk about working a job the right way, though.

But no, the reason they didn't get to Second Avenue before the morning rush hour got into full gear wasn't his fault, and it wasn't Tooter Browning's, neither, sitting back in the rear seat of the car all by himself. Good thing he was the only one back there, big as he was, Randall Eugene thought. I'd hate to be sitting by him, having to hug the door to get enough room to lean back and having to smell him up close while we rode along with the windows up, cool as it is this early in April. Tooter didn't stink, really, didn't smell dirty like many a white man did uptight in a confined space, but he had that smell a nigger will have. Kind of a musky, old timey, spicy aroma. It wasn't like the sweat coming off a white man or that old Mum and powder stink you'd sniff off a old lady. It had a tang to it that would put you on edge. Tooter smelled like he might do something any minute now, something that would surprise you and might work against you, real quick and strong. He smelled nigger dangerous.

Nope, here we are crawling along Second Avenue with all these delivery vans and buses and people in their cars going to work in all these buildings downtown in Nashville because it's Thursday, the day we're going to do the thing on the wig shop. Thursday, that's the day when the week's numbers money is going to all be there for them four or five hours late in the afternoon, according to what Tooter Browning says, who ought to know what he's talking about from just looking at him and listening to the way he says his words and looks out of his eyes and, goddamn, the scary way he smells. We're late getting here for the look-see because Milton Drummond's chickenshit and always has been, and will put off doing what he has to do until it's too late, every damn time.

"Can't you get around that damn bread truck, Milton?" Randall Eugene said, feeling an itching start up somewhere on his back, not high enough to be reached to scratch, but bad enough to make him squirm against the seat back. No relief, though, and there sure wasn't nobody around to scratch it for him. Like every damn thing else, Randall Eugene was on his own in this thing, having to deal with whatever come up without a lick of help or appreciation to move things along. People might be all around him, up in his face close enough to take the breath out of his lungs, but they sure wasn't about to provide any kind of advantage to him.

"He's looks like he's fixing to move here in a minute," Milton said, jiggling up and down behind the steering wheel and leaning forward as though another few inches less of distance between him and what he was looking at might make something happen faster. "See, his brake lights done went off."

"Honk your horn at the motherhumper," Tooter Browning said from the back seat in a lazy sounding voice. "Put a little pressure on the Ideal Bread van he be driving."

"I would," Milton said, hammering once on the center of the steering wheel hub, "but see, the horn don't usually work." It didn't that time, allowing Milton to throw up his right hand in justified aggravation.

"We close enough to see where we got to be going this afternoon, anyway," Tooter said. "You can read that sign up yonder off to the side, where it says about wigs and shit."

"We don't have to go in there right now, do we?" Randall Eugene said. "Just ride by it slow, take a look, and get it located."

"Naw, it ain't nobody in yonder needs to see me before the real business start up," Tooter said. "Little Lou catch sight of me, she going to know it's liable to be some shit coming down, and the first thing she going to do is get on that phone and let Pearly Red Mungo hear the news that she seen me. That's the last thing we want to have happen."

"He's the one supposed to be doing the pick up, right?" Randall Eugene said, turning in the passenger's seat to speak over his shoulder into the back of the Pontiac. "Or is he the man bringing that bag of money for her to hang onto until eight o'clock?"

"What you want to know for, Hoss? You ain't needing to know who do what when. All you got to do is walk in that door about seven and get Little Lou to start asking you what you want. And then you tell her just what I said she needs to hear. She going to hop up off that stool and come around the counter to show you what you asking for. Then I'll come in behind you, and that's when we'll hit our lick."

"Well, yeah," Randall Eugene said, keeping his voice low and friendly, but thinking goddamn I hate to have to listen to a nigger talk to me like that. It galls my ass. "I'm just, you know, wondering."

"You ain't got to wonder. All you going to do is get Little Lou out from that counter where she keeps the shotgun, and then I'll take over. Get her to show you a nice wig for your old lady that's got the cancer and had them treatments that's made her hair all fall out. That's your part of the job, and it ain't your business to worry about folks's names and shit. Keep your part in the deal clear in your head, and don't put nothing else in there along with it. You don't want to overload that fucker."

"Can I ask you something, Tooter?" Milton Drummond said, beginning to ease the Pontiac forward a little as the Ideal Bread van started to creep ahead in the morning traffic. "Why is Little Lou, like you call her, why is she going to want to wait on a white man wanting a wig for his wife? What I mean is why would she get up from where she keeps the shotgun and walk around the counter to help Randall Eugene find the right wig for his wife with the cancer?"

"That question's a good one," Tooter said, beginning to chuckle deep in his throat. "First good one I heard this morning that makes good sense. See, Little Lou is got a special thing about women that's lost all their hair to them cancer treatments. Her old mama died of that shit, and so did Little Lou's girl. So she got a soft spot for women wanting to cover up their heads where them chemicals has worked the hair all loose before that shit gets done killing them."

"That's the advantage we got then," Randall Eugene said, "when I ask to see about wigs for my sick old lady's head."

"You got to find a man's weakness or a woman's, either," Tooter Browning said. "And you got to exploit the living hell out of it. His weakness is your strength, see."

"Huh," Milton said, giving the Pontiac a little more gas, "where'd you learn that? Working at the co-cola plant when we was there?"

"Naw, I ain't never learned nothing working nowhere except I be getting exploited. I learned about looking for a weakness when I was boxing. Manny Elledge taught me that lesson over in the Jefferson Street gym when it used to be one there. Find where a man can't stand to get hit, Manny said, and then bust the hell out of that very spot. And then keep on doing it until he falls down."

Damn, Randall Eugene said to himself, the more Tooter talks the more I can smell that damn musk coming off of him. Out loud, pointing to the façade of the gray stone building coming up on the left, he said, "You can read that sign real good now. Off a little bit to the side of the door. Wanda's Wigs."

"That's right," Tooter said. "Right next to the whorehouse sign where it says about music city and magic fingers massages. That's where it's all going to come down just about dark."

"Ain't it supposed to rain tonight?" Milton said. "Y'all reckon the streets might be slicked up some?"

"Who gives a shit?" Randall Eugene said. "We ain't going to be trying to plow up no goddamn cotton field."

"Heh," Tooter said from the back seat. "You boys still a country bunch of fuckers, ain't you?"

I got to roll this window down, Randall Eugene thought, making himself cough like he needed air as he reached for the handle. It smells so funky and scary in this car I'm about to pass out. I don't know how to talk about goddamn cancer wigs. If I ask Maureen back at the house about it, she'll look at me like I gone nuts. I'll tell her I'm worried about her maybe getting sick. She ain't about to buy that shit, though. And I can't say a word back to this big black bastard sitting behind me.

"You going to want to write on the wall with your spray can again, Tooter?" Milton was saying, sounding like he was asking a football player if he was going to strut his stuff in a game he was about to play. "I mean like you did in the Stop 'n' Shop that time?"

"Shit, yeah," Tooter said back to Milton, on the verge of laughing as he spoke, "I got to get in my licks for Black Power, man. I be writing a message, and I done got thought up what I'm going to say."

"What's that?" Milton said in a way that made Randall Eugene want to lean across the seat and slap him upside the head for sucking up like that to a nigger.

"Oh, something like this," Tooter said, leaning forward in his seat and moving his right hand as though to point out a line of words one by one. 'Wig Up for the Race War, Bro.' I might even write it on the outside of the building."

"Lord have mercy," Milton said, speeding up his Pontiac a little there on Second Avenue so he could get through the light a half block ahead before it turned red on him.

When Ronald Alden left the house on Graystone, he knew he'd be late for his Thursday morning class, at least by ten minutes, if not more. He'd thought to call one of the departmental secretaries to ask her to tell the students to wait until he arrived, but he'd had to do that twice already in the last two weeks, and one more request to Dot Smothers to leave her desk and walk across campus to hold a group of surly scholars in place for a tardy professor would likely cause her to complain to the department chairman. The last thing Alfred Buchanan needed to hear in this tenure-decision year for Ronald Alden, assistant professor probationary, was that this candidate for lifetime appointment was forming the habit of being late to class on a regular basis.

Ordinarily, students would count it a great boon to be able to miss ninety minutes of staring at the lyrics of Shelley and being asked about the import of word placement, metre, and image by the man in the cheap suit standing in front of the classroom. But not today, since Dr. Alden had scheduled a written exam, and those that had prepared for it would be royally pissed at having wasted their efforts looking at notes and cheat sheets the night before. They expected salaried staff not only to be competent, but on time.

Ronald was leaving the house late through no immediate fault of his own, though he couldn't deny he had brought his troubles on himself, not anticipating several years before when he'd married the first woman to give him full and regular access to her body that she'd end up being a manic-depressive bitch of the first water once the vows were said and his fate was sealed. This Thursday morning Lily was in the down phase of the nut cycle and had been for several days, refusing to leave her bed when he was in the house, leaving all the care, feeding, watering, dressing, diapering, and transporting of his three spawn to him alone. The fucking you get for the fucking you got, as one of his college roommates had called the aftermath of marital commitment. Not an original thought, of course, but nothing he'd ever heard or thought was original, Ronald had come to realize. All he could do was recast, not create.

So Lily lay in bed, head covered with a pillow to muffle the outcries of rage, hunger, fear, resentment, and bad humor of her actual children and her putative husband. When Ronald had asked her if she could do them this morning because of the Thursday class and its scheduled exam, Lily hadn't even bothered to answer, making that four days in a row she hadn't spoken to him. At least, though, she had ceased to moan and cry for hours on end as she'd begun doing one morning almost a week before.

That had gotten so pronounced and so old that Ronald had called her shrink begging for help, and Dr. Tribble had finally, with great reluctance and a grumbling lecture against short-term measures, accommodated the plea by issuing Lily a new prescription for downers which proved to be strong enough to stun her into silence and a state of sleep bordering on coma. Better that than the steady moans and tears, though, Ronald considered as he loaded the last squirming Alden offspring into the Chevrolet for the ride to the all-day sitters at Southern Airs Day Care just off Peabody.

"I don't want to go to Southern Airs," Emily stated, after having refused to walk on her own to the car. "And neither does Rum Tum."

"Oh, is Rum Tum with us this morning?" Ronald asked as he forced his eldest child into the back seat. "Where's your other friend, Sarah? I bet she'd like to go with us. It's her turn to take a ride, isn't it?"

"Sarah's not in my room any more," Emily said. "I haven't seen her in a long time."

"That's too bad," Ronald said, firing up the engine and backing into the street. "She's nice."

"I think Rum Tum has hit her on the head real hard," Emily said. "She's knocked out."

"Why would he do that? That's not nice."

"Because Sarah cried too much. Rum Tum hates that crap."

"Don't say crap, Emily. That's not a nice word."

"You say it, Daddy. You say damn it and shit. You say goddamn."

"Stop that right now."

"See, you get to holler when you want to, and Rum Tum is fed up with it," Emily said and then turning to the empty space beside her, "Rum Tum, I know it's no use talking to him. But there's nobody else around. Just you and me."

The children delivered, all of them plus Rum Tum and the gear for a day out of the house except for the snacks forgotten on the kitchen table, the Chevrolet driven at high speed to campus and parked illegally in a maintenance department space, and a hard run across the quadrangle to Confederate Hall accomplished, Dr. Alden entered his Thursday morning sophomore survey of English lit class to discover that most students were still there. Only a few of the faithful looked up as he burst through the door in a stumble with the exam blue books in hand. Two or three cheered in a mocking fashion, and the rest sat silent, staring at him as though he was a waiter so late with his delivery of their entrees from the kitchen that the food was congealed and stone cold. Only one student smiled at him. Josephine Longineaux, Josey, Joey, Jo Jo, Jo Sweet, her blue eyes clear and sparkling, her wonderful legs crossed at the ankles, and her head tilted in that slant of invitation she projected so well. Kiss me, it said. You can't bear not to.

Fortified and burning, every cell at tingle with life and purpose and full presence in this moment before his love, Dr. Ronald Alden distributed the exam blue books and the questions to which his students were to respond: thoughtful queries into essence, into poetic strategy, into a meaningful grappling with issues of what it means to be human in an insensitive world, into the universe of the word. With a few quiet sounds of foot scrapes, pen and pencil scratchings, and shiftings in seats, the students settled into the most blessed moment of the classroom: concentration of their attention away from the teacher and toward the immediate empty space before them. They would read and write and erase for an hour, and Ronald Alden would be able to stare unobserved over the book held before him at the shifting planes of the face of Josephine Longineaux, at the perfection of her calves, and the rise and fall of the breasts beneath her blouse as her breathing calmly moved the fabric fortunate enough to be touching her.

"It's Thursday, ain't it?" Blanche Ann Weaver said, looking at an appointment planner on the desk before her, a piece of furniture which had once served the professional needs of a vice president of the Bank and Trust of the Cumberland but had been abandoned and left as trash with the rest of the furnishings in 1930 when commerce in downtown Nashville shuddered, slipped, and slid into the river to add to the flotsam of dashed hopes and sunk finances flowing toward the Tennessee, the Ohio, the Mississippi, and finally into the Gulf of Mexico. Blanche had found the desk among a bunch of other discards in a back room of the B and T building, dusted it off, rubbed it with linseed oil, and created herself a handsome physical center for the paperwork of the Music City Magic Fingers Massage Salon. She liked to run her fingers over the solid mahogany surface of her desk as she sat and brooded over the daily business appointments of the building's current enterprise, enjoying the soothing feel of solidity and worth the dark wood provided.

"Thursday, April the fourth," she said to the woman sitting before her studying her fingernails and their newly applied polish as she listened to her boss go over the work schedule of the day. "I see you got the usual coming in as the last appointment of the afternoon, right?"

"Yes, ma'am," Lurleen Blankenship said, automatically deferring verbally to a person older than she and occupying a higher rank to boot. By turning each hand slowly in a counterclockwise manner while stretching her arms out before her, she discovered she could make the polish glitter in the light from the large brass fixture above Miz Weaver's desk, and that soothed her to do. She did it again, looking from the left hand to the right and back before speaking again.

"My regular old fellow's scheduled to be here again, for sure. He hadn't missed a Thursday in I don't know how long."

"Dr. Flange, I got wrote down here for today's date in your column in my book," Blanche Ann Weaver said, reaching for the lit filter-tipped cigarette in the ashtray on her desk. She coughed in anticipation before she got the Kool up to her mouth. "Seven o'clock it says. That's kind of different, ain't it? He's usually in here before suppertime. Wants to get his session in before he goes home from work, don't he?"

"Yes, ma'am, he does come in on Thursdays right about four in the afternoon usually. But today's a special day for him, he done told me. It's like kind of an anniversary for him, the way he sees it."

"Anniversary of what? When he got married to his wife?" Blanche Ann said, beginning to chuckle a little. "On the ordinary basis, a man is going to have to celebrate being married to a woman by being with her on their anniversary, not stopping at a whorehouse first to get his ashes hauled. Later, yeah, but not before the observance."

"You'd think that, wouldn't you? But it ain't his wedding anniversary he's talking about when he says it's a special day, though."

"What is it then? What's so damn unusual about a Thursday in April? It ain't even the weekend."

"Well, I had to bite my tongue when he told me to keep from laughing at what he had to say, but here's what that old boy told me last time. He said to me, do you know what next Thursday is? And I said no. He said, it's been one year to the day since you first tended my wound. And I want to make that next time real special for you and me."

"Jesus Christ, his wound?" Blanche Ann said. "I didn't know he had a wound. Girl, you ought to have told me that. That kind of thing is just eat up with germs. It ain't no telling what you might have caught from that. Is it something that don't heal up? Is his dick dripping blood or puss or something?"

"No, ma'am, I wouldn't get near nobody with any kind of sign of a disease on them. And I go to the doctor to get checked out just as regular as clockwork, like you showed me how to do. No, Dr. Flange ain't got no real wound. He thinks he does, all right, but what's wrong with him is in his funny old head."

"He thinks you're a head doctor? Does he just want to talk to you? I've had dealings with nuts like that, and I thought it would be a lot easier than letting them fuck me the first few times I just let them talk while they paid me to listen. Didn't take long, though, for me to learn it's a lot better to have some old boy wallowing around on you with a semi-hard dick than to have to listen to him tell you how crazy he is and then prove it by just jabbering. That kind of shit ain't normal. It's tainted, girl. Let me tell you."

"I mainly go along with that," Lurleen Blankenship said, "but it's kind of different with him. I about got him broke of talking about his wound, whatever that is, but I do have to listen to him go on and on about Shiloh."

"Shiloh? What's that?"

"Oh, it's some little old town somewhere on the Tennessee River. He's done told me that enough to make me remember it. They had a battle at it or some kind of a shooting a long time ago. I guess they grow peaches there. He's always telling on and on about a peach orchard."

"Huh," Blanche said, reaching for another cigarette and thinking the ashtray on her desk was so little and tinny looking it was out of place on that piece of furniture. She promised herself she'd look around for something better, if she planned to keep on smoking while she wrote in her appointment book. "Kiss my ass, if that ain't a story. Well, what's he going to do on y'all's anniversary today? Bring you a cake to eat?"

"Naw, but I wish he would," Lurleen said, rechecking the gleam of her nail polish. It didn't seem as sparkling as it had earlier. Maybe the sun was shining too bright for the overhead light to look as nice as it had been doing before. "Today Dr. Robard Flange is just going to start right off being that other fellow, Major Rooney Beauchamp, and he's going to dress up like him in the clothes Rooney would have been wearing back at Shiloh in that old battle he's so nutty about. He ain't going to wait until I lick his arm down for him from armpit to finger tip before he starts talking like he's Rooney Beauchamp of Benevolence Plantation. He's going to start off as him, and he's going to bring me a long dress to wear, so I can take it off before I go Bald Uniform on him, and then we're going to spend the whole hour just carrying on."

"Lord God on crutches," Blanche Ann Weaver said, her cigarette forgotten. "Is that all? Tell me it is."

"Not exactly. He's going to read me this poem he's done wrote about me, and then he's going to give me a autographed copy of it. The name of it is going to be 'Old Tennessee's Daughter'."

"What kind of a tip will the lunatic give you, do you imagine?"

"I don't know, but it'll be big. He done told me that. Like an anniversary dowry, that's what Rooney called it."

"You just called him Rooney. Did you know you did that? Was it on a purpose?"

"It was a slip of the tongue, I reckon. But that's what Dr. Flange wants me to call him all the time now, so I do it. That, and lick on his arm until he finally gets off."

"Well, whatever makes them lay their money down is fine with me, as long as you can stand it, honey. But Lord God, licking down his arm? Don't anybody just want a straight fuck any more?"

"Well, lots of them do want that still," Lurleen said. "But you know what, I got to where now I'd rather just lick on somebody's arm instead of letting him put his dick in me, I mean if he's give his arm a good soapy wash first and all. I don't never get nothing out of it much, whichever way one of them ends up doing it, so I'd druther lick than suck or fuck."

"The times is got so different in Nashville," Blanche Ann said. "I thank the Lord I've got so fat and old enough nobody wants me to get naked for them no more. I wouldn't know what to do if they did, these days."

"Yes, ma'am," Lurleen said. "I'll let you read my poem after Rooney gives it to me, if you want to. Do you think this nail polish is too pinkish?"

"What's the name of it, sugar? What do they call it on the label?"

"Maiden's Blush."

"Shit, yeah," Blanche Ann said. "Honey, that shade suits you just fine. Wear it."

22

JULIAN WAS PLAYING with his plastic tricycle in the corner of the backyard, the only piece of bare ground smooth enough for him to be able to ride around in tight circles without running over the exposed roots of the magnolia tree shading that area behind the house on Graystone Lane. He'd be occupied by that activity until he wanted something to eat, Lily knew, so she had opened a bag of store-brand Oreo-style cookies and left that perched in plain view on the back steps of the house going up to the kitchen door. When Julian finished the ones he held in the hand not in use to guide his tricycle, he'd be able to refill with as many others as he could stand to cram in his mouth and clutch against his chest as he ran back to his ride.

Lily had just put Dylan down for a nap, having kept him awake for two hours past his regular schedule of sleep time, thus insuring he'd be unconscious long enough for it all to happen. She hadn't allowed Emily to take more than two cookies from the open package of Wow Chocolaty Middles, knowing that would keep her focused on thinking about what she'd be able to do as soon as Mommy went into the bathroom, closed the door, and took her special bath while Emily watched the Bozo the Clown show on Channel 2 for the whole hour.

"I want some more cookies now," Emily was saying. "I promise I won't ruin my supper by eating too many. Why can't I have as many as Julian has? He's got three or maybe seven."

"Because you're the big sister," Lily said as she bent over the bed of spring flowers now showing their heads, some in full bloom and some only buds as yet, ready to burst into fullness but never to be allowed that natural development, sacrificed now to a need more significant than mindless growth, maturity, and the inevitable withering in due time. "Big sisters have to show little brothers how to act, how to do what's right, and how to be all grown up."

"I don't want to act all grown up," Emily said. "Grown up's not fun. I'm not ever going to be that."

"Oh, do you want to take a nap, then, like Dylan has to do because he's a baby?"

"No, I'm too restless to take a nap now. I've got too much on me that I've got to think about."

God, Lily thought as she worked her way one by one through the bed of flowers, choosing only those which spoke the message she would need as accompaniment, even a six-year-old child has learned to feel what every female does, the burden getting heavier day by day, the unending road ahead that must be taken with no chance for rest and relief along the way, the hope for a relationship that will make it bearable, the inevitable discovery that there is no such remedy ever. Never. Not to be. No matter who the man holding out a hand with a promise of escape happens to be. The way out does not belong to another and cannot be conferred. It may be offered, it may be promised, but it must not be accepted. It is false. Each woman must find her way alone and unaided, in the face of all the lies and deception and cruel indifference each and every one of them finally deals you.

"Help Mommy find enough pretty flowers and leaves, and I'll let you have as many Wow cookies as you want, and you can eat them while you watch Bozo, the whole show this time, not just the nice parts."

"How many flowers do you have to have, Mommy?" Emily asked, beginning to pull with both hands on each stem she came to, some snapping off and some coming up by the root with clods of dirt still attached. "Is this enough?"

"No, I want lots of flowers, and I want most of them to be pretty, but some have to be ugly and nasty looking."

"What about rocks, too? Sticks and dirt?"

"Some rocks with nice colors, maybe. No dirt, though. Some sticks would be good, though. That's a good idea. Some dead sticks. Make them be ugly."

"Both my hands are full already, then," Emily said, stopping her picking to watch Julian climb off his tricycle and run toward the package of cookies on the steps. "Look, he's getting some more. Julian'll take them all. Piggy, piggy!"

"No, he won't," Lily said. "He'll take just what he can carry and cram in his mouth at one time, and then he'll run off. He'll leave, like they all always do. He won't even look back. He won't care enough to."

"I'll stop him," Emily said, letting the flowers and stems she'd picked fall back on the dirt of the backyard. "I'll catch him, and make him give them to me. I'll make him pay."

"You can't, sweetheart," Lily said. "You can never stop them from doing that. That's what they do, and they don't care what you want. They'll take it all."

"I'll get Rum Tum to help me. He'll knock Julian down and bring all his cookies to me. Rum Tum will make him cry."

"There's more left," Lily said, dropping into a paper bag from Hill's Food Mart the blooms and buds she'd selected so far. "Help me get your flowers into the sack. I've got enough now."

"Will you put them into a vase, all the flowers, so they can live? Even the ugly ones and the sticks, too?"

"I'll put them into water. Don't worry. Now, go get yourself some Wow cookies and watch Bozo. Mommy's going to take her bath."

"Rum Tum doesn't like Bozo any more. He growls when I watch the clown. He wants the Stooges."

"The Stooges aren't on now. You'll have to settle for Bozo. Let Rum Tum stay outside."

"I would," Emily said in a thoughtful tone, "but he wants to be with me all the time now, and I better let him come into the house. If I don't, Rum Tum will wake me up at night."

"All right," Lily said. "I'm going to go in the house and take a bath now. Be a good big sister, and make Julian behave. Don't wake Dylan up."

As Lily gathered the rest of the blooms, buds, twigs, and a couple of small stones into a pile for placement into the paper bag, she could hear Emily lecturing Julian about his behavior, but she didn't bother to listen to what her daughter was saying. Instead, she began to hum to herself the air she'd been hearing for the last couple of days, a tune a madrigal group accompanied by flute and drum and dressed in Renaissance costume

might sing, the girls in long dresses with high waistlines, garlands of flowers in their hair, and the boys in varicolored tights with doublets above
the midline and full billowing sleeves enclosing their arms and moving in
a cool breeze from the sixteenth century, all the lips of the singers pursed
in perfect ovals of pink.

"Too roo lay, too roo lay," Lily sang, part now of the song, as she
headed for the flowing brook overspread with the branches of willows
weeping and dapples of sunlight shining on the surface of the stream,
glittering among the shadows. The water would be cool, and it will hold
you up for a good long time if your gown be full and your petticoats be
many. You'd be able to hear the madrigals' song until its very end, sadly
sweet and soft and mellow, as it has fallen on the ear since time began and
the first heart broke.

"For bonny sweet Tollman is all my joy," Lily sang. "I'm Lily named
for the flower, and now all my flowers are lost."

23

THE PLACE WHERE Ronald Alden stood late in the April afternoon, waiting for his wife to pull up in the Chevrolet filled with his children, at least two of whom would be crying in full voice or at least in a swelling snivel halfway to a complete bay, had been mindfully and carefully chosen. His location was a little to the west of the entrance to Cole Hall, a women's dormitory across a dead-end street from the campus heating facility with its great pile of coal waiting to be consumed in flame, and as Ronald stood on his spot near the street itself, his briefcase beside him bulging like a tumor with its load of freshman essays not yet diagnosed but in urgent need of the doctor's attention, he glanced to his right as though he'd heard a sound requiring identification.

What that shift of attention away from the slim volume of poetry held open in his left hand and toward the building across the side street allowed him to do was to catch a glimpse of an antebellum-themed house standing a good distance back from the intersection of College Street and Vanderbilt Place. He could see clearly, if only for a brief spell, as he turned his attention away from a book of sonnets by a lady poet in Maine, the front portico to the brick house with white columns and a wide set of stone steps leading to its massive door. It was the home of the sisters of the Kappa Delta Sorority, where typically at that time of day the inmates began to drift in from the classrooms and laboratories and lecture halls of the sunlight hours to change outfits and freshen makeup jobs for dinner, darkness, and dates. Dr. Alden didn't see the KD he wanted to glimpse, and he lowered his eyes again to Marietta Mulrone's pallid Italian sonnets.

He'd promised himself he would grant his grinding need only two looks toward the KD house while he waited for Lily to pick him up for transport home, and this would be the second one. If he didn't see Josephine Longineaux on the second try, he would not look again, no matter how hungry he was for sight of her. If not all of her, at least a flash of golden hair as she walked through the door in a gaggle of others or maybe the sound of her voice or her laugh at some stupid remark made by one of the KD sisters. It didn't take much to be able to recognize her in the swarm of lessers she walked among. The more he'd come to be obsessed by Josey, Jo Jo, this Child of Light and Love, the less evidence of her existence he needed to pick her out of the drab surrounds of the world she moved in. She was in it, but not of it. That he felt in his bones.

If he heard one syllable spoken by her in the midst of a welter of sound from other sources, he knew her. If he glimpsed her for a second as she moved through a doorway and out of sight, her image was burned into his brain. What did it mean physiologically that he was able to know her so readily on the basis of so meager a supply of presence? What had happened internally to his nervous system to cause such instantaneous and utterly reliable comprehension of Josephine Longineaux? What had been so transformative to his synapses, Ronald had asked himself countless times. She was simply a human, though a wonderfully organized member of that class of beings, and his knowledge of her was so brief, rich though it was in touch, sight, smell, and—God—taste, that it did not seem possible to possess her selfhood so completely in his brain, heart, liver, hands, and essence.

And it was slipping away from him, this magic, this transcendence, this removal from all mundane, ordinary, and capturing in his life. Josephine Longineaux was not solely and completely with him any longer, even in the coils of the intimacy of physical lovemaking. She had begun to show signs of an awareness of time and place and obligation elsewhere, even as she shrieked and moaned in ecstasy. In the early days of their first tender times, she would often weep gently afterwards, so moving to Ronald that he'd joined her, tears wetting their cheeks together. She never cried now, usually rising instead after a session of lovemaking to look for Kleenex or a T-shirt to wipe things up. At the end of a recent session together, Josephine had even asked him, after getting dressed to hurry back to campus for a meeting at the KD house, if he could smell anything on her.

What had been utterly sweet between them had undergone a shift of emphasis. More precisely, Ronald said to himself as he stood before Cole Hall late in an April day, staring dead-eyed at black marks on a page before him, the very notion of emphasis has become possible now. She is showing consciousness of varying levels of importance and need. She has begun to demonstrate an awareness of choice. That realized, an ability to sense options, nothing but an ending could come. Like everything else in life, decay was inevitable.

"Dr. Alden," a voice said, "Waiting for a ride somewhere?" Acting properly startled at the intrusion of the world outside the interchange between himself as reader and the words upon the page before him as text, Ronald looked up in the way a skin diver returning from too long in the deep widens his eyes and gulps at air as he surfaces from another reality. One heavier, more dreamlike, essentially alone and treasurable for that reason, has been left behind.

"Robert," he said. "I didn't see you come up. I was standing here waiting to see what Marietta Mulrone was going to do with this sestet. She has worked herself into quite a little uncomfortable corner in the octave."

"I don't know her work well," Robert McLean said, never having heard the name of the poet before, but making a nice recovery nonetheless. He'd established he couldn't be questioned about the way of Mulrone with the sonnet form, and he couldn't be expected even to know she wrote sonnets. He'd shown, however, that he knew enough to appreciate her work from afar, and he was willing to be instructed about her and her poetic production, man of letters that he happened to be. He'd done all that with six words, demonstrating he'd been a graduate student at Vanderbilt long enough not to be pinned on the ropes and pummeled into submission. He could slip a punch.

"Neither do I," Ronald admitted, demonstrating respect for the acolyte before him and avoiding having to say something insightful about the unknown work of an unknown poet he happened to be toting around a book by. He could slip a punch, too. "I just ran across this collection and saw it was sonnets. So it's my first experience with Marietta Mulrone."

"Not with sonnets, though, eh?" said Robert McLean of Memphis birth and Washington and Lee baccalaureate education, adding a collegial chuckle.

"I've read a few of those all right. At least early on, when I was first discovering poetry. And yes, I'm waiting for the wife and kiddies to show up and take me home for a few hours," Ronald said. "Before I have to return to the salt mines in the morning. And Lily's a little late."

"I'm about to leave for the day, and I'm headed your direction. You're still on Graystone, right? Can I give you a ride? Save your wife a trip?"

"Let me," Ronald said, looking at his Timex, "give Lily a call, and if she hasn't left home yet, that could speed things up. I know she'd appreciate the favor."

"Sounds good," Robert said. "You can use the phone at the desk in Cole Hall. I'd like to talk to you a little about my orals coming up, if you don't mind, as we ride along. I know you're sitting in on the orals for the nineteenth century, right?"

"I am on your committee, they tell me, but all I can tell you about the nineteenth century is read, read, read." They both laughed at that, and Ronald threw back his head in so doing, some distance further than was called for, but doing that allowed him to take another quick look at the walk up to the KD house, his third one of the last fifteen minutes. He knew she wouldn't be there, but he looked anyway. There were girls treading up the steps into the house where Josephine lived, dark-haired and drab and chattering, but she wasn't one of them. Not a single synapse chose to fire in his central nervous system, and his tongue felt again the bitter taste of absence and non-stimulation.

Inside the reception area of Cole Hall, after having to prove he was an employee of the university by showing his ID card, Ronald was allowed to use the telephone on the clerk's desk while the monitor watched him closely. Who is he afraid I might be, Ronald thought as he listened to the ringing of his phone in the rent house on Graystone Lane, a potential rapist trolling for victims in a women's dorm? Does he think I'm trying to lure a stray independent female student into my clutches? Tear off her clothes for a quickie here in the reception room?

Thinking after the fourth ring that he had called too late to catch Lily at home before she got the kids all herded into the car to come pick him up, tardy though she was, as usual, Ronald was about to hang up when he heard the click of the instrument being lifted and in a second or two his daughter's voice.

"Hello," Emily said, adding what she'd been instructed to say when allowed to answer the ringing phone, "this is the Alden's house."

"Emily, this is Daddy. Let me talk to Mommy."

"Hello, Daddy. When are you coming home?"

"Soon, sweetheart," Ronald said. "You did a good job of answering the phone. Now let me talk to Mommy."

"She can't come to the phone."

"Let her know it's Daddy, and she'll come talk to me. Go do that for me now, please."

"No, she can't. She's in the bathtub, and she can't come."

"Why is she taking a bath now, Emily? She's supposed to be picking Daddy up at school. Tell her to come talk to me."

"She can't. She's in the bathtub with the flowers and the ugly sticks and the colored rocks. She's not taking a bath. Mommy's got her dress on. The long pretty one, and it's all wet now, and her hair's wet, too. She didn't want me to come in the bathroom, but I did. I heard her singing and saw her laying down in the tub with the water all the way to the top."

"To the top?" Ronald said, taking the Cole Hall phone from his ear and looking at the earpiece. It had to be broken. There was a malfunction somewhere, a misconnection. Had water got into the wires somehow? Emily was still talking when he put the instrument back to his ear.

"Mommy says it's hard to keep her face under the water. It keeps wanting to come up when the water gets in her nose. She can't make it stay."

"Emily, stay in the bathroom with Mommy. I'll be home as quick as I can," Ronald Alden said, slamming the phone down into its cradle so hard it bounced out again. "Here," he said to the desk monitor, pushing the receiver across the desk. "You do it."

Out in the street, Robert McLean was talking to a young woman, probably from one of his freshman composition classes, judging from the lean of his body toward her as he smiled and chatted in the course of edging into her personal space. The term *jailbait* sprang into Ronald's mind, uncalled for and inappropriate to the moment and situation, and it stayed there, repeating itself over and over as he told Robert McLean that he must get him to the house on Graystone as fast as he could, as he jumped into Robert's VW bug, leaning forward all the way down each street they traveled at a speed which made the car skitter and slide around turns, as he jumped out into the street in front of his house before the vehicle stopped moving, as he rushed through the front door and past Julian sucking his thumb in total focus on Jerry the mouse slamming a flat iron against Tom the cat's head on the TV screen, as he ran down the hall toward the bathroom, slipping on a throw rug and catching himself against the wall, as he grabbed the doorframe and spun into the bathroom, and as he saw Emily bending over the tub to pat her mother on the forehead with a sopping wet towel.

The phrase didn't stop recurring until after he'd pulled Lily from the bathtub, heavier than she'd ever felt to him before, dressed as she was now in a sodden long gown and a layer of petticoats, a garland of flowers and yard weeds wound into her hair, her face bluish and her mouth gaped open like a fish stranded on a bed of ice in a market, limp as he turned her to lean forward over the edge of the tub so he could push against her waist and belly. She moaned twice, began to vomit water with lumps of something yellow in it, and began to struggle against Ronald's chest, throwing her head back abruptly with enough force to smash into his nose hard enough to make his eyes water and a sharp pain shoot through his head. It stopped then, the voice saying *jailbait,* and it remained quiet through all the rest of the night, the calling of the ambulance, the arrival of the rescue team, three of them, who forced Lily to lie on a stretcher and be strapped down for transport to the Vanderbilt Hospital, the trip with no siren blaring, though Emily had asked the driver to turn it on as she rode along with her father, her two brothers, and her pinioned mother down West End Avenue, and during the final business of admission of a patient, the signing of forms and agreements, the dismissal of the person financially responsible for Mrs. Ronald Alden, and the doling out of cherry lollipops for all three children.

"Do you want me to call anybody in the English department, Dr. Alden?" Robert McLean asked as he drove Ronald and the children back toward home. "Dr. Buchanan, maybe? Or Dr. Flange?"

"Jesus, no, Robert. But thanks for asking and for coming along through all this chaos. I'm really indebted to you. I'll take care of things now. The main thing is to get the kids in bed and arrangements made for them so I can meet my classes tomorrow."

"Will they keep Mrs. Alden in the hospital for long?" Robert McLean said, sounding conversational and therefore probing for information, background, and any additional juice he could squeeze out of the distraught husband, as Ronald judged it.

"We'll have to see," Ronald said. "We'll just have to see."

"I think legally that a suicide attempt is treated as a crime in Tennessee. It doesn't make sense in most cases, certainly ones like this with folks like you and Mrs. Alden, but you know, if they didn't call it a crime for rednecks to do it, they'd be offing themselves more than they do now. They wouldn't be able to keep enough ambulances on the road to handle the volume, if they didn't discourage it legally."

"I don't know if you'd call what Lily did an actual suicide attempt," Ronald said, beginning to hear the first whisper of the phrase he couldn't get out of his mind earlier beginning to announce itself again. Jailbait. Jailbait.

"What Mommy did in the tub," Emily said, always a listener to the conversations of adults, "was to sing and wear a pretty dress and let flowers float in the tub and try to keep her head under water. That's what she was doing. I helped her pick the flowers and find the ugly sticks."

"There you go," Robert McLean said. "As Ophelia said, rosemary is for remembrance. And something something for rue, isn't it? Or did some other character say that about her? Maybe Ophelia didn't say it. I ought to know that. What if Dr. Vallandigham asks me that in the oral?"

"Why's there all this traffic on West End this time of night?" Ronald said, hoping to avoid having to quote any lines in response to McLean's sally and to prevent him from adding to what he'd already intoned with such gusto. Orals, for Christ's sake.

"It's going to be a lot worse than traffic pretty soon. Who knows what they'll do now in Nashville, once they get cranked up? It's already well underway in Memphis. It is coming down hard there by now. My folks are trying to decide whether to ride it out at home or head for their cabin on the lake in Mississippi. They're kind of stuck. Afraid to stay home in Central Gardens, but not daring to get out on the streets in a car. I should go over there to be with them, I guess, but I don't know what the authorities are saying we should do."

"What're you talking about?" Ronald said. "Has something happened?"

"Has something happened? Wow. I'm not surprised you haven't been paying attention, what with Mrs. Alden's condition and all, but everybody at the hospital and the guys in the ambulance were all talking about it. It's all over radio and TV, but I haven't turned the car radio on to listen because of what you're having to deal with now."

"What? Tell me."

"You haven't heard at all?"

"Let me tell Daddy," Emily said, hanging over the back of the passenger's seat in the VW. "I know what it is. Rum Tum told me."

"Rum Tum?" Robert McLean said.

"Her imaginary friend. A nice little dwarf she's invented."

"He's not nice, but he told me. He said to me, Emily, he's dead. Bad people killed him, and it'll be bloody bones now."

"Emily," Ronald said. "Where'd you hear such words as bloody bones? That's not a nice thing to say."

"No, it's not nice, but that's what Rum Tum said it was. Dr. King is dead, and it'll be bloody bones and fire now."

"Couldn't have put it better myself," Robert McLean said. "Rum Tum got it right. The dwarf nailed it. They shot and killed Martin Luther King today in Memphis, and the blacks have already started setting fires all over South Memphis. North Memphis'll be next, and the white folks are shaking in Central Gardens and Midtown. It'll go nationwide. They've already put the torch to Detroit again, and the night's hardly begun. Rum Tum the dwarf speaks the truth. No more water, the fire next time."

"Shit," Ronald said. "Goddamn."

"You said it, Daddy," Emily said, patting her father on his head. "You said it. All the bad words."

24

IT WAS JUST past six thirty and most of the street lights were coming on in downtown Nashville as Milton Drummond eased the Pontiac around a new-looking brown van double-parked with the engine running in front of Wanda's Wild Wigs. He hadn't thought there'd be any vehicle located in front of the old bank building when the time came to move on the numbers money deal, and he wondered what that meant. Had somebody got out of the van and gone into the wig shop where there was supposed to be just the one woman sitting behind the counter with all that money gathered in one place waiting to picked up around eight o'clock? Had some of that bunch of bad niggers heard that Tooter Browning and Randall Eugene were going to nip in there and take that eighty thousand dollars when it was just Little Lou by herself there to watch out for it until the pickup?

Maybe two or three of them were in there waiting with shotguns right now, hiding behind some of the racks of lady's clothes in the store or in a closet or somewhere, just aching to blow the hell out of the ones trying to take that week's worth of numbers money away from them. It'd be just like a bunch of black badasses to do a ambush, just for the fun of it. They want to shoot the shit out of all of us, not just keep us from snatching the money. They have got it in for the white man these days, no doubt about it, the whole damn bunch of jungle bunnies. Goddamn, Milton told himself, I'm scared to even stop this car, much less sit in it waiting for Tooter and Randall Eugene to go busting in there and getting their heads shot off. And the mean bastards hiding inside would figure out there's got to be a wheel man waiting, and they'd be bound and determined to take him out, too. They'd come piling out of that door like a bunch of apes, just blasting at me.

"Why's that big old van parked there?" Milton said out loud, pushing on the accelerator and brake at the same time and making the Pontiac get that grinding noise started in the front brake pads, like it would do.

"Ease off the damn gas," Randall Eugene said from the passenger seat, craning his neck to look around Milton at the wheel. "It looks like it's just somebody making a delivery. Toting some wigs or some kind of shit in there."

"Y'all didn't say nothing about nobody else going to be in the store but that lady, Little Lou," Milton said, the car now far enough past the van to allow him to move back into the lane nearest the curb. "It don't look right to me."

"The thing is," Tooter Browning said from the backseat, "the delivery folks don't make it a habit to let everybody see their schedule, you see. They didn't never check with me before they decide to tote in a box or two of merchandise for Little Lou to try to sell."

"Yeah," Randall Eugene said, starting to laugh a little, "nobody's done told the UPS man to ask us when we planning to go in there and take that money away from that woman holding it, Little Lou. See, Milton, we ain't been coordinating none of what we doing with what the delivery man's up to."

"I know, I know," Milton said. "I just want to be, you know, careful about things."

"I can see that truck driver leaning across the counter talking to Little Lou," Tooter said. "She's going to sign some papers and shit, and he'll be out of there in a minute or two, and then you can park and let us go in there to buy a cancer wig for Mr. Puckett's old lady. Just drive around and circle the block, and he'll be in that van and done and gone by the time we get back."

"Well, all right," Milton said and eased off the brake, making the Pontiac buck a little as they moved down the block past the Chop Suey Shop two doors away from Wanda's Wild Wigs. "I'm just asking, you know. Keeping my eyes open, and being careful."

Being chickenshit, Randall Eugene told himself and leaned forward to turn on the radio, hoping to find him some music he could stand to listen to long enough to last him around the block before he had to go into that wig shop and walk out with all that money. Being chickenshit, that's what Milton's being, and Tooter Browning's sitting back there with a damn gun as big as a horse's head stuck down in his belt, his eyes all squinted up as red as fire. Listen to that black bastard snorting through his nose like he's mad at something. And what is it that's stinking so much in this damned old Pontiac?

As soon as he heard the news on the radio in his car and had it verified on a special bulletin that ran across the TV screen before which his wife was sitting transfixed when he walked into the family room, DeWitt Vallandigham went for the telephone on the kitchen wall. He called Robard Flange's number first. His wife Marie said he was not yet home from a physical therapy treatment but he was due any minute and she'd pass along the word that DeWitt was getting a little impromptu gathering together of like-minded folks to discuss the implications of the assassination in Memphis and maybe lift a few glasses of sour mash in the process.

"It is a school night for Robard," Marie had said, "but I know he'll be mighty tempted to get together with you fellows tonight. He has a class tomorrow to teach, I know. Will it be the usual bunch? I mean if he asks who's going to be there?"

"Oh, Marie, we're so stuck in the mud we can't think of anybody else but each other we want to see. Truth of the matter is nobody but us wants to be around a bunch of rounders like we are."

"Well, that's certainly not true, I know, DeWitt, but I expect he'll be showing up there a little late. I know one thing, though. He'll be eager to converse and express an opinion."

"I've never heard Robard Flange fail to speak his mind," DeWitt Vallandigham said in a chortle. "I do declare."

By the time everybody had got to the Vallandigham place on Charleston Lane and got the first glass of Jack Daniels safely deposited where it belonged, DeWitt was already ahead of the bunch and was not likely to be caught up to in the stretch. "Come on in here, Gareth," he shouted to the last man to enter the door, "did you ever think you'd see this day?"

"No, Dr. Vallandigham, it never crossed my mind we'd see such a deliverance granted us in this fallen time. I am humbled."

"Well, come on in, and let everybody know what you just opined, young fellow. Not a one of us has said exactly what you just got through stating, and I do believe you've hit the truest note that's yet been sounded on this glorious night."

As the two scholars worked their way toward the rear of the house where DeWitt's study was located just off the family room, DeWitt thought to ask Gareth Lamb if he'd heard anything from Robard Flange about the news blazing from Memphis, knowing that Robard would be the first Gareth would seek for commentary on any event of great moment. Gareth had not, though he'd called the Flange residence and had much the same conversation with Marie as had DeWitt. "Oh, well," DeWitt said, "Robard's a little out of pocket for the time being, but as soon as he's free to join us, he'll be here. He wouldn't miss this for all the bourbon in Kentucky."

"All the sour mash in Lynchburg, you mean," Gareth corrected, knowing the tastes of his mentor in all things consumable.

"Gentlemen," DeWitt Vallandigham said, his hand on the small of Gareth's back as he escorted him into the study where most of the senior members of the Vanderbilt English Department stood, sat, and stumbled about the room with glasses and cocktail weenies in hand. "Here's our last member to join us tonight, unless Robard finally shows up to lift a toast in honor and celebration of events, and Gareth just said something I want you to hear."

"When I learned of the shooting of Martin Luther King Jr. in Memphis at around six this evening, I was at my desk correcting papers from my graduate seminar in medieval literature. The paper in particular I was reading happened to be on the topic of the audience of Piers Plowman, and it was proving to be quite a good one, really. Amateurish, naturally, and every sentence horribly qualified and undercut. Our students are afraid to make any claim forthrightly." At this statement mutters and nods of agreement along with a couple of deep sighs arose from the listeners.

"My attention to the paper on Piers Plowman's audience—it was by Houston Stride, by the way, known by some of you surely—was broken suddenly and abruptly by Doris Dowling bursting into my office to say that on her way out of Old Central at end of day—she'd stayed late at her desk to take care of some correspondence by our esteemed little chairman from Harvard—she'd been told by another secretary in the history department about the shooting of King. Doris was quite distraught, I gathered, and most upset."

"Oh, dear," David McDavidson said, "you'd think she'd know on which side the bread of her people is buttered." Murmurs of assent and a chuckle or two arose, and again Marvin Slope did not acknowledge the ongoing hiss and bubble and effect of sour mash and giddiness on his literary colleagues. Unimpeded, he plunged on.

"Looking up from the paper by Stride, I said almost instantly the line which sprang into my head upon hearing of the death of that nigra agitator and charlatan. It is one familiar to any student of medieval English literature. You'll remember the vision the speaker in the poem describes in the prologue. Here from that section is the line that burst into my mind. 'A fair field of folk found I there between.' That is the line I spoke aloud."

"Good God, how apt," Gareth Lamb said in a tone of awe. "The implications for irony and meaning are staggering."

"Not as staggering as that high-powered rifle slug was in Memphis," Shoul Lambert said, looking about him, tongue in cheek, to judge the effect of his wit and getting a dose of what he wanted, though not the full measure he thought his remark deserved.

"Subject what you just said in that quote from Piers Plowman to analysis and intellectual unpacking in light of this event, and you'd have the basis for one of the finest critical articles ever written about the intersection of timeless art and contemporary events. It would be worthy of publication in the *Sewanee Review*," Henry Hallam Horsham said.

"I think you are the man to write that article, Gareth," David McDavidson said. "Give poor Emily Dickinson a rest and turn your attention to the hurly burly of here and now in today's America."

Again arose laughter, joshing, yips of camaraderie, embellishments on the instant literary analysis by Gareth, the taking of drink and the eating of cheese and pigs-in-blankets, and above all, jubilation and expressions of relief at the resolution of a vexing problem. All due to an act of vengeance which no gentleman nor scholar nor Episcopalian would have taken, but one roughly seized in hand and executed by the common man, the yeoman, the creature of body and not of mind, the man unparalysed by thought.

25

"ALL I WANT to do is go outside, walk down Jefferson Street and see what all's going on," Tee Arnold Monroe was saying to his wife. "Damn, woman, that ain't nothing."

"Don't you be saying damn woman to me," Minnie said, turning the dial on the TV set against one wall of the living room where she and Tee Arnold were watching Walter Cronkite look serious as he brought more details about the news of the shooting death of Dr. Martin Luther King in Memphis. "I ain't taking that kind of talk from nobody I don't work for. Shut up, now, and see can Walter tell us if they know who did it yet."

"I can tell you who did it. I don't need no TV to tell me who that was. It was a redneck motherfucker white trash cracker pulled that trigger on Dr. King, and I tell you something else, too."

"I know what color he was," Minnie said, "I mean what his name was. Where he come from, who is he. That's what I want to hear Walter tell us if the police done got that figured out."

"Shit, woman. That man could be named anything. What his name is don't make no difference. Who he's working for, that what we ain't never going to know, and that's something they ain't never going to tell on the TV or put in the newspaper. They going to find somebody, all right, to throw in jail for it, but he ain't going to be the one that made it happen. Naw, you can count on that, woman."

"I done told you to quit calling me woman, and I don't want to have to say it again. You know what my name is I reckon, by now, or you ought to, anyway. I'm the one totes the groceries in here and cooks them up for you to eat them, so don't be saying no shit like woman this and woman that. I ain't about to put up with it. What if I was to call you man, instead of your Christian name? Huh?"

"That ain't the point, Minnie. Not a bit of it. And everybody better call me man. I flat guarantee you that."

"You drunk?" Minnie said to her husband. "You talking awful prosperous here all of a sudden. You bound to have got into some old busthead whisky or some mess like that. I won't have that poison around my house."

"Naw, Minnie, I ain't drunk. Only thing I am is fed up. It's done happening again and again and again. Sometime I think it going to ease up, and goddamn if it don't come back like a wildfire in the woods. Some kind of a wind gets to blowing, and the old fire ain't dead yet like you thought it was. It's just been burned down to coals, but when that new wind come up, it fan them coals up into flame again. And it's new wood done growed up for them to feed on, and Child they start doing that. Fire starts roaring again."

"I don't mind you calling me that—Child," Minnie said, looking away from the TV screen toward where her husband was sitting on the sofa under the picture of an old black man dressed in a suit and tie, a woman beside him in a long dress with white cuffs and collar, both standing in front of an unpainted house with a porch running the full length of the structure. "You use to call me that when we first hooked up back there in Dixon."

"It wasn't Dixon, Minnie. It was out in the country from Dixon, and you was just like a child when I first run across you." Minnie looked at Tee Arnold for almost a minute and then turned back to the TV set.

"Walter Cronkite stopped talking about Dr. King getting killed," she said. "Now he's on to that war over yonder. Something bad happening there, too."

"I just want to walk down Jefferson Street," Tee Arnold said. "That's all. I hear they's going to be people talking to us niggers in North Nashville, telling us what we ought to be doing about that mess that happen in Memphis."

"Memphis is way over yonder on the river," Minnie said. "It's a long way from there to here."

"Memphis is everywhere now, Honey," Tee Arnold said. "Memphis done come to Nashville, and it's going to be all over this country now. Everywhere you look is going to be Memphis."

"You better hope Memphis go back to where it belongs," Minnie said. "Just as soon as it can happen."

"It's always something cooking on a hot fire in Memphis. Sometimes it's that good barbecue they make over yonder, sometimes it's something else. But I tell you what. It's always hot and smoking, everything is in Memphis."

"Dr. King ought not never to gone to Memphis," Minnie said. "No good could've come out of that. And now he's done got killed for being over there. Lord, Lord, have mercy."

"I know how you feeling, a Christian woman like you always been, Minnie. But now ain't the time to be calling on the Lord and praying and crying and singing them old nigger church songs. We done been put up against the wall this time. We got to stop all this crying, and take a lesson from the other side of this thing."

"What you talking about, the other side?"

"I'm talking about fire and brimstone, Honey, that's what I be meaning. I mean we got to lay down the Bible and the song book and the crying to the Lord to help us out, and we got to pick up the devil's tools."

"Don't say stuff like that. God is listening to you. He hears every thing you think and all you say. He knows what all's in your heart."

"It's about damn time He started listening, that's what I mean. That's what I'm hearing in the streets out there in North Nashville. God ought to been paying attention a long time ago."

"You about to put your immortal soul in danger, Husband. Saying things like that. You don't give orders to God. Listen to yourself."

"It ain't God's turn no more, the way I figure it. He done had his chance. Now we got to see if the devil's tools will get the job done. We got to use what Satan does. He depends on heat, don't he? We got to use fire."

"You sounding like that little crazy nigger I done fed a meal to at the chancellor's house last year. That little skinny fellow with them big staring eyes, the one that talked all that mess and got them spoiled little brats at Fisk all crazy last year. That little vegetarian fool that dressed in new overalls. He the one got that riot started up last April, sure as the world. Niggers burning their own houses and the stores they use to buy stuff from. Tell me that ain't crazy."

"Stokely Carmichael might have sounded crazy then," Tee Arnold said, getting up from the sofa and moving toward the front door. "He don't now. People out yonder listening to him real hard now the white folks done killed Dr. King in Memphis."

"You talking about him yelling about black power when he was at Vanderbilt last year? Carrying on and getting everybody all riled up? You think that done anybody good?"

"He here right now. I done heard that news from Tederick Ruggins and Lem Richardson and Ned Jackson. Stokely Carmichael is in Nashville tonight, and niggers are going to be ready to listen to him. What he done last year ain't going to be a circumstance to what he got to work with this time."

"What's he going to be saying? Telling all you niggers you got to get mad and holler and protest or something like that? He got a big mouth, I give you that. But them speeches ain't going to mean nothing."

"Nuh-uh, Sugar," Tee Arnold said. "It ain't just talk this time. He be saying burn the fucker down. And you know what? He mean that, and people be ready to do it. The fire's done been lit, and all you got to do is let it take its natural path."

"That ain't nothing for you to be messing in, Tee Arnold. You're too old for that craziness. You got more sense than that. You done learned how to get along with the white man a long time ago. You still here, alive and walking around, ain't you? That shows you learned how to do. You hadn't learned it, you wouldn't be here able to talk about burning things down."

"Maybe I got to unlearn some stuff. Maybe I got to do that thing so easy a child can do it."

"Sit back down on the sofa. Mayor Briley fixing to talk to all of us in Nashville on the TV set. Let's hear what he got to say. He means business this time, not like it was back last April. That man is ready this go-round. What you mean when you talking about a child? What you talking about?"

"I'm talking about the first thing you tell your kids not to do. Here's what you say to them. You say whatever you do, kids, don't play with no matches. Learn that by heart, we tell them. What I'm saying is niggers like me need to forget that teaching. We got to learn how to play with matches. We got to learn how to set a fire."

"Don't go outside the house right now, Tee Arnold," Minnie said, grabbing at her husband's shirtsleeve as he moved to open the door. "Wait until morning. The mayor said they going to be calling in army troops. The white folks ain't going to be caught short again. It's going to be guns and tanks, and I don't know what all, everywhere all over Nashville. White folks be scared this time, and they be out for blood from the very first minute. You know they ain't nothing scarier than a nervous white man. You ain't got no business out yonder in the street."

"I ain't never had no real business being nowhere," Tee Arnold said. "I just want to watch how people do when they do have some business to take care of for a change. I be back in a little bit. Rest easy."

"You going to come back holding your head where a police or a soldier been whipping on it. And that's if you lucky. Listen to all them sirens blowing, fool. Just listen to all that racket and noise starting up tonight in Nashville."

26

IT WAS AFTER 2 A.M. when Felice Foldman heard her husband making soft noises as he came stepping carefully up the stairs to the second floor of Cherry Mount House headed toward his bedroom across the hall and one door down from hers. The telephones in the chancellor's residence had been ringing constantly since the news had come about what had happened to Dr. Martin Luther King in Memphis, every one of the lines connected to Vanderbilt, naturally, and even the personal number reserved for her use. At one point Malcomb had been so busy speaking to someone he couldn't hang up on, probably the chair of the board of trustees or the chief of university security or the mayor of Nashville or a senator or someone else powerful enough to hold the chancellor's sole attention, no matter the competing voice, that he had pointed to Felice to pick up an instrument ringing on a separate line. She'd found herself answering a phone not her personal one for the first time in two years. It made her feel almost nude.

It had been the editor of the student newspaper, Jonathan Seth Matthews, wanting a quote from Chancellor Foldman about the assassination of Dr. King, and prying into what measures would be taken to protect Vanderbilt students from the hordes of blacks that might come swarming from North Nashville across West End Avenue to attack the campus, rape the women, and steal all the late-model automobiles.

"Mr. Matthews," Felice had told him, "I can assure you that the safety of students is the first priority of the chancellor and that nothing will

243

happen that the Vanderbilt authorities haven't anticipated and planned for." That seemed to stop the little weasel for a moment or two, and Felice felt quite proud of herself for having come up with language that had the effect of quelling questions from a newspaper reporter, even if it was only for a student rag named the *Hustler,* for goodness sakes. The budding journalist went on to put other questions to her designed to undermine the chain of command and cast suspicion on the work of the chancellor, but Felice had played ignorant, promised to have her husband call Jonathan Seth Matthews as soon as he could, and after a few more attempts to catch her up in contradictions and to imply she was lying, the little creep hung up.

Felice considered her performance worthy of rewarding herself a treat. She had sounded on the phone just like a higher education administrator saying nothing actionable, and she deserved a nice hit from her store of feel-good powder in the carved jade box in one of the closets in her bedroom. She was still feeling up enough from the episode and its aftermath that when she heard Malcomb seeking his room and a couple of hours of rest before the menagerie would continue at full throttle, she felt lively enough to step out into the hall and invite her husband in for a chat.

"What a day for you it's been," she said. "You must be more spent even than usual."

"Mentally exhausted, but all right physically," he said, coming into his wife's room and taking a seat in the overstuffed chair she liked to read in. Felice sat on the edge of her bed, made herself not look pouty as her husband occupied her special chair, and reached for a cigarette.

"Do you think the Negroes will attack the campus?" she said. "That Seth Matthews brat is acting all concerned about it, though I can't believe they'd be that organized."

"Our little editor would act concerned, of course. All the Negroes'll do is burn down their own part of town. And besides that, there are literally over three thousand trained army troops on the way to Nashville and almost here. Over two hundred of them have been promised to us to patrol the campus."

"How'd you do that?"

"I didn't. It was the governor's doing. Not Tennessee's, though. Arkansas's chief executive."

"Oh, it was Win's influence," Felice said. "The Rockefeller name still has clout, it appears."

"Well, this is still America, isn't it?" Malcomb said, rubbing his eyes. "I really don't think it'll be as bad for us as last year's riot was, though. That time they were able to say I caused it by letting the students invite Stokely Carmichael to campus. And then all the hell he helped to raise was put on our tab. This time the trouble started in Memphis, so they can't pin this year's riot on me. Oh, and something else you'd be interested to hear. If it had happened any day but this one, it'd be the major news story in Nashville. Certainly at Vanderbilt, anyway."

"Is it good news?"

"Good and bad, as the saying goes. The bad part is that a professor in the department of English at Vanderbilt, a holder of an endowed chair and a scholar of note, at least in his own opinion, was involved early tonight in a dust-up in a whorehouse in downtown Nashville."

"Good God, who?"

"Dr. Robard Flange, that's who. And here's some of the best part. He was dressed in full Confederate uniform, and he was using as a weapon in this fight a sword he was wearing."

"Was he fighting with one of the whores?"

"No, he tried to prevent a robbery of a wig shop attached to the whorehouse, I think it was, and when the police carried him off, he said he was defending a young woman, a great and good friend in peril. She had been made afraid, Robard said, and it was his duty to attack the Negro who'd frightened her by robbing the wig shop. I think there was another guy, too."

"Do they sell wigs in whorehouses? I thought their stock in trade was just spreading their legs. And did Robard Flange tell them he was a Vanderbilt professor? Did he explain why he was wearing a costume? I guess it was to disguise being at a whorehouse, right?"

"Robard claimed he was someone else, a major something in the Confederate army from Mississippi or maybe Alabama. He said part of him was dead, and this young woman he was protecting had been helping him bring the dead part back alive."

"What? I bet I know which part that was," Felice said, giggling so hard the bed she was sitting on began to move. "No secret about that."

"I wish I could have seen the police take him down. He'd have been swinging his sword and cursing nigras all the way to the floor."

"Malcomb, did you just say niggers?"

"I did not. I said nigras, which is what passes for the polite designation for the race among the professional Southern gentry in Robard's gang."

"That was the bad news, you said. Robard getting caught in a whorehouse. You claimed there was a good part. What was that?"

"Oh, there is a good part, and it's real good, my dear. The publicity the university will get from this nuttiness is not welcome, naturally, but it couldn't have happened at a better time in terms of being a minor story in the Nashville newspapers on today of all days. But the good thing about it is that now I can fire the crazy bastard. We won't call it that, of course. Robard will be taking an extended sabbatical which will end up never ceasing, but getting rid of him will be like the first cut at removing a tumor that's been becoming more and more malign."

"I know who'll be happiest about Robard getting axed," Felice said. "I can see the prep school grin on his face now."

"Alfred Buchanan, of course."

"No doubt. That little pedant will be smirking like a jackass eating briars."

"Where did you hear that phrase? It's so rural," Malcomb said, beginning to laugh for the first time since his night began.

"I read books, dear, all the time that I'm not passed out from consuming controlled substances or eating dinner with rich strangers. Let me ask you something, if you don't mind."

"Go ahead, everybody else does."

"Would you like to spend the night in my room? It's been a while, and talking about whorehouses and dead parts coming back to life is making me pleasantly tingly and uncomfortable."

"Why not?" Chancellor Foldman said, rising from his chair and doing a little dance step toward where his wife was perched on the edge of her bed. "Maybe it'll change my luck."

The black studies program people at Northwestern University had put their visiting speaker up in a hotel near the campus for the two nights he would be in Evanston, a lodging not nearly so well appointed as the accommodations he enjoyed on visits to universities in Southern cities. He'd remarked to Tilden on the difference in quality between the treatment he received as visitor in the northern and southern sections of the country, saying it was what he would call counterintuitive, and Tilden had explained it all to him.

"Son," Tilden said, sitting on the edge of a bed with his tie loosened and his belt taken out a notch, "they may call you a spokesman for the black man in America, but if them honkies heard you asking that question about the reasons for you getting sorrier treatment in the North than in the South, they'd know you wasn't born in America. Hell, the best treatment you ever going to get and the best money they ever going to give you to talk to them is always going to come when you in places like Tennessee and Georgia and Virginia. White liberals in the South got something they want to prove, see, and these folks in Illinois and New York and California, they don't figure they got to show you or nobody else a goddamn thing. Hell, you lucky to get a bed to sleep in up here around Chicago. They ain't studying what you think you deserve and need."

"You got me again, Tilden," Stokely Carmichael said. "You're making sense like always."

"Hell yes, I make sense. I was raised in North Nashville, just off Jefferson, so I started learning the facts of life as soon as the air hit me. I wasn't born in a manger in the islands like some folks I know. I ain't no transplant."

"I will admit I do get a lots nicer sheets on my bed once I get below the Mason-Dixon Line. A bigger check and better vegetables, too."

But that conversation had taken place earlier in the day in Evanston before the news about the killing of Dr. King in Memphis got out, and now only an hour before he was scheduled to speak at Northwestern on the topic of "Whither the Black Man, Whither America?" Stokely Carmichael was considering whether to cancel his speech and pile into the lead car of a caravan and head south, or make the opportunity to speak in Greater Chicago into a platform for a new statement on where the movement had to head now, given the death of the great spokesman for non-violence in the struggle.

"Look what's happened to Martin," Stokely was saying. "He preached that shit, and he got killed anyway. It is a lie, and his death proves it."

"That ain't what killed him," Tilden said, shaking his head back and forth. "What he was preaching. He got killed in Memphis because he was a nigger who stuck his head up. It didn't make no difference what he was saying, one way or the other. He could've been calling for a restoration of slavery right now, and nobody would have heard what he was saying. They'd have still pulled trigger on him for being a nigger showing out."

"I'm thinking we ought to get in the car and take off for down there somewhere. I don't know if I should chance Memphis, though, right now. It's going to be raw there for a while. Maybe we ought to go to Nashville, show up at Fisk again, see if we can't stir the pot one more time. It's worked before real well down there."

"Memphis is already on fire," Tilden said. "And the kind of folks doing that burning ain't going to pay no attention to you. They ain't listening to talk no more for a while, no matter who it's coming from. They too busy knocking glass out of store windows and toting off TV sets and washing machines and taking potshots at the police and all kinds of fun stuff. You go down there, and it won't do you a bit of good. I know that. Nobody's going to notice you in Memphis. Not now. Nuh-uh."

"You're probably right. I guess we should head for Nashville. Let's tell Darnell and that bunch to get ready. I'll call the Northwestern woman and cancel out the appearance."

"You're wrong again, young man. Two reasons. Word is from our people in Nashville that you're already there in town. They saying it on all the TV channels in town. The brothers in Nashville are claiming you, son. Stokely Carmichael's back. That crazy nigger's in the city, running the show one more time. That old mayor, Beverly Briley, done made a statement about it. Said Stokely Carmichael's here all right, just like you was last year, but it ain't going to be this time like it was then. No sir. The mayor says he's got army troops already getting to town, and they are going to treat you and any outside agitator like common criminals on the prowl."

"I'm already there, huh," Stokely said, walking around the hotel room and rubbing his hands together. "That's what they dread and believe."

"Oh, you threw a scare into all the white folks in Nashville last April. It ain't no doubt about it. You just like the booger man to them. But you know the scariest thing about the booger man, Stokely? You know what makes little kids so scared of him when you tell them the booger man's going to get them? I'll tell you why that is. You never see him. You just hear about how bad that fucker is. So he's got it made, the booger man has. He can just lay back and not let nobody see him, and everybody gets more scared the less they see of him and the more they hear about him. He don't never show his face. But he might any minute. See what I'm saying?"

"I believe I do, but spell it out for me, Mr. North Nashville."

"I will do that very thing. Here's your alphabet lesson for you to get by heart. A, you got them all them honkies in Nashville scared up and the niggers encouraged anyway, so they don't need to see you. B, if they do see you, they'll get less scared. C, you better off staying right here in Illinois and talking to all them reporters and getting in all the papers and on the TV news. You want to hear the letter D spelled out for you, too?"

"Yeah, what is D?" Stokely said, not smiling now. "Let's hear it."

"D stands for dead. If you show up anywhere in Nashville, Tennessee, that's what you going to be. Martin got hit with one bullet just the one time, and that's all it took to stop him forevermore from making speeches about having a dream and all that business. You go to Nashville, and it'll be so many bullet holes in your ass your own mama wouldn't be able to know you by nothing but your shoe size."

"You think a soldier would off me."

"Naw, it'd be some nigger or a combination of niggers that did it, and the law would be able to prove that finding beyond a reasonable fucking doubt. So you still want me to call Darnell up on the phone and tell him to start getting things ready for our road trip down to Tennessee?"

"Tell you what, Tilden," Stokely Carmichael said, smiling again now, lots of teeth showing, "I feel like I got something to say tonight to that bunch of smart folks at Northwestern that they need to hear. I'm going to make them one hell of a speech."

"Now you're talking," Tilden said. "I can't wait to hear what you're going to tell them honkies and their house niggers here in the Land of Lincoln tonight."

27

"**TOLLMAN," CAMERON SEMMES** was saying, calling through the door of the little room next to the stairs to the attic in the big house on Belmont Street, the room Tollman called his garret, the one where he wrote his songs. "Tollman, I know you're in there because the door's locked. If you're not passed out or dead, tell me if you want something to eat. I'm hungry for a change, and I want to take advantage of an appetite while I still have it."

Her voice was flat, expressionless, and insistent, and calculated to be that way. Tollman Briggs did not respond to speech laden with emotion, and he was constitutionally unaffected by pleading, whines, or supplications. The less you sounded like you gave a shit whether he responded or not, the more likely he was to suspect somebody might be offering a thing he might be able to get on the top side of. The only exception to this pattern of behavior occurred when Tollman was doing the nasty with a woman. Then, and only then, was he pleased to hear a verbal response, the more helpless, defeated, and grateful the woman sounded, the better for him and for his wood.

"Get bent, then," Cameron said to the slab of the oak door between her and Tollman in his den. "I'm going to score some fried chicken while I still believe I can keep it down."

"Bring me back some dark meat," Tollman called through the door. "Just knock on the door, and leave it outside when you get here."

"Dude, you will never live long enough to see that happen. Trust me on this thing. I'm gone."

"Wait," Tollman said. "I'm working on a song, and it's going to be the one. The one, I tell you. I know it."

"Not about love and heartbreak, is it? That shit won't fly these days."

"I'll show it to you when you get back, Cameron. Go on now, and leave me alone, and make it thighs, not drumsticks. And no, it's not about love. It's about death and hate."

"You're just trying to get me hot, talking like that," Cameron said. "I might come back or I might not, but don't wait up for me."

Hearing the stairs creak as Cameron left on her quest for fried chicken, Tollman Briggs looked deeply again into the surface of the tablet before him on which he'd been writing, trying to decide if it was time to take up the guitar leaning against the wall and strike a chord or two, maybe see in which direction the words would drive the music. He decided not to do that, afraid suddenly that an arrangement of musical notes might take over and begin to drive the words instead. The words were too powerful for him to take that chance, he knew, feeling a stirring deep in his belly kick up as he read again the phrase that had come to him as soon as Wrong Hand had told him about Martin Luther King being offed in Memphis.

He automatically didn't believe what Wrong Hand was saying at first, since anybody who'd known the bass guitar player for more than fifteen minutes realized the boy's grip on reality was loose at best and completely slack and nonexistent at worst. He saw things that weren't there, he heard words that hadn't been spoken, he smelled rot and thought it was flowers. He claimed walls moved of their own volition. So when he came through the door into the house on Belmont, saying to anybody who'd listen that Martin Luther King had just been shot in Memphis, only Susie Creamcheese bothered to look up at him.

"That's right, Susie," he said. "I saw it on the TV. That's what they said."

"You hadn't got a TV, Wrong Hand," Susie Creamcheese said. "Or is it the one inside your head you watch Heckle and Jeckle on?"

"No, Susie. It was the one in the laundromat on Blair. I was washing my clothes, see, and the TV set they got bolted to the wall was where I saw it. King's been shot, the TV on top of the big dryer said. It said it over and over."

"That's bullshit," Tollman had said. "You don't wash your clothes. You don't even have any clothes to wash if you wanted to."

"I do, too," Wrong Hand had said, and started to list the items of his wardrobe. By the time he got to the description of the blue jean jacket he claimed was his, everybody but Susie had tuned him out, and before Wrong Hand began counting up his socks, he'd forgotten himself why he was doing it. "Do you count socks as two or one, Tollman?" he asked. "It's one pair, but it's two socks, right? So is that one or two?"

"It's three," Susie Creamcheese said. "One and two is three."

But a few minutes later when Cameron Semmes came in wet to the skin from walking in the rain all the way to Belmont from Twenty-first Street, she confirmed what Wrong Hand had claimed had happened in Memphis. It was at that moment as Tollman studied the way the rainwater in Cameron's hair dripped down her face and gathered on the point of her luminously pale chin that the phrase jumped into his head, the arrangement of words which he knew was the seed corn of the best song he would ever write. His legs began to tremble, but by the time he'd reached the third floor of the decaying mansion on Belmont, bounding over the shoes and articles of clothing and discarded cans and bottles and newspapers littering the stairs, he was strong and capable again.

The notion of turning to the guitar for a chord or two now rejected, he began to read over once more the words that had burst from his pencil and burned their way onto the writing tablet which Susie Creamcheese had lifted from McLemore's Five and Dime to use to write home to her parents in Indiana asking for money. Luckily, she had not gotten around to that yet, so she gave up the tablet to Tollman to write on without much of a struggle. "Maybe you'll be nice to me sometime, Tollman," she said. "Take a look in my direction. See my tongue, how long it is?" He promised her he would, just as soon as he got a chance, and now the formerly blank and worthless writing tablet had become a lasting artifact, transformed by a creative act into the record of a moment of intense inspiration that might well live forever in the lore of Music City.

"Memphis Murder Blues," Tollman said aloud in a flat conversational tone, and then repeated the phrase with the intonations and variations that song required. It would be a dark sound, the dictates of his art informed him, and it would play off the traditional blues rhythm, rhyme, and repetition from the soulful wails of the Delta. It would not be an anthem of lost and vanished love, of the end of a thing between a man and a woman at close of a day of passion and regret, of the death of a private joining of hearts. No. It would be public; it would be a Whitman-like use of the inner self to announce public woe, loss, and dark resignation.

"They's been a murder in Memphis," Tollman sang, his voice deep like the Mississippi itself, "blood upon the ground. Murder done come to Memphis, blues has left the old river town. Now the blues be spreading all around. They done killed King, didn't want to listen to what he sing. Done killed the messenger on a pretty day in spring. Done killed the man of truth, just like him killed by John Wilkes Booth."

Beginning to tremble again, his knees weakening and his eyes starting to mist, Tollman spoke to himself, congratulating that self within the self, that essence from which all true art springs, saying with the quiet certainty of a man of the folk, sure in his blood and bone of the truth of his belief and his claim, words that rang true. If that tune won't work on Eighteenth Avenue in Nashville, Tennessee, eggs ain't poultry, grits ain't groceries, and Mona Lisa was a man.

"I am going to eat me some dark meat chicken when my woman get back," Tollman sang aloud in a bugling tone, "and if she ain't back when I get on, I'm going downstairs and slip Susie Creamcheese the big old bone."

Gregory Donaldson had already taken off his rat costume for the day and begun to think again about the second cartoon series in progress for the new issue of *Cook's Night Out.* He had run into a creative stone wall, he was starting to believe, and he was in danger of repeating himself. How many ways can you present the Magic Chef debating God about free will, the existence of evil in the world, and the most effective ways to seduce Tri Delts without drawing some of the same panels over and over? This question was looming large as he placed the head of the rat high on a shelf of his closet in the dorm room he shared with Philander Lanier in Ransom Hall, and he was a bit slow to turn around when his roommate burst through the door, screaming something about troops at Vanderbilt.

"Isn't it great?" Philander said. "Can't you just see it? They'll be in lock-step, bayonets fixed, driving the Sigma Chis and the ATOs before them. The Greeks'll be crying and running and falling down and slobbering."

"Who? What?"

"Because of the riot that's going to happen. The blacks are fixing to burn down Nashville again, but this time the 102nd Airborne will be waiting for them."

"You mean Mayor Briley's gone nuts because King's got killed?"

"Nuttier's more like it. He's calling up troops, and it's not just ROTC. It'll be real guns and tanks, son. I can't wait to see waves of soldiers moving on Vandy."

"Well, Philander," Greg said in his best John Wayne voice. "I see I have a job to do."

"Have you told him yet?"

"I don't need to tell him," Greg said. "The Rat knows these things. He senses disaster, chaos, and old night before it's fully formed. We'll see how American soldiers stand up to the Rodent Erectus. Step aside, Pilgrim. Get me Wardrobe."

"Chambers," Lacy Bodean was calling as she looked for her husband on the first floor of the mansion on Fox Run, one of the most select addresses in Belle Meade, "oh, Chambers, you better not be hiding from me in the dark down here somewhere. You know how I hate surprises. Don't you dare jump out at me."

The two of them had spent the last hour at a meeting of the Neighborhood Security Task Force, which Chambers thought it was witty to call the John Bell Hood Lost Brigade, and Lacy was dying to get into something comfortable and have something comfortable slide down her throat in liquid form. The meeting had taken place in the Oak Room in the club, where wedding receptions and coming-out events usually were held, that nice big space just off the main bar, not the Golfer's Hole Out or the tiny little dark cave called The Rufus Roost which used to be reserved for men only, but had recently been voted open to ladies for two days of the week. The ones running the Security Committee this year, in particular Marshall Fallston and Rupert Weathers, had ruled that no orders for drinks were to be placed at the main bar in Belle Meade Country Club or in any of the others during the meeting, with the weak excuse being given that the event was not social but preventive.

"The topic of our hasty gathering, which I among others would identify as one of immediate emergency, is the gathering storm of violence and pillage which looms before all us in Belle Meade," Marshall Fallston, a physician of distinguished family lineage but not one whit of medical talent, had said, looking about him as though daring a contradiction from any quarter. The word on Dr. Marshall Fallston was that he could not diagnose, but he could prescribe with the best of them.

Chambers had raised his hand, waving his arm back and forth like one telling others on a far horizon that he had found the thing they had all been seeking and now they could relax and go about their business. "Marshall, are you referring to the possibility that some sort of invasion by the colored citizens of Nashville may occur? Are we to understand there are indications they may be set to swarm down West End, take a left onto Belle Meade Avenue, and scatter through all the dwellings and outbuildings to see what they might find loose to pick up and carry back home?"

"That is precisely the topic I seek to elucidate, investigate, and impress upon this goodly company," Marshall Fallston said. "I could not have phrased it more succinctly if I had taken an hour to compose the statement."

"Well, that's all very well and good, Marshall. But that happens every week day morning of the year, doesn't it? I see the colored brethren and sisteren getting off buses and out of old automobiles every morning starting a new day devoted to just those activities you say you fear."

Chambers got what he wanted from that, general chuckles from the men and a titter or two from some women, and a great guffaw from his loyal wife, Lacy. That didn't count for much, though, since anyone acquainted with Lacy in person or by reputation knew she'd laugh at a public drawing and quartering if there was the slightest excuse she could find in the event to do so.

"Thanks for that bit of leavening, Chambers," Rupert Weathers said, stepping up to the lectern and gently pushing Dr. Fallston aside. "I think we all needed and appreciated that for what it was. But the facts are that we are well prepared to defend our property and our persons in this time of peril, and the Security Committee of Belle Meade wants to explain how that is so and how you may aid personally in the efforts to keep our home place the safe haven it is." Murmurs of hear, hear and shifting in seats to more comfortable positions arose at that statement, and details supporting Rupert Weathers's assertions were laid out, analyzed, restated, caressed, and fondled until most of the property owners of Belle Meade there represented felt tendrils of reassurance begin to creep into the crannies of that part of the brain where anxiety and fear set up their dwelling place.

"I didn't know before today we had an army of peace officers here in Belle Meade," Lacy had said to Chambers as they drove home from the meeting at the club. "Be careful how you're steering the car now."

"I pray we don't have an army of our own of any sort anywhere in Davidson County," Chambers said, swerving to take a run at a squirrel or a raccoon or some other night critter crossing before the vehicle in search of nourishment. He missed whatever it was and snorted in brief disappointment. Next time, maybe. "Judging by history, the bringing together of military arms to repel invaders has never worked well for property owners in this domain."

"Don't start talking about the Battle of Franklin and the one in Nashville and the Gallant General Hood of Texas," Lacy said. "You do that again, and I'll not only stick my fingers in my ears and start hollering to drown you out, I will lean over and slap you up beside the head. I can't bear to hear those old stories not even once more again."

"If you hit me while I'm driving this car, I might run off the road and collide with a tree and kill us both, Miss Lacy. How would you like that?"

"It would be a much easier death than listening to how five Southern generals died in the same battle and ended up as corpses on the same front porch of that old country house in Franklin. I'd welcome the swift embrace of a tree trunk over suffering through another recitation of that. I would hope the tree would be a magnolia, though, and there'd be blossoms to fall on the wrecked car where we'd both be found with our hands interlocked as we'd reached out for each other in our final moment together."

"Well, I wouldn't want it to be a magnolia," Chambers said. "I do hate the way those old hard seedpods roll under your feet when you step on them and make you feel like you're about to fall and break your neck. They are shaped like unstable little footballs. No air in them, though. Not a speck."

"We'd be inside the car, and it'd be blossoms, Chambers, not seedpods descending all over the vehicle."

"A magnolia sheds something all year round, just like a sycamore. If it's not seedpods and blossoms, it's little branches and dead leaves and hard old bark. Magnolias on the place are an eternal nuisance."

"They smell good, though, and the blossoms of the magnolia are as white as cotton against a blue sky," Lacy said, harking back to an afternoon in early May some years ago, spent with and under Mathis Boroughton, an SAE from Mobile come all the way north to enroll at Vanderbilt. No, she thought, he was from Fayetteville, Arkansas, Mathis was. Was it him or that Deke from Indiana, David something or other? Hard to remember the exact boy during each and every precious moment, but the blossoms were so white outlined against the blue sky, drifting down from the magnolia and falling onto the plaid blanket. My Lord, my goodness. Maybe it hadn't been plaid, but a solid color ground cloth, come to think of it.

"See, Miss Lacy," Chambers was saying, "It would be only strange darkies that might concern me. Ordinarily I wouldn't fear the disloyalty of colored servants, at least the ones who've been with a family a good long while. But I did read enough about betrayal by family retainers to alarm me in this book everybody in Nashville's all talking about now. They have been known to turn on you. *Nat Turner Confessing,* I believe that book's called."

"I have dipped into that, Chambers," Lacy said, "and it's about stuff that happened a long time ago and it's all made up. It's fictionalized. None of what's in that book matters. You can't predict what the Negro will do now based upon what he used to do. It's different, altogether."

"I'm afraid you're right. They've changed, the whole race has. Use to, they loved us, all our servants did. They'd carry us children around on their backs and just whistle and sing and make us laugh. Dance a little bit when you told them to. Not any more, though. They stopped doing that. Seemed to've lost their rhythm."

"Chambers Bodean," Lacy said. "Are you telling me you're actually afraid of Negroes knocking you in the head and getting your stuff in Nashville? In Belle Meade? Colored folks on the rampage? Has it come to that?"

"Well, this William Styron fellow, he's got all worked up about them enough to write that book. And now with Martin Luther King dead and gone, the coloreds are all worked up, too. I wish Dr. King'd left a letter or something, you know, addressed to his people, saying something like y'all just cool down, Negroes and coloreds and blacks. Just work real hard and pay attention to what you supposed to do, and don't worry about worldly goods so much. Everything's going to be jake."

"If that's what you'd be counting on, I'm scared now, for sure," Lacy had said. "Get me home, and let me get drunk. I hope all the doors are locked and the army troops and Beverly Briley are out roaming the streets with their guns all cocked."

Now, hunting for her husband on the first floor of their home on Fox Run and knowing he'd try to find a way to hide in the dark so he could jump out and surprise her, Lacy Bodean steeled herself for the instant he'd do it. Chambers thought he was being cute, like always. Fun's fun, but cowering drunk in your beautiful home in Belle Meade worrying about niggers was just a royal pain.

28

THE ALL-RISE COMMAND from the clerk had come just before midnight, and it was followed by the processing of a few cases involving petty break-ins and push-and-shove scuffles in and around drinking establishments in the jurisdictional environs of metropolitan Nashville, which took more time to handle than they were worth. Drunks would always be on one edge or the other, Randall Eugene Puckett knew, having lived with, observed, and been one himself all his life. Either they'd be quietly sulled up with their heads hanging down as though they were looking for a two-bit piece they'd lost on the floor, or they'd be loud and hollering, demanding their rights and denouncing the people who were trying to deprive them of what the Constitution of the United States promised to every citizen, big and little, old and young, rich or poor, white or colored, law-abiding or with a record a yard long.

Two of the drunks who'd been run in for fighting with law officers in front of separate bars just a block apart on Nolensville Road were of the second variety, and the legal dealings with them took longer than you would think, enough so that Randall Eugene was feeling pain beginning to kick up in various parts of his body, especially on his upper left arm where the sword had cut him almost to the bone. Compared to that one, the others were just scratches and scrapes. The EMTs had wound up the arm with a bandage, stopped the bleeding, and told him to shut up complaining, and all that had helped keep his suffering tamped down for a good long while. Now it was starting in for good, though, really cranking up, and Randall Eugene sat slumped over on the bench where the big fat black woman had directed him, feeling the misery in his arm grow as the judge listened to assistant prosecutors ask for folks to be bound over to one jail or another to wait for grand juries to meet.

Sometimes it seemed like it took more time and trouble to get located somewhere that satisfied the justice system than it did to serve the sentence they finally came up with for whatever it was they claimed you'd done. Thinking about that and paying attention to the way the sword cut on his arm was starting to pulse up and throb with pain stronger and stronger every time his heart beat, Randall Eugene didn't even hear his name called when the clerk told him to rise and face the bench.

"Stand up, asshole," the fool sitting next to him said into his ear, "that old judge is looking right at you." I don't even know you, Randall said to himself, though he meant the words for the wall-eyed man sitting beside him, the one giving off a stink like a boar hog and with a breath that would knock a skunk off a gut wagon. Who do you think you talking to, son? I'm in here for armed robbery, not for fighting in a bar. Imagining himself saying that to the petty brawler gave Randall Eugene some relief, and he rose and lifted his gaze to the man behind the bench dressed in a faded black robe which was showing wear and tear. "Are you Randall Eugene Puckett, as named in the document which you've read and signed?" the man said, reading from something in front of him and acting like he didn't even want to have to look at the man he was talking to.

"Yessir," Randall Eugene said, and then added, "My arm's hurting real bad."

"It is, huh, Randall Eugene Puckett. Then maybe you should have considered the possible outcome when you chose to do hand-to-hand battle with a soldier of the Confederacy," the judge said. Everybody who wasn't sitting on the bench where the men in jumpsuits waited their turn to be dealt with laughed real big at that, and Randall Eugene felt worse at that point than at any other time during the whole night behind him and that left to come.

"Remand him to custody, officer," the judge said to the fat black woman in the police uniform with the gun on her hip, "but be sure you don't let him get anywhere near any more swordsmen."

"Hah," the fat black woman said, lazily jerking at the chain on the cuffs binding Randall Eugene's hands together to get him started in the right direction. All he could think about as he walked toward the door into the hall they took prisoners down to put them away behind bars until the next thing happened to them, people chuckling as he passed them, even some of the ones in jumpsuits joining in to show they too knew what was funny when they saw it, was one question. How in hell did Tooter Browning get away with all that money in the bag and him not be able to find a way out the door of the wig shop? And besides the nigger getting away so easy, that goddamn Milton Drummond drove Tooter off in his old wreck of a Pontiac, leaving Randall Eugene there in the wig shop, crying and begging and rolling around on the floor as he worked at dodging that silver colored blade the crazy man in the gray uniform was swinging at him.

Randall Eugene could still hear the gutted muffler of the Pontiac fading out as Milton drove down Second Street to take that nigger to a place where there likely wasn't somebody waiting to try to cut your head off with a sword. If it hadn't been for the whore in the long dress that came running up to stop the old man from swinging that blade, saying "no Major" to him, and if the police hadn't got there quick because somebody reported that nigger woman's shotgun blasting right after she touched it off three or four times at the ceiling, Randall Eugene would be lying dead in a morgue somewhere with his head probably cut off rather than being stuck in a jail cell.

Bound and determined as he was to write something on the walls with his spray can, Tooter just had to spend time on leaving his message, well after they'd got the bag of money in hand and Randall Eugene'd had been forced to stand there ready to go, watching his partner squirting away with that black paint. That woman behind the counter never would have picked up the shotgun, neither, and shot into the ceiling with it, if it hadn't been for Tooter taking his mind off business, shaking up his paint can, and going to work writing that revolution shit on the wall.

Goddamn downtown Nashville, Randall Eugene said to himself, afraid to speak out loud and let anybody know what he was thinking anymore and knowing he'd have to watch what he said now for a long time to come. Goddamn a wig shop. Goddamn a whorehouse. Goddamn a old Confederate soldier with a sword in his hand.

"Okay, Slick," the fat black woman said, stopping in front of a cell with its door standing open and giving Randall Eugene a push in the back. "Step inside and stick your hands back out to me through the slot. You safe now. You done home."

The two phones downstairs in the reception area of the KD house and each one in the rooms where the officers of the sorority were allowed to stay as a special privilege had been ringing steadily or being talked into ever since the news about Martin Luther King's death had swept the nation. The parents of Vanderbilt students, especially of those who were daughters and granddaughters and nieces and girl cousins, were sensitive to the manner in which current events of national moment affected them and theirs personally. To whom much is given, much is required. Such is true not only in the case of the obligation to do charitable work but in the recognition that any disturbance of civil order will loose the have-nots upon the haves as soon as the barricades go up.

Come home immediately was the call sent by the guardians to the fe-males in their care, if you can do so safely. If you're not able to make it to the home fortress, stay indoors on campus, and we'll begin importuning the authorities, who must and will listen to our demands.

"Surely they won't get as far as West End Avenue, will they?" Allie Winchester was saying to Josephine Longineaux in between fielding phone calls from Mountain Brook and Vestavia Hills. "Claire said she'd heard there'll be army troops here to, you know, stop them from getting on campus. Did you hear that, too?"

"No need to worry, Allie," Josephine said. "They might steal some cars from the parking lot, but they won't be breaking into the Greek houses. Security won't let them do that."

"Well, I'm going to stay in my room in the house with the door locked just to be sure, I'll tell you that. Until it's all over. Aren't you?"

"I'm not a KD officer," Josephine said. "I'll be in Cole Hall in my dorm room. Or maybe not."

"What do you mean maybe not? Where else could you be?"

"Well, I've got a friend who's concerned about me just being in Cole, so I don't know where I'll end up. He thinks security may be weak in the big dorms."

"Is it Dr. Alden? I forgot about that. But isn't he married? You couldn't stay at his house, could you?"

"I won't name names, ever. Let's just say my friend Ronnie has been trying to reach me all night. He's just a nervous wreck and worried sick about me."

"Are you? Nervous, I mean, like him. Are you afraid?"

"Are you kidding? Allie, men are so possessive and afraid, especially when the relationship is teetering. They get just crazy."

"Teetering?"

"And about to fall, I'm afraid," Josephine said. "It's a shame, really, how attached and dependent a man will get."

"So you're not still fucking him?" Allie said, ignoring the ringing of the phone on the bedside table in her room.

"I didn't say that. I just don't think I really love him in the way you're supposed to. Everything ends. Like it says in all those poems, carpe diem."

"I understand," Allie said. "You want to use this phone?"

"Are you kidding?" Josephine said, tilting her head to the side and smiling at her KD sister. "I try not to ever call anybody. It's up to them to call me."

29

T 3100 WAS THE LOCKED FLOOR in the Vanderbilt hospital where they'd taken Lily after the trip up Twenty-First Avenue in the emergency vehicle, and that's where Ronald ended up after getting the children back home and leaving them with Robert McLean who said he'd stay until their father returned from seeing their mother safely contained in the pyscho ward. Stay as late as you have to, he'd said. You had to give the graduate student credit for stepping into the line of fire like that, Ronald considered, particularly since he wasn't by nature born to the task as he would have been if female. The minus for that, though, was that McLean would be in a professor's house unsupervised, and he'd certainly take advantage of the opportunity to pry and snoop. Ronald knew he certainly would have if he'd been turned loose in the same situation back in his graduate school days.

All right, yes, Robert McLean can look into whatever he can find on my desk or in Lily's stuff, Ronald told himself as he waited at the double-locked steel door into T 3100 after pushing the call button once, but what can he find? Not a single scrap of paper containing an idea for an article bound to find its way into print or an outline of a proposed book by Dr. Ronald Alden, assistant professor of English, up for tenure consideration this year, his plan for a monumental and groundbreaking work that would change thinking on the poems of Wordsworth about livestock or the effect of Keats's medical training on his physical height. Such documents do not exist, and rumors about their presence are nothing but myth, fabrication, and dream.

264

The worst thing Robert McLean could come up with if he started rooting around for something juicy to share with his fellow graduate students would be a diary by Lily, if she kept one. She probably doesn't, Ronald considered as he peered through the foot-square piece of glass cut into the steel door to T 3100, shot through with steel wire reinforcement to foil any inmate hoping to bust out, since I have never seen her write anything down since college but grocery lists and letters to her mother, but the mentally unstable do like to record the ramblings of their minds, don't they, hoping to document and justify their nuttiness. Let's be honest, though, the real reason Robert McLean stepped in to give me a hand was not out of the goodness of his heart, or from Christian charity, or pity for my children, but because he knows I'm going to be on his orals committee and he figures he's now nailed down one positive vote to grant him a pass, whatever happens.

One damn thing for certain, Ronald knew. Rummage around in the belongings of the Alden household though he may, Robert McLean wouldn't find any written evidence of a relationship between Dr. Alden and a female undergraduate student at Vanderbilt. Nothing substantial in this world linked him with Josephine Longineaux. He had made certain all that existed between them had no documentation. That was the blessing, that was the caution, and that was the sorrow.

A face appeared in the steel crosshatched pane of glass in the door, and its voice sounded from a small speaker. There was a lag between the movement of the lips behind the glass and the words coming from the speaker, and Ronald had trouble understanding what was being said. "What?" he said through the glass. "I can't follow you."

"Everybody says that," the speaker said. "Don't look at me talking, and don't try to figure it out from that. Just listen to the wall."

Ronald nodded, said okay, and looked up at the speaker. "Who's your patient?" it asked.

"Lily Alden. She was just brought in tonight."

Ronald could hear some shuffling of pages coming from the wall speaker, and then the voice spoke again. "She's already three down on the list of admissions tonight. I see her now."

"A busy night, huh?"

"Not really. At least not yet. I predict it'll pick up real strong a little later, once all the soldiers get here and the curfew sets in."

"The Dr. King death?" Ronald said. "There's a curfew?"

"You hadn't heard?" the wall said. "Citywide. From six at night until six in the morning. No citizen on the street, short of emergency. You've been too busy to get word, I expect. Our people, the ones we see, will start going to pieces later tonight, once they get that news and start to brood and fantasize. It'll be a real run on us."

"Can I see my wife? Can I talk to her?"

"Yep. Listen for the two clicks and pull the door toward you. You can make it in first try, if you do it quickly. Step lively. I don't want to have to open the door to T 3100 any more than I have to."

Once inside, Ronald was escorted by a different person, a male attendant, to the door of the room in which Lily had been put and allowed to take a look at her. All he could see was a mound of bed covers, no sign of her head or hands or any other part of her body visible outside the white coverings.

"Why's she all covered up like that?" he asked. "Won't she be uncomfortable?"

"That's what most of them do the first night they're here," the attendant said. He was tall, a good sixty pounds overweight, his head shaved, and he was wearing boots that reached halfway up his calves, his white pants shoved inside in neat folds. "They cover their heads all up like that and stay that way, some of them do, for up to twelve or fourteen hours. I saw one spend two whole days in her foxhole. Didn't show her face for forty-eight hours."

"Why do they do that?" Ronald said. "Isn't it hard to breathe under that blanket?"

"Doctors will tell you one thing about that presentation, and people like me will tell you something else. Which reason you want to hear about presentation?"

"Presentation? Both, I guess. She's my wife, after all."

"A doctor will say that specific presentation is a hibernation response, an escape from the reality they can't bear to be in. Me and people like me, the ones that's got to handle these types day and night, we'll tell you something else about these presentations."

"Why do you call it a presentation? And what about the breathing difficulty under there? Won't they smother?"

"That last question, sir, is easy. Both of them's easy, really. They can breathe fine. The human animal will have his oxygen, no matter what his head might tell him. The body demands it. Nobody's ever held his breath until he died. That's why they got to use ropes and carbon monoxide and stuff like that when they're doing a suicide presentation. If they mean for it to succeed, I'm saying. Now you ask why it's called a presentation, this kind of behavior. You ready to hear it?"

"Yeah," Ronald said, staring at the lump under the cover that was his wife. "Sure."

"Everything they do, the ones that come in here and find their natural home waiting for them, is not being done to satisfy something they want. They ain't trying to deal with themselves now. No, the reason they do what they do is to work on the ones that's got to deal with them. They make purpose presentations, see, and if you think back, being her husband and all, you'll be able to testify to the truth of what I'm saying. Every crazy thing she's done, she did it for you to see. Now didn't she?"

"Shit," Ronald said. "Presentation, huh? That's what it is."

"That's it, buddy. I told you that because you asked. Now will you do me a favor?"

"What? If I can, I will."

"Don't," the attendant said, elaborately looking about him for eavesdroppers though it was clear no one was around but the two of them. "Don't tell nobody I said the word crazy. They will not stand for that in T 3100. That word is a no-no. It's a firing offense, son."

"I promise you," Ronald said. "That's an easy one to keep. I'm trained not to say a whole set of words. But why are you telling me all this? Don't get me wrong. I'm grateful, but why are you letting me know what you think?"

"I will tell you, buddy, because I can't *not* tell you tonight. To put it simple, I got into the medicine cabinet early on today and took me some feel-good. It makes me want to tell the truth, and I know how funny that must sound to you. Living with a presenter, you ain't used to the truth."

"You took a drug? Won't it impair your judgment?"

"I'm not required to have no judgment. I don't make decisions. I just move things around when they tell me to. It's easy work, for the most part."

"I think I follow what you're saying. Now, I believe I'm ready to leave for the night. Can I say something to my wife before I go?"

"You can say whatever you want to, buddy. I will tell you one thing, though. She ain't going to answer you. Answering is not part of her particular presentation at this time."

"Got you," Ronald said to the attendant, and then looking toward the lump that was Lily, he called out in what he hoped was an encouraging tone. "I'll be back tomorrow, Lily. Sleep tight." The lump did not move.

"Don't you worry about her," the attendant said. "She's happy as a clam, snug as a bug. She's right where she's been aiming for, right where she wants to be. And she's presenting to her heart's content. You ready to leave T 3100 now, huh?"

"Yeah, I am," Ronald said, heading for the steel door between T 3100 and all that was outside. "I got to call somebody. I've got to go make a presentation."

The gravesite of Bishop William McKendree was located on the Vanderbilt campus between Calhoun and Confederate Hall near a magnolia tree and the stump of a massive white oak cut off at ground level. Upon the burial of the old Circuit Rider for Christ Jesus back in the early 1840s, his grave had been on the edge of the property in a copse of hardwood trees, all gone now save for the rotting oak stump, and Ronald had asked Josephine Longineaux to meet him there since the memorial was now so well hidden by the sheltering magnolia and the stand of perennial flowers planted to shield the above-ground tomb from people passing by on the nearest sidewalk, that itself a good distance away. Under the limbs of the magnolia spreading low to the ground was one of the most private places in that part of Nashville, on campus though it was, solitary and hardly ever visited except for the occasional secret drinker.

Ronald had found the tomb a year or so earlier when he had taken Emily and Julian off Lily's hands for a Sunday afternoon, and had spent a couple of hours letting the two children run and tumble on the grass as he sat holding a book of poetry in hand, in case anyone who knew him happened to see him wandering the sward. The book was one he hadn't read and had no intention of ever doing so, but there was nothing like a book held lightly in the hand to frighten off prospective conversationalists on a university campus. It was to buttonholers like garlic or a midday mirror is to a vampire. He'd heard there was a tomb of an expired Methodist bishop somewhere on campus, but had never seen it until Emily came running up to him to let him know what she'd found and wanted him to see.

"Come on, Daddy," she'd said. "Come look at the ghost place. Rum Tum told me where to find it. He whispered it in my ear so nobody but me could hear it."

He'd gone with her to look at the moldering vault, read the name of its inhabitant to her, explained about death and assured her she herself would never die, since that failure of nerve and persistence happened only to worn-out old people, and fielded the other questions his daughter peppered him with as well as he could. When I'm old, will I die? What will happen to me after I die? Will I have to stay buried or will I go somewhere it's nicer to be? Will I come back alive again? Will you and Mama be here when I get back? Will I live my same life again? If so, will I have the same parents again? Ronald had told her all the lies she needed to hear at her current stage of life, and she seemed satisfied until she turned to the subject of the dead bishop in the vault.

"Rum Tum says he's in there," she said. "He's dead all right, but he comes out at night and walks all around here looking for somebody to grab and take back into his little house made out of rocks. He wants them to stay with him and be his friend. That's what worries me."

"Little girls shouldn't worry about that kind of thing, Emily," Ronald said. "Just think about fun things to do. Think about birthday presents. Rum Tum was wrong when he told you about that."

"Don't say that loud enough for him to hear you, Daddy," Emily had said, looking back toward the bishop's tomb. "Rum Tum doesn't like it when you say he's wrong. He don't make mistakes. If he hears you say he does, he will get mad and give you bad dreams. He'll make bad things happen."

So when Ronald had finally reached Josephine Longineaux on the telephone in the reception area of the KD house sometime after ten o'clock, the only place that came to mind where she might be able to meet him was the bishop's grave under the magnolia, the house made of stone where the dead man spent the daylight hours. Anywhere else on the Vanderbilt campus was too open to view, and as late though it was on the night when Martin Luther King had been killed, students were milling about, defying the curfew, drinking out of cans, bottles, glasses, paper cups, and anything that would hold liquid, smoking joints and snorting coke and sucking on bongs, running from campus security officers who were assigned to keep them inside, shouting and falling and shrieking with glee, and racking their brains to think of another verboten thing to do.

"I tried to call your room in Cole," Ronald said to Josephine. "But when you weren't there, I thought I'd take the chance of phoning the sorority house desk."

"I'm not talking on that phone right now, though. I'm in Allie Winchester's room, and the desk lady transferred the call here. I'm about to have to go back to Cole for the night because of the curfew, though. So I can't talk long."

"I didn't tell the woman who I was, Josephine," Ronald said. "Don't worry."

"Thanks for wondering how I am. I'm fine. All the KDs are fine. So I'll see you in class next week."

"Don't hang up. I'd like to see you."

"Tonight? How? I can't leave campus. Soldiers are all around the place now, and I know my parents will be calling my Cole number again. They've already called three times since the news about Dr. King. So later, okay?"

"On the way to Cole, can you come by Bishop McKendree's tomb?"

"Whose tomb? What?"

"Remember I talked about it in sophomore survey one day as an example of Victorian kitsch? You know, the culture's love affair with death and all its trappings. Remember that theme appearing in poetry? Remember it in Tennyson?" Josephine was silent, but Ronald could hear her breathing over the phone. Her lips would be pursed as she thought, and she would be staring into space with her eyes fixed on distance. A lock of her golden hair would swing forward, and she'd raise a hand to move it back where it belonged, brushing against her ear, the color of pearl touched with pink.

"Remember we walked by it once late at night, coming back from where we'd been out on the interstate, and I pointed it out. And then I stayed there by the tomb, standing in the shadow of the magnolia, while you walked on across the campus, going back to Cole Hall, and I watched you for as long as I could see you. The last thing I saw of you that night was the flash of your hair, so gold in the light of that lamp by the sidewalk, and then it was gone."

"Yeah, I guess so. I think I remember some of that. Well, it's really late, and I've been on this phone long enough that Allie is looking at me sort of weird."

"Weirdly," Ronald heard himself correcting. Idiot, he thought. Fool, he thought. English teacher, he thought. "Can't you come by the tomb for a minute or two? Josey? Can you?"

"Tell you what. I'll try, but I can't promise, you know. Things being the way they are right now."

"I'll be there," Ronald said. "I'll wait. I want to see you. I need to."

"Uh huh. Well, good-bye."

Ronald hung up the payphone outside the Texaco station near the Vanderbilt Hospital on Twenty-First, decided not to try to call and arrange for a taxi to get him home later, wondering if they'd even be allowed to run taxis at all during the curfew, and headed north away from the hospital toward the heart of the campus. It was a good several blocks to where he was going, and he began walking quickly, almost at a jog, and then thought that gait might look suspicious at this time of night, especially with a curfew in effect and soldiers roaming the streets. They'd be armed with assault rifles, on edge, probably just back from or going to Vietnam, and they'd be ready to crack open with a rifle butt the head of anybody they saw running on a deserted street, if not shoot him dead on the spot. At least I'm not black, and I couldn't be mistaken for a looter or a revolutionary, he told himself. But my skin color's something they could tell only in the daylight. I might look as black as the ace of spades in the dark.

Should I stay in the streetlights where they can tell I'm white? But if I do, they'll see me breaking the curfew and maybe throw me in jail. Maybe the army will have set up holding compounds by now, and I'd be put in with a bunch of angry blacks, all drunk or doped up and mad as hell at any honky they see, and they'd put a shiv in me just because I'm the wrong color. Would they even listen to me tell them I'm a liberal, that I'm down with the cause, that I'm going to vote the straight Democratic ticket in November, just like I've always done? Maybe I could show them I know a little Negro dialect. But if you try to talk the talk like a black man, they may take offense at that. If I tell them that I'm slated to teach the first course in Black American writing ever offered at Vanderbilt, how will they take that? Will they give a shit? Would the ordinary Negro on the street even know who Paul Lawrence Dunbar was, much less Charles Chesnutt? What about Jean Toomer? What about Ishmael Reed?

Jesus Christ, Ronald said aloud, what about Josephine Longineaux? He looked ahead at the empty and brightly lit street, quickened his pace and ducked into the shadow of an alley just past the last hospital annex, aiming for a darker way to the tomb. The moon was down, and he could not see a star in the sky.

Nobody was under the magnolia tree shading the tomb of Bishop McKendree when Ronald worked his way to the spot twenty minutes later, after dodging between houses to get across lighted streets without spending time on sidewalks visible to the patrols of police cars and military jeeps and trucks cruising slowly past the campus. As he'd trotted through the dark yard of one house on the south side of the university, he'd almost run into a clothesline that he saw nearly too late to avoid getting knocked off his feet. In swerving and ducking to get under the length of white rope strung between two posts, he'd stumbled up against a kid's plastic swimming pool that made a booming noise so loud when he hit it and fell that lights went on in both houses he'd been trying to sneak between. He'd scrambled to his feet, a little dazed, put on speed, burst across the street into the safety of a collection of university maintenance buildings, and hid behind a parked truck until his breath slowed enough for him to proceed in the direction of the quadrangle at the heart of the oldest part of the Vanderbilt campus.

He'd met roving bands of students, male mostly, as he walked at a good pace, trying to look all business, head down and eyes on the sidewalk, and someone in the third group of chattering and laughing drunks called out his name as he went by them, adding some insult which he didn't hear but which caused others in the bunch to laugh long and hard. Fuck you very much, Ronald said to himself as he hurried on toward what he hoped was an assignation with the woman who'd stolen into his head, his heart, his guts, his being. You ignorant little shits. That kind of silent response generally lifted his spirits when he'd found himself taken lightly, but it didn't succeed this time. Nor did it help him achieve psychic invulnerability when he'd imagined the unidentified sneerer reduced to a final weeping paralysis. That mental trick should have worked for him. It didn't.

Josephine wasn't there when he arrived at the vault, and he was disappointed for at least two reasons. He was desperate to touch her, to feel the fresh tightness of her skin beneath his hands and against his face and lips and tongue, to smell the scent defining her at this moment of blossomed perfection in her life, and to know she would still allow him access to her body and mind. That first reason was visceral, fundamental, and above all physical. But in addition to the urgency of that need, Ronald had another reason to feel disappointment at the absence of Josephine Longineaux when he ducked under the spreading limbs of the magnolia and found nothing there but a slab of stone covering a clerical body dead since the nineteenth century.

What he had imagined as he struggled to make his way from the hospital where his wife lay covered of her own volition head to toe on a bed in a locked room in a psychiatric ward to a rendezvous with a beautiful and willing young woman who'd never given birth, never had to work for a living, never had to run a household, never had to make out grocery lists and write checks to pay overdue bills, never yet suffered the true and certain boredom of day-to-day existence with no change in sight, was to find her languishing in blonde and weeping perfection near a tomb, the emblem of loss and death and finality, while she waited for her lover to come to her. And he was that lover, Ronald Alden, teacher of English to the unwilling and listless on a daily basis, a man burdened with a mad wife and three children and the whole dreary calendar of life's responsibilities. But not tonight, not at this moment, not in this dark wood sheltering beauty and youth and promise. Tonight with her would be a fiery moment in the glowing present tense with the past dead, the future not a worry.

But Josephine Longineaux was not there in the dark. She was not waiting, pensive and pining, for him to come to her. Ronald groaned and lowered himself to the vault of Bishop William McKendree, sat upon the cold stone covering beneath which the bones lay, and tried to think of an appropriate line of verse to say to himself from a poem by a nineteenth-century English poet, preferably one of the Romantics, Keats or Shelley, perhaps. Maybe Byron. That's not to say the Victorians didn't produce some wonderfully moving expressions of lost love and non-fulfillment of desire, he told himself. Let's be fair. But the best of that subgenre of verse, it must be admitted, did come from John Keats, dead at age twenty-four.

He ran over every line he could recall from poems by Keats which he thought might prove appropriate, telling himself he must be certain he made no mistake when he spoke the words aloud, discarding any and every line and phrase that he couldn't recall faithfully, truly, and completely, and that process allowed Ronald Alden to sit upon the tomb of the dead Bishop with lines of poetry running through his head until well after midnight of April the fourth, the day Martin Luther King was killed in Memphis and Lily Alden was admitted to the T 3100 unit of Vanderbilt Hospital. If you set for yourself high enough requirements and limit choice to only the most suitable, Ronald told himself, if you are stern and unyielding in the vision you allow, you can see infinity in a grain of sand, eternity in an hour.

A little after midnight, someone rustled the leaves of a branch of the evergreen magnolia, its scent heavy in the night, and stepped from the light of the nearest sidewalk lamp into the darkness of the tomb area, causing Ronald to jump up from the cold stones where he'd been sitting, a crucial line from "La Belle Dame sans Merci" vanishing from his head. "Is that you?" he said, his voice strangled and weak in his own ears. He was instantly gratified he hadn't added Josephine's name to his outcry as soon as he recognized the shape of the figure coming into the shadow of the overhanging magnolia to be male, a small man certainly, but undeniably not a woman.

"Who's that?" the man said. "It sounds like somebody I used to listen to every Monday, Wednesday, and Friday yammering on about paragraph development."

"Greg," Ronald said. "Greg Donaldson. What are you doing out so late tonight of all nights? You're violating the city curfew, I hope you realize."

"Dr. Alden," Greg Donaldson said, "it is you. I'd recognize that voice from the grave, no matter who's buried in it."

"So you know about the old bishop's final resting place. Not many people do."

"Only the horny, Dr. A," Greg said. "And those in need of a quick snort or two. What are you doing here?"

"I had to take my wife to the hospital tonight, and I can't find a way home with the curfew on. So I came here to wait until daylight."

"That's too bad. Is she very sick?"

"A little sicker than usual. It's really just precautionary, putting her in the hospital. She'll be fine."

"Oh, well," Greg said. "Campus Security won't bother a professor who's on campus, would they?"

"Nobody can be out and around but security and police and the troops, Greg," Ronald said. "It's a full curfew, they say. So I'll while away the hours thinking of dead poets."

"Maybe you'll want to come along with me, if you're bored here with the bishop," Greg said. "I'm visiting the old boy at home to get ready for the next labor of the Rat."

"The Rat? Where's your costume?"

"I'm wearing it, all but the head and feet. I guess it's too dark for you to appreciate my lovely fur. I stashed the head and feet behind the tombstone in that hidey-hole before they chased us all inside at six today. I'll be puttin' on the Ritz here in a minute."

"Oh, what will the Rat be doing tonight besides getting locked up or maybe shot?"

"The Rat," said Greg, "has a major job of work tonight, and he does not shirk his responsibility, Dr. Alden. He will feed the troops, the gallant young men who defend us from the Viet Cong of South Asia and the Negroes of Nashville. It will be a cheese-less situation the Rat will face and redress."

"You are one crazy bastard, Greg," Ronald said. "Determined to be nuts."

"I'm not the one sitting in the dark on a tomb waiting for my honey chile to show up," Greg said. "Come on and go with me. She's not coming, Dr. Alden. Face it."

"I think you're right, Greg, though I don't know what you could be talking about. Not a word of it."

"That's right, Dr. Alden. As the Rat says, never apologize, never explain, and never 'fess up. Let's go feed some Yankee soldiers."

"Shit, why not?" Ronald said, moving away from the tomb and shivering when a draft of cold air hit him. "I don't suppose you've got an extra Rat head on you?"

30

AFTER GREG HAD DONNED the Rat's head and feet and offered to let Ronald borrow a bandana to tie around his head as a disguise, which Ronald had rejected immediately, imagining what a trigger-happy army inductee or a Nashville cop would do at the sight of a masked man approaching, the two of them worked their way north on the campus toward West End. It was well after midnight, or in Ronald's way of accounting for the night about eight or nine ransacked Keats poems deep into it, and they saw no one else before they reached the street.

"No traffic at all," Ronald said. "Not a car. Not a pedestrian. Talk about eerie. All I hear is a train somewhere."

"Not a train, Dr. A," the Rat said. "Look toward downtown. That noise is coming from tank engines. See them on the way toward us? Four of the army's finest."

"This is a bad idea, Greg. It's no time to play now. We better move back off the street. No, let me put it another way. We have to move back off the street."

"Can't be done, Dr. A, and don't call me by any other name but Rat, please. I have put aside the old skin and taken up residence in a new and improved one."

"Oh, for God's sake," Ronald said. "Come on, Greg. We've got to get out of sight. Why are they sending tanks this direction? It's completely quiet around Vanderbilt. Nobody's anywhere to be seen on the streets around here."

"Because they can hook a right up there at the corner and take that street all the way into North Nashville. That's why the tanks're coming this way. Look over at the sky straight across. Toward Fisk and Tennessee State."

"They're doing it again," Ronald said, looking north at the red and yellow leap of flames above the horizon. "Just like last year. The way it's burning you'd think every building in that part of Nashville is on fire. Listen to that crackling noise. Is it just the fire or is that guns going off?"

"Both, the Rat says. But here's what puzzles the Rat. What's left to burn this year? Did they get enough built up since last time to be able to set it on fire again?"

"There's always something left to put a match to again, I guess," Ronald said. "This time they'll be finding new fuel for the bonfire. They've got a lot to work with tonight."

"You know what a Sigma Chi asked the Rat tonight after the news about the killing of Dr. King in Memphis? Came right up to the Rat's executive desk outside Rand Hall to put the query."

"I can imagine, but tell me."

"No, it wasn't the usual stuff about our black brothers being lazy and homicidal and smelling bad and drinking Thunderbird. It was real thoughtful for a Sigma Chi, what he asked was. It was Gatewood Dunn. You may remember him from the sophomore survey course last year. He sat by Josephine Longineaux. Remember that loving couple?"

"I think so," Ronald said, wondering instantly at the sound of her name what the exact words were of "This Living Hand" by Keats, that one about Fanny Brawne, so short and fierce, that to read it was like watching blood shoot from a just severed artery. "I think I may remember him."

"The Rat would hazard his all that you would, Dr. A. Well, what Gatewood asked the Rat today was why was it the nigras would burn down the houses they lived in and leave themselves nowhere to go after the fires were set. That's the term he used, nigras, so the Rat knew Gatewood was making a serious inquiry. That's what Nashville society folks call blacks when they're being thoughtful. The Rat told him, said it's because their houses ain't worth staying in, that's why. Their houses make a whole lot better fire than they'd ever make a place to live. It's a matter of profit and loss, the Rat told Gatewood, like all things. It's an economic decision. The Rat put it to him in a way he could understand."

"What did he say to the Rat when he heard that?" Ronald asked, able to recall only part of one line from "This Living Hand," something something, then "see, here it is, I hold it toward you." What was the rest, what came before that, what started things up? Can you ever tell what makes a thing happen and from where the right words come to record the event? Is it like a fever with a culture of microbes trying to grow and prosper in an unwilling host? Or is it just a low-grade slide of a heavy weight, finally giving way after resting at an angle impossible to maintain forever? Beware of falling rocks. Gravity's bound to have its way.

"He said the usual thing one of them says to the Rat, and the Rat was glad he did. Gatewood Dunn said and I quote him exactly, you crazy fucker. You don't make sense."

"That made you glad, huh?"

"It did make the Rat glad, and I ask only one thing at the demise of this rodent and that's that Gatewood's sentiment be inscribed upon my tomb. The Rat sees the letters glowing now on the stone. He never made sense. That will be my epitaph, short but apt."

"Rat, that makes sense to me, what you just said. He never made sense is a statement that makes sense. But look over there now, those four tanks are almost at the corner, and what do you see behind them?"

"Troops," the Rat said. "I wonder what the military term is for that many together. A squad? A battalion? A horde? A swarm?"

"Greg, I know this much. That bunch, whatever it's called, does not respond to or appreciate the absurd, and that's what you and the Rat deal in. We've got to get off this sidewalk and fade back into the groves of academe behind us. Let's go."

"Dr. Alden," the Rat said. "I hate to admit it, but reason dictates we do so. I say that, but the Rat does not agree."

"To hell with the Rat. Leave his head for them to puzzle over, if you just have to make a statement."

"What a great idea. The Rat approves, and I will leave his head as commentary on the situation. I also brought with me a bag of cheese chunks the Rat wanted to hand out piecemeal to the soldiers. Maybe even sticking them in their rifle muzzles as they stand at ready. They wouldn't have liked that."

"No, they wouldn't. They would have knocked the Rat on his ass if he'd been lucky. Just pull off your head, throw it down and let's go,"

Ronald said. "Look, the fire in North Nashville is so big now you can see it billowing and lighting up the clouds. It's casting shadows on the Parthenon and on buildings way over here on campus."

"The Rat's judgment is that the nigras of Nashville are trying to set the night on fire. The Rat predicts the blaze they make will cast shadows for a long time to come," the Rat said, throwing his head onto the sidewalk by West End Avenue and scattering his bag of cheese chunks after it, most of them not falling in neat separation, but sticking together in awkward wads.

Jesus, Ronald thought as he fled in front of the Rat crashing through a stand of wisteria just the other side of the wall marking off Vanderbilt from the rest of the world, we're all making our best presentation, every damn one of us. And with that, another piece of the dead poet's plea to his lost love popped into his mind, something about Keats's hand's being "now warm and capable of earnest grasping." That shit will not last, Johnny Boy, Ronald said to Keats as he charged through the new spring growth of ornamentals on the university grounds. Trust me. It won't even outlast the cheese. Behind him the screech and grinding of steel tracks mounted as the tanks swung around the intersection and headed for the burning streets and buildings of North Nashville, the boots of the following troops marching in a ragged rhythm and time.

Ronald focused on the tramp and beat of that regular sound. Stay with that, he told himself. Don't get outside it. Don't let a single thought stray. He ran, breath whistling in his throat. He ran. Ran.

Lily Alden had been seeing many different people, most of whom she knew but had not seen for a long time, ever since she came out from under the blanket on that quiet bed they had let her lie on for as long as she wanted to stay in that cool silent room. She had appreciated that. Staying in bed with no one expecting her to rise, no one wanting attention, no one thinking they had a right to come before her in any way. The people who let her stay in bed covered head to toe were kind, the ones of them who came into the room now and then, most of the time saying nothing, but now and then letting her know there was something to eat if she wanted it. Or offering her water or juice. Or reminding her again that there was a bathroom for her sole use when she needed it.

The people she began seeing in the room when she'd eased back the covers and let her eyes open again were mainly from Ohio, where she grew up and went to school during the week and church on Sundays and sometimes Wednesday nights for prayer meeting, but not too much of that. A once a week dose of church was enough, her father often said, joking mainly but meaning it, too, enough medicine taken to keep in good graces with the angels and saints and Jesus and God Almighty until the time came to do the final accounting of profit and loss and figure out which direction you'd have to take for the rest of eternity.

The first person she saw from that time in Ohio when she peeped out from beneath the cover was her English teacher from senior year, Mrs. Nell Scarber. She was sitting in a chair against the wall of the room where they'd put Lily to lie down covered up in a bed with nobody else around, and Mrs. Scarber had somehow managed to bring her desk from Warren G. Harding High School with her to Lily's room in the T 3100 unit of Vanderbilt Hospital. The desk took up all of one wall, and behind it on the wall beneath the picture of George Washington was the quotation from the Bible for everyone in the classroom to read daily, if they wanted to, the one about studying to show thyself approved. Mrs. Scarber's desk was covered with student papers, as it always was, and Mrs. Scarber was marking them one by one, now and then shaking her head at some mistake she'd found and then writing with her red pencil in the margin to show the student where she'd gone wrong. Lily spoke to her, said hello Mrs. Scarber, but her teacher had shushed her, and told her to lay her head down on her own desk if she wasn't feeling well. She'd be better soon. It was just a cramp.

Nobody from Lily's whole four years of college at Denison showed up in her room, though, and she was glad about that. She had not taken a single minute to look at herself in the mirror and put on fresh makeup or brush her hair, even, and she certainly didn't want anybody from Denison to see her looking such a sight. Even after she'd gotten out of bed, feeling a little weak from resting under the covers so long, and made her way to the bathroom, not able to do much there even though she couldn't remember the last time she'd relieved her bladder, and finally opened the door to her room and looked outside to see where she was, Lily didn't see a single person from college she'd have to deal with.

Her father was there in the big room, at one point, though he didn't notice her, maybe because he was busy talking to Dr. Martin Luther

King, really giving him a lot to think about, Lily could tell as she watched her father shake his finger in the air in a friendly fashion, letting Dr. King know the opinion of a good middle American small businessman trying to keep afloat in this changing time. Dr. King had his lips pursed in thought, nodding his head as he listened, and he had blood all over the collar of his shirt, but he didn't seem to notice it much, just dabbing at it now and then with a white handkerchief, trying to keep it from getting on his tie, Lily supposed. Lily had to admit she felt a little proud to see Dr. King paying such close attention to Arthur Schmidt of Mansfield, Ohio, obviously impressed by what he was hearing from her father about race relations and Vietnam and the mess the country was in.

Tollman Briggs was there, too, and when Lily looked away from her father and Dr. King to see what Tollman was doing off in the corner of the room—playing his guitar, of course, with his shirtfront all open so you could see that tangle of chest hair, and some hippie girl sitting down on the floor in front of him, licking her middle finger until it shone in the light, rubbing the tip of it on Tollman's bare foot and then doing it all over again—Lily was surprised when she looked back to see her father and Dr. King again to discover that they were nowhere in sight. No big deal, though. They've probably found some conference table where it was more convenient to sit, take notes, and continue their discussion.

After seeing in this strange new room people she knew or had known or had heard about somewhere along her way, some she was pleased to encounter again and some she was not, Lily was not surprised to glimpse someone from the English department at Vanderbilt sitting by himself in an overstuffed chair near a bank of windows with heavy wire mesh fixed in front of them. The man had put up his hand to touch the wire and push at it a little, though he'd had to strain to do it while still sitting in the chair, and he had a cross look on his face. He looked around him, as though to find someone to help him do whatever it was he wanted with the wire mesh, and he caught sight of Lily as she stood watching him.

"Young lady," he said. "I think I know you. Are you not married to one of the lieutenants in the Fourth Mississippi? Not a very promising young officer, as of yet, but perhaps the fires of battle will prove him, test his mettle, and burnish him in the flame."

"I don't know who I'm married to," Lily said. "I was married, dressed in a white gown with little pearls down the bodice, I do know that, but I swear I can't remember the groom's name now. It just will not come to mind. Perhaps you can help me, Dr. Flange. I seem to recall that my husband was in your department."

"That was precisely the intent of my question to you, my dear, about the young lieutenant. But you seem to have confused my identity with that of some other person, I believe. I am Major Rooney Beauchamp of the Fourth Mississippi, and the name you called me earlier is not mine own, I must declare. My home county is Panola, where my people's holdings are located on the Benevolence Plantation."

"I do apologize," Lily said, coming closer to the windows through which a weak ray of sun shone, lighting up the brass work on the man's military blouse. "I am having some difficulty with details these last few days. Could you tell me where we are, Major Beauchamp? And what time of day it is? When I pulled the covers over my head, it was dark outside and now it's not, I see. I'm a little confused."

"I can and will inform you of our location and the time of day and the situation in which we find ourselves, my dear. It will please me to do so. May I inquire your name?"

"It's Lily. Lily Schmidt," Lily said, automatically lifting her right hand to touch her hair.

"Like the flower," the man in the overstuffed chair said. "A lovely name for a lovely young lady. Who are your people, Lily Schmidt? That name does not smack of the South. Its form as Smith is assuredly of the yeoman stock of the British Isles, but the pronunciation you give it is Germanic. Is it not?"

"Yes, Major Beauchamp. My family came to Ohio after the 1848 troubles in Europe, I was always told. From Germany, as you said."

"Your location and your people in Ohio are not of your own doing, Lily. You must not be ashamed of that," he said, finally disengaging his right hand from the wire mesh between him and the window and scratching at his left arm with it. "Look to your conduct now as a young woman, the way you live in this time, not to that of your people in years gone by. Your present demeanor will suffice, and it will honor you."

"Thank you, I will," Lily said. "Will you let me know where we are now and what day it is?"

"We are in a military hospital, Mrs. Schmidt, in Nashville. The year is '64, and prospects for success are dire. The battle at Franklin has come near to breaking the back of General Hood's corps, but we soldier on. We persevere. Hood is at the gates of Nashville, even now. Undaunted and unbowed, he prepares to move on the Union works."

"I guess I've gotten ahead of myself," Lily said, putting her hand to her forehead as though to add up a set of figures difficult to hold steady for computation without the aid of pencil and paper. "I knew we are in Nashville and that Franklin has troubles of its own, though not so bad as Nashville's. But I could have sworn the year was '68."

"It's a strenuous and difficult time," Rooney Beauchamp said, "particularly for ladies. Don't be upset at the tricks your mind is playing upon you. I will tell you with great assurance that you are a Northern woman who's fetched up somehow in Nashville during this dire time. I had thought you wife of a lieutenant in the Fourth. But I see I am doubtless mistaken. Could you be wed to a merchant, perhaps? It makes no matter, whoever your good husband may be. Do not be afraid. Let not your heart be troubled. Our quarrel is not with you, and it is my fervent belief that any one of my men in the Fourth Mississippi would defend your honor to the death. You have the word of a gentleman and an officer from the Delta on that matter. We have no enmity toward Northern women, though our armies are locked in a struggle to the death. We do not make war against women and children as do some commands in Mr. Lincoln's battalions. Be assured of that, and be not afraid."

"Oh, thank you for those words," Lily said. "I haven't heard anything like that from any man for years. May I ask why you're in this military hospital, Major?"

"I am here for treatment for wounds suffered in battle," Rooney Beauchamp said. "I am not so harmed as to be hors de combat, but the medicos insist I must lie down and rest me a while. I am eager to rejoin the fray, however. My men need me, as does my nation."

"How were you wounded?" Lily said. "Is it your arm that's been hurt?"

"The encounter was of no real consequence, my dear. Merely a brief skirmish with a Union squad attached to an Illinois regiment. But out of such small matters do great events arise. And yes, as you have observed, the wound I suffered is to the left arm. See how it droops, much like that of the broken wing of a shot hawk perhaps, brought to ground but defiant yet."

"Were you shot in the arm, Major?"

"No, not in this encounter. The real damage to that limb was at Shiloh. The wound that I suffered most recently came from a knife thrust, I believe it was. It's of no real consequence, and I was not unduly slowed in my response. I swung my saber with my good right arm, and I made the miscreant pay for his low and despicable action."

"Were you forced to take his life?" Lily said. "Had he so offended you? Wasn't it self-defense? You had to do it. You had no choice."

"The offense was not his action in itself, my dear. A soldier in battle bears no personal animus toward the enemies of his country. He acts from duty and honor. But in this case, I must say, concepts of that sort did not obtain. My opponent was not properly a soldier, but a nigra armed with a firearm and a great blade. Yes, the Union has descended to using nigras in the ranks of their armies. The end of civil and manly behavior in war has come. All is now sheer barbarism. And as far as the status of this so-called soldier is concerned, he was not seriously injured. You couldn't kill one with an axe, as the old East Tennessee saying goes."

Lily reached out her hand and patted the wounded Major on his shoulder, careful not to upset the way in which he was holding his arm, lifted and curled as though it were a baby in a cradle. From across the room somebody said something which seemed to be directed at her, Lily could tell, when the voice continued speaking. "Miss," a woman was saying, "no touching. A patient cannot come into physical contact with any other patient. Not ever."

"Oh," Lily said. "I was just patting the major on his injured shoulder. I'm sorry."

"Just remember after this. No touching. No patting. No feeling up."

"I appreciate the gesture, Miss Lily," the wounded major said. "These attendants continue to do all they can to postpone my amputation. I cannot apprehend their reasoning, but we must deal with their mistaken notions until we are allowed to return to the field."

"Amputation? Is your arm that bad?"

"I will say this. I have come to believe a severing of this limb from my body proper is my only recourse. But do not be alarmed. I intend that removal of this dead and dependent thing and will finally achieve that goal, God willing. But tell me, Miss Lily, why do you find yourself in this military hospital?"

"I think it must have been the water," Lily said after pausing to consider what the most accurate answer to Major Rooney Beauchamp's question might be. "The brook I lay in. Yes. Either that or the flowers. They didn't like the water, and they didn't like the flowers, either. They kept talking about the flowers, acting surprised and even laughing at them, but the flowers were beautiful, along with the green twigs floating beside them over the pebbles. They all moved so slowly downstream, all the parts of what I wanted, and I drifted with the flowers and leaves and twigs. And I sang too roo lay, too roo lay, loo, not to call attention to my voice or musical ability but to accompany the flow downstream. And do you know what I liked most about it, the drifting in the stream with the flow of the water and the flowers? Can you guess, Major?"

"Please call me Rooney, Miss Lily, and do tell me what you liked best about it."

"The feeling I had. I couldn't find the word for it while it was happening, but that didn't matter then. You don't need words when the moment is at hand, do you? Only afterwards do you have to know what to call a thing that's caught you up in it. And so it wasn't until they were pulling me out of the stream and away from the flowers that the word came to me. It grew in my mind like one of the flowers. Guess what it was."

"Peaceful, perhaps?" Major Beauchamp said.

"No, not exactly. That's close, but it wasn't that. It was languid. That's the word. Languid was the word, and languid sounds like what it means."

"A lovely comment, Miss Lily. Your soul is in it."

"All right," someone was saying to Lily and the Major. "Dr. Flange and Mrs. Alden, here's your meds and your cups of water, and it's four more hours that's done come around again. It's time."

"What are these?" Lily asked, but the black man in the white uniform didn't answer except to rattle the pills in their container and hold them out toward her. She took them, to be polite, and put them in her mouth, ready for the water to help them down. It was too warm to drink—you could tell it had been held in somebody's hand too long—but Lily forced it down right behind the pills. Major Beauchamp didn't want to take his pills, though, and another Negro in white, a woman, had to follow the Major across the room when he got up out of his chair and moved away, almost at a trot, trying to avoid swallowing his dose.

"I won't have it," he was saying. "I don't want it. No, no, no."

"Come on, Sugar," she was saying. "You know you going to end up doing just what I tell you to, so might as well save us all some time and trouble. Give it on up now, and save your ammunition." Other voices began to chime in at that, some laughing and some calling out encouragement to the major as he ran across the room, his feet skittering on the polished floor. As soon as the noises and laughs started up, Lily closed her eyes and began to watch herself stepping into the stream filled with spring buds and petals, the water cool against her feet and ankles, its murmur enclosing all other sounds in the colors, white, purple, and pink. She lay down gracefully, one hand out to cushion her descent into the brook, not making a splash or slipping on the wet stones, and she heard the song begin as she lay back in the stream, her eyes half closed as the guitar's strings began to sound. She blended her voice with the plucked notes of the guitar, and a troubadour joined in, his voice deep and melodious, layered just below hers. It was his, he was the singer. Tollman, of course.

31

THE MEETING was an extraordinary one, called for early on Tuesday morning and including all fulltime members of the department of English, untenured and tenured, probationary and permanent. Peggy Newstead, head secretary, had been forced to scramble to find a room large enough to hold all of them, given several conditions limiting her choices. First, the chairman had set the meeting for the time of day when most classrooms were filled with students and therefore taken; second, the citywide curfew of 6 p.m. was still in place with no end to it declared yet, even though most of the fires in North Nashville had burned themselves out over the weekend and the bands of roving blacks had either been beaten back or held at bay by the tanks and troops; third, several professors had not appeared on campus since the news of Dr. King's death had broken, some claiming they were making a political and moral statement of solidarity with the Negro race by refusing to work, and others afraid their cars would be hijacked on their way to campus by Mau Mau raiders and they'd be subjected to death and even worse for being teachers of rich college students.

George Gwaltney described best the quandary in which a right-thinking individual found himself. "If you did get ambushed by a raiding party," he said to a cluster of fellow assistant professors before the extraordinary departmental meeting got underway, "would they be willing to listen to your views on civil rights for the Negro? Could you prove to them you were sympathetic to the cause? Would they listen to reason?"

"Well put, George," Lodge Draper said. "And imagine the irony of being assaulted or worse by blacks because they mistake you for a racist oppressor. A hideous prospect. Eminently unfair."

"Gentlemen," explained T. M. Randstool, a man who'd begun his career with great enough early promise to be granted tenure and then became a revealed drunk of such magnitude that he was doomed to be a lifelong associate professor. "Here's the truth, whether you want to hear it or not. The ones that make up the Negro raiding parties don't give a shit about politics. Hell, they're perfectly satisfied that King got killed. They're glad it happened. It gives them cover to pillage TV sets and shiny wheel covers for their rusted-out old Cadillac DeVilles and cases of Crown Royal out of the package stores. It's an iron-clad license to loot."

"I hope you're being satiric, T. M.," Lodge Draper said, "or at least facetious when you talk like that. That's the kind of language one is likely to hear from the White Citizens' Councils."

"Hear, hear," George Gwaltney said, looking about him for sounds of seconding of his sentiment, but getting none. Lodge Draper was giving signs of preparing to make a fuller statement, though, by drawing his head back as though to set himself to spit out something foreign which he'd just sensed in his mouth, an insect, maybe, or a bit of gristle that had finally worked its way loose from between two molars. He added to this expression a deep frown that suggested after long thought he had reached a conclusion which no other person would been able to formulate, much less voice.

"It seems to me," he was beginning to say in preface to a summation of his opinion on the matter in question when a sound of brisk rapping came from the front of the room in which the department was gathered. Murmurs, coughs, and shufflings and shiftings in seats followed, widespread enough to cause Lodge Draper to sink back within himself, his thoughts unexpressed and destined to fester in a low seethe until he'd be able to disgorge them later. He frowned again and joined the others of his colleagues, tenured and untenured, probationary and permanent, in looking toward the source of the pounding coming from the lectern. It was a wooden gavel being wielded by the chairman, an action which in the memory of the department had never been taken before at a meeting.

"To have us meet in the small chapel of the Divinity School seems most apt, I would say," Alfred Buchanan began, "and I'll so inform Peggy that she should always attempt to reserve this chamber for you in future."

"Now to our matters of concern today," the chairman continued, pleasantries well completed. "I have called us together in this extraordinary meeting to address a few pressing matters, mainly informational. It has been a most astounding last few days for the nation, for our students, for the institution and for members of this department, individually and as a group. Let me begin with announcements and some ground rules for our discussion today.

"Let me convey my first bit of news a bit obliquely. When the department of English meets in its initial gathering in the fall term, there will be discovered at least two major differences in personnel. First of all, you will not be any longer an all-men's club. I'm delighted to inform you that Dr. Muriel Laager of Columbia University has accepted our invitation of appointment to the endowed chairship, which we have been searching so manfully to fill. She will join us as the Mildred Smith Townsend Professor of American Literature and Women's Studies, a newly endowed chair."

"Is that the Jew woman?" Gareth Lamb asked Marvin Slope in a not-so-soft whisper.

"What do you expect?" Slope said. "That's the name of the one we said was completely unacceptable, wasn't it? So here she'll be."

"His nerve, his gall, his impudence," Henry Hallam Horsham said to the man next to him, David McDavidson, who leaned away, his face averted, as if to avoid a blast of halitosis. The old bastard, Henry said to himself, he'll insult me unfairly, but he won't face up to King Alfred. You're just a gutless old closet queen, David McDavidson. So there.

"The next major change in personnel in the Vanderbilt Department of English will involve its chairman," Alfred Buchanan said. "You will be wanting a new one, a man to replace the current occupant who has accepted a new post, that being the chairship of the department of English at Stanford University." If that doesn't knock them over, I don't know my agrarians and fugitives and new critics, Alfred told himself as he watched the congregation before him swell individually and as a group in their seats like suddenly inflated balloons and then subside as if the air was rushing out of each empty rubber bag through a sudden rupture. The sound of the spontaneous intake and expulsion of departmental breath was unique, Alfred considered, one he hadn't enjoyed before, but it came to him as sweetly as the imagined swish of angel wings would to a holy roller somewhere in deep East Tennessee.

"Dr. Buchanan," Lawrence Hill Dunham shouted above the ensuing hubbub, "I know I speak for the department when I congratulate you on such a superb appointment. And there will be ample time to thank you for your contributions and leadership at Vanderbilt later. But I have a question, and it's this. What about Robard Flange? What can you tell us about him and his situation? We've heard such wild rumors and read such strange accounts in both Nashville newspapers."

"Thank you, Larry, for your kind words about me which mean so much professionally and personally. I will speak to you about Dr. Flange when we conclude our business as a full department and move to an executive meeting of the tenured members. I can say nothing about that matter until then."

"When will we go into executive session?" Shoul Lambert said.

"Now," Buchanan said. "All but tenured members are now dismissed."

"My advice to you," George Gwaltney said to fellow assistant professor Ronald Alden, "is to come with me and let's go get hammered."

"I want to, but I can't. I've got to go see my wife. She's in the Vanderbilt Hospital."

"Is she sick? I hadn't heard. Sorry to learn that."

"She's sick all right, George, and you'll be hearing about it from every graduate student and secretary and janitor and preacher on campus. You'll hear this, too. The kind of sick she is does not yield to treatment."

"Oh, shit," George Gwaltney said.

"Oh shit is right. And oh dear and oh fuck me and all you can think of to add to those sentiments."

"I'm going to go get drunk by myself, then," George said.

"I will, too. Later. Bad drunk. I deserve it, I earned it, and I'm counting on it."

The curfew was driving Marlene Mercer mad. She had done nothing since the assassination of Martin Luther King on Friday but teach her two classes of freshman composition, go to her graduate courses, one on the MWF sequence and the other Tuesday-Thursday—a schedule not her fault but that of the lazy senior faculty bastards who deigned to teach only at times convenient to themselves—and then scurry back to her apartment in Hillsborough Village before running the danger of being arrested for being out after six in the evening. By noon on

Tuesday, she couldn't face the idea of being cooped up alone for another twelve hours in those two depressing little rooms on Fairfax during the night to come.

By not buying her lunch on Tuesday and telling herself she couldn't eat at noon for the rest of the week, Marlene had scraped together enough money to buy a gallon jug of Paisano table wine, a package of off-brand water crackers, and a plastic container of onion dip on sale at Hill's supermarket just past the Vandy hospital. When she asked Betsy Ames and Jennifer Smithing if they'd defy the curfew that night and come to her apartment for some relief from isolation, they'd jumped at the chance, both arriving a good half hour before the soldiers and police were reportedly approved to start shooting to kill anybody that dared to move on the streets of Music City. That very morning Robert McLean had memorably said in the graduate seminar on Alexander Pope that open season on anybody that read books or stepped away from the TV set after dark had finally been declared and made official in Davidson County.

By the time Jennifer and Betsy arrived at her garage apartment, Marlene had already gotten two glasses deep into the gallon jug of busthead red, put albums by the Doors and the Stones on her stereo, and begun singing along with Jim and Mick. "Girl," Jennifer said, coming into the kitchen area to locate a glass, "you know you're not supposed to have fun on a week night. What is all this uproar?"

"I have decided I'm not a serious person," Marlene said. "Nobody else in the PhD program in English at Vanderbilt is. Why should I be the only one to bust my ass in the study of literature?"

"Woo," Betsy Ames said. "I can drink to that. Give me that jug, and tell me what you know."

"I know whose wife is in the psycho ward at the Vanderbilt hospital," Marlene said. "And I'll swap you that story for what you've heard about Robard Flange."

"Who's the lady in the nut ward? Tell me. Is it Ruth Gwaltney?"

"No, she ought to be, married to the asshole she's hooked up with. But no, it's not Mrs. George Gwaltney."

"Well, it's got to be the wife of one of the assistant professors," Betsy said. "The ones married to the old farts have already had their crackups years ago and been pasted back together."

"Not too damn well," Jennifer Smithing said. "I saw Denice Vallandigham in Old Central the other day and she looked like Baby Jane sitting on the beach after everything had happened to her."

"I love Bette Davis," Marlene said. "She takes shit from no man."

"That's why the homos all like her, too," Jennifer said. "I heard Dr. Horsham talking about her last year at one of the classic movie series nights. He said she was divinely righteous."

"Oh, Jesus," Marlene said. "He is just too precious for words. The thing I hate about homos is not that they like boys but that they take some of the best ones off the market away from us girls. Especially the way Henry Hallam Horsham hawks them."

"Surely not," Jennifer said. "There can't be many guys who'll go both ways."

"In English departments," Marlene and Betsy said almost at the same time, laughing at themselves and reaching for the jug of wine simultaneously. "You'll find the switch hitters there," Betsy went on to say as Marlene poured. "The men in English departments don't know who they are or what they like to do half the time. They don't know if they're going or coming."

"Tell us whose wife's had to be locked in the cuckoo's nest, Marlene," Jennifer said. "If it's not George Gwaltney's roommate, who is it?"

"Lily Alden," Marlene said. "That's who. My landlady's daughter works in housekeeping on that floor of the hospital where they keep the wigged-out ones. As soon as she found out who one of the new freshmen in the nut house was, she recognized the name and she told her mama. Mama told me."

"She's got a bunch of kids, doesn't she? Lily, I mean," Jennifer said. "That'd help drive you crazy."

"Maybe she found out about her husband fucking undergraduates," Betsy said. "That could have tipped her into going off the deep end."

"Yeah, but she was acting real nutty last year at Timbo's fish fry," Marlene said. "Remember how she was dancing like a whore and how David Mullins was all over her at first until he got scared and bailed out."

"That's right," Betsy said. "I was kind of tipsy myself, but everybody noticed all that going on. It got too real for David Mullins. That lady was acting like she meant business."

"Everybody saw that but the ones watching Robert McLean and Houston sniffing around Dr. Buchanan's daughter. That was ridiculous to see. Like two dogs quarreling over a bitch in heat."

"Do you think either one of them got to fuck her that night?" Marlene said. "They were after that precious Barnard princess hard and fast."

"Houston's tongue was hanging down to his breastbone," Jennifer Smithing said. "I thought he was going to start humping her leg any minute."

"Don't start talking about Houston Stride's tongue, now," Betsy Ames said. "I'll get faint and have to lie down and let y'all loosen my corset."

Everybody had a good laugh at that, Jennifer so overcome she snorted busthead red into her nose, which led the other two to an even greater display of merriment. "Oh, Lord," Betsy said, "it is so good to get out of my goddamn apartment for a while."

"Tell me about it," Marlene said. "But let me ask you something before Betsy gives us the latest word on Dr. Flange. Has Houston come knocking on either one of y'all's doors in the recent past? Tell the truth now."

"I will confess that no he hasn't, and I will also admit I wish he would again, whenever he can work me into his schedule," Betsy said.

"He did before, though," Marlene said. "I remember you telling me that last year in the spring sometime."

"He did, and that's the only time he did me. I really fucked up, I think, by acting so glad he was there and telling him that. They do not want to hear that shit. Start acting grateful, and the sons of bitches are long gone. He never came back again, the hard-hearted little shit."

"That's true what you say about if you act grateful and how that scares them off," Jennifer said. "Why is that, do you think? If a man acts grateful to me for letting him do me, I like it. And I'm more inclined to let him do it again, too. Turnabout's fair play. That's the way I see it."

"Let me tell you what I think," Marlene said, one hand held out as though to quell a set of objections to what she was about to declare and the other holding her glass of sour red wine at drinking ready. "I think the reason a woman likes it when a man acts like he's grateful for her letting him fuck her is because she's a normal human being. She has not been raised by a pack of wolves. Your ordinary man does not possess human responses. He acts like he truly has been raised in the wild by beasts. When he thinks you're grateful, all his antenna go up and he thinks uh oh, this bitch is fixing to tie me down if I don't watch it. She's going to want me to fuck only her from now on, and shit, I just finished fucking her. I do not have to do this one again."

"Miserable bastards," Betsy Ames said. "You nailed it right on the head, Marlene. Where's that cheese dip? I got to eat something or I'm going to fall over. And one other thing. How do you get them to do you again without scaring them off?"

"It's onion dip, not cheese, and it's right there," Jennifer Smithing said, pointing in the general direction of the kitchen table. "And the way you get a return fuck is to act like they didn't do it right the first time. You know, act a little unsatisfied. Make them feel inadequate is what I'm saying. They might rise to the challenge. But let me ask you something, Betsy. Would you let Houston Stride back into your apartment and into your pants if he came knocking again, after the way he treated you that one time he lowered his precious self to do you?"

"Hell, yes," Betsy said, lifting an onion dip loaded cracker toward her mouth. "In a New York minute I would."

"Would you, Marlene?" Jennifer asked. "He's done you, hadn't he?"

"I got to confess something I'm ashamed of," Marlene said. "Houston has never tried to get in my pants, but I did get into his one night at a party at Bruce Edge's apartment."

"What do you mean?" Jennifer said. "Tell us. Please."

"Oh, I cornered him in the hall, the one that goes to the bathroom and the back bedroom in that house. Remember how it's laid out?"

"No, and I don't care about that part. What happened?"

"We all had been doing some grass and drinking, too, of course, and I went up to him and gave him the big eye and the open mouth thing, and he kissed me. We did that for a while, a lot of tongue, and I could feel him get hard, so I just reached down, unzipped him and let it pop out of his fly and jerked him off real quick."

"Why didn't you, you know, drop to your knees?" Jennifer said. "I couldn't have kept myself from doing that."

"Somebody might have seen me, girl. I got scruples." That got the biggest laugh of the night, which lasted until the Paisano jug was near empty and Jennifer and Betsy had sneaked out of the apartment and walked to their places in utter defiance of the curfew. A squad of 102nd Airborne troops down from Fort Campbell noted them as soon as they ventured onto Hillsborough Road, but their commanding officer had good sense and ordered his men to let the drunk ladies pass in peace.

32

THE SUN WAS BENDING toward the west, getting on toward leaving Nashville to its own devices, and Tee Arnold Monroe was feeling a little chill coming in the air as he sat on the front porch of his house just off Eighth Street. He had leaned his straight-back chair up against the wall behind him in a posture that let him extend his legs and ease the low back pain which had got to kicking up on him now and then, and he knew that meant he had to keep an ear cocked for Minnie. She might be at the door any minute, and the last thing she wanted to see was her husband adding to the scarred place in the paint on the wall behind him by leaning his chair up against it.

It was a balancing act, Tee Arnold considered, as he sat in his preferred position on the front porch of his house, and the two things he had to keep in equilibrium was whether it was better to sit the way Minnie approved or at least allowed and thus be able to focus on watching the street and measuring the damage that had been done to the houses across the way and up and down as far as he could see—the burned-out cars, the broken glass and scattered debris, the puddles of water left from fire hoses here and there, the black circles where tires had gone up in flames, and the other evidence of what had been taking place in North Nashville since last Friday. If he sat with all four legs of the straight-back chair well and truly resting on the porch floor, he'd be able to consider what the evidence of destruction everywhere before him might mean and predict for the next night to come and then the next one and the nights and days after those. He could let his mind roam, touching where it wished, dwelling for as long as it wanted, being restless and moving if and when it chose, settling for a spell, and maybe coming up with new things to think about, to include in his estimation of what was and what was likely to be.

But that luxury of thought could be bought only at the expense of staying flat and level in his seating posture and feeling that low-grade discomfort build and wane and build again in his back as he pondered. Sit that way long enough, and the pain would begin to interfere with thinking about anything but it. Pain is selfish, it came to Tee Arnold's mind, letting him know instantly he ought to tell somebody he had just thought up that idea. Maybe he should write it down if he could locate a pencil and a piece of paper somewhere in the house to record the truth he'd just come up with. Pain is selfish. It wants all it can get of your attention. It wants the whole damn world, come to think about it. Pain is a white man. And a nigger is who it steps on.

Lord, Tee Arnold said to himself, listen to what all I'm coming up with in my head, sitting here reared up on my front porch looking at all them burned houses and cars and smelling all that smoke in the air. Fire from plastic and old rotted-out lumber and Sheetrock and asphalt shingles and car bodies and gasoline and wore-out upholstery, that kind of fire does make a bad mixture of stink. It sure don't smell like lightwood pine and split hickory logs did in the fireplace back in Dixon, Tennessee, in them old days. That smelled wholesome like it was coming from somewhere worth being at and going somewhere worth going to, and this stink here smells like it was mixed up by the Devil himself and brought to a hard boil in Hell over a fire made out of a bunch of shithouses.

It was at the very moment, just at the point where all Tee Arnold's thinking in the proper position for mental activity took place, that the other part of what he had to keep balanced in his mind when he was considering how to sit on his own damn front porch kicked into action. That was Minnie pushing open the screen door, stepping out of the house and instantly seeing what she had known she would see.

"It ain't going to do you no good to let them front legs of your chair come down and slam against the floor," she said. "I done seen you, how you was sitting. Some more of that damage to my house paint's done been done. I swear to Jesus Christ himself you sit here on this front porch looking more and more every day like my old granddaddy did back in them woods when I was too little to get my own drinks of water. Jaw full of chewing tobacco and just as country and careless as the day is long."

"I'm sorry I forgot and leaned up against the wall here, Honey, but I got to thinking about what all this burning and looting and letting off gunshots means. I'm talking about what's been going on here in this part of town with these young fools running and hollering and burning everything down. So my mind got to wandering, and I forgot to remember how I was sitting and what the chair back does to that new paint job."

"It ain't that new," Minnie said. "That's the problem with that paint job. It's old, but it's all we got, and we got to take care of it. There ain't no new paint for my house coming any time in the future that I can see. Can you?"

"They still making paint in this country, and they still selling it to folks to get their houses all fixed up nice. I know that to be the truth."

"How we going to buy it? We just lucky to have this house still standing," Minnie said, beginning to gesture at the street before her, her forefinger jabbing as she swept her arm from one point to the other of the prospect. "The way these fools been acting. Burning their own places down. Houses, stores, churches, everything. Shooting at each other and everybody and every thing."

"They ain't burned no church, though, has they?"

"They sure have. Little Redeemer of Man over yonder on Oriole Street, they done put the fire to that last night. Burned slap to the ground. That was that Holiness Promise Church, where it used to be Baptists going before they moved into that new one they got now."

"I wonder if Bloomer knows that down at the barbershop. I expect it's probably safe to go over there by now and tell him, if he don't. Everything seems to be quietening down today."

"You ain't going to find Gus Bloomer cutting hair in no barbershop, I don't care how quiet it done got today."

"What you talking about? Gus ain't been hurt by nobody, has he? He still all right, ain't he? Is he took sick?"

"That barbershop was burned down night before last, Tee Arnold. You knew that. We talked about it yesterday, about Gus's Hair Today and the whole block it used to be on, how all that's gone. All that's burned, Baby. We done talked about it. Don't you remember me and you sitting in there at the kitchen table, eating on the last of that roast beef I brought from the chancellor's house middle of last week? You scaring me now talking like that. Don't do that."

"I remember that, Sugar," Tee Arnold said, standing up from his straight-back chair so he could reach Minnie to pat her on the shoulder. "I sure do. It just slipped my mind for a while. I was turning my attention to how nasty this old riot smoke smells all up in the air around here now. It ain't nothing like it was out in the woods out yonder close to Dixon. That old country smoke had a sweet smell to it in the fireplace, didn't it, Sugar?"

"It sure did, Tee Arnold. Tell you what. I'm going to go in there and see if they's anything left in the icebox for us a little snack. Sit on back down in your chair. If it eases your back any, lean on yonder against that wall. You right, baby. It's always going to be some paint to cover stuff over. They ain't never going to run out of that."

"All right, Minnie," Tee Arnold said. "I just sit here a little longer. It's getting cool, though. I be in the house in a minute."

He sat back down in the straight-back chair, careful not to lean back since it would be only a little while before he'd go inside the house he and Minnie lived in. His back wouldn't get to bothering him that quick. Had Minnie told him about the barbershop burning down, he wondered. He couldn't bring it to mind if she had, but she didn't need to know that. She had a lot on her. What was it I thought about pain a while ago, that good idea that come to me, Tee Arnold asked himself, sniffing at the stink in the air. Was it something about how bad it smells when something's hurting you and you can't get no ease from it? Was that my good notion about pain I done figured out? That must have been it, maybe. Sure. Sure it was.

"Rum Tum," Emily was saying in a quiet voice, the kind Mama was always telling her to use when she was talking to somebody, especially a grown person, instead of yelling out loud to make them turn and listen to what she was saying. "Rum Tum, don't you want to watch *Romper Room* instead of the Stooges? Are you hearing what I'm saying?"

Rum Tum didn't show any sign that he had heard what Emily said or cared what it was, so she said it again, this time loud enough to cause Mrs. Peebles to look up from the knitting needles and yarn she was holding in front of her, her mouth moving as she sat counting one number after another. She was wearing the same dress she always did, and it was the one color Emily didn't like. Green. Mrs. Peebles didn't want to have to start over again when she was counting, and she looked over her glasses at Emily without smiling a bit. She didn't like to lose her place, she'd told Emily whenever she had to look up from the things she was making with her needles and yarn. She called it that, losing her place. Emily couldn't imagine how you could know you were in the place you were supposed to be and that you knew you had a place. Where did it go when you lost your place? Where is the place of your place? How could you know where to start to hunt for your place?

"Who you talking to, Emily?" Mrs. Peebles said. "The TV set? They can't hear what you're saying to them, Sugar. It just looks like they're real people inside that box. They ain't in there at all. They're not real. It's just some kind of electricity makes them come on the screen and talk to each other. They can't hear a word you say, no matter how loud you holler at them. So if you have to play like you're talking to them, make it real soft and nice. Be like Julian. See how quiet he is?"

Emily didn't have to look at Julian to know what he was doing. He'd be sucking the first two fingers on his right hand, and staring at the TV set the same way he stared at everything. He didn't ever know what anything was, but he wasn't bothered by that. Emily already knew the stooges inside the TV set couldn't hear her talk, and so did Rum Tum. He turned his head toward Emily to let her see how he was laughing at how dumb Mrs. Peebles was, saying something like that to Emily about electricity making the TV work. Rum Tum wasn't really laughing, though, Emily could tell, just lifting his top lip to show his teeth, how sharp they were and how he never brushed them like you're supposed to do every day. They weren't white like Emily's, but the color Daddy's were, darker than white and not as yellow as lemon Kool-Aid but like it.

Emily knew Rum Tum wasn't looking at her because she had asked him to let her watch Miss Nancy on *Romper Room* instead of the Stooges, but to make fun of Mrs. Peebles. He wanted Emily to be bad and not polite just the way he was. See me and be like me. That way of doing was not nice, though, like Mama would say when Emily was doing a thing she didn't like. Maybe when she was making Julian cry or yelling real loud at the TV set or throwing tinker toys up in the air high enough to hit the ceiling so they would come down faster than they went up. She wasn't at home, now, though, Mama wasn't, and Daddy was at work a lot of the time, so Mrs. Peebles was there to take care of her and Julian and Dylan. To change her brothers' diapers and make cheese sandwiches and English peas for lunch and not let them get out in the street. And sit there being dumb while she looked at her needles and yarn and not letting Emily do what she wanted.

"We know they aren't real, Mrs. Peebles," Emily said. "The people inside the TV set, but what they do is real. And that's why we talk to them. The way they act is real."

"Julian doesn't talk to the TV people the way you do, though, Honey," Mrs. Peebles said and started making her lips move again as she looked down at her knitting and said numbers under her breath, starting over from the beginning.

"Julian's too little to know what's real," Emily said. "Rum Tum always knows what's real and what's make-believe. He's always right. Julian's never right." Rum Tum liked hearing Emily say that about him, enough to look away from the Stooges on the TV screen and back at her, letting her see his yellow teeth again. He had his boots with the sharp-pointed silver toes on now, she could see, and he hadn't when he started watching Moe pull Larry's hair and hit Curly on the head with a hammer. Rum Tum had been wearing his house slippers when he sat down to watch the Stooges, but something had happened on the TV to make him change to his boots. Emily knew what that meant when Rum Tum put on the boots with the sharp toes, but she decided to ask him what he was going to do anyway. He liked that.

"Why are you wearing your boots, Rum Tum?" Emily said, putting a nice smile on her face, the way you're supposed to when you're talking to people. "What are you going to do?"

Rum Tum pointed toward the TV screen, showing his teeth again, and Emily looked to see what he meant. Curly had a box of matches, and he was striking one on the rough place on the side of the box where you have to do it to make the fire start. He couldn't get one to stay lit at first, and that made Curly frown and let whiny and growly sounds come out of his mouth—that made Emily laugh whether she wanted to or not—until he finally got one to burn bright enough to look real on the TV screen. Then Curly stuck the burning end of the match to Larry's messy hair, and the fire got big then. Larry had been sleeping, and when he woke up his head was on fire, and that made him yell and run to the sink to stick his hair under the faucet. Curly laughed, and Moe laughed, and Rum

Tum laughed, and then Emily decided to laugh, too. The only ones not laughing at Larry's hair on fire were Mrs. Peebles and Larry.

Mrs. Peebles was still counting, her lips moving up and down as though she was chewing something sweet in her mouth and making the skin under her neck wiggle back and forth, and she didn't look up when Emily followed Rum Tum out of the living room toward the kitchen where Mama kept the box of matches to light the gas burners on the stove when they didn't start on their own the way they were supposed to do. If something wouldn't burn by itself, Mama told Emily one time when she was watching Mama cook supper, you had to help it out. That's why you keep matches in the kitchen drawer. Not to play with, but to help make things that are supposed to get hot get that way.

"What are you going to do with the box of matches, Rum Tum?" Emily said, close enough behind the little man to see the points of his boots shine as he ran down the hall and into the kitchen. They looked like they were on fire themselves, the silver-colored sharp toes of Rum Tum's boots, flashing with sparks as he led Emily toward the drawer where the matches stayed as they waited to be struck against the box so they could become fire and make things get hot and burn. Rum Tum wouldn't answer with words any question Emily asked him, usually, wanting her to guess again and again until she got it right. Then he would stop shaking his head no and lift his lips to show his yellow teeth and move his head up and down with one big nod. That showed he was happy.

This time, though, when Emily asked him about the matches and what he wanted to do with them, Rum Tum looked over his shoulder and said one word to her. "Play," Rum Tum said. And then again, "Play." Now he was wearing his red shirt, instead of the blue one he'd had on when the Stooges came on the TV set, and his bright yellow pants, the ones covered with little black birds that looked just like each other. When had he changed his clothes, Emily wondered. You could never catch Rum Tum getting dressed to do something new. Every thing he did was a secret.

"All right," Emily said to Rum Tum, careful not to touch him on his shoulder, though she wanted to. Rum Tum hated for anyone to touch him. "We'll play with the matches. We'll strike matches, and make them burn. We'll make fire come live with us and be in our house. It'll burn for us, fire will. It'll burn."

PART THREE
ASHES

33

APRIL AGAIN, ALWAYS AGAIN the light green of the leaves and buds and branches and tender shoots touched with gold by the rays of the rising sun, all come anew in the same old way to Tennessee, the Cumberland Valley, to Davidson County, and to Nashville. The birds gave announcement, sounded the eternal alarm, and set the clock to signal the sap and juice of all things living to arise. Mindless and urgent, the music of the birds of spring worked its way into the senses of every creature still present, yet alive, and capable of hearing in the declines, slopes, waterways, and rises of the spring landscape of the Athens of the South.

Of these, one was Tollman Briggs, removed now from the crumbling mansion on Belmont Street and residing in a spacious loft apartment downtown near the river. He woke quickly, alone in his bed, thinking of the recording session to begin today at the RCA studio on Eighteenth Avenue, the album of his original songs set to follow up the mammoth success of his singles of last year, "Memphis Murder Blues" and "Idiot Savant." He arose clean, purified, prepared to do the honest work of an honest craftsman, womanless, and free in the world.

Cameron, he allowed himself to think, gone now finally for good. Now returned to Little Rock, like a dog to its vomit, wrench in hand, to take up the Semmes family plumbing business. There's a song there, lost some place in those leaking pipes and burst connections in Arkansas, looking for a way out. I'll make that song mine someday, while Cameron screws nuts on and off and counts billable hours. Tollman stepped to the bank of windows opening on the Cumberland, drew a deep breath, and attempted to whistle accompaniment to the trill of a blue bird perched on the sill, singing its heart out. I'm off tune just a bit, Tollman admitted, lips pursed, but close enough for Nashville, off a little everywhere, still close enough to settle for just about right.

"Chambers," Lacy Bodean said to her husband in their home on Fox Run in Belle Meade, rousing from a strange dream in which she'd found herself in a large company of people with all her hair fallen out and her face completely scrubbed of all makeup, pale and colorless enough that no one recognized her, not even the men, and none wanted to say a word to her, "do I still look good to you in the morning? Tell the truth now. Don't just try to make me feel good."

"I haven't tried to make you feel good in years, Sweetheart," Chambers said, reaching for his glasses and turning to face Lacy. "That's somebody else's job, ain't it? You look to me like you always do, far as I can tell."

"Well, good," Lacy said, mollified. "That's a relief. I feel better. Let's go see what Tawanda's got cooked for us this morning, and we can look out through the breakfast room window and watch the birds play and sing and carry on."

Randall Eugene Puckett woke to the sound of all the doors clanging open at once on his level of the cellblocks in the Tennessee State Penitentiary, a bang of metal followed immediately by a voice on the speaker system telling everybody to get ready to form up and proceed to the corridor. Before he rose from his place on the top bunk, Randall Eugene took time to look again above him at a flaw in the paint job on the ceiling of his cell. It reminded him a little of the way the water stain on the ceiling of the bedroom in the trailer house in East Nashville looked like a duck riding a tricycle, if you held your head just right. This one here in the Pen looked like a turkey, though, a real thin one with no head on it. What kind of noise would a turkey make, Randall Eugene wondered, if it tried to sing? Nothing but a damned old gobble, he guessed, as he swung his legs over the side of his bunk, careful not to let them violate Rufus Washington's space below. There ain't nothing this nigger I got to live with for the next ten years won't take wrong, Randall Eugene said to himself as he eased his way to the cold concrete and metal floor. He just looks for trouble, and me here with him every day. And that scary damn Tooter Browning and that weak-assed Milton Drummond still outside walking around loose.

"Oh, God," Marlene Mercer was saying as the headboard of her bed banged against the wall behind her at an increasing rate of speed. "It's almost here, oh Jesus, oh Houston, now, now, yes, yes."

"Well then," Houston Stride said in another few seconds, collapsing onto Marlene's chest and belly, but careful not to let all his weight come into play at once. "That did me good, Marlene. How about you, girl?"

"Absolutely," Marlene said. "And the best thing is that I've caught up."

"Caught up? What do you mean?" Houston said, rolling off Marlene to an easier position beside her on his back. "What time is it? I've got to go home and babysit while Brenda goes to her exercise class."

"It's time for you to leave, all right, I imagine," Marlene said. "I could have predicted that. And to answer your question, what I've caught up to are Betsy and Jennifer. You've never given me a total fuck before like you've done for them, and now I don't have to feel left out."

"Oh, all right. But how do you know about me and Betsy and Jennifer?"

"They told me, Houston. Lord, what do you think?"

"I think that's got to be some kind of a violation of confidence or something. Do women talk to each other about that kind of stuff?"

"Do turtle doves moan in the morning? Hear that pair of them carrying on outside my apartment right now? Keep your ears open, and you'll hear all kinds of moaning coming from everywhere in Nashville this time of year."

"I still don't think that's nice," Houston Stride said. "Talking behind a man's back like that."

"You fuck behind your wife's back. What's the difference, Lover Boy?"

"When you get married, you'll find out the answer to that, Betsy, to your everlasting sorrow."

"I'm Marlene, motherfucker," she said and laughed. "But I don't care whose name you call me. I'm all caught up with Betsy now. On the way out don't let the door hit you on the ass."

Henry Hallam Horsham felt a little strange, a bit out of phase. Not ashamed at all about the identity of the person lying beside him on the deep blue silk sheets of his king-sized bed, still asleep as yet, the lovely lad, but a bit nervous about bringing an undergraduate student to his digs and allowing him to spend the entire night there. That he hadn't done in years and had sworn off doing the last time he'd lapsed. Not that it hadn't been a ravishing evening, and Lord knows the young ones do have incredible powers of recuperation. True, all that, true, true, true, but mercy sakes, what if one as new to himself as this one seems to be doesn't have enough depth of experience to realize the accurate measure of what's happened. Just two ships passing in the night, a brief interlude, that's all it was, but what if the young man thinks he's fallen in love with me. Which he might understandably do. Oh, my soul, it could get messy. Best to get him roused and out of here and sworn to secrecy and agreement that it was an irresistible moment of madness and never again and so on and so forth. I've got to handle this delicately, Henry Hallam Horsham told himself. Let's get it going. Steel yourself, you foolish thing, and do it.

"Jonathan," Henry said softly but insistently, "Jonathan Seth Matthews, time to rise and shine. The birds are all atwitter outside, and soon they'll be on the wing to pastures new. Let's not let them fly away without your going with them."

"Sure, Dr. Horsham," Jonathan said, thinking I hope he doesn't want to get all lovey dovey now. I wouldn't be able to stand it if he did. He looks so truly old in natural light. Not as ancient and hairy and wrinkled as Allen Ginsberg, but there is a difference. This guy here I let get off on me is not the King of the Beats, not the author of *Howl*. I have seen the best minds of my generation destroyed by madness, as the man says. Let me leave here now without having to be starving, hysterical, naked. Don't let Dr. Horsham try to kiss me. Please.

"So when will you make the official announcement, dear?" Felice Foldman asked her husband as they sat in the nook just off the official dining room of Cherry Mount House, alone for a change and almost knee to knee in the special booth built for two to enjoy a private breakfast. The inset booth for two had given them both a good laugh when they'd been first introduced to the nooks and crannies of the official home of the Chancellor of Vanderbilt University almost ten years ago. Actually, they had waited that day to laugh until they were alone in the room in the Hermitage Hotel where they were staying until the formal announcement of Malcomb's appointment and then the move-in date. There had been a little dread, too, Felice admitted to herself as she sipped coffee and watched chickadees working on the bird feeder overflowing with seed just outside the breakfast nook window. Dread at realizing she'd now be having to deal with people for an unforseeable period who thought special nooks for certain meals were charming. All that prissiness will be in the past soon now, though. Hallelujah, as the Methodists of Tennessee like to say in conscious self-parody. Hallelujah and pass the sour mash.

"I'm working that out with the PR people," Malcomb said. "Stuart Longmire is concerned, properly, I've got to admit and applaud his insight, really, that for the chancellor to leave Vanderbilt for another institution after less than ten years is a first for people here. They want and need to dance around that new fact, not miss a step, and charm all those who matter."

"The donors?"

"Those, of course, and the newspapers and the politicians and the alums, the alums, the goddamn alums," Malcomb said. "The tradition here has been for the chancellor to stay at the helm until he's too ancient to find the men's room any more. And my leaving is a surprise to all, and could be considered an insult, taken wrongly."

"But, Malcomb," Felice said, "It is Duke, after all. You aren't leaving for the presidency of some podunk place."

"True, true, but that in itself makes these Nashville types itchy. It plays to their sense of being just a little less fine-haired than the better East Coast universities."

"That's what I love," Felice said. "It's the sweetest taste of all. Oh, look, the chickadees are mating in the bird feeder."

"Don't those birds know one's not supposed to do that," Malcomb said, beginning to chuckle, "Don't get your honey where you get your money."

"Oh, God, I love it," Felice said. "I love it all. Go to it, birdies. Get some."

"Ain't you going to work this morning?" Tee Arnold said to Minnie after he came into the house through the back door, the one into the kitchen, after taking his usual inspection walk around the backyard each day after being waked by the usual noises of the morning in North Nashville. People grinding away at the starters of old cars with bad timing and worn plugs and weak batteries, women hollering at the menfolk staying in their houses, children fussing with each other as they drug their way up Eighth toward Dunbar Elementary and Pearl High School, trucks and buses blasting by, and this time of year the way the birds started squawking and carrying on at the first sign of sunrise and kept hollering way past the time they ought to have calmed down a little. "You still sitting there drinking coffee, Minnie. Look at that clock up yonder on the wall."

"That clock's wrong, and if you'd have looked at it during the last week here you'd a seen it says the same thing all day long."

"Hmm," Tee Arnold said. "I ain't noticed that. It do say it's almost three o'clock. You right, girl. It's wrong."

"It look like it fixing to be no difference to me what time it is, Sugar," Minnie said, looking into her coffee cup as though she was suspicious about what she might find waiting inside at the bottom. "Every time look like it's going to be the same now."

"What you talking about?"

"I'm talking about my job. That's what I'm talking about. Whether I'm about not to have one or be able to hang on for a while longer."

Tee Arnold looked long and hard at his wife, then up at the dead clock on the wall and asked her what she meant and how did she know what she seemed to know.

"Chancellor be leaving his job. I learned that from Maurice. He seen it on a letter in the man's study, and I don't know if they going to want me to keep on running that kitchen or not. That's what I mean."

"They done fired the man over yonder at Vanderbilt?"

"Naw, he ain't fired. He got him a better job, I reckon. But I ain't worried about him and where he going to work. I'm studying the new one they be bringing in once this'un and Miz Foldman clear out."

"Who it going to be? Why you worried about your job? People got to eat, no matter if they new or old at the job. You be cooking, running things still. They going to keep on needing you, no matter what they name happen to be. Why you worried, Honey?"

"I ain't worried about the new big man at Vanderbilt. I'm worried about the woman that's going to be with him, about what she want. A rich new white woman come into a house, she got to find things to change. She ain't going to be doing no work, and she sure got to stay busy. It ain't no rest for somebody that don't need to work. It's a fulltime job not having to make a living."

"She ain't going to fire the cook," Tee Arnold said. " I don't care who she is. You done showed you know how to run a rich man's kitchen. You done proved yourself in that job."

"You don't know nothing about white women that's got money and time on their hands. Don't try to tell me my business."

"So you ain't going to work today?"

"Sure, I'm going to work. I'm just going to drag in late with my mouth all pooched out, and I hope old Felice Foldman notice that and ask me what's wrong. Then I can act all scared and worried and she might feel sorry for me, and put in a good word with the next white bitch I got to work for. If they give me the chance, I mean."

"It's a lot more to being a cook than I knew," Tee Arnold said. "You done showed me that."

"It's a lot more to being a nigger woman than you know," Minnie said. "I tell you that. It's a lot harder than being any kind of a man, no matter what color he is."

"I'm going to get that clock fixed while you gone to work, Sugar. I promise you that."

"You do that, husband," Minnie said. "You do just that."

Birmingham News, April 4, 1969, *Engagements*

Dr. and Mrs. Palmer Sterling Longineaux of Mountain Brook announce the engagement of their daughter, Josephine Carol Longineaux, to Mr. Gatewood Crawford Dunn, son of Mr. and Mrs. James Forrest Dunn of Buckhead, Georgia. Miss Longineaux is a senior at Vanderbilt University, with English literature her major field of study. She is a member of Kappa Delta Sorority, an honors student, and was elected Miss Vanderbilt of 1969. Mr. Dunn is also a graduating senior at Vanderbilt, a major in economics, and a member of Alpha Tau Omega Fraternity in which organization he has served two terms as Pledge Master. The wedding will be held on June 4th at 11 a.m. in St. Matthew's Episcopal Church in Mountain Brook, with a theme in keeping with Miss Longineaux's love of literature, an Aubade of the Birds of Spring.

Lurleen Blankenship wasn't able to leave the Music City Magic Fingers Massage Salon until just after dawn, what with there being two big conventions in Nashville the same week. One had something to do with

insurance agencies in Illinois and Indiana and Missouri and some of the
rest of those states up north that Lurleen had heard a good bit about since
she'd moved to Nashville, but had never visited and had no wish ever to
do so. From what she could tell from the men from those locations who
came into Magic Fingers looking to spend a little money and lay a little
load, the states they called home must be real flat, ordinary, and quick
on the trigger.

That was an advantage, Lurleen had to admit and had said so to
Blanche Ann. "They in and out real quick, Miz Weaver," she said. "And
most of them don't argue much about what different stuff is going to cost
them when you tell them. That's all good. But it gets kind of old, you
know, one just like the other one flopping down the same way as him
before and him after. Saying the same things, you know. It makes the
time just drag."

"I know what you're saying," Blanche Ann said, she and Lurleen
talking in the reception area of Magic Fingers early in the morning. That
was unusual, Blanche Ann being there in the building after ten o'clock
at night, much less in the time the next morning when the light began
coming up in the East over the Cumberland. They had had a real run
of business from the conventioneers all night, though, two of the Magic
Fingers therapists claiming to be sick so not even there and the other
three fully employed every minute. It finally had come down to Blanche
Ann being called into service, a situation she hadn't experienced in so
long she almost didn't know how to act. It comes back to you, though, as
she'd told Lurleen, just like swimming or riding a bicycle.

"Tell the truth now," Blanche Ann said to Lurleen, beginning to grin.
"What about that other bunch, all them disc jockeys from their conven-
tion. How'd it go with them boys?"

"It was different all right," Lurleen admitted. "They wasn't any better
qualified than the other bunch to do something worth remembering, but
they would forever talk to you. Make jokes and brag and say what they'd
done and how good they did it. One of them even offered to get me into
the music business."

"Hah hah," Blanche Ann said. "Playing what instrument? The skin flute?"

"That's one I hadn't heard before. It's a little bit funny."

"Why you hadn't heard it is because it's so old," Blanche Ann said.
"There ain't no new way to talk about fucking, I don't reckon. It's all been

said and done. Every new bunch says and does the same thing and thinks they're the first ones to do it."

"I'm beginning to believe that," Lurleen said and yawned real big. "I got to go lie down."

"That's what you been doing all night, idn't it?"

"By myself, I mean. My goodness, you sure are full of life this morning."

"Sugar, I guess it's from seeing all them little-dick naked men," Blanche said. "I ain't had that opportunity in a while."

"I seen all I want to. I tell you that. I'm going home and get in that bed."

"Today's Thursday, ain't it? I guess you won't ever be seeing your steady Thursday boyfriend no more, will you, Lurleen?"

"No, I reckon not, and you know what? I kind of miss that old fool. He was soothing to be around."

"Except when he pulled out that big old sword that night and start cutting with it, huh?"

"He just got over excited, Rooney did. He did the best he could to take care of me."

"You the last person needs taking care of, Honey."

"He didn't think so," Lurleen said. "I liked that about him. Poor old boy. I wonder what's happened to him."

"Well, wherever he is, he's still crazy as a bedbug. Go on home and get some rest. I'll see you tonight. Both of them conventions end tomorrow, and all them old boys'll have to go home to their wives and girl friends."

"I pity that poor bunch of women," Lurleen said. "I am going home now. I feel like I been whipped like a stepchild. Listen to all them birds hollering outside. I didn't know it was all that many birds downtown like this."

"Honey, it's birds all over Nashville this time of year. Singing their fool heads off. They don't know no better, and they don't care where they are, downtown or out in the trees and bushes. They just pop open their damn beaks and sing."

The Rat was set up on the terrace of Rand, in complete costume, what little of it that remained wearable, but he had no portable card table with him and nothing to lay upon it in display. No stacks of *Cook's Night Out,* no leaflets he'd scrounged from various holiness churches and faith tabernacles, no clippings from newspapers involving stories about rats, mice, insects, starlings, feral felines, and abandoned dogs, all those pests that might plague homeowners of Middle Tennessee, none of the ammunition the Rat had used over the last years to appeal to the audience he'd worked to build at Vanderbilt University.

The time was early morning, a few minutes before the bell in the administration building would chime the hour to begin the first class of the day, and students were streaming by the plastic chair in which the Rat sat as they sought infusions of coffee and sugar inside the snack bar for the day to come. There were many more of them than usual, the time of year being what it was, late enough in the term for realization to set in that the day of reckoning was at hand, the end of the academic year when the professors took their turn at lashing those who'd mocked them, played sluggard, and demonstrated the futility of depending on education to effect human progress. No students took note of the Rat in passing. The time for parody, irony, and play was past. Brutal May was slavering near at hand.

"My people, my people," the Rat called out once or twice as clots of students flowed by him, but he did so in simple observation of a duty, not in expectation of being noticed or heard. "Attend, attend, behold the Rat as he prepares to assume the raiment of commencement. It's your last chance to see him before he shucks off the old skin and emerges full blown and new, pink as an infant rodent."

Dr. George Gwaltney, assistant professor of English, one of a group recently denied tenure by a unanimous vote of the senior members of his department, slowed his progress as he stepped up on Rand Terrace and stopped to speak to a former student. "Greg," he said, shaking his head in mock sorrow, "to what a state has the Rat fallen. Just look at what's left of your feet."

"Dr. Gwaltney," the Rat said, "I'm glad you came by this morning, so alive with the energy of spring and the promise of new life. Listen to the birds, how they sing in chorus."

"What's next for you, Greg?"

"When I was a Rat, I spake as a Rat. Now I am about to become a man, I will speak as a man. I'm going to law school. Got me a full ride to Virginia, Dr. Gwaltney. The ruminations and ruination of the Rat have paid off. What about you?"

"I'll be headed for East Texas State College in Commerce, Texas, Greg. It's not going to be like Vandy, but they have contracted to pay me a salary for next year, unlike the Princeton of the South."

"After I've spent my time in law school, I'll give you one free legal action of your choice, Dr. Gwaltney. Step right up for a free tort, hot out of the oven."

"I'll keep that in mind, Greg," George Gwaltney said. "Have you seen Dr. Alden come by this morning?"

"I have not, although I've looked. The Rat wishes one last meeting with him to chew over the cheese with the good doctor. Where'll he be going now?"

"He hasn't found a job yet, Greg, the last I heard. Somebody told me he was interviewing at a small college in the Midwest. Iowa, maybe? I don't know. He's not around campus much these days. I understand he's living in an apartment complex way out on Charlotte Pike. Word is they lost all their belongings in that house fire last year, and they've had to rent almost everything they use. If you see him, tell him I asked about him."

"I will do so. He and I share a love of secluded tombs, you know. Rat-like, we've gathered to skulk and gibber among the headstones. I consider Dr. Alden an idol to all Ratkind."

"You are going to leave the costume in Nashville, aren't you? I don't think this act would play well in Charlottesville at Mr. Jefferson's university."

"No fear, Dr. Gwaltney. Old skins stay in old places. The rat suit's now for the birds. Time to twitch my cloak about my shoulders and head to pastures new."

"At least you've learned some literary quotes to use in the big world, Greg."

"Why sure," the Rat said. "Isn't that what Vandy's for?"

"Dear," Marie said after opening the driver's side door of the Buick and scurrying around the car to pop the handle by the passenger's seat, "here we are at home again. Another nice visit you're going to have today. We'll eat lunch and talk and listen to some Brahms and maybe a little Mozart, and you'll have time to take a little nap in your own bed. And then we'll go back to Mockingbird Acres later in the afternoon. We don't have to be there until five o'clock, so we'll have the rest of this glorious spring day to be together. It'll be just like the old days, won't it, Robard?"

Dr. Robard Flange stepped out of the car carefully, his left arm adangle, and looked about him at the expanse of lawn, ornamental bushes, newly blooming flowers, and trees touched with pale green, all to be traversed before one could enter the building standing beyond all this evidence of new and unconstrained growth. "What is this place, woman?" he said, fumbling in the floorboard of the car to find the rubber-tipped cane he needed for support. He picked it up in his right hand and swung it about his head in a gesture that included all the visible world. "This is not the Delta. Where are the new rows of cotton plants?"

"Oh, Robard," Marie said. "Let's just go in the house and have some lunch."

"I'm worried about the lateness of the plantings at Benevolence. The rains of spring have delayed the field hands from carrying out their tasks. Late planting, late harvest. Too much weather in between one task of cultivation and the next. Too much disturbance in the atmosphere."

"Please just look at the flowers, Robard," Marie said, pointing to the beds lining the stone walk leading to the house. "Listen to the songbirds." She had lost a great deal of weight since April a year ago, and she felt much lighter and easy on her feet as she led her husband toward the front door of the house. At first as the pounds dropped away with her making no effort to reduce, she had found solace in at least that part of the way she had to live now, but one night lying awake in the small hours it had come to her that the slimmer and healthier she became the longer she would live. I should eat all I can to regain the excess weight and go beyond where I was and feel my blood pressure rise until finally my blood clots and my heart explodes and I can get some relief, she'd told herself.

Mrs. Robard Flange tried that, cooking fattening foods for herself and buying cakes and candies and pastries and ordering the most caloric entrees in restaurants when she ate out with ladies from St. Andrew's Episcopal, but she'd been unable to eat more than a bite or two of any rich offering set before her. She grew increasingly slimmer, quicker, more resilient physically, more able to suffer for a longer time, defeated once more by her appetite, no matter from what direction she approached it.

At least, she thought to herself as she helped her husband through the door and into the house, he hasn't screamed at me today when I called him by his real name. When I said Robard, he looked at me as though he knew I was referring to him. That's a good sign. He didn't explain to me again that he is Major Rooney Beauchamp of the Fourth Mississippi and of Benevolence Plantation in Panola County. He didn't call me Lurleen, and beg me to do that nasty and terrible thing to his arm. He didn't ask to be given his sword to keep the Negroes from seizing Lurleen and doing all those horrible things to her that he seems to relish describing and that he is so determined to spell out to any who will listen. Today's visit may be a good one. I might not have to call Gareth Lamb to help me get him back in the car. Dr. Lamb does keep finding excuses these days not to come around Robard any more. He's not reliable in the way he once was. Let today be a good visit. Oh, I hope it will be.

"Lurleen," her husband said, looking at her the way he used to when he wanted some intimate event to take place, his eyes visible only as slits. "Come sit by me, Daughter of Old East Tennessee, and let us tell sad tales of love and woe. Speak to me of the birdsongs of spring in the Smoky Mountains. Here on this settle, Child. Sit you."

"Robard," Marie said in a voice broken once more on a Sunday afternoon early in another April in Middle Tennessee. "Robard, you know I was born and reared in Nashville. I have never been able to stand East Tennessee."

The interview had gone well at Bonar College. Ronald Alden, Ohio State University PhD, presently an assistant professor of English departing from Vanderbilt University, and a scholar of nineteenth-century prose and poetry, had been met at the airport in Sioux City by a student driver, identifiable by the Bonar College Titans gimme cap he was wearing, and had been led along with his bag to a large GMC van painted in the Titan team colors, purple and white. The van was large enough to hold an entire basketball team or the defensive unit of the football squad, but Ronald and the student driver were the only occupants as they pulled out of the Sioux City airport lot and headed north toward Providence, Iowa, the seat of Bonar College, just thirty miles from the South Dakota line.

The dark highway was dry and clear, but snow was still on the ground, and as Ronald looked out the window of the front passenger seat—the student had insisted on carrying Ronald's bag and had explained in a sincere tone that Ronald did not need to ride in the seat beside the driver but could have his choice of any of the other fourteen available—he could see that the snow and ice in the roadside ditches had melted into a small flow earlier in the day but were now refreezing as the later afternoon came on. The ice was black, and the grass beneath it was the color of cane syrup.

"They told me you got three children," the student driver had said, "and that'll make you really like Bonar if you come here. It's a family-orientated college, and we're real proud of that. All the professors have their students come over to their houses for tea and conversation about just all kinds of things and all. And you'll never have to worry about finding baby sitters for your kids. We love children at Bonar."

After his meeting with the entire faculty and the sub-meetings with the search committee and the curriculum committee and the English department of Bonar College, and the one-on-one sessions with the dean and the president and the human resources director, Ronald knew he'd be offered the job before he left the campus for the return to Sioux City in the puddle-jumper prop plane which would make a stop at the St. Louis airport for transfer to a real aircraft and the final landing in Nashville. He knew that because the president had told him he was just the sort of faculty member Bonar needed to move forward programatically and because Ronald had responded to each query in the properly agreeable and deferential way. The study of English was not of consequence in itself, the dean had said, a statement the president had repeated, his eyes sharp for any sign of challenge. Such disciplines were designed only for service to the real purpose of Bonar College, he went on, its mission having been, still being, and to be in future the preparation of elementary and secondary teachers to staff the public schools of Western Iowa and East South Dakota. Ronald had agreed to the centrality of such purpose, had foresworn all notions of any emphasis on literature for its own sake, and pledged himself to be a born-again lover of the purposes and definition of small regional private church-related colleges.

"You have about an hour before the student driver will pick you up for the return to the Sioux City airport, Dr. Alden," the president said, beaming pleasantly at the Ohio State PhD he was about to add to his roster. "Would you like to wander about the campus for a while on your own?"

Ronald said he would and he did, leaving his bag in the lobby of the administration building, Brailow Hall, fastening his overcoat all the way up to the top button against his throat in the coming chill of late afternoon of his second day at Bonar, and heading down a tree-lined street toward the west and the obscured sun hanging above the horizon, not yet fully into its plunge into darkness.

As soon as he walked three blocks or so on Union Street, he saw that no trees of any size were to be found any longer, and by the time he'd reached the western city limit of Providence, Iowa, not a living thing higher than a ordinary-sized man was to be seen. He stopped and looked toward the western sky, knowing that in due time he and Lily and the children would be located in a house somewhere behind him with maybe a tree or two in the front and back yards for camouflage.

Here on this street is where his wife would take healthy walks with him in the afternoons, winter and summer, spring and fall, and they would look in the direction he faced now, their view of the open fields before them unshielded by vegetation or buildings or hills, and they would be able to see to the far horizon, the sky huge above them and all things, its maw open and empty and hungry to be fed. If they would be able to find an elevation high enough where they could strain to stand on tiptoe, it came to Ronald to know as he stood facing west, the cold wind of April blowing in his face hard enough to cause his eyes to water, he and his mate Lily would be able to see the earth laid out before them all the way to its edge, stretching to the open water of that ocean where America leaves off, where nothing is all there is and all you see and all you hear and no birds sing, all the way to the end of the world.

35674057276181